# UNFORGIVABLE

"*Unforgivable* is a truly great read! Wainscott creates finely honed tension in a first-rate thriller where no one is who they seem and everyone is someone to fear. Don't miss it!"

—Lisa Gardner, *New York Times*
bestselling author of *The Third Victim*

"Tina Wainscott kicks off her foray into the suspense genre in a very big way. *Unforgivable* is gripping, gritty, and quite terrifying."

—*Romantic Times* (Top Pick)

"How Mary Higgins Clark used to write . . . I will be keeping a sharp eye on this author!"

—Detra Fitch, *Huntress Reviews*

"Tina Wainscott delivers hard-hitting suspense with a touch of romance. With each turn of the page, the plot moves in surprising directions. The characters are finely crafted and complexly layered—nothing is as it seems. Be warned, this is not a story for the faint of heart; Wainscott's writing is often brutally direct and forthright. *Unforgivable* is unforgettable, romantic suspense of chilling intensity. Readers who appreciate well-written thrillers will enjoy this book."

—Megan Kopp, *Romance Reviews Today*

"Ms. Wainscott shows another side of her true talent as a writer . . . [The] suspense . . . grabs the reader from the very beginning and keeps the reader hooked until the very last page . . . I look forward to Ms. Wainscott's next mystery."

—*Interludes Reviews*

## ST. MARTIN'S PAPERBACKS TITLES
## BY TINA WAINSCOTT

*Now You See Me*

*Unforgivable*

*Back in Baby's Arms*

*Trick of the Light*

*In a Heartbeat*

*Second Time Around*

*Dreams of You*

*Shades of Heaven*

*On the Way to Heaven*

# I'll Be Watching You

## Tina Wainscott

St. Martin's Paperbacks

*To my bud, Doris Geyer. Stay kewl . . .*

*This book is also dedicated to my BC girlfriends, including Kim M., Karen S., Pamela B., Sigrid Albert, Kat, Murphy O., Robin D., Delilah Schroeder, Shannon K., Barbara, Catherine T., Ann Mathes, and Aussie Barb. May all your dreams come true . . .*

## ACKNOWLEDGMENTS

Many thanks go to Joe Agresti for his continued assistance in matters of law enforcement. His help and patience is immeasurable. As always, any misinterpretation of the law is the author's.

My appreciation goes out to good friends Amy and Andrew Winch for helping me with both plotting and research. Cheers to you both.

My gratitude to Michael Ramsey, who shared so much about his life with alligators. Not only did you contribute greatly to Zell's profession, you inspired it to begin with.

And a big thank-you to dear friend Kim Wooten, who not only inspired a few of the characters in this story, but shared so much of her Everglades wisdom and knowledge.

# PROLOGUE

Elva Lyons closed Southern Comfort after the last customer pulled himself off his bar stool and left. She turned off the neon beer signs and televisions and finally the overhead lights. After hours of music and conversation, even the silence was a wall of white noise humming in her brain.

"Ready to go home, Oscar?"

Oscar lifted his head and emitted an assenting grunt.

"I thought so." After closing the front door, she and Oscar walked to her rusty truck where she helped hoist his large rear end in. "I'm getting too old for this. We're going to have to install springs on your hooves." She slid in next to her potbellied pig and closed the door.

Oscar was a by-product of the last moneymaking scheme turned money-losing mistake. She'd given up on the pig-breeding venture, but kept one of the babies. She reached over and scratched his head. Her "baby" weighed well over a hundred pounds now.

During the drive through the dark Everglades night, the warning she'd received earlier that day rang through her head: *I got a bad feeling about you, Miss Elva. Please be careful.*

"Ah, the kid's strange." Her friend Smitty swore Tullie Macgregor Kendall was psychic; she'd had spooky "feelings" since she could talk. And Elva had, after all, put herself in a precarious situation, even if she had taken precautions. Maybe that's what the girl had picked up on. She patted her rifle. "Nothing's going to happen to us while we got this, right, Oscar?"

She wouldn't mention that the old Remington Fireball was really for varmints and small game. If necessary, she could shoot someone in the leg. She doubted she could bring herself to actually kill a person.

She remained in her truck long after pulling into her yard. She surveyed her small home tucked in the middle of a hammock that was far from screaming distance of anything human. No shadows moved other than the ones she'd grown accustomed to. Just the normal sounds: crickets and frogs and maybe a raccoon sloshing through the water looking for dinner. Sounds she'd heard most of her life.

She got out of the truck, waited for Oscar to jump down, and walked quickly inside. She set the gun near her bedroom door and went about her nightly ablutions. She'd given in to the wrinkles and sagging body parts long ago. Still, there was no point in letting her skin get dry and cracked. After washing her face, she sat on the edge of her bed and smoothed on a lotion smelly enough to mask the cigarette smoke. Oscar settled onto his cushion next to the bed with a prolonged snort and seemed to drop right off. In ten minutes, Elva hoped to be in the same blissful state.


It was easy to see what Elva was doing from the shadows of the closet. She'd thrown her clothes in the hamper, and soon she would fill a glass with tap water and set it on her nightstand before slipping between the sheets. That seemed to be her routine. When she walked into the bathroom to fill her glass, it was time to slip from the shadows.

A moment later, Elva came to an abrupt stop and dropped the glass. It landed on the floor with a thunk. Water pooled and then seeped into the carpet. "What are you doing here?"

"Oh, I think you know."

"But . . . how did you know it was me?" Elva stammered.

"Because I'm smarter than you, old woman." And smart enough to wear rubber gloves.

"How'd you get in here?" Elva slid a glance to where she'd propped the rifle. It was gone.

"You never do check those windows in the second bedroom, do you? One's been unlocked for weeks."

Elva was trying—and failing—to look calm. "It's the fair thing, you know, after what you did to my family—and his family."

Nothing was fair in life, but there was no point in mentioning that. What was so damn fair about Elva buying a box of junk at the church fair and discovering a dead woman's journal hidden at the bottom? A journal with one entry that could start up an old investigation. Luckily, Elva had been greedy and hadn't turned it in. Yet.

"I suppose you want the journal," Elva said, and had the nerve to let resignation color her voice.

"I already have it."

Elva's eyes widened as they settled on the white journal with the pink rose on the cover.

"All right, so you found it. Go on, then. You got what you wanted. It's over."

"Oh, no, it's not over yet."

Elva didn't have time to move before the butt of her own rifle slammed her in the head.

# CHAPTER 1

"Kim, someday that attitude of yours is going to get you in trouble," Ray said as he wiped the last margarita glass dry and set it in the rack.

It already had, but she wasn't going to tell her boss that. "So I'm supposed to just take everyone's crap around here with a pleasant 'Thank you, sir, may I have another'? I never was good at getting down on my knees."

He narrowed his beady eyes. "You better learn to kiss some ass. That's what'll get you promoted around here."

"You'd have to be *much* better looking *and* pay me more before I'd even think about kissing your fat, pimply ass." She added a smile to temper the words.

"If you weren't such a damn good bartender—and you know it pains me to give you a compliment like that—I'd fire you six ways from Friday night."

He would probably have to fire her before she ever quit. She called her stick-to-itiveness commitment and perseverance; her friend Becca called it "too chicken to step out of your comfort zone." Kim liked her own explanation better. She wiped down the copper-clad bar top until the muted lights picked up every indent. "I'm your best bartender, and you know it. You might hate it, but you know it. And speaking of promotions—"

"Yeah, I know, you finished your degree."

This time her smile was genuine. "You did promise me a management role when I got my BA in business." Managing City Lights was a temporary goal. She really wanted to put all those classes at FSU to work by owning her own place someday.

"I know, I know. I'm working on getting enough to let Carrie go without risking backlash."

"Glad to hear it." She tossed the rag in the bin. "I'm outta here. G'night."

Ray's voice followed her into the employees' room. "And it wouldn't hurt to unbutton that blouse a little, show more cleavage. Wouldn't hurt at all. Bring in more tips that way."

Her body went rigid, but she bit back two immediate responses. One was, *What cleavage?* and the other was an unkind suggestion that was no doubt anatomically impossible. She wasn't going to dress like a bimbo—or more precisely, like the cocktail waitresses. City Lights' policy was for the waitresses to wear skimpy black shorts and white dress shirts open nearly to the belly button. The guys didn't have to bare skin, but that argument had gotten her exactly nowhere.

It wasn't as though she was ashamed of her body. She'd finally gotten comfortable in her skin, accepting that she'd never fit into a size 7 or be petite. She'd starved herself for that image of petite perfection once and had looked like a refugee from a war-torn country. At five nine, she was straight, straight, straight; not a curve to be found. Though she could stand to tone up, she just wasn't motivated to pursue a workout routine.

And damn him, she got more tips than anybody. Not that it mattered, since they all had to throw their tips into one jar and split them. Still, she took pride in the fact that she hadn't had to show butt cheek to get them.

Ray's voice followed her as she walked across the lot to her car a few minutes later. "Park in the employees' section, Lyons! And stop telling the other girls to park in the customers' section."

Telling him a thousand times about the lack of safe lighting hadn't worked before, so she simply said, "Bite me!"

She ignored his rude gesture and closed her car door. The guy was a pain, but she gave as good as he did. He wasn't the worst boss she'd ever had, the pay was decent, and the nightclub wasn't far from where she lived. She went through this every night, when the lack of traffic gave her too much time to think about her life. The thought of getting another job didn't relieve the heaviness in her chest. It wasn't the job or working into the wee hours that dragged at her bones—and her spirit. Heck, she'd grown up in a bar.

*That was a long time ago, kid.* She ignored the hitch in her throat and pulled into her apartment complex. City life was getting to her, too. Tallahassee wasn't the worst place to live; it just wasn't her.

An old van had taken her designated parking spot. "Great. Thanks again, bucko." Apartment living was also dragging her down.

She hiked from the faraway spot she'd found to her upstairs apartment. Simon would be asleep. He had left the foyer light on for her, as always. She smiled at the thoughtful gesture, but her smile faded when she saw the bowl where she was to put her keys. Everything in its place or Simon would go off for twenty minutes about how simple it was to put her keys in the bowl when she came in so she wouldn't have to undertake the daily key hunt. She figured, why mess with routine? He was the same with dirty dishes. God forbid one glass should rest in the sink.

Kim hadn't really wanted to shack up with Simon, particularly without a marital commitment looming somewhere in the near future. But when he'd proposed it, he'd said the magic word: *home.* It had been a long time since she'd had a home.

Due to time restrictions, they'd ended up renting an apartment. She had the distinct feeling that Simon was giving their relationship a test run. He'd signed on for a year's lease without balking. Since they'd moved in together six months earlier, every time she brought up a stronger commitment, his beeper went off. Every single time.

Still, they were—all right, she'd say it—comfortable with each other. There was nothing wrong with predictability, was there? She knew Simon's moods, both of them, and because of their disparate hours, they didn't spend enough time together to get on each other's nerves.

Becca's lecture on her choices in men echoed through her mind. *You choose emotionally safe men, Kim. Men who can't give you their hearts, so you won't be tempted to give them yours.*

Ah, what did she know, Miss Married-for-ten-years-to-the-perfect-guy?

A night-light in the kitchen illuminated the anally neat place. Her memorabilia, neon Budweiser lizard sign, Everglades prints, and bottle of tequila she'd bought on a trip to Mexico, complete with the worm, were stashed in a closet with the rest of her "tacky" stuff. The place looked like something out of a catalog. Yuck.

She tiptoed through the bedroom to the bathroom, turned on the shower, and stripped out of her clothes. Her "chicken cutlets" bounced on the linoleum floor. She didn't wear the cutlet-shaped boobie pads for the added cup size, though that wasn't a bad benefit. They gave her an extra layer of padding so when someone brushed against her they weren't actually touching her breasts.

She scrubbed the smoke off her hair and skin. She never dried her shoulder-length blond hair, because she didn't want to wake Simon. After a brisk towel-drying, she slid into bed.

"How was work?" he asked, surprising her that he was awake.

"Same as always. Though Ray did intimate he was getting ready to let Carrie go soon."

"He's said that before."

"Yeah, I know. I'm afraid he's going to keep stalling me."

"Then get another job."

She rolled onto her side facing him. "I want to open my own bar."

"You still talking about that?" He traced circles around her nipples. "Think of the liability, the setup costs, obtaining a liquor license—and you know you're not good at politics. You gotta schmooze for one of them babies."

When his fingers went lower, she placed her hand over his. "I wish you could see my grandma's bar. Everyone went there, everything happened there, the whole town revolved around Southern Comfort." When his other hand grabbed her breast, she said, "Simon, can we talk for a minute?"

He let out a huff of impatience. "You keep talking about these idyllic memories, but you were a kid then. It probably wasn't as great as you remember, for one thing. For another, you won't create anything like that here; this is a city. Besides, your hometown can't have been that great. You haven't been back in ten years, other than for your mother's funeral."

"But it *was* great." Her voice trailed off. Cypress was still inside her, a bittersweet ache deep in her belly. Tucked in the Everglades wetlands, surrounded by the dangerous beauty of nature, the town still sang to her soul. She wanted to visit her grandma, who wouldn't step foot out of the town limits since moving there in 1957. Kim wanted to soak in the smells of the wild orchids and feel the electricity in the air before a summer storm let loose. She wanted to see black, roiling sky behind a sunlit prairie. She'd never told Simon about the circumstances that made her leave the only town she'd ever known. The only town she'd ever loved.

His hands had come to life again. He couldn't relate to dreams and memories. Sex was the only way he knew how to relate to a woman. She had to admit it was easier that way. Easier, but not necessarily satisfying.

They made love in the dark. She called it making love, because she did love him. But without eye contact, it always fell short. When she insisted on having the lights on, he chose a position that allowed no eye contact. In the one and a half years they'd been dating, he'd never once spoken an endearment to her during the act.

Within two minutes of finishing, Simon disengaged and got out of bed. She pulled up the covers and waited for the inevitable. The shower kicked on a second later. He told her it was just a thing with him. It wasn't personal. But it was way personal. She pretended to be asleep when he returned to bed, and knew something had to change.

Something changed the next morning when the phone jarred her out of sleep. Kim fumbled for the receiver. Simon had long ago gone to work.

Her voice sounded froggy when she answered, "Hello?"

"Is this Kim Lyons?" The voice sounded official, even with the Southern accent.

She blinked the sleep out of her eyes and sat up. "Yes."

"This is Samuel Wharton from Cypress. You may not remember me—"

"I remember you," she said, her body going rigid. "You helped defend my stepfather." He'd made a fool of her on the witness stand. Why was he calling her now, ten years later?

"Yes, I did," he said, drawing out the words with pride. "But this doesn't have nothing to do with him. This has to do with your granny."

A stinging sensation burned across her skin. "What about her?"

"Well, now, she's dead."

He dropped the words like little bombs that shattered her insides. As much as she tried not to let Wharton know how his casual words had affected her, she could hear it in her voice. "That can't be right. I just talked with her last month. She was fine." She wanted to think this was a cruel joke.

"I'm afraid she's not fine anymore."

"But . . . how? When?"

"Last week. She died in a way fittin' of Elva Lyons. She took her skiff out late in the night, apparently tipped it over, and hit her head on a log or cypress knee. The official cause of death was accidental drowning. Everyone in town went to the memorial service."

Her words stuttered out of her throat. "M-memorial service? It's already happened?"

"Well, now, we couldn't track you down right away. It was right touchin', too, with everybody in town wailing into their hankies. Elva was a good woman, and she'll be missed something awful. Anyway, I called to tell you that your granny left you something in her will. She left you Southern Comfort, to be precise, with its land and inventory. She also left you her house, including twenty acres of swampland. You're the sole heir."

"The bar . . . she left me the bar?"

"Yes, indeedy. Now I know you ain't gonna be coming down here to run the place, and I also know that no one here is gonna run it for you. So here's what I'm proposin': you sell the bar to a client of mine for thirty grand. It's off your hands, and you got some cash to roll around in. I told my client—"

"Who's your client?"

"He prefers to remain anonymous. But don't you worry, he'll treat the bar with the same respect your granny did. All the pictures will remain on the walls as a tribute to the history of the place."

The pictures. She'd forgotten them, all those old photographs from way before her time that used to fascinate her. Pictures of her dad growing up, and the old-timers, and even herself. They were her history. Her legacy. And so was the bar. She owed that much to her grandma, to not sell out to someone who was too chicken to own up to it. Her chest swelled with resolve and fear and grief. "I'm not selling it."

"I don't think you understand," Wharton said as though he were talking to a child. "No one's gonna run this bar for you. It's gonna close up. Your granny sure wouldn't want that, would she? Take the money and run. That's what you did before, only there wasn't any money. You just ran."

His words, right that they were, jabbed at her. Leaving was the only choice a teenage girl had when most of the town hated her, even one with more attitude than two redneck boys put together. But she wasn't that teenager anymore. She was a woman who longed for her home in the wetlands, who longed for a bar to call her own. The conflict between what she wanted and what she would have to go through to get it burned bitter in her mouth. "Who's handling the place now?"

"Smitty."

The rascally old fart who'd helped Grandma run the bar since Kim could remember.

"If you're lucky, I may have a buyer for the house and land, too, though it ain't in good shape."

Her bar, her house, her land. It had been in her family for years. Now her family had all but petered out, but she was still here.

"I'll be down to meet with you. I'll call later to make an appointment. Good-bye." She hung up and dropped back on the bed. Her heart was racing; she could feel the pulse in her throat. Go back to Cypress. She'd never wanted and feared something so badly at the same time.

"Grandma, what do I do?" She squeezed her eyes shut. "I'm sorry I left. I'm sorry I didn't visit."

Tears filled her eyes and spilled down her temples. She had to say good-bye to her grandma, who had been there for her when her mother had betrayed Kim, and then when Kim had betrayed her mother. Even though she'd stayed neutral, Grandma had stood beside Kim during the trial and all the ugliness after that.

It was time to return home and face the ghosts and demons that waited there. It was time to see what else was there for her.


"You're going to do what?" Simon asked when they met for lunch.

"I'll only be gone for a week. I need to go down and see what's what."

"I can't take that kind of time off without notice. Unless you can wait until"—he pulled his ever-present laptop computer closer and punched the keys—"the last week of September. And honestly, the thought of spending any time down in the swamps in the summer doesn't appeal. Maybe in the fall."

"I can't wait that long. Don't worry; it's only a week."

She wanted to think that he'd miss her. He might, but he wouldn't tell her. They didn't share that kind of thing. They loved each other; they didn't have to say it regularly. That's why they got along so well, she figured, because she didn't need to hear it every day. There were plenty of ways to show affection besides throwing herself all over him, getting carried away by emotions . . . she reined in her thoughts. Despite Becca's know-it-allness, Simon was her perfect mate. At thirty-seven, he was settled professionally and mature, which was why she liked men who were at least ten years older.

She shoved her untouched Caesar salad around with her fork. "I didn't expect you to come with me anyway. Ray's got someone to cover for me at the club, so I'm heading out this afternoon."

He stopped mid-chew and stared at her for a moment. "Isn't there someone else who could take care of this for you?"

"There's no one." The words stuck in her throat. Maybe because that was true of her life. Her grandfather Pete also lived in Tallahassee. He was the reason she'd moved there when she'd left Cypress. As far as she knew, Pete and Elva hadn't spoken since he'd moved there in 1976. Even so, when she'd called him that morning, he'd sounded deeply affected by her death.

Simon set his silverware across his plate. "I'm sorry about your grandmother." His brown eyes reflected sincerity, if not depth. He'd probably never loved someone so much it ripped your guts out when they left. She'd loved only two people with that intensity: Elva and her father.

His cell phone went off, and as always, he answered it immediately, no matter what they were doing. Yes, even then. She waited until he wrapped up his conversation about data security and apologized to her. "What were we talking about?"

She got to her feet. "I was saying good-bye."

# CHAPTER 2

Night cloaked the earth as Kim drove through the Big Cypress Swamp. A sheen of moisture covered the asphalt, evidence of a late afternoon storm. Highway 20 led from US41 south to Cypress, flanked by mangroves that visually blocked miles of marsh and swampland. As soon as she pulled onto 20, she felt an odd commingling of homecoming and dread. Wharton was right; she had no friends or family here.

Who might still hold the past against her? The Macgregors, of course. They more than anyone, and not only because Macgregors held grudges. Their pasts and their families had intertwined a long time ago.

Cypress and the Macgregors went back to the beginnings of Cypress itself. The Seminoles had first claim on the land that was only a few feet above sea level and surrounded by either bay or swamp. The Macgregors were among the first white people to settle there, drawn by the abundant wildlife and promise of a fresh start. Stories of why the Macgregors left their native Scotland included feuding clans, unrest, and escape from murder and mayhem.

They, the Waddells, and a handful of other hardy families had homesteaded here five generations ago. The Macgregors owned land from the bay to US41 on the west side of 20. The Waddells owned a tract of land east of town where they'd set up the Gun and Rod Club, their hunting and fishing lodge.

Kim passed the fancy entrance to the Macgregors' estate. Two stone columns with a carved plaque of a heron and the words HERON'S GLEN adorned a paved road that wound through a break in the mangroves. She knew that straight out was the alligator farm Winnerow Macgregor's father had created in the eighties. South of that, overlooking the bay and mangrove islands, was the home she had lived in for a while.

If she continued down the road she was on, she'd end up in town. Cypress consisted of two marinas, the fish houses that processed incoming seafood, and such tourist attractions as airboat tours of the national parks. The southern part of town held homes scattered throughout a grid of streets. That's where she had lived with her Southern belle wanna-be mom and a dad who lived a life that often led him to trouble, though he never hurt anybody.

Not like Winnerow Macgregor, who also lived life with passionate abandon and had the money and family name to get away with it. He'd not only hurt someone; he'd killed her father.

Kim slowed down so she wouldn't miss her turn. Elva's entrance was much less ostentatious. No columns for her, just a cut through the mangroves and a shell road built high enough to withstand the seasonal rising of the water. Elva had never recovered from her son's murder, either, and yet, as feisty as she was, she'd never pursued justice for Donnie.

Winnerow claimed it was an accident. Supposedly when Winnerow had mentioned he was hunting two gators that had escaped from the farm, Donnie asked to go along. While they were out in the swamp, Winnerow's gun had gone off and shot Donnie in the chest.

Sure, it had been investigated. But Winnerow had no motive, and folks attested that they'd heard about Donnie going out that night. That Donnie didn't much go in for hunting and wasn't even friends with Winnerow hadn't bothered anyone. That Deputy Kinsey, who *was* a good friend of Winnerow's, had been first on the scene didn't bother anyone, either. The shooting had been deemed accidental, and that was that. But it wasn't that. Kim knew there was more to the story.

As much as she disliked Winnerow, she had to admit he had always been a man to pay for his mistakes. When Dewey, one of the farm's employees, fell off the roof and suffered a brain injury, the Macgregors took him in and appointed him estate caretaker. So while Kim pressed her mother to seek some kind of recompense, Winnerow made a surprising offer: he'd marry Kitty Lyons and take care of her and Kim.

It was unthinkable, but her mother did think about it— for about fifteen minutes before accepting. And while she claimed she was doing it for Kim, she'd had a gleam in her eyes when they drove up to Heron's Glen that first time. Kitty hadn't cared that Kim detested the thought of living with Winnerow and his two teenagers, Zell and Charlotte. She hadn't cared that it was the ultimate betrayal to her daughter and dead husband.

Zell and Charlotte had made it clear that they saw the intruders as another mistake they had to contend with. It was well known that since the death of Winnerow's first wife, his children—Zell in particular—had become parents to their father. Zell had come into Southern Comfort numerous times to retrieve his father. He'd spent two days searching the Ten Thousand Islands when Winnerow had gone off boating without a radio.

Kitty was too distracted by the large home and prominent name she'd found herself with to worry much about her stepchildren's resentment or Kim's trouble fitting in. She lectured Kim about her attitude and told her to be grateful. Never mind that Zell and Charlotte put a baby alligator in her bed, tricked her into lying in poison ivy, and played other pranks on her.

While she was back in town, Kim would do whatever she could to avoid the Macgregors.

She almost missed the break in the road. The brown mailbox blended into the background and the drive itself was grown over with clover. Elva didn't like guests, evident by the sign advising trespassers to keep out. She was happy enough to serve just about anybody at the bar, but nobody was to enter her domain without an invitation. She'd say, "I talk to people all the livelong day; I don't want to talk to them in my home."

Kim's throat thickened as she drove down the rutted shell road that took a left turn. Elva and Pete had chosen a dense hammock in which to build their small house. Now the hardwoods and palms formed a tunnel, and Kim had the sensation of driving into another world. The vegetation had grown a lot in the eight years since her mother's funeral, the last time she'd been here. Her headlights illuminated dewy ferns that clambered onto the road and the red reflection of a coon's eyes before it turned away from the intruder.

She *was* an intruder who didn't deserve all this. But it was hers nonetheless. All she wanted was to gather her thoughts and courage and get a good night's sleep. She'd need all of that for tomorrow when she faced Cypress.

Mosquitoes clung to the windshield and dive-bombed her window. She hadn't thought to bring repellent. Surely Elva would have a can or a dozen; folks here bought them in quantity, even though they became immune to the painful blood thinner mosquitoes inject after the first five hundred bites. Kim would have to make a quick dash to the front porch.

The house came into view in the distance, a specter from her past. Wetlands surrounded the house and patch of land it sat on. Two huge oaks and assorted hardwoods protected the dwelling in a branchy cocoon. The yellow bug light on the front porch was burning, no doubt on an automatic timer. Still, it was a welcome sight.

The truck parked in the clearing was not. The lump in her stomach quickly turned to fear. In the dim light, she could tell it was a new, black Ford with extra suspension and lots of chrome. That wasn't Elva's old truck; hers was parked off to the right. Someone was there, and she was pretty sure it wasn't a welcoming committee.

"It's Sam Wharton," he said when the other party picked up the phone. "She's in town, or at least I think it's her. Billy Bob and Clem spotted a white Toyota sports-car-looking thing turning onto 20 and said it looked like her driving. She called yesterday and made an appointment for one o'clock tomorrow. How do you want me to handle her?"

"She doesn't know it's me who wants to buy the bar?"

"Nope. Just said a nameless client."

"Good. I don't know how she feels about the likes of me, and she might refuse to sell it out of spite. If she accepts the offer, I'll have you handle everything and then sign it over to me. By then she'll be long gone with no reason to ever come back."

Wharton propped his feet on the corner of his desk. He didn't usually work late, but he'd had an appointment with a particular lady who was seeking a divorce. If they conducted their business behind closed blinds late in the evening, well, it wasn't anybody's business but theirs.

"What if she stays?" Sam said.

"Huh? Is that what she said, she was coming back to stay?"

"Calm down, that's not what she said. But we have to be prepared for the possibility. She's stubborn enough to do it, too. If she thinks you're lowballing the offer, and with no one I know willing to manage that bar for her, it's kinda like cornering a wild hog. She might just attack."

His client seemed to consider that. "Well, you're the one who said to make that offer. I can up it."

"You probably should. The bar is on that nice corner lot with the river on two sides. I'd up it to sixty grand."

The man on the other end let out a spew of cuss words. "I ain't got that kind of money, Sam, you know that." He stewed for a few seconds. "All right, offer her forty-five and go up to sixty, but only if you have to. I'll talk to the bank tomorrow morning and see if I can wrangle that much."

"Let me know." There was a glob of cum on his calendar desk pad, and he smeared it with his finger. He'd have a reminder of their fun for the rest of the month. "What if she does stay?"

"That can't happen. I want that bar. Elva told me she'd sell it to me. She was thinking about retiring next year. That bar is mine. Kim ain't gonna stay. She's got nothing here."

"And if she does stay?" It wouldn't hurt to keep him riled up, just in case. Sam didn't want her to stay, either.

"I'm going to get that bar one way or the other," he said in a confident voice.


Tullie Macgregor Kendall's bare feet padded down the circular staircase at Heron's Glen and took her into the leisure room where her mama and grandpa Winn were playing backgammon. Daddy was out fishing, and the big house was so quiet she'd thought everyone had left her alone. Mama was dressed in a silky blue gown and matching robe fringed with white fur. She was so beautiful, the most beautiful woman ever. She dyed her hair auburn—Mama hated when Tullie called it red—and kept it short. Wasn't it better to have a pretty mama than having one who messed up her nails and hair playing in the park or tickling her?

"Hey, frog, whatcha doing up so late?" her grandpa asked, swiveling his wheelchair around to face her.

He'd called her frog ever since she was little and liked catching the green frogs that lived around the house. She climbed up in his lap but looked at her mama. "I'm nine. Shouldn't I be allowed to stay up later now?"

Charlotte Macgregor Kendall tamped out her cigarette. "It's almost ten o'clock. Why are you up?"

She knew her mama didn't like when she talked about her feelings, but she couldn't ignore them, especially not after Miss Elva died. She couldn't help but wonder if it was her fault somehow. "I got one of my feelings, Mama. I saw Uncle Zell and some lady I don't know. Something bad was gonna happen." She turned to Grandpa when her mama wrinkled her nose. "I was right about Miss Elva. I had a bad feeling about her, and she died. And now I saw Uncle Zell and . . . I'm scared."

Grandpa hugged her close. "Not every bad feeling comes true."

"I know, but this one came with pictures." Most of the time she just got a feeling. The pictures scared her most. "Where's Uncle Zell?"

"Who knows where that boy is?" Grandpa said with a laugh. "But he's been taking care of himself for a long time, frog. I wouldn't worry none about him."

She shifted on his lap. "What about the lady? I didn't know her." She turned to Mama. "She was as old as you, with short blond hair, almost as short as yours."

Mama dropped one of the game pieces loudly on top of another. She gave Grandpa a funny look. "When is Kim Lyons due back in town?"

"She might already be here."

"Who's that?" Tullie asked. "I never heard of her."

Her mama crossed her legs in that quick way she did when she was irritated. "Wish we hadn't, either."

Tullie turned to her grandpa for the answer, since her mama was now taking a long drink from her wineglass.

He said, "She . . . well, she lived here at Heron's Glen for about two years. I married her mama. You were too young to remember Kitty before she died. Kim is Kitty's daughter and Elva's granddaughter—"

Mama leaned forward, slamming her glass down on the table. "We don't talk about her. She betrayed us."

"Betrayed?" Tullie asked.

Mama said, "Remember that baby raccoon we found? We nursed it back to health and then it bit you. For no reason, just turned on you."

Tullie looked at the faint scar on her finger. She remembered all the shots she'd had to get.

"Well, that's what Kim did to us. She bit us. That's why we don't talk about her."

Even Grandpa had a hard, mean look on his face. He softened it when he saw her looking at him. "Forget about her. She'll be gone before you ever meet up with her."

Mama lit up another of those nasty cigarettes. Tullie particularly hated them because sometimes when Mama got to gesturing, she lost track of where that hot tip was. She'd burned both Tullie and her daddy a few times. Boy, did he get mad. "Honey, give your mama a kiss good night and get on up to bed."

Tullie kissed her grandpa's soft cheek and slid down to the floor. Her mama's lips were always cool as they brushed her own. She started to leave the room, but paused. "What about my bad feeling? What if that Kim is the lady I'm seeing and something bad happens to her?"

Her mama smirked. "Well, that'd be the best thing to happen in a good long time."

That wasn't nice, but Tullie didn't say that. Her mama could be mean sometimes. Tullie walked out of the room, but remained just out of view.

Her heart tightened when Grandpa said, "You ought not to dismiss the girl's feelings. She had a feeling about me right before my stroke, remember? And before the fire broke out in the shed."

Mama made a sound of frustration. "Why must my only child be so strange? I know it was because I smoked weed before I knew I was preggers."

"Charlotte—"

"There's a reason why animals eat their young, you know."

"Charlotte!"

"Well, Daddy, it's true. All right, all right. What about Kim?"

"She's got an appointment with Sam Wharton tomorrow. He's going to make her an offer for the bar. If she's smart, she'll take it and run. Can't imagine her staying in town much longer than a few days."

Her mama's voice sounded as sharp as ice cubes dropping in a glass. "I hope so, for her sake."

Tullie ducked out of the shadows and ran up to her room. She *was* strange; all the kids in school told her so. But it wasn't right, her own mama thinking that, was it? It wasn't right at all.

Her pink nightgown puddled on the carpet when she pushed the straps off her shoulders. She kicked it away and changed into long pants and a shirt. Without making a sound, she crept out the front door and climbed on her bike.

# CHAPTER 3

Kim pulled her small canister of police-issue tear gas from the glove compartment. How long ago had she bought it, anyway? Years ago from a hairdresser who was selling them illegally. Maybe too long, but it was all she had. She waited for a minute or two, hoping the owner of the truck would come out. Of course, that'd be too easy. No, he or she was going to make her come to them.

She'd expected some trouble, but mostly in the form of bad attitudes and being snubbed. She hadn't thought about anything worse than that. Who knew she was going to be in town? Well, just about everybody if Cypress was as close-knit as it used to be. She was sure that as soon as she'd called Wharton and set up an appointment, he'd called somebody, who'd called somebody . . . and so on. The two thousand residents kept tabs on everyone and enjoyed every minute of it.

She pushed the car door open and couldn't breathe. Warm, moist air poured down her throat and tightened her lungs. Wearable air, Elva used to say, so thick it felt like a coat. Before Kim could get used to it and draw a deep breath, she was assaulted by what made the air even thicker—mosquitoes. She made a quick dash to the front porch door, avoiding the gaping hole where a board on the steps was missing. The porch ran the length of the house and was screened in. A hundred mosquitoes followed her in.

She slapped as quietly as she could as miniature needles pricked her skin. The light illuminated a can of Bug Off right outside the door. She closed her eyes and doused herself with the cool spray. One problem down, one bigger problem to go.

The keys to the house and bar were beneath the mat as Wharton promised. She grabbed the can and held it in front of her as she unlocked the door. The house was dark inside. As her eyes adjusted, she searched for movement or a flash of light. There was nothing. In the movies, people always called out "Hello? Is anyone there?" thus giving away their location and presence. She remained quiet.

The smell of old wood reminded her of days spent here with Elva, fixing a big pan of buttery eggs and greasy bacon, laughing at Elva's dirty jokes, and thinking it would last forever. Kim moved away from the door and listened to the dark silence. She remembered the layout of the house: kitchen to the right, living room to the left, Elva's bedroom in the rear left and the extra room to the right.

She flicked on one light in the living room. Elva liked things dark and cozy. The walls and floors were rough-hewn wood and the couch was brown. A few cheap porcelain knickknacks lined the mantel of the small fireplace. She started at the sight of a fox peering around the couch. Not the owner of the truck, obviously, but just as startling. How had it gotten inside? After a minute, she realized it didn't look quite right. It hadn't moved, twitched, or even breathed since she'd spotted it. It didn't react when she walked closer. She reached down and touched it.

"Eww." It was a stuffed fox, a real one.

A barn owl was poised to take flight from above the kitchen cabinets, and a raccoon held a fish in its paws on the coffee table. Sometime in the last eight years Elva had gotten into having dead animals around her home. Charming, real charming.

A hallway led to the two rear bedrooms and one bathroom. Holding the can aloft, she snapped on the light and surveyed Elva's bedroom. Aside from the stuffed alligator— God, she hoped it was stuffed—all looked as usual. She even checked behind the shower curtain imprinted with tropical fish. When she opened the door to the second room, she spotted something more disconcerting than a stuffed alligator. Through the rear window she saw a structure out back with a light on inside.

Kim walked back outside and down the steps. Mosquitoes buzzed around her but didn't alight. What did people do before spray? she wondered, waving them away from her face. When she walked around a bush, she saw what the structure was: a hothouse. Wood beams were covered in an opaque plastic that served as roof and walls.

A silhouette moved inside, a tall silhouette. Her fingers tightened on the can. For the first time, she wished Simon had come with her. He would have insisted they call the authorities, which wasn't what she really wanted to do her first day back. She was tough, this was her property, and she'd handle it. If only her heart would stop pummeling her rib cage.

She wasn't sure what the hothouse contained. Who knew what Elva's latest interest was? Hopefully it wasn't taxidermy, and there weren't dead animals in various states of preservation inside. Her stomach clenched even worse as she advanced across the damp ground toward the structure. Anyone sneaking around on someone else's property at this hour was probably up to no good.

The door was closed, but she could hear faint music inside. Did the person even know she was there? Maybe it would be better to call the sheriff's substation and hope Kinsey wasn't still the shift commander. Before she could think better of it, she'd pushed open the door, held out her can of tear gas, and said over the music, "You're trespassing on private property."

The man standing amid a mass of orchids didn't appear

to be stealing them. In fact, he held a plastic spray bottle in his hand. He wore a shirt covered with mountain ranges and surfers. He took her in with eyes the color of the curling water on his shirt, glancing at the can in her hand briefly before meeting her gaze. Unfortunately, he didn't look at all concerned. He misted the orchid he'd been poised over. "You gonna deet me to death?"

She blinked. This was as bizarre as finding the stuffed fox in the house. "What?"

He inclined his head toward the can. "Deet. The chemical in swamp sucker spray."

She dropped her gaze to the can—of Bug Off. Crap, she'd grabbed the wrong can. She set it on a flat board crammed with pots of orchids. "Zell," she said in a sort-of greeting, the kind you give one of the last people you want to see.

"Kim," he said in that same way, but added a slow appraisal that foolishly made her hope to see approval. He gave away nothing. He reached over and turned down the small CD player on the upper shelf as the Black Crowes sang about a remedy.

Her former stepbrother. He'd been just about gorgeous back then, if a bit rangy. Now he'd filled out some, more than some as evidenced by the slice of bare chest she could see since he hadn't buttoned his shirt. The problem was, he knew he was gorgeous. Add that to his family's money and name, and it was just about disgusting. Not that he rubbed his money or his name in anyone's face; at least he didn't use to. He'd probably matured into a bigger jerk, so forget that lurch in your stomach, she told herself. Forget that Cupid's bow mouth of his that had intrigued her even as she'd hated him. Despite her thoughts, she involuntarily ran her hand back over her hair as she looked around the hothouse.

He continued misting the orchids. "I was wondering when you were going to make your way out here."

"You knew I was here? Why didn't you come out?"

"Like I said, figured you'd make your way out here

eventually. Didn't expect you tonight, actually. Thought you'd be coming in tomorrow to meet with Sam."

Zell hadn't done much in a hurry, she remembered, always thinking through new situations at his leisure. If he hadn't been expecting her, he'd probably been thinking through her arrival. Which didn't excuse his giving her the heebie-jeebies, though she wouldn't admit that to him.

Whatever he was spraying on the orchids smelled like soapy dishwater. He was focusing on his task while she focused on a muscle in his forearm that moved with every squeeze of the trigger. "What are you doing here, anyway?"

He slid her a look. "Trespassing on private property, it would seem."

That was something else she remembered about the exasperating Zell Macgregor: he didn't answer questions straight-out.

"Well, you *are* trespassing."

His mouth quirked at the corner. "I suppose I am, technically speaking."

He leaned past her and sprayed the orchids next to her, accidentally—or maybe not—misting her. He smelled like mosquito spray, cologne, and male, a combination that was oddly intriguing. He ought to look silly, wearing that tropical shirt and misting orchids, but he managed to pull it off somehow. She wasn't going to back away as he brushed by her.

When he seemed absorbed in his task, she decided not to let him bother her and looked around. There were squares of screen that acted as windows, letting in what constituted a breeze and keeping out the mosquitoes that were itching to get in. She realized then that she'd slid back to her old ways, closing the door as soon as she'd entered the hothouse to keep the buggers out.

*Hothouse* was the right word for it, too. It was like a steam bath scented with earth and flowers. The humidity wrapped around her and dampened the hair at her neck. The place was crammed with orchids of every kind, from the showy to ones with prissy little flowers. Larger plants were mounted on the wood support beams. Toward the back was a table with bags of bark pieces and pots. Elva was definitely into orchids. Or had been, she thought as a shadow crossed her heart. She turned back to Zell, surprised to find him watching her.

He hung the bottle on a hook and rubbed his hands on his jeans. "Guess these are yours now. Best take care to keep them alive before you sell them."

"That's what you were doing here? Taking care of Elva's orchids?"

He leaned an arm against the support beam. "It would appear so."

The man was infuriating. Not once had he smiled at her, though she supposed her entrance hadn't warranted a warm welcome, armed with bug spray and accusing him of trespassing and all.

"So you're helping Elva? Or . . . me?" Those words had come through a tightened throat.

"Now, don't go thinking I'm doing anything benevolent. Particularly on your behalf."

She crossed her arms over her chest and hoped she didn't look defensive. "I wouldn't expect you to."

He grabbed the portable CD player, hit the stop button, and headed to the door. "I was merely protecting my interests."

"And those would be?"

"These orchids. Elva borrowed the money for these from me. She had a mind to start an orchid-breeding business. Started out with a couple dozen and then bought out some guy's collection in Miami."

She could only stare at him for a moment. Great. Now she was probably into Zell for a couple hundred dollars. "She borrowed money from you?"

"I've got a contract at the house. She insisted on having it drawn up legal-like. I can get you a copy."

She shook her head. "I believe you." Zell didn't need to lie for money. "I'll pay you back when I get everything settled." She turned back to the orchids. "I guess this means I have to keep these things alive."

"If you want to get your money out of them."

She took in the hundred or so plants. "Are they easy to take care of?" Of course, she was probably asking too much; like he'd said, he wasn't going to help her. He'd help anyone but her, she imagined.

He seemed to weigh being helpful against family loyalty and past betrayals. In the end, he set down the player. "Sure, as long as you know their individual needs. I'm no expert, I just remember what Elva told me." He walked over to a shelf of plants with beautiful orange flowers. "In general, they like humidity and music. Some people talk to their plants, but Elva played music for hers. I don't play that country stuff she liked, but they've been okay with rock and roll." He nodded toward the section closest to the door. "Here you got your Oncidiums, otherwise known as dancing ladies because that's what they look like." They did indeed look like Spanish dancers wearing flowing yellow dresses with orange bodices.

He pointed to a section of tall plants with white flowers going from the top down to the base of the plant. "These are Phalaenopsis. They like humidity but no sun. A slice of sun cruises through that far corner during the day so they get just enough. The ones in the hanging pots are vandas, and they're about ready to be repotted. Those are Dendrobium Nobiles, and since they're flowering, they like to be in a cooler area. Cattleyas like to dry out between waterings. Miltonias, on the other hand, can't dry out at all. And that group of Phalaenopsises have some kind of bacteria on them."

He nodded toward the bottle he'd been using. "Spray them with that once in a while. Wash your hands after touching them so you don't spread it to the others. That'll get you started, anyway."

"Yeah, thanks." For nothing, she wanted to add. He knew exactly what he was doing; giving her so much information at once, he was no help at all. "How about you take these in payment for what Elva owed you?"

"I don't do orchids. Just keep them alive and you'll get your money out of them."

No way. She was the biggest brown thumb she knew. It was all she could do to keep her philodendron and fern alive.

"How much did Elva borrow, anyway?"

"Five thousand."

Her mouth dropped open. "Dollars?".

"She was serious about this orchid thing. So don't let those plants die now. Some of them are rare. That one in the back corner is worth about three hundred dollars by itself. The one next to it will probably net you four hundred. The rest of them are worth from twenty to seventy apiece."

"Dollars?" she repeated.

"Orchids are big business." He nodded, the closest he'd get to a civil parting, she supposed.

She watched him walk to his truck through the screen window, though all she could see was his silhouette in the shadows. She felt a twisting in her stomach she was sure was frustration and irritation, both at Zell and herself. Why should she care if he hadn't smiled or asked how she was doing? They may have been loosely related once upon a time, but there wasn't one warm fuzzy between them. And that was before the murder trial.

Only after he left did she pull her gaze back to the hothouse. Zell's CD player was sitting on the table near the door. Oh, well, she'd get it back to him. When she picked it up, she realized it wasn't a CD player; it played digital music tracks. She turned back to the orchids.

They were odd-looking plants. They all seemed to be looking at her, clamoring for care and attention: *Feed me! Feed me!* She imagined them marching slowly forward, closing in around her, and then like that movie with the man-eating plant, they'd start nibbling on her.

She shook her head. Grief and frustration and waning adrenaline were all warping her brain. Add nine hours of driving on top of that, and it was no wonder she was nearly hallucinating. She was pretty sure it wasn't her imagination that many of them looked as though they were sticking their tongue out at her, though.

"Elva, what kind of mess did you leave me in? In charge of keeping a couple hundred orchids alive and in debt to Zell Macgregor. Can it get any worse?"

Even as she uttered the question, she thought, *Famous last words . . .*


Zell paused at the end of Elva's driveway and glanced back at the dark hammock. So Kim was back. He was sure she wasn't going to stay long. No reason unless she had some crazy idea about running the bar. He tensed at the thought of her living there again. Nah, she didn't have the guts to do that. He pulled out onto the highway and headed north. It was then that he realized he'd left his music player in the hothouse. He'd get it tomorrow when he brought her a copy of the agreement. Maybe she didn't have the nerve to call him a liar, but he'd just as soon make it on the up-and-up. And he had another little surprise for her, too. He grinned at the prospect.

He drove between the stone columns announcing Heron's Glen. His dad had just put those in. To Zell's thinking, it was a bit like rubbing it in. As if Winn were making a point since the big house couldn't be seen except by air or boat. Zell stopped at the crossroads. The alligator farm loomed in the near distance, lit up for security. To the left a ways sat the big house, Heron's Glen itself. To the right was his place. Charlotte and her family had taken over the house, with Winn in residence, and Zell was happy to let them have it. He'd built his octagon house himself, with the help of a few friends. It sat on short stilts at the edge of a marsh prairie. The bay was pretty enough, but looking out over a vast prairie with palmetto heads in the distance was more his style.

"Holy—"

Out of the darkness came Tullie on her bike, her long blond hair swaying as she turned toward him. He swerved to the left and came up beside her. "What are you doing out this time of night? Does your mama know where you are?"

The girl was as pretty as one of those orchids and just as mysterious. She had the trademark Macgregor blond locks that would turn darker with the years (unless she dyed them like Charlotte did), but she'd gotten her daddy's lighter blue eyes. She hardly ever smiled or laughed, and that bothered him more than anything else about her.

She was breathless, looking as serious as always, but not panicked in a the-house-is-on-fire way. "Uncle Zell, I gotta talk to you."

"Let's put your bike in the back." He jumped out and set the bike in the bed of his truck.

She climbed in and slid across the driver's bench. He got in and closed the door, letting the cold air wash over them. The colder the better, though he turned the fan down for Tullie's sake and turned on the interior light. "What's up, angel?"

That endearment always got a ghost of a smile out of her. This time she hugged him harder than he thought she'd be able to. When she sat back, he said, "What was that for?"

"I'm glad you're okay."

"'Course I'm okay. Well, according to most folks, anyway." Some of the women he'd dated would call him self-centered, and they were right. Others might call him full of himself, but he wasn't so sure about that. "What's got you so worried?"

She folded her hands in her lap. "You believe me, right? About my feelings, I mean."

"'Course I do. Did someone give you a hard time again?"

She shook her head, but that solemn look said otherwise. Charlotte was probably the worst offender, dismissing the child altogether. Not that she called Tullie names, but Charlotte should accept her child no matter what.

"I had one of those dreams with the bad feeling again. You were in it."

He ruffled her hair. "And you were worried about me." She nodded, and his throat tightened at the love he saw in her eyes. "Well, I'm just fine, see." He held out his arms.

"Will you be careful, Uncle Zell? At least until that Kim Lies leaves?"

"Who?"

"Kim somebody, the one who betrayed us." She rubbed her finger.

"How do you know about her?"

"I think she was in the dream, too, her and you. Something bad was happening, but I couldn't tell what it was."

He leaned against the steering wheel. "What did she look like?"

"She had blond short hair, short like Mama's, and she was tall, for a girl, anyway. Not as tall as you. Pretty, but not as pretty as Mama."

He considered that for a moment. "That does sound like Kim." She wasn't as pretty as Charlotte, but Kim had surprised him by being prettier than he'd remembered. Her blond hair wasn't as short as Shar's, though. It flipped up at the ends, grazing her shoulders. Her mouth was full and wide. She'd filled out that gawky too-tall frame of hers some. The unthinking male part of him might even be interested in her if it didn't know any better. "But she'll be gone soon enough."

"I hope so."

"Is that all that's bothering you?" When she nodded, he said, "I'm going to take you on home. I'll cut my lights so you won't get in trouble. I presume no one knows you're out here?"

"Nope." Again, that ghost of a smile. "Thanks, Uncle Zell."

He put the truck in reverse, speeding backward until he reached the intersection. As promised, he cut the headlights and then grabbed the bike out of the bed. In the yellow glow of the running lights, Tullie's solemn face looked at him.

"Uncle Zell, what's 'smoking weed'?"

That took him aback. "Why would you ask something like that?"

"That's why I'm strange, 'cause Mama smoked weed when she was preggers."

He knelt down to her level. "Who told you that?"

Her voice went soft. "I heard her say it to Grandpa. She said that's why animals eat their young."

He swallowed a curse so it came out as a hiss and put his hand on her shoulder. "You're not strange, Tullie. Different, but not strange. And there's nothing wrong with being different. In fact, it's a good thing. We got our own personal warning system in you. Nobody else around here has that." He gave her shoulder a squeeze and stood. "I'll be careful, I promise. Go on in, now. I'll watch you."

She rode the rest of the way down the drive, waved, and disappeared inside. Now he let the curse out. He was going to have another talk with his sister, damn her loose mouth.

He remained leaning against the front grille of the truck for another minute, thinking about the warning he'd promised to heed. Had Tullie ever seen a picture of Kim? Not likely. Any pictures of her had been cut out and thrown away. The description was too close to discount. Even if Kim was back for a short time, her presence was bound to cause turmoil just when life was settling into a pleasant routine.

Winn had always been the baby of his family, even after he'd married and had two kids of his own. Though tragedies had flattened Winn's spirit, his stroke had made him finally take responsibility for himself and his family. It wasn't easy to get used to, but Zell was too happy not having to baby him to mind much. Except for Elva's unexpected death, for the first time in years, he was enjoying a selfish, easy life.

Kim's reappearance was going to change that. He just had a feeling about it.

# CHAPTER 4

Kim left a message for Simon that she'd gotten there safely, leaving out the part about being scared halfway to the afterlife. He sure hadn't wasted any time setting up plans for the night.

She'd started to change the sheets on Elva's bed, but realized she couldn't sleep there. She took a shower, put some sheets on the old but fabulously comfortable couch, and dropped in exhaustion. Then she lay there thinking for the next few hours. She'd forgotten how many sounds filled the swamp night air: something scurrying across the roof, the low twang of the bullfrogs, the plaintive cry of the whip-poorwill, and . . . *footsteps?*

She crept through the darkened house and looked out the windows. Every shadow was shaped like a human or monster. She waited to see if they moved, but nothing stirred in the airless night. All right, it was probably her imagination then.

Elva didn't own a radio, and the television's rabbit ears only pulled in three snowy stations, so Kim turned on Zell's music player. Her thoughts ran from Elva and the bar to her dad, whose pictures were scattered around the house in various stages of his life. "He was always into something,"

Elva would say when she reminisced. Unfortunately, that was the truth.

Kim's thoughts moved to her encounter with Zell, and finally to the music itself. He had a mix from the eighties to the present. "That Don't Satisfy Me" by Brother Cane; a romantic ballad, "Angel," by Aerosmith; "Bent" from Matchbox 20; "Love Stinks" by the J. Geils Band; "Love Ain't No Stranger" by Whitesnake. Some she knew only because the title scrolled across the small screen, like the rap-rock "In the End" by Linkin Park and the poignant guitar ballad "Bokeelia" by Andy Wahlberg.

She realized she was trying to find Zell in those songs and she was too tired to question why she even bothered. Was he involved with someone? Married? Somehow she didn't see him married; he was too hard to get to know.

Unfortunately, listening to his music made her dream about him when she finally did drop off, which put him in her thoughts when she woke up in the morning. She was sure she was only thinking about him because he was so damned irritating. Or maybe because he disliked her; it always bothered her when someone disliked her, though she'd never admit it. She made a mental note to buy some batteries to replace the ones she'd worn out on his player.

She scrounged up some tea bags and brewed a pot of raspberry tea. She planned to go to the bar in the morning when no one would be there. She needed some quiet time to take it in and think. Her appointment with Wharton was at one; he'd probably try to buy the place from her again. Maybe she should counteroffer and sell it. Sure, she wanted her own bar, but if she didn't live here to enjoy it, what was the point?

She took her cup and walked around the house. This place would be harder to sell. Nestled in the swamp a good ten minutes outside of Cypress, and not a neighbor to be seen for miles . . . who would want to make this their home?

Elva, for one. She'd loved this place. Kim remembered her picking up odds and ends, sometimes even things other people had put out in the trash. The coffee table was missing a leg; Elva had made do with a leg from another table. None of the chairs at the kitchen table resembled one another. Her dishes were a collection of interesting plates and cups and saucers, mostly unmatched. A wooden étagère was filled with knickknacks like cranberry glass, old perfume bottles, and bowls of shells. Mediocre paintings depicting Florida scenes adorned some of the walls, all done by someone named P. Witherspoon. On top of the old television were a group of framed pictures. One was the shell frame she'd made for her father, and inside was the picture of her and her dad. Lying around the frame was a shell necklace her father had made for her in return. She picked it up and fingered the smooth edges.

Elva met her husband, Pete, in Naples. Soon after they'd married, Pete took a job at a seafood-packing plant in Cypress. He didn't bother to ask Elva how she'd feel about living in the swamp far from any city, and Elva, being a good Christian woman, never thought to object.

Elva had hated Cypress at first, but she'd grown to love it. She and Pete had built their home and made their life together with their son. Pete then announced he'd taken a job in Tallahassee, probably not coincidentally around the time their grown son announced he'd gotten Kitty Parsons pregnant. Well, Elva was still a good Christian woman, but she'd had enough of being told where she was going to live—and she wasn't leaving Cypress. She did, however, help him pack.

Kim took in the house, trying to ignore the animals looking at her with their glassy eyes. She had always felt just as at home here as she had in her childhood home. Maybe even more so since there wasn't any turmoil. Her dad was always into some kind of trouble and her mom was always yelling at him about it. She'd warned him that his hijinks were going to make her a widow someday, and she was right. But oh, her daddy lived with passion while her mom spent her days wishing she had more money and more dignity and felt she deserved more than she'd gotten.

Kim finished her tea, grabbed her small purse, and stepped out onto the front porch. That meant dousing herself with spray. Because Cypress was surrounded by parkland, mosquito control didn't send their planes down this way. The only relief was the trucks that drove around the town puffing out smoke. Those didn't do a lot of good way out here.

A cacophony of bird sounds greeted her. Just past the driveway two great blue herons prowled the shallow waters for a late breakfast. She loved the birds down here, especially the wading birds. Herons and egrets and the wood storks—or iron heads as they were called locally—that were making a slow but strong comeback. A pileated woodpecker drifted from one tree to the next as it kept a wary eye on her. Kim felt a swell in her chest as she took everything in. She'd missed this.

"Grandma, what am I supposed to do with this place? And all those orchids?"

She lifted her head at a familiar sound. She knew what her grandma must have felt at hearing that crunch of shell beneath tire—trepidation. Unannounced visitors weren't usually good news, that's what she'd always said.

She wasn't sure what she felt when Zell's fancy truck pulled into view. Trepidation, sure, until she realized he was probably bringing a copy of the loan agreement. So what was the buzz that felt as though she'd walked into an electric cattle fence? Listening to his music and dreaming about him half the night hadn't helped, either. That reminded her of the music player, and she went inside to get it.

When she reappeared outside, he was unhitching the rear gate of his truck. He wore another colorful tropical shirt and jeans that were faded in just the right places.

"Thought I'd scared you back into the house," he said by way of a greeting. Not that she expected a cheery *good morning* out of him.

She walked to the truck. "You forgot this last night."

"Thanks." He tossed it into the cab of his truck and then went around to the back.

"I'm afraid I owe you some batteries. I listened to it last night and fell asleep with it on."

He paused. "You listened to my music?"

She shrugged. "It was better than wondering what every little sound was. Not that I was afraid or anything, just not used to the sounds out here anymore."

He stared at her for a moment, making her feel self-conscious. Making her wonder what she'd admitted to. No way could he extrapolate that she'd been thinking about him while listening to his music.

"Did you enjoy the selection?" he asked at last.

"It was . . . interesting. You have eclectic taste, that's for sure." She ruffled her fingers through her hair, still getting a strange feeling there was a subtext going through their conversation. "I liked it. Most of it, anyway."

The corner of his mouth tugged, just barely a smile. Before she could wonder if he was, in fact, smiling, he pulled a folded piece of paper out of his back pocket and handed it to her. "Here's a copy of the agreement. Elva already made some payments. I wrote the balance on the back. We can settle up when you sell the bar or the orchids, whichever comes first." He pulled out a large box filled with blankets and pillows. "Don't worry about the batteries. Can you get the door?"

She opened the door to the porch and then to the house, waiting for some kind of explanation. After he'd set the box down in the living room and headed out again, she asked, "What is this?"

"That goes with this." He opened the passenger door to his truck and let out one of the ugliest pigs she'd ever seen. It was black and hairy with a saggy chin and a belly that nearly scraped the ground. Its ears were erect, and its snout was long. She surmised it was happy because its little tail was twitching. Then again, it could have been hungry. She took a step back as it approached. Zell said, "This is Oscar. He's a potbellied pig—and he's yours."

Without further explanation, he lifted a large bag from the truck bed and hoisted it over his shoulder, then grabbed up a mesh bag. He walked into the house after leaving the door open for Oscar the pig and letting him enter first. She was left to follow. Why was it that every time she saw Zell, she felt discombobulated? She was chagrined to admit how much he threw her off.

He'd set the brown bag against the wall and was filling one large bowl with water. Then he poured brown pellets from the bag into another bowl, and from the mesh bag dumped out a bunch of toys. Oscar snurfled (that was the word that popped into her head, anyway) everything and then roamed the living room as though he were checking it out to make sure she hadn't changed anything.

Zell was already out front again, removing a wooden box filled with smooth stones and setting it on the ground. "Owen made this. It's a rooting box. Better that he roots out here than in the house. Throw in some popcorn or Cheerios once in a while."

She grabbed at his arm and then pulled back. Touching Zell after a long, lonely night thinking about him wasn't the best idea. "You can't leave this . . . this pig here."

One side of his mouth lifted in what was no doubt a smile. "Sure I can. This is Oscar's home." He walked on out to his truck, forcing her to follow once again.

"It is?"

He leaned against the door of the truck. "Oscar was Elva's pig. For a time she took to breeding them, but she grew out of it and got rid of the other pigs. She kept Oscar. They had a special friendship, she and Oscar. When she died, I took him 'cause there wasn't anybody else to do it. But since you came back, I'm giving him to you. Consider him part of your inheritance."

"You can keep him. I mean, I'd like you to keep him." She forced a smile even though she wanted to call him a few ugly names for enjoying her discomfort so much.

He shook his head. "Oscar's okay, but I'm not a pig person. Besides, a gator'll likely eat him out at my place. He's easy to take care of."

Oh, no, not this again. "Easy," she said, the word etched in doubt.

"Feed him twice a day, including lots of leafy vegetables, make sure he has plenty of water, let him outside a few times to attend to his business, give him a brushing once in a while, and don't feed him from the table. He likes carrots, and pickles are great for getting him to do what you want. But don't feed him much human food. It'll make him fat."

"Fat! He must weigh a hundred pounds!"

"A hundred and twenty-five, I'd figure. Pigs are smart so don't start him on any bad habits. Just like people, they pick 'em up fast and don't shed 'em too easily." He gave the truck cab a couple of taps with his palm and opened the door.

That's it. He was going to leave her. "Zell." He paused. Instead of trying to get more information about the pig, she found herself asking, "You knew my grandma pretty well, didn't you?"

The smirk left his face and was replaced by a melancholy shadow. "She was good people, your grandma." He got into the truck and pulled away.

Mosquitoes buzzed around her. Swamp suckers, Zell had called them. She waved them from her face and watched his truck disappear around the bend. She turned and looked at the house. The exterior wood was stained dark brown, as though Elva wanted it to blend in with the dirt yard and surrounding hammock. Fishing nets were strung from the gutters, and Kim wondered if it was for decoration or just a place to hang them. With Elva, you never knew.

A pain worse than a thousand bloodsucking mosquitoes crushed her chest. She'd run away from all this, from what she loved—she swatted at a mosquito hovering near her nose—and the things she hated. More than anything, she'd loved her grandma, but she'd left her behind, too. She turned around and found Oscar looking at her. This was crazy. First the orchids and now a pig! And Zell tangled up with all of it. Well, she probably wouldn't see him again. That was fine with her.

She took in the house, the hothouse, and the surrounding wilderness. A haunting song from Zell's music list played through her mind. "One Simple Thing" by the Stabilizers. They swore that one simple thing was all they needed to make it complete. There was one thing she needed to feel complete: a home. Someplace she could hang her tacky beer signs and leave her keys wherever she damn well pleased.

Oscar snorted.

"What am I going to do with you?" Now that she'd thought about it, she'd seen a picture of Elva and a pig in the house. "All right, fine. We'll figure something out. I hope." Maybe one of the locals would take him. And not eat him. Did people eat potbellied pigs? She wouldn't put it past some of the folks she'd known around there. Great, something else to worry about. "How'd you get outside, anyway?" Her gaze went to a large dog door inside the screen door. "Oh." She'd left the front door open. She tried to get the pig into the house, but he wouldn't go in. Some smart pig. "All right, spend some time out here then. There's plenty of water."

She walked to her car and opened the door, ready to jump in as quickly as possible. Which wasn't possible, because Oscar was now standing in her way. For a large animal, he sure moved fast. "Oscar, move! Mosquitoes are getting in."

Instead, he clambered into her car. It wasn't a pretty sight, but he managed, "Oh, no you don't! I'm going to the bar. A bar's no place for a pig."

Apparently it was, and apparently he was used to riding to work with Elva. He sat in the passenger seat and waited for her to stop letting in the mosquitoes and get in. Unfortunately, she wasn't going to get a hundred-pound-plus pig to go somewhere it didn't want to go. Resigned, she got in and slammed the door shut.

The city had put in a vibrantly painted sign just before the bridge that read, WELCOME TO CYPRESS. The sign depicted the Ten Thousand Islands at sunset with a white egret in the foreground. She wondered if Amy Macgregor Burton had painted it. She'd had quite a talent for painting, among other things that foddered plenty of gossip back in high school. Her mother was Winnerow's sister, Sue, who'd stabbed her abusive husband twenty-two times for killing her boa constrictor. Sue was spending her time in prison nowadays. Her son, Dougal, was so disgusted he'd taken the Macgregor name and refused to acknowledge either of his parents.

Oscar made a snorting noise that drew her from her thoughts. He looked odd sitting on the passenger seat. She crossed the bridge and took a deep breath as Cypress came into view. It was more built up than when she'd last been there. A sign for a quaint inn pointed down Sheepshead Lane. Signs of increased tourism were reflected in the new welcome center and billboards announcing the area's attractions. Macgregor's Airboat, Swamp Buggy, and Helicopter Rides had added eco tours, according to their billboard. Zell's aunt and uncle weren't the only ones offering such tours now.

She passed her turnoff and continued through town. A new gas station made the total two, and the convenience store had changed names. She breathed a sigh of relief that things hadn't changed too much. No apartment buildings or large-scale businesses, just the same quaint, simple town.

She intended to make the loop on Cypress Road, which traced the west edge of town along the Lost River, but she ended up cutting through the center of the residential area and stopping in front of her childhood home. Someone had put a small boat out front along with some crab traps, for decoration, she figured, since flowers bloomed through the slats. The homes scattered in this open area were small wooden refuges built decades ago up on short stilts to protect from flooding. Some of the homes were undergoing renovation, particularly the ones overlooking the river.

She circled back to Cypress Road, past the industrial

part of town where the local seafood was processed and the docks where the charter fishermen kept their boats. The small building that used to be the post office was now . . . well, what was it exactly? Kim paused and read the hand-painted sign: BEER, WORMS, AND WEDDINGS. Beneath that in smaller letters: WEDDINGS PERFORMED BY REV. HAM MACEY. BEER AND WORMS ARE SELF-SERVE.

"Well, okay then," she said, blowing out a breath. "Good to know."

As she crossed the main road again, she passed the marina, which had doubled in size since her last visit. And there was Southern Comfort, like an old friend waiting for her arrival.

It sat in the back corner, with the larger Lost River on one side and the smaller Snake River it split into on the back side. Beer signs, including one like hers with the lizards, invited a person to come in from the muggy heat and cool down with a brew and some music. The building was a small, oblong box that Elva had recently extended by several feet. The front door had been moved to the right; the previous door's opening was filled in with wood that didn't quite match the rest. A ramp had been installed for disabled persons. She wondered if Elva had ever taken her advice and built a deck out back. "Who wants to sit outside with the mosquitoes?" she'd said.

Kim glanced at the clock in her car: eleven. Where had the morning gone? It was already opening time. But there wasn't a car in sight and the lights weren't on. Where was Smitty?

She helped Oscar out of the car, and he ambled right up to the steps. He was definitely used to coming here. Her hand was shaking when she inserted the key. She realized she was afraid things had changed inside, obliterating all of her childhood memories. She'd spent so much time here, helping Elva after school and sometimes hanging out when her parents were either working or not getting along. Oddly enough, the bar had been her comfort zone.

She pushed open the door to the familiar smells of stale

smoke, beer, and old wood. And an unfamiliar one: the lingering aroma of fried food. Oscar walked right in and did the same checking-out routine he'd done with the house. She wondered if pigs lifted their leg to claim their territory. Ahead of her was a wall that she guessed enclosed the new kitchen.

She switched on the lights and took in the bar—and smiled. It was almost exactly as she remembered. The tightness in her chest eased. Like Elva's house, the interior was all dark wood. A long bar stretched along the back wall, its mirrors reflecting an impressive array of bottles. That bar had been Elva's pride, coming from an old saloon in Georgia. The piece had been hand-carved a century before from mahogany, stained dark and polished until it gleamed. The mirror had been broken in transit, and Elva had cried.

The rest of the open room had the usual smattering of tables, some small and cozy and some long enough to accommodate large groups. She'd added a second television. Most importantly, the pictures were still there adorning much of the wall space. They dated back to the beginnings of Cypress. There wasn't as much dust on the pictures as she thought there would be, only a thin layer. Grime filled the cracks in the floor, though. She imagined it sanded down and covered with a thick coat of varnish.

The addition was indeed a kitchen, a small one. She grabbed a plastic-coated menu off the table and read down the meager list of offerings: chicken wings five different ways, four different sandwiches, and a selection of fried veggies. She frowned. A kitchen meant a cook; all these tables meant a waitress. She glanced at the clock. Where was everybody?

The door opened and two scruffy-looking guys walked in. They stopped cold when they saw her.

"Hi, come on in. I'm Elva's granddaughter, Kim."

"We know who you are," one said.

"Where's Smitty?" the other one asked.

She said, "I . . . I don't know."

They turned around and left.

She did remember them, now that she thought about it. But she didn't remember having done anything to offend them.

An older couple came in. Kim vaguely remembered them too and greeted them the same way she'd greeted the men.

"Heard you was back," the woman said. She outweighed her husband by about a hundred pounds. "When you leaving?"

"I don't know." Bitterness burned her throat. As they turned to leave, she said, "Wait a minute. I don't remember kicking your dog or burning down your house. What's your problem?"

"No, but you tried to punish a good man for sins he didn't commit. The Macgregors been good to us over the years. We don't take quarter with people who done them wrong."

"Where's Smitty at?" her husband asked, scanning the room.

"He's not in yet."

He gave a *hmph* sound that his wife mirrored, and they left.

Kim dropped down to the nearest chair. What was going on here? Had the Macgregors asked everyone to boycott her? She rubbed her hands down her face. Is that what had happened to her waitress and cook? "Oh, Oscar, this isn't good."

The pig ate a French fry off the floor and looked up at her. He waddled over and touched his snout to her leg. She patted his head. He smelled like shampoo, which meant that Zell had bathed him before bringing him over. And that also meant that pigs required baths.

Before she could ponder the implications of all that, the door opened again. JoGene Waddell, her first love, walked in. Her heart did a funny skip-beat. He still looked rangy, not having put much meat on his five-eleven frame. His straight brown hair was parted on the side, and he sported a goatee that made him look all kinds of interesting. She'd lost him when she'd lost everything else. He'd broken things off, and she'd understood. She had, after all, implicated his father in a murder.

"Heard you were back," he said, walking with the same swagger he'd always had. He glanced around. "Where's Smitty?"

"The million-dollar question." She came to her feet and then didn't know what to do with her hands. "How are you doing?"

He took her in with a gaze that didn't reveal what he thought. "Good. Still working with my dad over at the Gun and Rod Club, managing the cabins now." He didn't sound thrilled about it, either.

He knelt down and petted Oscar, who leaned into his hand like they were old friends. It made her feel so left out she felt tears prick the backs of her eyes. She blinked quickly as JoGene straightened.

"How about you?" he asked.

"I don't know yet. Ask again in a few more days."

They both laughed in that awkward kind of way.

He looked around. "So, this is yours now."

"Yep. Did you . . . come in to eat?"

He hesitated. "Sure. I always get a BLT and a Budweiser."

She headed to the kitchen. "I didn't know Elva had a kitchen. I'm not sure what happened to the cook."

He followed and watched as she searched for foodstuffs. "Elva added this a few years back, because people kept asking her to serve a bit of food. She didn't have a cook during lunch. Linda May used to wait tables at night, and Elva and Smitty did the cooking and cleaning. It's not the kind of place you go out to eat dinner, but if you're coming here for a few brews, might as well eat, right?"

She figured out how to turn on the grill and separated slices of bacon. A large window above the grill allowed the cook to set the food on a counter for easy access. "You said Linda May used to wait tables."

He glanced away. "Her parents wanted her to take some time off . . ."

"While I'm here." She finished what he didn't say. "There *is* a boycott, isn't there? People keep coming in, asking for Smitty, and then leaving."

He leaned against the open swinging door. "I probably shouldn't be here, either. My dad'd have my hide."

"So your dad's still a controlling, tyrannical bastard, huh?" Buck had been a major drawback to dating JoGene.

"Yeah, I guess you could say that. And leave it to you to say that. You never did hold back your words."

"No point in it."

The bacon sizzled while she searched for the potato chips the menu said were served with the sandwiches. Next she found a plastic plate and dumped a pile of them on it. When she looked up, he was watching her again. She remembered hot kisses in the backseat of his Wrangler and how he'd try every which way to get her to go all the way.

"So about that boycott," she prodded.

He shrugged. "It's not like anything official. Everybody just knows you're in town and they remember. People around here remember things for a long time. You did try to nail their favorite son to the wall, after all, along with my dad."

"My dad was a favorite son, too. Nobody jumped to see that justice was done on his behalf."

JoGene lowered his head and his voice. "Kim, you have to let that go. It was an accident. That was always your problem, not letting things go."

Even though it was his father's best friend who'd killed her dad and not his father, JoGene looked uncomfortable with the conversation. Too uncomfortable. Before she could ask him why, he said, "So, how long are you staying?"

"The other million-dollar question. I'm not sure." She didn't know why she wouldn't say a week. That's all she had off from work. "So why are you here, then? To see if I'd gotten fat and dumpy?"

He chuckled and took her in. "You haven't gotten fat and dumpy, that's for sure."

She crinkled her nose. "Words to warm a girl's heart." She pulled out the toast and set the bacon to drain. "You want mayo?"

"Lots of it. So whatcha gonna do with this place, anyway?"

"I don't know yet. I wasn't expecting any of this. All of a sudden I've got a pig and a bunch of orchids and a bar and a house. It's a lot to take in."

"I imagine so."

"Wharton's got somebody who's too chicken to come forward and identify himself who wants to buy this place for next to nothing. You wouldn't happen to know who it is, would you?"

He surveyed the place. "Not sure how much this place would be worth. It's sitting on decent land, but it's a locals place. Doesn't attract many tourists, except for the folks who come to our club."

She handed him the plate. "Draft or bottle?"

"Draft."

A couple of guys had come in while she'd been in the kitchen. Though they didn't leave after her spiel, they asked about Smitty and then reluctantly decided to stay since they'd driven over and all.

When she dropped the draft off to JoGene, she asked, "Where can I find Smitty?"

"Maybe at his trailer over at the park. He's at the Sunset Park, south of our place."

She nodded and then got started on the other men's orders. No waitress, no cook, no Smitty, and hardly any customers. The longer she stayed, the more strain it was going to put on the bar's finances, whatever they were. She glanced at the clock. She wondered if Wharton and his secret client had anything to do with this.

When she dropped off JoGene's bill, he said, "You look good, Kim." He looked at her work-worn hands with short nails that wouldn't grow no matter how hard she tried. "You married yet?"

"Boyfriend. You?"

"Nope." In the awkward silence that followed, he got to his feet and handed her some bills. "Be seeing you around."

Would she be seeing him? And how did she feel about that? She only nodded as he wandered to the restroom. Who cared? It wasn't as though she were going to have a fling.

Why did Zell's sexy smirk come to mind at that thought? He was the last person she'd ever find appealing, other than in a purely aesthetic way. Even when they'd been forced into their stepsibling roles, even when she'd hated living among the Macgregors, she'd admired his looks. Especially when she'd accidentally walked in on him as he was drying himself off after a shower. She'd just stood there gawking at him for a few seconds before decency roused her.

Forget about that! Remember those vicious three-hour Ping-Pong matches played in the recreation area beneath the big house, and the way he'd smashed the ball at her and never once let her win.

All right, she might have had an itty-bitty crush on Zell. Except for that, JoGene had captivated her teenage heart. But now she had Simon, calm, predictable Simon who still hadn't returned her call. She was sure she missed him, or would when she got past her irritation with him. She threw JoGene's debris in the garbage can with a jerk of her hand and went out to see to her customers.

On his way out, JoGene stopped beside her and said, "I thought I should tell you . . . be careful, you hear?"

The warning, spoken in a low voice, tiptoed up her spine. "Why do you say that?"

"People are watching you. A few want to make sure you don't get any ideas about staying. I don't know how far they're willing to go to make that happen." He touched her cheek. "I just want you to stay safe."

# CHAPTER 5

Once Wharton had given her the necessary paperwork at the office, he said, "Lucky your granny put your name on the house and bar. That saved you from having to go through probate."

It was lucky. And odd. Elva always said she was going to live forever. She'd never drawn up a will and said she never would. Swore doing things like that invited death. "When did she add my name?"

"About five months ago." He turned to the shelf behind his desk and picked up a simple, metal urn. "This here's your granny."

Kim took the urn and tried not to think how unfair it was that her grandma, full of life and piss and vinegar, was ashes in a plain urn. What had made Elva think about dying? Then she realized something. "She was cremated? On whose authority?"

"It was a mistake, actually. The funeral home thought they were supposed to cremate her while we were still trying to track you down." He gave her a smile. "If you give it some thought, you'll agree that cremating her was best. You can spread her ashes somewhere that meant something to her. Now then." He pulled out a file and opened it. "We need to talk about my client's offer. As I said, no one here is going to run the bar when you go back to Tallahassee. You don't have any family here. There's no reason to hold on to it. The way I figure it, you're lucky someone wants it."

His words stung, but she kept her mouth in a tight line and didn't let him see it. She wanted to tell him that he couldn't be sure of that. There might be someone who'd help her out. Smitty's absence didn't bode well, but you never knew. Maybe he had the flu. "You're going to try to get me to take thirty grand for my bar again."

Wharton looked like a fat version of Uncle Sam, with a pointed white beard and white suit that smelled like he'd worn it a few too many times between washings. An unfiltered cigarette dangled from his mouth. "Nope, I'm not going to do that. He's willing to go up to forty-five thousand. I told him he was crazy upping his offer that much, but he figured you should get something out of it."

Acrid smoke drifted her way, but she made no move to show him it bothered her. "He. Who is it, and why isn't he man enough to identify himself?"

"Nothing to do with manliness. He just prefers to have me do the dealing part of things. Keeps it simple." He pulled out a contract. "All you have to do is sign here."

She wasn't sure where the words came from, was surprised when they came out of her mouth. "I might just stay in town, run the bar myself."

The cigarette dropped out of Wharton's slack lips.

Her instinct was to rush out words about not meaning it. Surely she didn't. As much as she loved Cypress, Cypress didn't seem to have much use for her. Simon sure wouldn't move there.

Wharton retrieved his cigarette. "No need to get nasty, Miss Lyons. No need for that at all. Forty-five's a fair offer, more money than you'll get from anyone else. If anyone else even bothers to offer."

"I wouldn't consider an offer unless I knew who it was."

He gave a wheezy laugh. "Money's money. Who cares where it comes from?"

That made her wonder if the Macgregors were trying to

buy Southern Comfort. Maybe even Zell. "Not interested. If that's all . . ." She got to her feet, relieved to get out of the office that smelled like smoke and some other odor she didn't care to identify.

"That is until you realize that owning a vacant, rotting building isn't going to do you much good. Thing is, Elva was talking to him about selling the place. They hadn't talked money yet, but she was interested in retiring. You'll just be following through on what she wanted anyway. I'll be here with that offer, if my client is generous enough to keep it on the table such as it is."

He hadn't even taken her statement about staying seriously, except for his initial reaction. She walked out of his storefront office space across from City Hall's historic white building. Before she could even take a breath of relief, she saw Buck Waddell leaning against his brown wrecked piece of a truck. He was tall and lanky like his son, though his brown hair was thinning something fierce. He'd done a comb-over with the remaining strands. His bloodshot eyes locked on to her and stayed there as she walked to her car. He'd parked behind her along the curb even though there were plenty of spaces in the lot. He took a drag off his cigarette and flicked it near her car. She knew there was no point in greeting him and didn't want to anyway. She did have the urge to check her tires and tailpipe, but she got in and pulled away without looking.

Southern Comfort's shell parking lot was deserted. She'd closed up for her appointment with Wharton and left Oscar in the bar. It was too hot to leave him in the car. She stepped out of her car and brushed the damp strands of hair from her neck. Though she'd curled the ends under that morning, the humidity had sent them curling up. Even the mosquitoes seemed to take a break at midday. Maybe the humidity weighed them down the way it weighed down everyone else.

She thought back to her encounter with Buck. That dead look in his eyes was enough to cool her down even before the air-conditioning sent her into a state of minishock.

Could he be the one wanting to buy Southern Comfort? She sure as hell wouldn't sell it to him, and he knew it. Wharton was buddies with both Winnerow and Buck so he could easily be representing either one.

"Forget them. You're mine now." She looked around the bar, and an odd sense of pride swelled in her chest. "You're officially mine." Elva had wanted her to have it enough to add her to the deed. Had she been feeling ill? Again, guilt spiked through her at not being there for her. She placed the urn on the bar.

Oscar got up from where he was lying on a pile of blankets and ambled over to greet her like a loyal dog. She'd wanted a dog for a while now. That was part of her dream of home: the house, the dog, and the fenced-in yard. When her dad was alive, they had a black-and-white mutt named Hobo. He'd gone to Heron's Glen with them, but disappeared one night. An alligator, the Macgregors had supposed. Part of living in a swamp. Sometimes in the dry season, a wild one got hungry enough to wander down near the house. Another reason to hate the ghastly creatures.

The first reason was Toopie Harding. Kim had gone with her dad to help out old Toopie, who lived in a shack down on the river. Donnie had been doing some repairs on her roof. Her dad never hesitated to help someone in need, even when chores at his own home remained undone.

Toopie was crouched down by the river washing her clothes when they'd arrived. She had no washer and no money to go to the Laundromat. Kim had gone because she wanted to help people, too. She figured she could do some yard work, even though she was only six. Toopie turned at the sound of their approach through the overgrown yard. What she hadn't known was that a ten-foot gator had been waiting for an opportunity to strike. While Kim and her dad watched, frozen to their spots in horror, the gator grabbed her arm and twisted it right off.

Kim shuddered even now, remembering all the blood and the woman's stoic mask of pain while her dad put a tourniquet on the stub. They'd stayed with her until the ambulance came. She'd survived, and her dad had gone out regularly to take care of things she couldn't do anymore, Kim had never gone back. Nightmares of that attack plagued her for years.

"Forget that." She reached down and patted Oscar's head. "I've got enough to think about, like what to do with you. Grandma obviously loved you." Oscar had more blankets than a hospital. Kim owed it to Elva to make sure whoever took Oscar would spoil him in the way he'd become accustomed. She needed to do that for the bar, too. Elva had worked hard after Pete left to build this place. There was even a rumor that Elva had run some marijuana up the coast of Florida back in the seventies when times got tough. Kim wouldn't put it past her. Elva would do whatever she had to as long as it didn't hurt anybody.

Kim went through the drawers at the desk in the far corner of the kitchen until she found the financial books. She spread out everything on one of the long tables and then went over to the jukebox. Elva had invested in a newer one that held CDs. That was a good thing. The CDs themselves were not a good thing. Elva loved her old country classics, and that pretty much dominated the selection: Willie Nelson, George Jones, and Johnny Cash to name a few. She found a couple of oddball CDs, like the Black Crowes and Kenny Wayne Shepherd, and wondered if Zell had had anything to do with those. Kim wasn't much into rock and roll, but they were better than the country and better than the silence, too.

She fiddled with the shell necklace her dad had made and settled in to figure out if Southern Comfort was holding its own financially.

Kim Lyons was in the bar. The exterior lights were off, indicating Southern Comfort was closed as usual between lunch and happy hour. What was she doing in there, anyway?

*Don't worry. You took care of anything Elva might have had. You went through the drawers and file cabinets at both the house and the bar. You looked through everything, right?*

Having keys to both places sure helped. Wouldn't hurt to hang on to them until Kim left town again. Just in case.

Had Elva told her granddaughter about the situation? No, Kim would have come to Cypress sooner and would already be checking into things. As long as she settled the estate and left town without causing trouble, no one else would get hurt. Murder wasn't pleasant, but sometimes it was a necessity. Elva had invited death upon herself. Kim would need to be kept an eye on. The two keys gleamed in the sunshine, bright enough to be blinding. Nothing like a visit here and there to make sure Kim behaved herself.

"Where were you last night?" Kim asked Simon a while later, hoping she didn't sound like a nagging wife. "I was hoping to hear from you this morning."

He sounded contrite, though he had as much trouble saying he was sorry as she did. "I went over to Cal and Anne's for dinner. We had one too many bottles of cabernet, and I ended up staying the night on their couch."

She propped her feet up on the corner of the desk. "Are you going to stay at their place the whole week I'm gone?" Simon hated being by himself. That was why he'd pressured her to move in with him.

"Of course not. So, how was the drive down?"

Obviously he'd been really worried, she thought with a wrinkle of her nose. "Fine. I'm at the bar now looking at the financial records. The place is holding its own, I'm happy to see. There's a small reserve for emergencies, too. I found some weird payments I have to figure out." A ledger listed five five-hundred-dollar payments, but not what they were for or whom they were to. Hopefully they weren't Zell's payments for the orchid loan, not that much a month. "There are a few snags." She told him about the orchids and Oscar.

"We can't have a pig," Simon said in the fatherly voice he used when chastising her for leaving her socks on the floor. "We've got six more months left on our lease. A lot of residential areas won't let you have potbellied pigs, either."

"I didn't say I wanted to keep him."

"You had that sound in your voice, like when you saw those puppies at Patsy's place."

She glanced at Oscar, who was snuggled in his pile of blankets. He was no puppy, that was for sure. "I don't plan to keep him. But I do have to find a home for him. And I've got to sell the orchids. It's a mess. I phoned in ads to the local papers about the orchids and Oscar, so hopefully I'll get some bites." She gave him the number at the bar. "If you need me." If he needed her . . . that was a laugh. Companionship, that's what he needed. Anyone would probably do. She wondered if he'd even remember her birthday on Monday. Heck, she didn't require anything fancy. Even some redneck roses, the wildflowers that grew by the side of the road, would do.

"I'm going out with Jackson and Cliff tonight. They're going to take me out to some hip-hop clubs. Should be interesting."

"I bet." She didn't mention the fact that he never took her out to the clubs. He seemed to think that because she worked in a club, she didn't want to spend her free time in one. "Have fun. I've got to get through these papers, so I'll let you go. Tell the guys I said hey."

She gave him plenty of opportunity to say something meaningful; at least an *I miss you.* All he said was, "Sure will. Bye."

"Yeah, me, too," she said to the silence and wondered why she felt as hollow as an empty beer keg. But she didn't want something heavy, she reminded herself. That's why she picked guys like Simon.

She got up and walked over to the jukebox, searching for one song in particular. She chose it for an upcoming selection. "Rocky Top" was the song that reminded her of the only man she'd given her heart to, and he'd broken it but good—her dad. Not that he'd meant to. Most people didn't intend to die. She couldn't forget that her dad had had alcohol in his system that last night. Winnerow had had only a trace amount, but Kinsey had probably given the alcohol time to leave his system before testing him.

When the song played, she kicked her feet up the way she and her dad had. Her dad was always the first one on the dance floor and he danced like a sinner on Sunday. And like a sinner, he tried to get everybody to join in, though no one danced as crazy and as vivaciously. He threw his whole body into it and didn't care what he looked like. When Kim was out there with him, she'd done the same.

She was halfway through the song when she got the impression that someone was there. It was just that eerie, unexplainable feeling, that change in the atmosphere that some part of the brain picked up on. She whirled around and saw a man with a rounded back and white, scraggly hair that stuck out at the sides watching her with a smile.

"Just the way you and your pa used to do it," he said, making himself comfortable in one of the chairs at the long table where her papers were laid out.

"Smitty!"

She pulled the plug on the jukebox to kill the music, irritation at being startled not nearly as bad as embarrassment at being caught dancing like a silly fool.

He looked worn and tired, but he had that same twinkle in his eyes. "Didn't mean to startle you." He lifted a key. "I just let myself in like I always do."

Oscar sauntered over and greeted him, and Smitty scratched his back. When he hit a spot on Oscar's side, the pig fell over, grunting and writhing in pleasure.

She joined him at the table, her irritation melting away. "I thought you'd deserted me."

He looked a little chagrined as he laid out a rolling paper and set a line of tobacco down the center. "Yeah, I suspect you would. I've had a lot on my mind, what with Elva being gone all of a sudden–like. It's been hard."

"I know you two were close." She'd sometimes wondered at Elva and Smitty's relationship. They were together a lot and acted like an old married couple, finishing each other's sentences and knowing what the other liked and didn't like. Back then it had grossed her out to think of her grandma in a romantic relationship. "I wish I'd come down more, called her more. I just figured she'd be around forever."

"We all did." He sighed as he concentrated on rolling a perfect cigarette with yellowed fingers and licking the edge of the paper to seal it. When he was done, he met her gaze. "I did desert you, young'un. Ya see, I'm in a bad position. Loyalties," he added when she waited for further explanation. "On the one hand is Elva. I owe Elva, and she did love this place. This bar and Oscar were her life." He studied her a moment. "Now I see that guilt coloring your face 'cause you're thinking you should have been part of her life, too, but you never came back around."

All she could do was swallow hard and nod. How had he seen it? She hoped she wasn't that transparent.

He nodded toward some of the pictures on the wall. "You were still part of her life. She has pictures of you all over the place. She knew it'd be hard for you to come back, even for a visit. And you did invite her to come up many a time. She considered it, even though she swore she'd never leave Cypress. She kept saying, 'I got to call that girl, see how she's doing.' When someone dies, you get left with a bunch of should-haves and could-haves. She had them, too, young'un, so don't beat yourself up over it."

"You were talking about loyalties," she said, unable to say anything else. Unable to thank him for that release. She kept rolling and unrolling one of the papers on the table.

He lit up his cigarette, filling the air with the scent of vanilla tobacco. "Loyalties." He said the word as though it weighed heavily on him. "I have loyalties to Elva. To the bar." He glanced around. "But I also have loyalties to the Macgregors. They're kin, after all."

Smitty's daughter, Nancy, had married Winnerow's brother, Calvin.

"How is Nancy? I saw their airboat tour signs coming into town."

"Nancy and I don't talk much. She's busy with her life. We pass a friendly word now and again, and she brings me a ham big enough to feed fourteen people for Thanksgiving and Christmas. I didn't mind; me and Elva had our holidays together."

And now he was alone. She could feel the pain of his loneliness as though it were her own.

He didn't dwell on it, though. "So you see, even though I'm not a blood Macgregor, I owe it to my daughter to lean in that direction should any strife come up." He looked her straight in the eye. "And you, young'un, are strife personified."

She crinkled the paper she'd been rolling. "I did what I had to do."

"I understand. Winn Macgregor took away your daddy—"

"It had nothing to do with that."

He regarded her for a moment. "You sure?"

"Of course I am." She was, wasn't she? Yes, definitely. "I never lied about what I saw. Zell and Charlotte were the liars. They said I made it up because Winnerow killed my father. But they were the ones making up stories about me." Even after all this time, the anger was still there. Maybe because the whole thing had cost Kim her home and ten years with her grandma. She felt it was important that she get her side across to Smitty. "I saw Winnerow's truck go down that road into the swamp. I'm pretty sure I saw Buck with him, which made sense because they were always hanging together. The next day when I walked down the road, I found that girl's body."

"It tore the town apart. Tore Elva apart, too. People stopped coming to the bar because she'd taken your side. It was hard times for a while."

"I . . . I didn't know that." Kim hadn't gone to the bar during the year between the investigation and the trial because people had been hostile toward her. "I'm sorry."

"It didn't matter to Elva, not all that much. Things were tight, but she was tough."

"I didn't know," she repeated, softer this time.

Finding Rhonda Jones's body was worse than seeing that alligator tear off Toopie's arm. At first Kim hadn't recognized the mass as a body at all when she'd seen something floating in the swamp near the old shell road. Her long, brown hair floated on the water and tangled in air plants that were growing on a log. Her skin had been gray, her eyes open wide and seeing nothing.

Kim had gotten sick twice before making it back to Heron's Glen and calling the sheriff's substation. Even now, her stomach lurched at the memory of it. Mack Kinsey hadn't wanted to believe her story about seeing Winnerow's truck. He'd tried to trip her up by confusing her about the timeline and making her doubt what she'd seen.

Rhonda had been hit on the head, strangled, and sexually assaulted with a stick. Because there was no semen found inside her, and since she'd been in the water, there was little useful physical evidence. Kim's testimony was all they had. Kinsey was pressing for the case to be dropped against Winnerow for lack of evidence, just as it had been dropped against Buck Waddell. Kim had contacted the *Naples Daily News* with information about the case, and they had run a story. What had pushed her to talk to the newspaper was seeing Rhonda's young son, Ernest. The boy had looked so lost and confused at the funeral. Kim knew that expression, knew those feelings too well. He was the catalyst for her to seek justice no matter the price. And it had cost big time.

With public pressure, the case went to trial. Investigating detectives found a witness who'd seen Winnerow giving Rhonda a ride two weeks before her murder. One of her hairs was found in his truck. The case had gone to trial in Naples, the city forty minutes north of Cypress.

The prosecution's best shot was Kim's testimony. For the first time, Winnerow Macgregor was going to be judged for his sins. Most of the folks in town thought Winnerow couldn't actually commit such a heinous crime. Sure, he'd killed her father, but that was an accident.

From the beginning of the investigation, Kim had moved in with Elva, unable to live with the Macgregors anymore. She knew Elva had sacrificed the town's good will to harbor her granddaughter and had appreciated it. She never knew how much of a sacrifice that had been.

And it had all been for nothing. Winnerow was acquitted. The hair in his truck? Sure, he'd given Rhonda a ride. Most people in Cypress would give a ride to someone walking along the side of the road. Half of the town were character witnesses, singing Winnerow's praises. Those same folks also testified that Kim was vindictive and spiteful. Zell and Charlotte had testified that Kim's behavior leading up to the murder indicated her venomous hatred toward her stepfather. They made up fights that hadn't happened. It was believable enough to make the jury doubt.

Kim had left town sure there was nothing there for her. But in the ten years she'd been gone, she'd dreamed about the swamps and waterways and everything that was Cypress. She'd wanted to come back. But not this way.

*Thank you* came almost as hard as *I'm sorry,* so instead of thanking Smitty for being there for Elva, she said, "You were a good friend to her."

"We were a lot more than friends, young'un."

"I kind of wondered about that." The thought didn't gross her out anymore as long as she didn't dwell on it. After a moment, she said, "You found her, right?"

His mouth tightened. "When she didn't show for lunch, I got worried about her. Saw her truck at the house, skiff was gone. I took my johnboat out and went looking for her." He shook his head. *And found her,* he didn't say. "I tied a ribbon to a branch near where I found her. So I could go back sometime."

Not knowing what else to say, she said, "I'm surprised she didn't leave *you* the bar."

He'd been scratching Oscar's belly the whole time, leaning slightly to the side to do it. "I'm happy enough with my little salary and something to pass the time. A man like me don't need much in life." Something in his expression told her he'd needed Elva, and it closed Kim's throat.

"I'm glad you and Elva found happiness together," she said at last. "Why didn't you two ever get married?"

"She wouldn't have me, if the truth be told. She liked her independence, liked her time on her own. Zell advised me to give her space or I'd lose her. I was happy to get what I could. That was enough."

A thought occurred to her. "Would you like Oscar?"

"Can't have a pig in the trailer park. Rabbits they'll let me have, but not pigs. Zell asked me, too, and he had that same desperate kind of look on his face that you do. It was nice of him to take in Oscar, especially when he had no obligation to do it. And didn't particularly want to. That boy is either here or out working, so he don't have time to tend to an attention hog like Oscar here."

Kim found it slightly bizarre that she and Zell had anything in common. And that he had taken in Oscar because he was nice. She liked thinking Zell was that spoiled, brooding teenager who would lie under oath to protect his no-good father. "Zell and Elva were friends?"

"I think he saw her as a sort-of grandma. He lost both his mama and grandma when he was young, see. He was closest to his grandpa Zelwig. Mighty fine man, he was, nothing like Winn. Zelwig passed on when Zell was fifteen."

"I remember him. You would have never thought he had as much money as he did. He was a nice guy. Zell was named after him, right?"

"They name every other generation's son Zelwig, some kind of family thing."

"Do you know about the loan Zell made to Elva?" she asked.

"Yep. She was lucky Zell didn't charge her interest. I told her that was a big responsibility to get into, them orchids. But she doesn't listen to anyone when she's got her head set on something." The smile on his face faded. "Sometimes she didn't say anything about it until it was a done deal. Like with the orchids. And other things . . ." He'd faded off and gone to some unpleasant place.

"Do you happen to know anyone who might want to buy the orchids at cost?"

"Not right offhand. Your best bet is to sell them off piecemeal."

She'd started rolling the paper again and realized what it was she'd been rolling: the ledger with the mysterious payments. "Do you know anything about these five-hundred-dollar payments?"

He didn't even look at the ledger. "Elva did all the paperwork and finances. I just helped out, that's all I did."

He was clearly uncomfortable with the line of questioning, and she realized that's what she'd been doing—questioning him. So she held back the next question, which was who he thought might want to buy the bar.

She pushed to her feet. "It seems to me that you need the money you make here as much as I need you to help me out. I know, I know," she said when he opened his mouth. "Loyalties. Can't you just look at it as a job and not a betrayal?"

"Things get tricky, and you know how the Macgregors are with holding grudges. I don't want to cause my daughter any problems, either. But there might be a way—"

"What?" She braced her palms on the table. "What way?"

He scrubbed his fingers through his mess of hair. "If Zell said it'd be all right, I reckon it'd be all right. People around here respect him." Before she could digest that, he added, "The thing is, asking him would put me in an uncomfortable position. So you'll have to ask him." He got to his feet, gathered his pack of papers and bag of tobacco, and stuffed them in his pocket.

"Me?" The word came out as a squeak. "I can't—"

"That's the only way it'll work, young'un. You let me know what he says. I'll be waiting to hear from you."

He shuffled out into the bright day, and she dropped her head to the table and groaned.

# CHAPTER 6

By the time people started trickling into Southern Comfort that evening, Kim had decided that she'd do whatever it took to keep the place running. She didn't have to like it, but she'd do it. She needed to figure out what to do, and there was no point in letting the place run into the ground in the meantime. Finding Zell was going to be the tricky part.

The first customers were Mr. and Mrs. Palmer, an older couple Kim remembered living one street away from her childhood home.

"We wanted to give our condolences," the tiny woman said after ordering a bucket of the "kick-ass" wings. "We'll miss Elva something fierce." She patted Kim's hand. "We've missed you, too."

She swallowed hard. She wanted to thank them, but the words would have come out all soft and mushy. She simply smiled and went to put the wings in the fryer.

Surprisingly, a few people came in over the next two hours. They either asked about Smitty or looked for him. But they didn't leave when she said he wasn't there. The Palmers left Kim with a warm feeling. At least not everyone hated that she was back.

It wasn't until the place was over half full that she began to wonder if something was going on. First, it *was* half full.

Second, an air of expectancy hovered thicker than the smoke. Third, nobody was playing the jukebox. Between taking orders and making food, Kim dashed over and bought some music. When her selections played out, no one picked up the gantlet. Unless times had changed, that was very strange. The place rarely went without music for longer than a few minutes.

She had a feeling it had something to do with the expectant air, and it gave her an uneasy feeling. It didn't help that some of the folks watched her with glowering expressions that reminded her of Buck Waddell. Sometimes she caught a mention of Zell's name, and inevitably the people at the table would look her way.

They couldn't know that she had to ask Zell's permission for Smitty to continue on there, could they? This was a small town, no doubt, but still . . .

Like everyone else, Kim glanced at the door whenever it opened. She felt an odd shift in her chest when Zell sauntered in. When several people broke into applause, he lifted his arms to the side and turned around to show off his eye-popping orange Hawaiian surf-at-sunset shirt. It was buttoned and hung over the waistband of his blue jeans. Alligator boots were the final touch. Somehow it worked, though she wasn't sure why.

"Dang, Zell, that's the brightest one yet," one guy said.

"I like the teal blue one you had on yesterday better," a woman said with a gleam that indicated she'd probably prefer him without a shirt at all.

Zell took the gawking in stride as he made his way to the bar. People tried to get his attention along the way, asking him for a minute of his time later as though he were the mayor. Kim was surprised when he walked directly to the bar and took one of the stools with an ease that said he did that quite often.

"Heard you wanted to talk to me," he said, leaning against the bar.

She blinked, trying to pull her thoughts together. "Well, yeah, I did. Did Smitty tell you that?"

"Yep. He's outside. Said you had to ask me about something."

Had Smitty set her up for this? When she shifted her gaze to the small crowd beyond, they were all watching. They reminded her of the time her dad took her out into the mangroves. Several hungry gators were assembled beneath a rookery full of egret nests waiting for a hatchling to fall out. Since she hated gators and loved egrets, that moment had stuck with her. Just like, perhaps, this one would. Dammit, that was why they'd all come out tonight, to watch her grovel to her former foe—and from the hungry expressions on their faces, they clearly expected Zell to turn her down.

"Let me just deliver this whiskey and I'll be right back." When she returned, she asked, "Want something?"

"Captain Morgan and root beer."

She lifted her eyebrow. "Spiced rum and root beer? Interesting combination. I doubt we have root beer, though. I've never worked at a bar that carried it."

He leaned over the bar, leaving his jean-clad rear sticking up in the air, and pointed to a shelf next to the icemaker. Root beer. His mouth quirked up in a half-smile. "Elva kept some on hand for me."

She squelched a comment about how often he must get his way. Even back when they were young, girls went out of their way to do things for him. She bought time while making his drink, hoping the hungry gators would lose interest. Of course, they didn't. When she set the drink on the bar, she said, "I'm supposed to ask you if Smitty can continue to work here until I figure out what I'm doing with the place."

He just sat there for a long minute, giving away nothing. Was he going to ignore her question? Oh, she got it. She hadn't exactly asked, and that's what he was going to make her do. Just perfect.

"Can Smitty continue to work here for the time being?" Forced meekness filled her voice.

"I heard you the first time."

All right, fine, he wasn't that big of a jerk. Still, he didn't answer. Conflict shadowed his expression, something akin to what she'd seen on Smitty's face when he'd talked about his loyalties. She didn't dare look at the folks also waiting for his answer, probably hoping she'd cry or beg. They didn't know her very well. Kim Lyons never cried and she never begged. But she was impatient.

"Well?"

"I'm thinking about it. Never rush a man while he's thinking."

She wanted to tell him, *Go on and say no, get it over with.* She folded a napkin to within an inch of its life. She noticed that he hadn't once glanced at their audience. She couldn't tell if he was enjoying his power position over her, but she figured he was.

He took a long sip of his drink and set it squarely in the center of the bar napkin, taking care to line it up just so. Finally he said, "You understand your request puts me in an awkward position."

"Wasn't great for me, either." She swallowed her pride and added, "I do understand. Believe me, you're the last person I wanted to ask." Her face flushed hot. "I mean—"

He waved off her fumbling. "I know. But Smitty's thinking of family, of family honor and loyalties. It's good to consider things like that."

Her stomach twisted at his words. She knew exactly what he was talking about. She said, "I'm not here to make a war or to dredge up the past. I'm fine to let sleeping dogs lie. I just want to keep things going while I decide what to do. If someone's going to buy this place, they ought to have a successful business to go with it, don't you think?"

"You gonna sell it?"

She could barely push out the words. "What else can I do?" That's when it hit her how hard it was going to be, how selling seemed a betrayal of her own family. "And there's Smitty to consider. He needs the money. It's not fair to keep him from working." She glanced at the crowd now. "And obviously this place means a lot to the locals. If

Smitty's not here and they don't come to drink, I have to close it. Where will they go?"

Was that the slightest glow of admiration in his eyes as he took in her argument? She kept going in case it was. "I know this puts you in a tough place, but I'm in a tough place, too." What she'd meant to say was *I'm sorry I put you in a tough place,* but that was too hard to say.

She figured he'd turn to look at the folks waiting for his answer and see what their temperature was. He hadn't taken his gaze off her, though.

"All right, he can keep working here." He grabbed his drink and weaved around the tables to the jukebox.

She just stared after him. People murmured, taking in first her, then Zell. He slid a dollar bill into the slot and chose a track from the Kenny Wayne Shepherd CD. Then he walked to the door and leaned out to say something to Smitty, who ambled in with a grin. Kim hoped she didn't look as shell-shocked as she felt. Smitty took three orders as he made his way to the bar while Zell settled in at the small table in the corner beside the jukebox and stretched out his legs.

She wanted to thank him, as hard as that would be, but he hadn't given her a chance. One of the men who'd wanted his time took the chair at Zell's table and started bending his ear. While he listened, his gaze slid to her before going back to the man.

"Two Miller Lites and a pitcher of Budweiser," Smitty said as he approached the service end of the bar.

Now that music filled the room, less attention was on her, which was just fine. She pulled her gaze from Zell. "Did you happen to tell the whole town that I was going to ask Zell about you working here?"

He lifted a shoulder, not looking the least bit sheepish. "May have mentioned it to someone. Why?"

She shook her head. "Well, maybe because half the town showed up to watch."

Seeing the bar full of people probably wasn't unusual to him. "It *is* Friday night, you know. Busy night usually."

Usually, but not when the pariah of Cypress owned the bar. "Whatever. What was that order again?"

While she filled the order, Smitty flipped a switch that started a fan somewhere above. The smoke disappeared through a vent in the ceiling. "Elva had it installed last year. She told the nonsmokers she done it for them, but she really done it for Oscar. He'd started to wheeze a bit. Didn't care about her own health, but she didn't want her pig getting emphysema."

"That sure sounds like my grandma." Kim set Smitty's order on the tray. "What's Zell doing over there, anyway? Holding court?"

Smitty chuckled. "In a manner of speaking. Ever'body goes to him for advice. He's got a good head for it. They call him the Sage, after another fella who used to dispense advice a long time ago."

When Zell glanced her way, she realized she'd been caught watching him again. She turned back to Smitty. "The Sage, huh? What's he give advice on?"

"Oh, just about ever'thing. Love, money, whatever you got on your mind."

She pictured herself sitting in that chair across from him, asking what she should do about the bar, Elva's house . . . her life. Turmoil bubbled inside her. Simon didn't understand her love for this place. Though he'd never been here, he knew it was swampland and rednecks who made their hard living from a hard land. She couldn't tell him how the sight of a rookery made white by egrets could stir her soul, how going out to the middle of the marshland and just sitting there watching stars and listening to the silence was better than taking a vacation to anywhere else in the world. Or how leaning against her own bar, the same bar her grandma had sanded and stained herself, could mean more than inheriting a million dollars. How one place could stir guilt, fear, awe, and belonging all at once.

Would Zell understand? She pushed the thought from her mind and headed over to take an order. All he wanted—all most of these people wanted—was to see her leave. And that thought simply tore her apart.

Zell had enough troubles of his own, but he listened to Angus's woes about how he thought his wife was cheating on him.

"Go on home, grab her, and throw her on the bed," Zell said. "Tell her you're gonna make love to her all night long, and see how she acts. If she's smiling, she's not cheating. And then make sure it does last all night. That means giving her hers for a good long time before the finale. There's plenty on a woman's body to keep you occupied." At Angus's questioning look, he added, "Just make sure you do something to every inch of her body, and spend extra time on the important parts. And make no mistake, my friend, they're all important."

Angus nodded vigorously, as if storing this all in his memory.

"Now, if she makes excuses, well then, you'll want to have a sit-down with her." As Angus balked, Zell added, "It's better than wondering. Confront her and see what she has to say." Strange words from a man who hated confrontation.

"All right, Zell, that's what I'll do. Your next drink's on me."

He waved that away as Angus got to his feet. "Don't worry about it."

Still, Angus wandered to the bar and tilted his head toward him as he paid his tab. Kim glanced his way again and nodded as she took his money. She'd been looking at him a lot, probably surprised he'd said okay.

He wanted to think it was for Smitty, though the guy didn't need much money to live on. He wanted to think it was for himself or even for the folks around here who called Southern Comfort their second home. The truth was, it couldn't have been easy for her to ask him, and that had been the deciding factor. As far as his family went, though, he was sticking to the self-centered reason—he'd done it for himself. Nothing was more important to the Macgregors than family honor. Didn't he know that well enough.

Smitty had wiped down one of the tables and then ended up joining the men who were sitting there for a few minutes. The man hid his grief over Elva's death as well as Zell hid his. The town wouldn't be the same without her.

He watched Kim as she carried a pitcher and frosty mugs to one of the tables. She knew what she was doing. She carried the six mugs with her fingers wrapped around the handles and poured each one with nary a trace of head or spillage. She glanced his way before heading back to the bar, this time checking his drink in the quick way of an expert.

Back behind the bar, she dug a spoon into a jar of peanut butter and stuck it in her mouth. Did she know how damned provocative she looked as she slowly drew the spoon out and then lathed the bowl with her tongue? A minute later, he watched her sling the bottle of Captain Morgan with a flourish before adding root beer.

He especially enjoyed watching her walk toward him with his drink. She wore black jeans and an off-the-shoulder top that reminded him of a white handkerchief. A sliver of her stomach showed, and even more interestingly, a belly button ring caught the light. It was a simple gold ring with a small diamond chip. She was long in the torso, long all over, really. She'd had a boyish figure growing up, and though she hadn't filled in all that much, there was nothing boyish about her nowadays. Her choker was made of tiny shells. Instead of the country gunk someone had chosen on the juke, the Cheap Trick song "She's Tight" flowed through his mind as a soundtrack to her trek toward him.

She set the drink on his table. "That one's on your friend who just left. Something about giving him advice on his cheating wife." When he only nodded in both thanks and acknowledgment, she added, "I think he was a little confused about the important parts thing."

Zell shook his head. "I thought I'd made it pretty clear."

"What do you consider the important parts?"

He leaned back, completely enjoying her curiosity. "From a woman's point of view, you mean."

"Yeah, well, I know what men focus on. T, A, and P."

He laughed at her succinct statement. "Yeah, well, the uneducated man, maybe. Angus is a pretty basic kind of guy. I was trying to enlighten him."

"Okay, so let's hear it."

He was trying not to let on how much he was enjoying this exchange. "Her feet, particularly the arch of her foot and her toes, which make for great sucking. The backs of her knees, which respond wonderfully to a flick of the tongue."

She rocked forward then, as though his tongue were flicking the backs of her knees as they spoke. "Okay," she said, a squeak in her voice.

"Her inner thighs, that soft, white skin that probably gets neglected due to the proximity of, er, P, which admittedly *can* be distracting."

She made a sound in her throat, but kept her expression passive. "Very true." The complete focus of her eyes gave away her interest.

He let his gaze settle on her stomach. "Then her belly, paying particular attention to her belly button." He decided to skip the more intimate parts since he didn't know Kim all that well. "The dip between her breasts, a great place for a dab of whipped cream, by the way. A woman's shoulders, surprisingly enough, can be very erotic with just the right attention. Then the place where your neck and shoulders meet, slowly, very slowly moving up to your neck, which by now is usually damp and tastes just the way you smell— your unique fragrance." He realized he'd slipped into saying *you* and reverted to a more neutral form since he was actually looking at Kim's body as he spoke. "By the time a man gets to a woman's ears, she can hardly stand it."

Kim shivered and then rubbed her neck. "I think that was good advice," she said in a high-pitched voice. "I hear you're like a guru around here."

He finished his first drink. Damn, he'd actually gotten rather, er, *interested* by his own words, or more particularly, the images that went with them. "That's what they tell me."

She shifted her weight from one leg to another as though hoping he'd invite her to sit, which would not be a good idea. "The Sage."

"Yep. Need some advice?"

She only uttered a nervous laugh. "Your first drink's on the house, too. For letting Smitty hang around."

He lifted it to her in salute and watched her walk away. Her ass had a nice shape to it and a nice, demure sway; natural, not deliberate.

Unfortunately, someone stood in the way, and he couldn't watch her anymore. He looked up to see Billy Bob Horter glaring at him. Billy Bob was a goon of a man, taller than Zell and probably twice as heavy. His buddy Clem was his polar opposite, short and skinnier than a cattail reed. Dumber than one, too.

"Why'd you let Smitty stay on? We was all waiting for a scene, her begging you to let him stay, you telling her what for. Did you lose your balls last time you went out in the swamp?"

Clem added, "Maybe an alligator got 'em." He clicked his teeth together and chortled.

"I got my reasons for what I do and no one to answer to but myself." And his father, of course. What were the chances that this would slip by Winn? Maybe he'd be in a drunk the whole time Kim was in town.

Even though the two men continued to stare him down, Zell glazed his eyes and thought about the busy night he was going to have tomorrow. He'd be trudging through the swampland collecting alligator eggs, sinking into knee-deep muck warmed by the sun all day. The mosquitoes would be buzzing all over, and all manner of critters would be slithering and creeping around him. It was one of his favorite things in the world to do.

"I think he's getting some of what Kim's got between

her legs, that's what I think," Billy Bob said, and Clem nodded vigorously in agreement.

Zell shook his head. He really didn't like fighting. Probably because he wasn't very good at it, and that was probably because he didn't have his heart in it. Bashing a guy had no appeal to him. Particularly when it would be one against two and probably him getting the bashing.

*All's fair in love and war.*

For some reason, his gaze went to Kim, who was watching them and not looking too happy about the tension she saw.

Zell took a leisurely drink. "Look, I'm not going to fight with you guys. We'd both get hurt and it wouldn't change anything. Let it go." He kept his body language casual and relaxed, though his muscles were ready for action. He might not like to fight, but he sure wouldn't sit there and take it, either.

"Is there a problem here?" Kim asked from behind the two men, making them swivel around.

Not good. Didn't she remember what jerks these guys were? They'd come back to town a few years back after getting out of prison. Because Buck Waddell gave them a job despite their prison records, they had a fierce loyalty to him. Zell was sure Buck had encouraged them to be their nasty best to Kim.

Zell stood. The two men looked at him and then at her. Instead of answering, they went back to their table cattycorner from Zell's. Their superior smirks weren't a good sign. Someone hailed Kim, and she walked away.

Angus walked out of the restroom and gave Zell a conspiratorial wink and a wave as he headed out to give his wife the business. He was still wearing his knee-high white crabbing boots with his blue jeans. Somehow Zell had become a sage to the local population. He wasn't sure how it had happened, guessed he'd given someone some good advice and they told a friend and so on. He didn't mind helping people out, but sitting here talking to no one was what he liked best. Sitting, and thinking, and people-watching, enjoying a drink and the familiar smells of fried wings and smoke.

He wasn't enjoying himself now, though. The two men were talking loudly enough for Zell to hear.

Billy Bob said, "I say we teach her a lesson about where she belongs—and where she don't."

Clem gave his trademark guffaw that reminded Zell of those obnoxious Beavis and Butthead characters. "That'd be fun."

Billy Bob's slow smile spread across his beefy face. "Yeah, it sure would. If ya know what I mean."

Another guffaw, louder this time. "Man, you got some good ideas."

Zell just listened. That's what he did. Some people might think he was slow, but he never rushed into things. He liked to give matters a lot of thought, play them out to their eventual end. He was pretty sure they were trying to goad him on. They knew what they were talking about wouldn't sit well with him. What he needed to determine was how serious they were. Would they jeopardize their jobs and freedom to reap justice for something they weren't even involved in? Or would they figure that no one would punish her attackers?

After a while, their talk grew quieter. He only picked up a word here and there: *parking lot . . . closing . . . scream.*

He didn't like it. He pretended to tie his boot and caught them in his peripheral vision. They weren't even paying attention to him. He didn't figure them to be smart enough to pull that off, making it seem as though they'd lost interest in goading him to plan a real crime. Billy Bob was watching Kim now, his mouth in a perpetual smile. A smug kind of smile.

With a sigh for his few peaceful moments at his table, he pushed to his feet and stuck his head between the two men from behind. "Whatever it is you're thinking, put it right out of your pea brains. Don't make me put a hurtin' on you."

They both got to their feet so fast, Zell had to step back. One chair fell to the floor with a clatter.

"You telling me what to do, pretty boy?" Billy Bob said.

"Pretty boy, good one!" Clem said.

Ah, hell. "This isn't about me, it's about you doing something stupid and wrong. It isn't right, a man hurting a woman. For any reason."

"You ought to be the one wanting to hurt her," Billy Bob said, puffing his bulky shoulders up even more.

Clem followed suit. "If you was man enough."

Zell's fists clenched, but he wasn't going to start something in the bar. Some of the other patrons had started paying attention to the discussion. He was pretty sure he'd have an ally or two, but he really hated dragging someone else into his trouble.

Billy Bob reached into his box of high school maneuvers and pushed Zell back. Zell took a step forward and crushed his foot beneath his heavy boots. "Outside," he said through gritted teeth. Several men nearby got to their feet and advanced toward the two idiots.

"All right, everybody out! Out!" Kim's voice pierced the tension as she put her hand on the two men's backs and turned them toward the front door. "All of you, out of my bar. I'm not going to have you trashing the place."

She was a big enough woman to carry it off, though even little Elva knew how to get rambunctious drunks out of her bar, too. Zell was surprised, though, to be included in the ousted group. Some of his friends also left. They walked out into the warm, muggy night air, the two factions eyeing each other with murderous looks. Finally the two men got into their beat-up truck and peeled out of the lot, sending a spray of shell and gravel onto nearby vehicles.

"You gonna let her talk to you like that?" one of the men asked Zell, indicating the woman in the bar.

"Not going to go back in and say, 'But he started it, Miss Lyons, I swear!' " That got a laugh out of them with his imitation of a whiny boy. "I'm done for the night. Thanks for your help, guys."

"No problem," they all said and headed to their vehicles. Zell started his truck and sat there for a moment, shaking his head in disbelief. His dad had been kicked out of here plenty of times, but this was a first for him. He supposed she had to nip problems in the bud and include anyone who might be a troublemaker, but it still didn't sit well.

He pulled out of the parking lot and headed home.

The remaining folks in the bar stared at Kim as she cleared the glasses from the now empty tables. She didn't need any troublemakers, even if one was named Zell Macgregor. Oh, yeah, Zell was definitely trouble. She'd much rather be annoyed with him than melting over his words about the important places on a woman's body. Especially when his gaze on her body seemed to follow his words.

Well, the patrons had gotten two shows tonight. One with her humbling herself and asking for Zell's help, and the other with her kicking him out.

Would he rescind his okay now? Was he that vindictive? Who knew, but it wouldn't surprise her if that kind of thing ran in the family. After a while, the place had cleared out except for Smitty, who was sitting there at a table not earning his piddling salary. He had the look of a coach who'd just watched his principal player goof up an important play. And because she didn't feel exactly right about ousting Zell, she sat down at the table and asked, "What?"

"Not a good enemy to make, young'un."

"Zell wouldn't hurt me, would he?"

He laughed at that as he pulled out his bag of tobacco and rolling papers. "No, not Zell."

"Those two jerks?"

"Billy Bob and Clem. Don't you remember them? They probably went to school with you, though I think they're a couple of years younger. Billy Bob Horter and Clem Johnson."

"Oh, yeah, I do vaguely remember them. They used to shoot frogs just to watch them explode. Billy Bob bit some girl on the arm and got expelled."

"It won't surprise you to learn they went to prison for a few years on assault charges. They both beat up Billy Bob's ex-girlfriend 'cause she had the nerve to break up with him. Buck gave them a job at the club; gave them a break. A break no one else was willing to give them, so they don't like anyone who crosses Buck."

Her muscles tensed. "They can't dislike me because of what happened—" At Smitty's nod, she said, "That's crazy. They don't even know me anymore."

"Doesn't matter. They'd love a reason to act up again, to justify it in their mind, ya see."

The feeling in the pit of her stomach twisted into a painful knot. "I'm glad I kicked them out, then."

He shook his head as he rolled his cigarette. "I understand your having to do *that* part of it. I'm just warning you to be careful, is all."

"What part don't you understand?"

"Kicking Zell out. Those two were planning something, and Zell was warning them not to do anything to you."

She dropped her head onto the table and groaned. "Please tell me that's just what you *think* he was doing."

"Heard some of the conversation. Now Zell, he don't like to fight, never did. Never provokes a fight. But he'll do whatever he has to do to protect a woman. Back in high school, some boys was doing that pushy kind of flirting with Charlotte, and he could tell she wasn't comfortable with it. There were three of them and one of him, but it didn't matter. He jumped right in and took two of them down."

"What happened to the third one?"

"Charlotte flattened his nuts."

She rubbed her eyes until the skin felt hot beneath her fingers. She'd jumped the gun and probably made a handful of enemies tonight. Jumping to conclusions was only one of her bad habits. "Guess I owe Zell an apology." For someone who hated eating crow, she was sure doing a lot of it lately.

"S'pose so."

When she looked up at him, he was smiling ever so slightly. "Why do I get the impression you're enjoying my discomfort?"

He stuck the cigarette in his mouth. "Hasn't been anything quite so interesting as your arrival since Bo Miller got stoned, whipped out his pecker, and pissed on Kinsey's shoe."

Billy Bob sat in the truck behind the darkened Quick Mart and narrowed his eyes at Southern Comfort. "Who does she think she is, anyway? Kicking us out like we was making trouble. We was just sitting there minding our own business when that son of a bitch comes up to us."

Clem chimed in, "Yeah, minding our own business."

"Somebody needs to put him in his place, too. Thinks he's God's gift to Cypress because of his last name."

"Maybe we ought to mess up his pretty face. Break a nose, poke an eye out. He wouldn't be so pretty then." Clem giggled at that.

Billy Bob wondered if he'd ever get used to Clem's girlish giggles. But he did like the idea. "We could have some fun with Kim, teach her who's in charge around here. Wreck her pretty face, too. Bet she'd pack up and hightail it out of here without saying a thing. That'd sure make our boss happy. And who would believe her anyway?"

"Who would care? Nobody as far as I can tell. Buck'd be proud of us, he would."

Billy Bob flicked his cigarette out the window as Kim and Smitty walked out of the bar. She'd parked off to the side in that little foreign job. There was a clump of bushes that led from the river's shoreline past her car. Enough room to hide, he bet. The nearest buildings would be closed at that hour. "And if Zell Macgregor gets in the way, we'll take him out, too." He waited until both Kim and Smitty had pulled onto the road. Nobody made a fool out of him like that, especially a woman like her. The woman he'd gone to prison over learned that real fast. So would Kim.

Or maybe they wouldn't have to wait. He put the truck into gear and pulled out onto the road behind Kim, gunning the engine to catch up to her.

Kim squinted as headlights suddenly glared in her rearview mirror. What the heck? The only two cars on the road, and it figured she'd have some jerk behind her. "So go around me."

The truck stayed right on her tail. She slowed, hoping he'd pass her. The increase in her pulse told her this wasn't about being in a hurry. That was soon confirmed when she felt the truck bump her, sending her car swerving furiously.

"Damn!" She gripped the wheel and fought to gain control. Gravel kicked up behind her as she tore up the shoulder of the road. The truck had backed off, the driver probably wanting to stay clear if she started rolling. As soon as she straightened the car out, he was on her again.

She gunned the gas and stressed out all four of her cylinders. She'd once kidded that the car didn't have horsepower, it had hamster power. It wasn't so funny at the moment. The engine whined pitifully. The headlights shot forward, closing in behind her. She flinched, ready for another jolt. Just then her car's engine kicked in and gave her boost enough to avoid the bump.

"Are you crazy?" she screamed. "You could get us both killed!"

She didn't want to take her hand off the wheel long enough to adjust the dimmer on the rearview mirror. She could hardly see the road ahead with the glare in her eyes. And she couldn't see anything of the truck other than the headlights.

She didn't have time to make the turn into her driveway, but leading the idiot to her house didn't seem like the best idea anyway. Heron's Glen passed by in a blur on the left as she continued down the highway, the truck close behind.

The sheriff's substation was located near the corner of US41 and Highway 20. Yes, that's where she'd head. If she could make it there before—

The truck bumped her again, sending her car's rear into a fishtail. She let out a scream of both frustration and fear as she tried to control the car again. Her fingers ached where they gripped the steering wheel. As soon as she had control, she gunned the engine again. As the truck gained on her, she swerved into the oncoming lane. When the truck followed her, she jerked back to the right lane.

The lights at the intersection shot relief through her. She cut through the parking lot of a gas station and headed straight for the small building with two police cars parked out front. She had barely put the car in park when she pushed the door open and jumped out. Her legs were wobbly, but she still ran toward the door. Only then did she look back.

The truck was gone.

# CHAPTER 7

Saturday morning tradition at Heron's Glen was a big family breakfast out on the veranda. Zell tried to attend as many breakfasts as his schedule permitted. He walked in the front door and headed toward the lanai. Heron's Glen was an eclectic mix of each generation's tastes. Great-great-grandmother Lydia Macgregor brought the china cabinet with its antique porcelain and silver service with her from Scotland. The family crest adorned one wall painted in the Macgregor plaid. Great-grandparents William and Mary had left the legacy of the hand-carved railing on the curved staircase that matched the crown molding and other accents.

Granddad Zelwig and Grandma Clarice added genteel, Southern furniture and wallpaper that Zell's mother, Andrea, had spent weeks removing years later. She had added her own touches, some of which still remained. Stepmother Kitty had had the couches in the living room covered in bright yellow stripes. Charlotte had purchased an elegant chaise longue at an estate sale and spent hours reading there. Zell figured she just wanted to look good stretched out on the red velvet wearing her matching pumps and robe.

By rights, Calvin and Nancy should have gotten the

house since Calvin was the firstborn. Lucky for Winn, born last and late, Calvin had no desire to continue the gator business. Winn had shown some interest in the then fledgling farm. By the time Grandad Zell died from emphysema, Calvin had started his airboat business and Sue had started her prison sentence. Winn got the farm and house; the surrounding land had been divided between the rest of the family.

Gisella, their part-time cook and housecleaner, had outdone herself this morning, laying out a spread of a veggie frittata, the little potatoes she called *papitas,* and an array of toasts and muffins.

He joined them at the long table out by the pool. Heron's Glen was perched at the base of the mainland surrounded by mangroves on three sides and looking out over Otter Bay toward the back. White sand, shells, and sea oats comprised a beach with a dock tucked in on the right. The opaque green water stretched out a half-mile before mangrove islands closed it in.

"Good morning to you, too," Shar's acid voice proclaimed from behind him.

He wasn't going to admit how the view always took him in to the exclusion of everybody else. "Morning," he said instead, adding a sheepish smile for good measure.

"Morning, Uncle Zell!" Tullie called from her place at the table.

Winn nodded at him as he tore into one of the tamarind muffins. Gisella had a tree in her backyard and used the soft, peanut-shaped fruit for all kinds of things. Shar's husband, Owen, lifted his coffee cup in greeting but didn't smile.

"Going spotting today?" Shar asked, getting right to business.

He dropped into the seat next to Tullie and remembered he had some hell to pay on his sister for her big mouth. "Scheduled the helicopter for one. I'm going to cover our land and the Marsh Point Company's land." He could hear the excitement in his voice. His uncle Calvin was taking him out over the plains so Zell could map out alligator nests.

Years ago spotting was primitive; throw out a marker from the plane, note a few landmarks, and hope you could find your way back via airboat later. Nowadays spotters downloaded digital quad sheet maps and global positioning systems and used sophisticated tracking systems. It had taken a lot of the fun out of it but made it much more efficient. The next part of the job made up for the loss. Over the next few nights, he'd go out in his airboat and steal eggs from alligator nests.

"I want to come with you when you take those eggs," Owen said. "I think I'd like that part of the job."

Zell piled food onto his plate. "One of these days." He didn't need Owen tagging along. All he needed was someone to drive the airboat, and his cousin Dougal was the best driver he'd ever had. The guy had a knack for finding his way around the prairies at night. Owen just had a knack for getting in the way.

Owen's mouth curved into a sneer. "Not right you having all the fun."

Wasn't right Owen marrying into money and opportunity, either, but Zell decided not to mention that. Especially with Owen still sulking. Zell wasn't sure what Shar saw in him. He guessed it was more his acquiescence than his good looks and charm.

"Gonna be a full moon," Shar said. She knew Zell loved going out on the airboat during a full moon.

He just grinned and said, "Yep."

Ever since he was knee-high to a mudbug, he'd been fascinated by alligators. When his granddad Zelwig started the farm in 1985, Zell had been thrilled—until the reality of it set in: two buildings housing hundreds, and then later thousands, of alligators at varying ages. The air inside so hot and rancid he could hardly breathe. He wanted to be outside in the prairies and marshes. He wanted the adventure of collecting eggs and harvesting alligators.

When the American alligator was removed from the

endangered species list, its numbers continued to flourish until there were too many of the animals. The government was spending money removing nuisance gators from populated areas. So it undertook studies to research how farming could help both the economy and conservation efforts.

It was ironic, then, that Zelwig, a man who had made a living hunting alligators before and even after the park made it illegal, had found a way to legally make a living from alligators once again. He hadn't liked being government regulated, but it was a small price to pay.

Shar had managed the farm since their father's stroke, though Winn kept his hand in the financial end of the operation. Nothing bothered his sister, not the heat and smell inside the buildings, not even the harvesting. She supervised it all and did a damn good job.

As Zell continued to eat, he picked up on an air of expectation similar to what he'd felt at the bar the night before. Ah, that was why Winn was watching him with blue-green eyes icier than a glacier.

"Heard you were down at Southern Comfort last night."

He shrugged. "Go there all the time."

"Not when Kim's in town. Not when she's there."

Shar said, "Sam said she threatened to stay in town."

Winn threw his napkin on his plate. "Heard you took up for her. Those fellas hadn't even done anything," he ground out in his low, ominous voice.

Zell pushed away his plate, knowing he wasn't going to get in an enjoyable breakfast after all. He did finish his glass of fresh-squeezed orange juice, though. "I'd take up for any woman who was being threatened. That's what my granddad taught me. It's what he taught you, too."

Winn's face reddened. "You better show me some respect and deference."

"Show you respect and deference. Why? Because you're my father?"

"Yes," Winn said with a hiss.

"You spent most of my life being the biggest child in

this family. Shar and I became your parents, cleaning up after you and wiping your ass. And now that you've started to look back over all your bad choices, responsibility is tugging at you. You're trying to be the patriarch now. Is that it, Dad? Well, I'll tell you what: you've got a long damn way to go before I feel obliged to listen to your directives." *Or to respect you,* he didn't say.

Shar's mouth dropped open. Owen busied himself with cutting another piece of frittata. Tullie looked down at her lap. Winn glared, but he knew the truth in Zell's statement. He jammed a piece of muffin in his mouth and fumed.

After a few minutes of awkward silence, Shar said, "What about letting Smitty work there? I heard it was up to you, and you said he could help that woman out."

"Wasn't right punishing Smitty for what she did. 'Sides, I don't want the bar to go under. That's been the only real local hangout for years now. Kim'll be on her way soon enough, and we won't have to worry about it anymore."

Shar said, "Oh, you just make yourself sound so damn honorable."

He gave her his most charming smile. "That's because I am." Owen snorted, but backed down from Zell's challenging look.

Shar laughed. "And then she thanked you by kicking you out!"

"She didn't know what was going on. She thought we were causing trouble." He pushed up from the table. "Well, if you're through thrashing me, I'll head on out now."

But Winn wasn't through. He wheeled into Zell's path as agilely as though he were riding a go-cart. "Don't go causing me trouble by panting after that girl."

That took him aback. "Panting? Kim's the last woman I'd be panting after." He leaned around and rubbed Tullie's head. "See you, angel."

Up until then, Tullie had been listening to the adults converse with her dark expression. She was no doubt thinking of her feeling. Zell was glad when she whined like any kid. "I wanna go with you! I like going up in the copter."

"Not today. But I'll take you out on the airboat later, okay?"

That brightened her pretty face. "Okay."

This was why he liked doing the fieldwork. He loved his family, but he didn't want to work with them day and night. That was way too much togetherness for him.


Kim knew it wasn't going to be a good morning when she stepped outside. The chorus of birds was an eerie backdrop to the dead rat lying on the broken steps. A wild animal or maybe even some stray cat could have left the mangled carcass. Footprints marred the dirt, but she couldn't tell if any of them weren't hers.

She didn't want to think further than that. She grabbed a handful of paper towels and picked up the rat. As she headed toward the hothouse to find a shovel, she saw the alligator tracks across the damp ground. The distinctive trail of the tail with footprints on either side gave her a shiver. She'd gutted fish and cleaned frogs that she had gigged out in the swamp with her dad, but alligators terrified her. She buried the rat, stomped on the alligator tracks, and tried to push both far from her mind. There were bigger things to think about.

Like nearly getting run off the road last night. It was her bad luck that Kinsey had been on duty. He had chalked her experience up as an impatient redneck with no manners or even a drunk driver. Nothing more sinister than that. Still, she'd insisted that he follow her home in case the boys had ideas about waiting at her house for her.

Oh, yeah, she was pretty sure it was the two boneheads she'd kicked out of the bar. Unfortunately, the truck was nowhere in sight. They'd probably figured she'd gone to the substation and hightailed it back to the rock they lived under.

The short dock caught her eye, and she walked to the

end of it. Her hands traced the edges of the skiff, smooth from wear and time. The skiff was the last place her grandma had been alive. It resembled a flat canoe, shallow and narrow. Elva often sojourned into the wetlands during the wet season. She used a pole to maneuver the skiff through the shallow waters, sometimes having to drag it across drier sections.

Kim climbed into the skiff and inhaled deeply in an effort to ease the turmoil inside her. She'd forgotten how clean the air was down here; only the faint scent of earth, leaves, and a rotting log before the water and ground absorbed it. That's what she loved about the swamp, how she could experience thousands of years of life and death, of symbiotic relationships that hopefully would forever continue the cycle. Everything was beautiful here, from the green moss on the trees to the pattern of the oil on the water left by mangrove pods.

This was Elva's world. She was strong, capable, full of sass and independence. She'd been paddling in these waters for decades. If she'd had a choice of where to die, she'd have chosen the swamps.

That she had died still didn't feel right.

Kim untied the skiff and shoved away from the dock. She hadn't intended to take it out, but there she was, following the winding route through the hammock. As she pushed her pole into the tea-brown water, she took in the beauty that Elva had taught her to appreciate. How many times had the two of them come out here? Elva would merely point out something: the pattern of orange lichen on a cypress trunk; a strangler fig wrapped around an old palm tree; air plants and orchids perched safely out of a poacher's reach. Every plant and creature took advantage of the limited space in the hammock, living on top of one another to grab a perch and a tiny bit of sunlight.

They hadn't said much during those forays, and when they did speak, it was in church-quiet whispers. Elva said this was God's sanctuary. Birds were the choir, stacks of bromeliads were the altars, and the skiff was her pew. This was where Kim would spread Elva's ashes, she decided. But only after she had come to peace with her death.

Smitty said he'd tied a ribbon to a branch where he had found Elva's body. After a half-hour, Kim found it dangling from a branch. The sight of it brought tears to her eyes and an ache to her chest. The old-timers seemed to take death in stride. It was a way of life in the swamps.

But something about Elva's death wasn't right. It kept nagging at her.

She shivered, even in the heavy air filled with buzzing insects trying to find a breach in her bug spray zone. She backed up and poled toward the sunshine.

Beyond the edge of the dense hammock lay a vast wet prairie streaked with thick patches of marsh and mangroves. Birds chattered from the stand of cypress trees in the far distance. She brushed away a web, sending the large golden spider with furry black tufts on its legs scurrying away. She paddled through a tight opening and went from dim and damp to bright and hot.

She followed a swath of water to the opening of a maze of mangroves she remembered exploring in years past. Maybe she'd go a little ways into them for old time's sake. She pushed the pole into the mud and was instantly surrounded by mangroves and isolated from the prairie. An egret prowled among the leggy roots of the mangroves, and dragonflies buzzed over the water looking for mosquito larvae.

The sun glared down as she continued to pole farther into the mangroves. She felt completely at peace until she heard the thud of a pole hitting the side of a boat. Three egrets abruptly took flight, and she realized that the chattering birds in the distance had grown quiet. She looked ahead and then behind her, but saw no sign of anyone. Suddenly being alone wasn't so peaceful. She'd come out on a whim, without her tear gas.

Her body stiffened as she strained to hear anything else. There. What was that? The sound of water stirring, the sound she'd been making as the pole slipped into the water and pushed the skiff forward. Ripples of water moved toward her through the mangroves to her right. She strained to see through the branches and leaves but could see nothing of what lay beyond. But she could still hear, and someone was definitely on the other side.

Since she was in the Everglades National Park, it could be anyone, though few people traveled this far from the park's paths and roads. Buck Waddell's land was a couple of miles to the south. What she was hearing, though, wasn't a hunting party. Hunting wasn't allowed in the park, and besides, it sounded like only one skiff, which meant one person or maybe two.

Did he—or they—know she was there? They could have spotted her from across the distance as she'd poled out of the hammock, she supposed. They could be hunting illegally, and she could be mistaken for a target. Or it might be someone out enjoying the peace and quiet like she was—or had been. She decided to play it safe.

"Hey," she called out in a strong, confident voice. "How're you doing over there?"

She heard another thunk of wood against wood. And nothing else.

A chill slowly spread through her despite the heat. She slipped her pole into the water and pushed forward, going deeper into the mangroves. Somewhere up ahead, she remembered a break that would allow her to exit. She would listen to whoever was on the other side and see where they were going.

A knot formed at her diaphragm. Through a thinning part of the trees she could see the vague shape of a boat roughly even with her. She knelt down but couldn't see who was in it. The movement sent out ripples that would radiate to her follower. What did he want? A flash glinted through the leaves. Binoculars?

Her fingers tightened on the pole. She could use it as a weapon if necessary. Wasn't that opening around the next bend? If he were following her, though, he would cut her off. Maybe that was his intent. When she came around the bend, she spotted the opening that was much smaller than she remembered. Her follower wasn't masking his sounds as he headed toward that same opening.

She decided to go back toward the opening she'd come in through. Then it was only a short distance to the hammock. Very quietly, she turned and headed back. Twigs littered the bottom of the skiff. She threw one behind her, hoping to make the follower think she was still continuing forward. A few seconds later, she threw another twig into the water.

Her heartbeat jumped when she heard branches scraping against the side of a boat. He was pushing his way through the opening. She shoved the pole into the mud and lost her grip. The pole fell into the tannin-colored water. She lunged for it before it sank. When she tried for another shove downward, her fingers slid against the wet wood. She gripped harder and pushed forward. Behind her, she could hear a boat sliding through the water.

At each bend, she hoped to find the entrance; instead she found more mangroves. Had she taken a wrong turn? Was the passage this narrow before? For all she knew, she could be heading to a dead end. She glanced behind her. No sign of him yet. But he was there, maybe gaining on her, maybe right around the last bend.

Fear propelled her on. Her fingers were cramping from her tight grip on the pole, but she pushed onward. When she turned the next bend, she gasped in relief: the opening to the marsh lay fifty yards ahead. The boat sounded just as close behind her. She only dared a glance as she glided toward the opening. No sign of him.

She pushed out into the prairie and kept going through the wet grasses until she reached the edge of the hammock. When she turned back, she could see the front edge of a boat tucked just inside the entrance. A reflection flashed through the leaves again. He was watching her. Enjoying her panic and fear. Bastard. Anger flared through her, making her want to pole right back and see who the hell was trying to scare her.

Instead, she glared defiantly in his direction for a

moment before heading deeper into the hammock. "I'm never leaving the house without my tear gas," she chanted over and over until she reached the dock. She jumped out, tied up the skiff, and headed inside.

A half-hour later, Kim had washed off the sweat and washed away the fear. Whoever had terrorized her in the mangroves hadn't come into the hammock. She kept checking, even during her shower. Damn, if she could have only seen who it was. Could it be Billy Bob and Clem again? Something told her that today's creep was more subtle than those clods could ever be. Either way, it was darn disconcerting. Now she was angry at the jerk, and at herself for giving him the satisfaction of scaring her.

"Forget about it," she told herself as she stripped the sheets off Elva's bed and ran a load of clothes. The washer and dryer were in the bedroom, which made it easy. She'd also discovered that Oscar liked his blanket fresh from the dryer. He'd stood in front of the dryer with the blanket in his mouth, probably annoyed that it took her so long to get the hint.

"You've got bigger fish to fry. Like apologizing to Zell." Who knew when he'd deign to return to the bar while she was still in town? Since she had no idea what he did for a living, she was going to have to go to Heron's Glen. The prospect churned her stomach.

Oscar followed her out the door and to the car. She turned to him. "You know, if you're going to insist on riding everywhere with me, you're going to have to get in the car yourself. I'm tired of shoving pig butt."

His only response was to twitch his erect ears at her. Today the ads for the orchids and Oscar would run in both the local and Naples papers. *And the bar?*

She'd put off placing an ad for that. First, she had no idea what it was worth. Unfortunately, of the two real estate offices in town, one was owned by Macgregors and the other by a Wharton cousin.

Okay, find out how much it was worth, and then what? The prospect of selling the bar was messing with her insides more than having to apologize to Zell, and that was saying something. Like Wharton had said, though, running it from afar wasn't an option. There wasn't anyone she trusted.

Except herself.

It wasn't a new thought. It had been hovering at the edges of her mind since she'd gotten the call from Wharton.

She glanced into the backseat where a raccoon, owl, fox, and alligator sat. They were going up for grabs at the bar, with Smitty getting first dibs. Not that she minded foxes, raccoons, and owls, but having them in the house was kind of creepy.

She tried to pass off her increased heart rate to too many Tums. "Nice try," she said as she pulled through those fancy columns at Heron's Glen. It wasn't the prospect of seeing Zell, either, she told herself; it was the apology itself. And possibly seeing any other Macgregors. "What am I doing here? This is crazy." She glanced at Oscar. "Why is this so important to me? Even the idea of sending a note or calling didn't ease this yucky feeling. Crap, I hate having a conscience. Why should it matter, especially with Zell?"

Oscar had no comment. He just continued to look odd and a little bit funny sitting in the passenger seat taking in the surroundings.

"I guess if he can be nice, so can I. Personally, I think it's easier to be a bitch."

At the crossroads, she remembered the road went straight to the farm and left to the house. A newer road had been cut in to the right. She could see a structure in the distance, maybe another farm building. Other dirt roads splintered onto the pieces of land owned by other Macgregors. She turned to the left.

She'd spent as little time at the farm as possible during her stay with the Macgregors. Charlotte loved the farm, but then again, she'd always been a little strange. Alligators were part of the wetlands, something to be hunted or saved depending on where you came from, or just gawked at if you were a tourist. But loved? Zell and his wild cousin Dougal had gone out at all hours whenever they managed to get assigned to trap a nuisance gator. Zell had been planning to get a degree in wildlife biology.

The large, brick house loomed ahead of her, tripping her heartbeat again. The entrance featured three arches, with a balcony above it. Flanking the entrance were the dueling turrets, one housing the curving staircase and the other the formal dining room. Palms, gumbo-limbos, and other native plants were part of the Xeriscape design. On the right side of the house, their estate caretaker, Dewey, toiled away beneath the hot, sticky sun.

Looking back, she understood what living here had meant to her mother. Kitty had been born poor, gotten pregnant right out of high school, and married a man who couldn't give her any more than she already had monetarily. Too bad she hadn't appreciated the other joys of being married to Donnie Lyons, like getting crazy and enjoying life. Kitty wanted class and money, and Winnerow's offer gave her both. Kim hadn't cut her any slack on her decision, and that had torn apart their relationship. The loss still hurt, even though Kim had convinced herself that it didn't.

Obviously Kitty hadn't been as happy as she'd wanted to be. She'd traded in one drinking, partying man for another, and this one didn't even love her. Even before Rhonda's murder had changed everything, Kitty had started drinking, too. She'd wrecked her car driving drunk. At least her one last act of dignity had been being buried in the Macgregor family plot.

Kim pulled beneath a sprawling gumbo-limbo tree with its reddish-brown, peeling bark and opened the windows for Oscar. "Be right back. How long does it take to say, 'I'm an idiot, sorry'?"

As she approached the house, she realized it was Saturday and that meant they'd just had their breakfast get-together. Which meant that they'd all be there.

"Well, pig poop." Though strictly speaking, pig poop wasn't all that bad of a thing. Just dry pellets. "Be strong, be strong."

She rang the bell and heard the chime sing throughout the house. Not much had changed since those tenuous days here. The trees were bigger and the driveway had been paved. The sculptured beds of mulch and plants had been added.

When the door opened, she saw no one at first. Just straight through the formal foyer and living room to the lanai. She shifted her gaze down and caught her breath. Winnerow sat in a wheelchair. Whatever had happened to him hadn't affected the hardness in his blue-green eyes. Half of his mouth was held in a firm line while the other half was slack. She was surprised and a little relieved to see him helpless. Only a little relieved, though. Winnerow had too many allies in town to be considered genuinely helpless.

"What are you doing here?" he barked.

She could see that there was no use making pleasantries, so she got to the point. "I'm looking for Zell. Is he here?"

Charlotte appeared around the doorway, looking as beautiful and crafty as ever. Her blond hair was now auburn and cut short, and her eyes matched her father's in color and animosity. "What do you want with my brother?"

Winnerow turned to Charlotte. "Told you he was panting!" For a half-slack mouth, there was nothing wrong with his booming voice.

Panting? "I just need a quick word with Zell if he's here. If he's not, I'll catch him later."

Winnerow growled, "You don't belong here and you don't belong in Cypress. I wouldn't plan on staying around town much longer."

She heard the movie line in her head, *Is that a threat?* If only something smart would come out of her mouth, something strong and sassy. But his words about not belonging tore at the edges of her heart and tangled up any sly comebacks. She glanced beyond Charlotte and Winnerow, but didn't see Zell anywhere. Owen Kendall stood several feet behind the door. She remembered Charlotte dating him in high school and she'd been married and had a baby when Kim's mom had died.

As Kim turned and walked back to the car, she caught sight of a young girl peering around the corner of the house. She ducked back. Kim kept her head high as the huge front door slammed shut. That was as much of a welcome as she'd ever got there, really. Winnerow had made token efforts, but his two teenagers hadn't. She supposed she hadn't been the easiest to welcome. They'd finally reached a tenuous peace when all hell had broken loose.

"Kim?"

The shy, tentative voice broke her out of those thoughts, and she looked down to see the girl. She was pretty in a solemn kind of way with long, straight hair the Macgregor shade of blond. Though she hadn't gotten the teal eyes, her eyes were startling just the same, so light blue, they rivaled a moonflower.

"Yeah. Who are you?"

"Tullie Macgregor." She glanced at the house.

"Charlotte's daughter. Hi." Even something as minor as a child's lack of hostility touched Kim in a soft, mushy way.

"I know where Zell is. Want me to take you there?"

"Sure. If . . ." She looked at the house, too. "If you're sure it's okay."

"Mama don't care where I am. I'll ride with you."

"Uh, you'll have to share the front seat with Oscar."

Tullie tugged open the door and squealed in delight at seeing the pig. "Oscar!" She gave him an unabashed hug that made Kim almost ask if she'd like the pig. When Tullie started to climb in, she paused at the sight of the animals in the backseat.

"Uh, those were Elva's," Kim said. "I'm trying to find a home for them."

"Smitty won't want 'em," she said, squirming right onto the seat with Oscar, though she only took a corner. "He doesn't have room."

"How'd you know I was giving him first dibs?"

Tullie pointed down the road. "Go back the other way."

Kim followed, wondering why this girl was helping. Maybe it was in retaliation to a mother who didn't pay enough attention to her. Whatever, Kim was taking the help.

"How old are you?" she asked conversationally.

"Nine." Tullie hadn't taken her gaze off Kim once she'd settled onto the seat. "You're the Kim who used to live here. The one who bit our finger."

"Pardon? I didn't bite anyone's finger, but I did live here . . . for a time anyway." She wondered how much the girl knew. Probably everything, if she knew the Macgregors. They'd probably added her to the trove of family stories, making her into an ogre along the way.

"Go straight," Tullie said when they reached the intersection. "Zell's house is up ahead."

Kim only nodded, not sure what else to say. Tullie kept staring at her, as though she were evaluating her—or looking right through her. "Is something wrong?" Kim asked finally.

The girl seemed to weigh what to say, which was a strange thing for a young girl to do. Most kids just spoke their minds. "Are you going to be here long?"

Great, even the kid wanted her gone by sundown. "I'm not sure. I've got some things to figure out."

She pondered that. "Like the truth."

Now that wasn't what she'd expected. "The truth?"

Tullie nodded. "You're looking for the truth."

"I don't think so. I'm looking for a life maybe. Direction, definitely direction." *A home,* her inner voice chimed in. "I'm looking for Zell—to apologize for my bad manners," she felt compelled to add. "But not truth."

Charlotte watched her traitorous daughter get into Kim's car. She knew exactly what the little freak was doing— taking her to Zell. All because of that stupid vision or whatever it was that she'd had. She supposed she could run down there and yell at Tullie to get out of the car, but that'd make her look like a hag.

"What's she doing, coming round here sniffing for Zell? I don't like it," her daddy said as he wheeled toward the large front window.

"It's not like Zell's going to give her anything. She's not his type." Shar pushed her father's wheelchair toward the study. "I'll call him after we do your physical therapy and see what she wanted."

He swatted her away, stinging her with his thick, gold ring and his rejection. "I can steer myself! I'm not a cripple."

She pulled her hand back and swallowed words about how she didn't like this new daddy. She'd been taking care of him for a long time, after Mama died and through his heavy drinking and withdrawal with each successive tragedy that had hit the Macgregors. She'd stepped aside when Kitty had come in, but reasserted her position when Kitty began to drown her disappointment in booze.

Shar had been afraid that the stroke would trample what was left of his spirit, but it had done just the opposite. It had made him into something he'd never been before: a father. She didn't like it. "Well, what do you want me to do about her?"

He narrowed his eyes. "I'll take care of her if she causes any trouble."

# CHAPTER 8

Tullie fiddled with the hem of her ruffled shirt that, not surprisingly, had grinning alligators on it. Green alligators, which always made Kim wonder where artists got the idea that alligators were green. They weren't nearly as cute as the ones on her shirt, either.

The structure she'd seen in the distance now came into focus. The light wood exterior of the octagon home made it blend into the prairie beyond. It wasn't a large house and was nothing like the big house. It was raised up from the ground like most homes in the area. Tall grasses surrounded the house and a stone walkway led to a covered porch on the left side. His truck was parked out front.

"This is Zell's place?" She couldn't take her eyes from it. Something about it made her feel at home, yet she'd never lived on a prairie or in an octagon house. "It's beautiful."

"He built it himself over the last couple years." She hopped out of the car and had to push Oscar back to keep him from getting out.

Even though it was cloudy, Kim rolled down the windows all the way. "I'll be right back, Oscar."

She glanced in the backseat and decided to bring Zell a peace offering. She grabbed up the two-and-a-half-foot alligator. Tullie had skipped on ahead, gone inside, and then come out again before Kim made it up the walkway.

"He must be out back," Tullie said, waving for Kim to follow. "He's going up in the copter later. I'm hoping he's going to take me with him."

The wet prairie here was adorned with palmetto palms that always reminded her of the extinct Truffula trees in Dr. Seuss's book. Of course, these weren't nearly as colorful, but they were in abundance as groups of them made up palmetto heads that dotted the prairie.

A trail led from the house through a mixture of grasses as tall as her waist in places, and in the case of sawgrass, as sharp as a blade. Tree frogs leaped away, but toothpick grasshoppers merely swiveled to the back side of the blade of grass to escape detection. Pink, purple, and yellow flowers dotted the sea of brown grass. It was quiet out here, with only the occasional call of a bird, a breeze rustling the grasses, and their footsteps on the gravel pathway.

Until the roar of an airboat filled the air. The blast of sound cut through the silence and made Kim fumble with the alligator. Not that she was jumpy, she told herself, giving Tullie a sheepish smile. The sound died down as they came upon a dock. The flattish boat with a large fan in the back that propelled it over waters as shallow as two inches sat at the end of the dock. Two seats perched in front of the fan accommodated the driver and a passenger. The sides of the airboat were painted to look like the skin of a diamondback rattler.

Tullie skipped down the new boards of the dock to the airboat that Zell was working on. He was shirtless, his tan skin glistening in the sun. He was long and lean and looked way too good in a pair of disintegrating jeans. He was wearing that music player with the headphones and was so intent on whatever he was doing he hadn't seen them. Which was all right, since it gave her some looking time.

Her fingers tightened on the smooth belly skin of the gator. Well, there was nothing wrong with gawking at a beautiful specimen of man, was there? Even if he was someone she didn't particularly like? When she managed to pull her gaze away, she saw Tullie watching her.

Tullie didn't giggle like a typical girl, though, at catching Kim gawking at her uncle. She gave Kim that eerie, contemplative look that no little girl should own yet. Then she looked at Zell. Kim wanted to say, *Don't worry, kid, ain't nothing gonna happen between me and him.* Just in case that wasn't what the strange look was for, she decided against it. Then she realized her thoughts were in dialect. Where had that come from? Well, from here. *You can take the girl out of the swamp, but . . .*

Tullie climbed onto the airboat and tapped Zell's arm. He gave her a warm smile before looking up to see Kim. His smile cooled somewhat, but wasn't unwelcoming. Curious, of course, but it was not the reception his father and sister had given her. He removed the headphones and stepped onto the dock. He smelled like clean sweat and the black grease that was smeared on his right forearm. For some reason his intriguing advice to Angus popped to mind, about throwing his wife on the bed and telling her he was going to make love to her all night long. So did his dialogue about all the important parts. Was Zell that kind of guy—*Nah, let's not go there.*

Tullie walked closer to Zell and whispered, "That's her, the one I saw. 'Cept her hair is longer." Zell nodded in response to the strange comment. She turned to Kim. "I'll go check on Oscar, make sure he's not too hot."

Once Tullie was out of earshot, Kim asked, "What did she mean, I was the one she saw?"

"She has feelings. Guess you'd call them psychic. She had one about you and me."

"What were we doing?"

"She just saw us, and it worried her. She's afraid something bad is going to happen." He glanced down at her midsection. "Is that for me?"

Her eyebrows shot up, along with her blood pressure. "Excuse me?"

"Thought you didn't like them."

"I, uh . . ." Oh, he meant the alligator! Her flush turned into one of embarrassment at where her thoughts had taken her. She shoved it at him. "I don't. It's for you, if you'd like it. Apparently Elva had a fondness for using dead animals as decorations. I thought maybe you'd like this one."

He took her in for a moment as she held out the alligator before finally taking the damn thing. "I suppose I could find a place for it. Thanks." He took it and set it on the cleaning station ledge. "She bought a collection a couple of years back. Sold most of them, but kept her favorites. You know Elva, always wheeling and dealing."

She wished she could just leave it at that and hope he got the peace-offering innuendo. But that would be cheating, and he was clearly waiting for some further explanation of why she dared tread on Macgregor property.

"About last night . . . I didn't know what was going on with those two guys. I mean, I didn't know you were . . . I just thought—"

His amusement halted her words, such as they were. "You trying to apologize for kicking me out?"

"Yes." She laughed at the relief in that word. "Yes, that's what I'm trying to do. Not very well, I know. Smitty said those two guys were talking about . . . well, doing something to me."

Zell grabbed a rag and wiped the grease off his arm. "At first I thought they were just pretending to plan something to get on my nerves. Then I wasn't sure. I didn't want them to get any ideas."

Her throat tightened at the gesture. This time she could enjoy his chivalry instead of feeling so guilty about it. "Thanks. I appreciate what you did . . . especially . . . considering . . ."

"You always have this much trouble talking?"

Never. She laughed it off, not wanting to admit it was he who was tripping up her tongue. "Say, how much are Elva's payments to you each month for the orchids?"

"Two-fifty, due on the first of the month."

Two-fifty, not five hundred. "I'll make sure you're paid on time."

"I don't doubt it." She wasn't sure if he was being threatening or he just had faith in her integrity.

"Tullie said you were going up in a helicopter."

"Yep, going nest-spotting. It's egg harvest time."

Seeing the anticipation on his face was something. "You obviously like it."

"I like anything that takes me out there." He nodded toward the marsh. "Especially when it has something to do with gators. Today I map the nests and tonight I go out and harvest the eggs. There's nothing like uncovering a nest and discovering it's full of beautiful, white eggs. It's like opening a treasure chest every time, never knowing what's going to be inside." He did love what he did; she could tell by the way his voice had changed from the usual reserved tone to one closer to a boy's on Christmas morning. The passion in his voice tickled through her stomach. Few of the men she knew had that kind of passion for their jobs. Or for anything.

"Do you take all of the eggs?"

"Yep. Alligators lay about thirty-five to forty eggs in one nest, but few live long enough to grow to three feet. At the farm, ninety-five percent of the eggs produce viable gators. My job is to survey the alligator population for both Macgregor properties and a few other properties we've arranged lease deals with. I map out the nests, take the eggs, and then monitor hatch rates. When the gators reach a survivable age, some are returned to the property to compensate for the ones that would have survived in the wild. It's good for the environment, good for the economy, and good for people who like alligator leather."

Of course, it was good for the Macgregors, too, but he was modest enough not to mention that.

"I'll bet you would have gotten into the park service if they weren't the enemy."

Locals resented the government's intrusion into their

livelihoods. When the national park was established in 1947, many gladesmen lost their fishing and hunting grounds. Not that the government could keep the natives from continuing to pursue their livelihoods. Laws just made it more challenging. Zelwig Macgregor was a legendary poacher and local hero.

Zell shook his head. "That's why I went to the University of Georgia instead of Florida. Up there they teach you how to preserve nature *and* profit from it."

"Now that you're back, I bet you never leave Cypress."

Zell obviously took that as a slam and affected a hick accent. "Wail now, every now and then they let me out of here. 'Course, those boys up in Tallahassee don't much like it when I show up in water-logged sneakers with my suit."

"I didn't mean— You go up to Tallahassee?"

He dropped the inflection. "To lobby for industry issues. They even let me sit on some committees for things like water conservation . . . long as I don't pick my nose and scratch my ass."

She gave him a playful shove before realizing what she was doing. "I didn't mean it that way. I'm impressed, really."

"Didn't tell you to impress you." He closed up his toolbox. After setting it beneath the cleaning shelf ledge, he grabbed up the alligator and gave it a look-over. "Nice specimen. It's still got its stripes. They lose them when they become adults." He carried it under his arm and indicated that she join him as he started down the boardwalk.

She walked beside him, amazed that they had shared a conversation and were now walking in companionable silence. Amazed more that she *liked* being with him. What was going on here?

"You really love those creatures, don't you?" she asked.

He held out the alligator. "How can anyone not like them, or at least respect them? First, the alligator is the only animal where every aspect of their ecology is salable. Nothing goes to waste. Second, this is the oldest living reptile, the closest we'll get to seeing a dinosaur. He's an engineering marvel, a study in survivability." He indicated the bumps on the back of the gator. "These scutes here are made of bone, and his hide is tougher than anything. He blends into both the water and land and moves around in either environment with ease. He's a killing machine from head to toe. He can use his tail as a weapon if someone grabs hold of it. Had 'em knock me on my butt a few times with their tails."

He swung it around so that its mouth faced her. "You're looking at a couple thousand pounds of biting power with up to eighty teeth that regenerate if needed. When he's submerged, only his nostrils and eyes are above water. They're exciting to hunt and they're exciting to preserve. There's a primitive power in hooking a ten-foot gator that could tear you apart. There's a different kind of feeling in setting a few four-footers free in the swamp to balance out the population, especially when you saw them come out of their shells."

He'd obviously noticed Kim backing up as he gestured with the gator. He didn't just love what he did; he was totally, completely into it.

"Why are you so afraid of gators, anyway?" he asked, pulling the gator back. "I remember we couldn't even get you to walk into the gator houses to look at the babies."

She didn't want to tell him about the old woman who lost her arm, so she shrugged. "All those teeth are reason enough."

He waved that away. "Gators rarely attack humans unless they're threatened, a mama gator's babies are threatened, or they're really, really hungry."

"That's comforting." She met his gaze. "Well, I'd better get going."

"I asked Smitty to walk you out to your car after the bar closes. Don't be sassy and all toughlike and tell him not to."

That uneasy thrum returned to her insides. She thought about telling him what had happened last night but decided not to. She couldn't prove it was them. "Do you think they'll cause trouble?"

"It's like being around a gator. It might just hiss. It might just sit there and watch you. Or it might attack."

"I've got tear gas."

"Your wits are your best weapon. If they knock it out of your hand, it's not going to do you a whole lot of good. And ole Smitty, he's not going to be able to keep two ornery buttheads from causing trouble, but he's a start. Mind yourself while you're here."

It was a warning, but she wondered if his motive was only to help her. "Are you trying to scare me into leaving town?"

He paused when they reached the covered entry for his home. "Be the best thing for you. Some folks'll be happy when you head on out."

"Including you."

"Including me." He set the gator down. It looked as though it were striding away from the door. "I want you to leave, yeah, but for different reasons altogether."

She swallowed hard. "And they are?"

"One, for what you did to my family."

"And the second?"

Tullie walked around the curved pathway. "Oscar's getting kinda hot."

She looked at Zell, waiting for his answer.

"You be careful," he said in his typical nonanswer way.

Why did every encounter with Zell leave her feeling . . . well, leave her feeling? Annoyance and admiration and, yes, even attraction tangled inside her. She felt a little tender at his blunt honesty. "Tullie, you need a ride back to the house?"

Kim felt some relief when Tullie displayed the typical coyness of a young girl. She batted her eyes at her uncle and said, "Unless he's gonna take me with him in the copter?"

He jerked his head toward the house. "Make us some sammiches while I take a shower. We've got to head out shortly." With a squeal, Tullie raced into the house, leaving them facing each other again.

"Sammiches," she said with a grin. "I haven't heard that word since I left town." She let her smile fade. "Funny the things you miss. You're not going to tell me, are you? The second reason, I mean."

Before he disappeared into the house, he said, "We'll just leave it at the family thing. That's reason enough."


Zell had seen the flicker of hurt in Kim's eyes when he'd said he wanted her to leave. Telling her why wouldn't have helped any so he'd used her reason enough line and left it at that. The first problem was he liked her. It was a weird tangle of sexual interest and something else he didn't want to examine too closely. Her coming there to apologize had notched her up on his scale of respect big time. He remembered how hard it was to wrangle an apology out of her. It had taken balls to come on Macgregor property and admit she'd made a mistake. Just like it had for her to ask him to let Smitty continue on at the bar. Damn, he really didn't want to respect her.

The second problem was she was inadvertently putting him in a bad place. Defending her meant opposing his family, at least that's the way they'd see it. And he didn't blame them. On the other hand, he couldn't stand by and let someone hurt her. So the sooner she left town, the better.

"Sammiches are ready," Tullie said when he stepped into the blessedly cool house.

"Hold on while I take a shower." He grabbed the phone on his way upstairs. When Shar answered, he said, "Is it all right if Tullie goes up with me?"

"No, it is not. That little traitor needs to get her butt right home. I suppose you saw Kim."

"She went to the house?"

"Yeah, asking after you. Daddy told her what for, and she left. But our little Tullie offered to take her to you. That's what happened, wasn't it?"

Talk about getting in the middle of things. Damn, he hated conflict. He started the shower to mask his conversation from Tullie. "She had the feeling. You know how tore up she was about Elva dying after having that feeling. And she was right about that, you know. She needed to see if Kim was the woman she'd seen." He thought it was strange, though, that Tullie "saw" Kim with shorter hair than she had.

"You can't believe that garbage."

"Doesn't matter whether I do or not. I respect that she does and so should you. Which reminds me, if I ever hear again that you talked about smoking pot while you were pregnant and that's why Tullie's strange, I'm going to whup your behind."

"I didn't say that to her."

"Well, she heard you anyway. Just what a little girl wants to hear from her mama. Made her feel real good."

"Dammit, Zell, stop making me feel bad. I can't help it if she creeps around listening to adult conversations. All right, all right, I'll be careful. Aw, why couldn't I have had a normal kid?"

"That's just what I'm talking about. You shouldn't even be having thoughts like that. She's your kid. You love her no matter what. Cut her some slack and let her come up with me. And don't give her a hard time about bringing Kim here. Don't drag her into family grudges."

"That's what we had to grow up with."

"Right, and it was bad enough for us. Let it go."

"'Cause you're so smart about raising kids. You're gonna be a bachelor just like Marvin and Dewayne."

Zell thought of the odd brothers who were their cousins. In their late thirties, they had never married, and they'd lived together since moving out of the house. They were content with their hunting dogs, homemade beer brewing contraptions, and each other. At the rate he was going, he might just end up a bachelor, alone with his stuffed alligator. Women were a fun addition to his life, but he didn't need someone else to take care of. Besides, no woman had ever passed his alligator test. But he'd never had a woman give him an alligator, and that was a fact. "Can Tullie come or what?"

"All right, she can go. Just don't lecture me anymore. And what did Kim want, anyway? She's not still there, is she?"

"No. She apologized for kicking me out of the bar last night. No big deal." He thought about her holding that alligator out to him and stumbling through her apology.

Shar huffed. "The sooner that woman leaves town, the better."

"I couldn't agree more."

Kim ran a few errands before heading to Southern Comfort. Smitty said he would open up for lunch. Saturdays were slow and leisurely in Cypress. What a difference from Tallahassee where you had to plan your errands strategically to account for traffic flow. Where no one knew your name or your business. Where most people hadn't seen you grow up. Of course, she'd also grown accustomed to all-night grocery stores, a variety of restaurants, and Blockbuster around the corner. Still, she'd never felt as though she belonged there.

She didn't belong here anymore, either. On the upside, neither the teller at the bank nor the clerk at the gas station was rude to her. A woman at Tiger's Grocery Store had even welcomed her back. That in itself was cause for celebration. "See, Kim, everybody doesn't hate you."

Oscar tilted his head in agreement. " 'Course, you don't hate me. I feed you. You're easy. Hopefully someone nice will call and offer you a home."

The pig looked away as though he knew what she'd said. Maybe she'd stipulate that he went with the bar. Unfortunately, the thought of selling the bar made her feel even worse.

"Elva, if you want me to stay, give me a sign."

When she pulled up to Southern Comfort, broken bits of glass winked on the gravel parking lot. Someone had broken the front windows and smashed the neon lights. She felt as though *she'd* been beaten up instead of the bar. She involuntarily reached over and stroked Oscar's head, though she wasn't sure if it was out of protectiveness for him or comfort for herself.

She parked next to the three trucks that were far from the glass and took in the damage again. Someone had wanted to make a statement: *Leave.* Her eyes stung as she walked into the bar that was lighter than usual with the sun streaming in the front windows. Nothing inside had been touched.

Smitty was talking to the two tables' worth of people. When he saw her, he ambled over.

"What happened to the windows?" she asked after giving her customers a welcome smile.

"The what?"

"Windows?" Was he deaf?

"Winders, young'un. Don't you forget where you came from."

She'd forgotten *winders.* "Yes, sir. What happened?"

He shrugged. "They were like that when I showed up. Called the sheriff's substation and they sent a man over. He took pictures and the rocks that made the mess, but didn't have much idea who it was."

The list of suspects was too large to contemplate. "I'm going over to the marina and see if anyone over there saw something."

"Already did that. Tubbs, the guy that owns it now, couldn't say whether your winders were okay this morning when he came in or not. All those stacked boats block the view."

She went into the storage closet and came out with an old hammer and a tape measure. Smitty helped as she measured the openings.

"I'll be back," she said a few minutes later.

"Where you going?"

"I've got to fix those winders."

He scratched his grizzled hair. "Aren't you gonna cry or stamp your foot or something?"

"What good would it do except give folks something to gossip about? Is that what Elva would have done?"

" 'Course not."

"I'm more like my grandma than my mom, thank gawd. I'll be back."

He handed her his keys. "Take my truck. You'll need it for the wood."

Half an hour later, she returned from the hardware store with sheets of plywood and a box of nails. The clerk promised he'd rush her order of replacement glass. She hauled the ladder out front. Smitty had already cleaned up a lot of the glass. She was going to double his pay for the night just for dealing with that.

He came out after her few customers left. "How's it coming, young'un?"

"Fine and dandy." Miserable and hot, drenched in sweat and swatting away flies. She pounded in the last nail on that window and turned to him. "You have any idea who did this?"

"No use pointing fingers unless you're sure."

She nodded because he was right and otherwise she might just cuss for the hell of it. Maybe he could help with her other quest. "Who was Elva talking to about selling the bar?"

"Who wasn't she talking to? Elva was always yammering about selling, it was getting too much for her, she was tired of working long hours, cranky customers, blah, blah, blah. But she'd never sell. She wanted you to have it."

She sat down on one of the ladder steps. "I don't know what to do with this place, Smitty. I feel like I'd be doing her wrong by selling."

"You would."

She winced at his blunt honesty. "But keeping it means staying, and some people don't seem too happy with me being here temporarily, much less permanently." She nodded toward the window she'd just covered. "Someone tried to run me off the road last night. That was fun."

Smitty instantly looked concerned. "What? Are you sure it wasn't just a drunk?"

She was already shaking her head before he'd even finished the sentence. "No, this was deliberate. Unfortunately,
I couldn't see the make or inside the cab." She scrubbed
her fingers through her damp hair. "I just don't know what
to do."

"Sounds like you need to talk to the Sage. Even the
mayor talks to Zell. One time he settled a dispute between
two fighting dogs. I swear he talked sense right into 'em."

"I'm not talking to Zell. He could even be the one trying
to buy the bar. And maybe orchestrating all this to make his
point."

He laughed, snorted actually. "Zell, take up vandalism
pranks? Not hardly. Besides, he owns ten percent of it anyway."

*"What?"* Just when she was chiding herself for suspect-
ing Zell, those words yanked her out of her thoughts. "He
owns ten percent of Southern Comfort?"

"According to his and Elva's agreement. He didn't want
her to, but she insisted on putting up ten percent as collateral for the loan."

She rubbed the bridge of her nose where a headache was
about to settle in. She hadn't had a chance to read the loan
agreement yet. "It's like circumstances are burying me
deeper in the muck, keeping me here in town. On the other
hand, most folks want me out of here, the sooner the better.
You'll think this is silly, but I asked Elva for a sign about
staying when I pulled in here and this is what I got." She
gestured to the windows. "I don't know what to do."

"It'll come to you in time."

Tullie had said Kim was looking for the truth. "Zell
says Tullie is psychic. Is that true?"

"I swear she knows just what move I'm going to make
when we play backgammon. She sometimes comes by
after school and plays a couple games with me."

"She saw me in one of her visions."

Smitty's face darkened as he leaned against the wall.
"She had a feeling about Elva. She made me promise to

keep an eye on her, said something bad was gonna happen. That was two days before she died. Wish I'd known she was going out that night."

She pushed away from the ladder and walked closer to him. "Something had made Elva think about dying, long before Tullie's premonition. Was there something wrong with her health?"

"Nope. She was as healthy and ornery as ever."

"But she thought to add my name to the bar and house. You know her. She never liked to think about dying. What made her do that?"

He only shrugged. "Maybe she was feeling her age."

"She wasn't that old!" Kim tapped her fingers against her cheek. "Elva went poling all the time in the summer. She could maneuver that skiff as good as any cracker. Don't you think it's odd—"

"It was just an accident." He shifted his gaze away. "Just a stupid ole accident."

"Do you really believe that?"

"It was her time to go, that's all. That's all. Don't want to talk about it." He walked back inside, leaving her to wonder what he knew. He'd been uncomfortable when she'd asked about those payments. She followed him in.

"If you're trying to protect Elva's memory, please don't. If she was involved in something—"

His keys jingled as he walked past her. "I'm going home for a bit. I'll be back before happy hour." She'd never seen him walk so fast.

She watched him pull out of the lot and decided she was going to invest in a bottle of Tums for the bar. She had a feeling she was going to need it. Had Elva been up to something, or was he just expressing his grief in a strange way? No, he knew something. To keep her mind from wandering down a dark path, she went to work on the last window. Maybe this was the revenge those two rowdy guys had decided on rather than running her off the road again. She hoped so.

When an old Cadillac pulled into the lot an hour later, Kim stepped down from the ladder. She kept the hammer in hand until Amy Macgregor Burton stepped out. Amy had gone gray prematurely and didn't care to cover the fact. Her silvery locks hung past her shoulders in the back and curled around her face in front. She had the Macgregor teal eyes and a pretty, heart-shaped face. Her linen skirt swished as she walked up to Kim.

"'Member me? Amy?" Her voice had a light, lyrical quality.

"Sure do." Kim glanced around. "Are you supposed to be here? Being a Macgregor and all?"

She handed Kim a business card with a Glamour Shots picture of Amy next to Cypress Real Estate's heron logo. "I came to see if you were thinking of listing this place. No need to harbor the past if it gets in the way of doing business, that's what I say."

Or making a commission, Kim thought.

"Looks like you had a bit of trouble," Amy said, surveying the front of the bar.

"It does, doesn't it?" She climbed back on the ladder and put the last nails into the facing wood. "Nothing I can't handle."

"So, are you going to list Southern Comfort? I do hope you'll list it locally. Surely no one in Naples could present it as well as someone from here."

Why did everyone assume she was going to sell it? "I'll give it some thought." To get off the subject, she asked, "How's your mom?"

"Still serving time, still as ornery as ever. She's petitioning the prison to let her have a pet snake."

"What happened to your painting?"

"Still do it, but it don't pay the rent. Even this real estate gig isn't doing it."

Before Kim could think better of it, out came the words, "Want to wait tables a few nights a week?"

Amy blinked, as surprised by the offer as Kim. "What happened to Linda May?"

"Quit." Kim hammered in the last nail and climbed down from the ladder. "Think about it."

Amy shifted her weight from one foot to the other. "Well, Zell did give Smitty the okay to keep working here. Maybe . . . maybe I will."

"I'm not sure what kind of tips you'll get or how busy you'll be. As I recall, Saturdays were always pretty busy with folks from out of town and from the hunting club." Unless Buck was sending them elsewhere. But the only other lounge in town was at the Everglades Inn. It attracted out-of-towners, but not the regular folk. "You can start tonight, say five-thirty. I'll have to see what Elva paid Linda May; that's about as much as I could afford right now."

"Okay." She smiled. "Okay, then. I'll be here."

When she left, Kim took a deep breath. It was a start. Now she'd just have to see how it went over having a Macgregor working for her.

JoGene watched Kim nailing the boards over the windows he'd smashed early that morning. Why didn't she look more upset? She'd just gone right to work fixing things like it was her bar. Legally it was, but in every other way it was his. Elva had told him she wanted to sell the place, and he'd said he was interested. She hadn't figured how much she wanted, but she promised to come up with terms the following week. And then she'd died.

Hiding behind Wharton hadn't been the greatest idea. He figured being anonymous would ease it along, but she didn't like that at all.

Kim hadn't made one move to put the bar up for sale, not even a sign in the window. Ads for the orchids and the pig had showed up in the paper that morning, but no bar.

His fingers tightened on the steering wheel. She'd better not be thinking of keeping it. Southern Comfort was his. He needed it. Maybe he ought to implement his backup plan, just in case.

He left his truck at the marina and walked over to the bar. "Hey, Kim. How's it going?"

"Just fine and dandy," she said in a voice that indicated it was neither.

"Need some help?"

She pounded in another nail before answering, "I've got it, thanks. 'Sides, I wouldn't want you to catch hell from your dad for helping me."

His hands tightened into fists, but she was too busy to see that or the red infusing his face. "He doesn't own me, you know," he said through rigid lips. "Nobody owns me."

"Come on, JoGene. I remember how it was."

He wanted to knock over her ladder, maybe slap her hard. Just to show her he wasn't impotent. Damn her. He wanted to crouch down over her and rip off her jeans and show her just how potent he was. He was surprised how even his voice sounded as he headed away. "See you around then."

He'd see her around. He'd show her.

# CHAPTER 9

"Dayum, woman, you like to scare my nuts right off me!"

It was the third time Kim had heard some colorful expression when one of the few customers saw the animals on the bar. "They're stuffed," she told Bo (at least that's what the back of his belt read) as he poked them to find out for himself. "The deal tonight is, buy a pitcher of beer and take an animal home with you."

Tullie had been right; Smitty didn't want the animals. No room in his Airstream trailer.

"Well, I might take the owl. Wife loves owls." He turned to his buddy. "Or is it woodstorks? Ah, a bird's a bird. Gimme a pitcher of Michelob, sweet thing."

Kim didn't know these two, so she figured they were staying at the camp. She poured a pitcher and set it and two frosted mugs on the bar. "That'll be seven-fifty."

When he settled his bill, she said, "And here's your owl."

The smell of wings and the tang of the vinegar in the Hotsy-totsy sauce competed with the smoke. Elva had designated four different types of sauces: BBQ, Burn-your-ass, Hotsy-totsy, and an expression for the mild sauce that young children couldn't even say. She doubted many men ordered it, that was for sure. Only Elva would put something like that on a menu. Kim intended to revamp it. She'd keep Hotsy-totsy in Elva's honor.

Amy brought up some empty glasses. "I swear that raccoon and fox are staring at me. It's downright creepy!"

"They'll be gone by the end of the night probably." And why did she feel downright guilty about that? Because they were something Elva had liked. Just like when a woman had called about Oscar, and Kim grilled her about the living situation. "I don't think so," she'd said after hearing that they lived in an apartment in Naples. Oscar needed his outdoor time. She owed it to Elva to do right by him.

She owed Elva.

*I owe her. I can't turn away from all this. And not only for her, but for me. This place is mine.*

*Oh, no, what are you saying?*

"I'll take the coon," Bo's friend said, reaching for it.

She slapped his hand away. "It's already spoken for. So's the fox." Her voice was tight. She grabbed up the critters and set them on the bar behind her where they'd have a place of honor. The blood had drained from her face and her heart was beating slightly faster.

She was staying. She was probably crazy—no, definitely crazy. But she was staying in Cypress.

"You all right?" Amy asked when she came up to grab a towel.

Kim only nodded, not ready to share her revelation yet. She took in the place her grandmother had loved all these years and left to Kim. She didn't believe for a minute that Elva was going to sell it to someone. Now all she had to do was quit her job, tell Simon, whom she hadn't even thought about all day, and then tell everyone here. That was going to be the hardest part. Not saying good-bye to the man she loved but who was all wrong for her, but telling the folks here that she was staying.

"I must be crazy."

"What?" Amy asked, stopping in her tracks.

"Nothing."

She sat on her decision for an hour, letting it roll around

in her head. It felt right. Crazy but right. This was her home, and even if the people here didn't think so, this was where she belonged. Pressure was building in her chest, a mixture of anticipation and fear. Of course, her subconscious had known all along that she was staying. Her soul had known from the moment she'd turned onto the highway leading to town. It had taken her head a little longer to come around.

The post-happy-hour crowd was nearly that—a crowd. The jukebox was playing those old country classics and people were actually laughing. She knew some had come in to check her out; she was sure she was a topic of interest. As Smitty had said, the most interesting thing to happen in a while. It looked as though he were talking about her, too, sitting with his cronies at the long table. That's why Elva paid him as little as she did. He was a part-timer even though he was at the bar full-time. That was all right; Amy was doing a great job even if she was a little too chatty. At least nobody was hollering impatiently for his or her beer.

Amy yelled, "Smitty, need a twenty-four order of Burn-your-ass!" She arrived at the bar and said, "Two long-neck Buds and a Jack Daniel's, no ice."

Nobody ever ordered interesting drinks here, like Screaming Orgasms and Slippery Nipples, though Kim suspected most folks only ordered those to say the words. But she had caught her groove with the fancy maneuvers an old boyfriend had taught her. At least making the drinks could be fun.

"That is so cool how you do that," Amy said, watching the bottle of Jack spin in the air. She nodded toward the room. "They're all betting you drop a bottle 'fore the night is out."

Kim forced a smile. "Great. Is anyone betting I *won't* drop one?"

Amy grinned. "Me."

"Thanks. You're doing a great job, by the way."

"I did a bit of waiting tables at Thelma Sue's place 'fore she went out of business. Wasn't my fault, I swear! Her nephew had his fingers in the till and run her out financially."

Kim laughed. "I wasn't blaming you." She set the drinks on the server's end of the bar and watched Amy saunter back to one of her tables.

Clem and Billy Bob had wandered in a bit ago. She didn't like the smug smiles on their faces as they watched her from their table. Either they'd busted her windows or they were planning something else. Or both. She stared right back at them before heading into the storeroom to get more Budweiser. But only after instructing Amy to make them pay as they drank. They'd already gotten a free pitcher of beer when she'd kicked them out last night.

She caught herself wishing Zell was there at his table drinking—what was it? Oh, yeah, Captain Morgan and root beer. She smiled and then realized she was smiling a little too much over him. She restocked the ice bin, flattened a box, and put it out back. Outside, the frogs were in chorus and a fish flopped in the dark river. A full moon was rising to the east, so close and bright she could see the craters. Across the river the mounds of mangroves were silhouetted against a slate-gray sky. She pictured a screened-in deck out here and maybe a place in the corner for a guitar player on the weekends. She only had a minute to dream, because the mosquitoes had homed in on her and were signaling fourteen thousand of their closest friends to join them for supper.

*Elva, I'm going to do this.* She walked back in and her pores shrank again in the cool air. She remembered Elva explaining why she didn't run the air conditioner in the house: *A body wasn't meant to be switching from hot air to cold air just like that.* She'd snapped her fingers. *I'm gonna enjoy the air just as God intended it.* Kim suspected she just wanted to save money.

Amy greeted the couple that came in with a quick hug and then went on to explain, no doubt, what she was doing there. Charlotte Macgregor didn't look pleased. Owen followed her, to Kim's surprise, to the bar where they took stools. Charlotte looked around as though she expected to see major changes. Her eyes alighted on the dead animals for a moment until Kim distracted her by asking what they wanted to drink.

"Jack and Coke, and Owen will have a Bud Light." When he was about to protest, she pinched his belly, which was protruding over his belt. "Bud *Light*."

Kim felt Charlotte's gaze as she flipped the bottle. Her moves felt awkward beneath the scrutiny. "Mug?" she asked Owen as she set the drinks on the napkins she'd placed when she'd taken their order. He shook his head and slung back about a third of the bottle.

Charlotte tapped her long, acrylic nails on the lacquered surface of the bar. She had a rhinestone imbedded in the bright pink polish of each nail. Frosty swirls surrounded each stone. "I understand you found Zell earlier."

"Sure did." She wasn't about to implicate Tullie and hoped the girl hadn't gotten into trouble. "I didn't know where he lived or I wouldn't have come to the house and bothered you."

"You didn't bother me. Nothing bothers me. It's my daddy that got bothered. I think it's *him* you should be apologizing to."

Great, now everyone knew she'd apologized to Zell. As for Winnerow, how could she apologize when she wasn't sure she was wrong?

"Surprised to see you here," was all Kim would commit to.

"Yeah, well, I figured I'd see what's what."

Owen polished off the bottle and asked for another, pointedly ignoring his wife's raised eyebrow. Kim wondered what price he paid to up his status, if that's why he'd married Charlotte to begin with, and how much he resented her rule over him.

"It's a shame what happened to Elva," Charlotte said. "She was a magamous woman."

"I think you mean magnanimous," Kim said.

Charlotte cocked that eyebrow at her now. "That's what I said." She was as cool as the ice she was clinking in her drink. Kim supposed she'd have to be to oversee the alligator farm. Working with creatures that could eat you had to teach you to keep your cool in any kind of situation. According to Smitty's ramblings, not only was she doing a good job running the farm, but she actually enjoyed working with the creatures. Kim figured anyone who liked gators was definitely off center. Which, she figured, fit Charlotte.

JoGene sauntered in and headed over to the bar. "Howdy," he greeted Charlotte and Owen before giving Kim a wink and taking a seat. "Bud." JoGene and Owen had been buddies back in high school and apparently still were.

When Kim realized he wasn't calling *her* Bud, she reached around and poured him a draft. Owen said to JoGene, "Your dad's going to have pissing fits when he finds out you're here."

JoGene swigged down a few inches of his brew, too, and slammed down the mug. "I don't give a damn what he says."

Owen shook his head like a dog shaking off fleas. "We're talking 'bout Buck here."

"I'm gonna get away from him, I am. You just wait and see."

"I have been waiting to see," Owen said, clearly having given up on the prospect. "Maybe if you win the lottery or something."

JoGene visibly tamped down the anger building on his expression, swallowing as though it were a ball in his throat. "Are we going fishing later tonight? Snook's supposed to be biting."

People in Tallahassee had made fun of the way Kim had pronounced *snook* with a long sound rhyming with *kook*. She'd tempered some of her pronunciation over time, but she wasn't bothered when someone called her a redneck. "And proud of it," she'd say with a lift of her chin.

"So," Charlotte mumbled around lighting a cigarette. "How come everybody notices Zell and those stupid shirts of his, but no one notices my nails? Every week I get 'em done

differently, but does anybody applaud that? Noooooooo."
She lifted her hands. "Do you know what I have to go
through for these babies? Zell orders a shirt out of a catalog,
and it's a big whoop-de-doo."

Owen ducked as her hand whipped through the air.
Even JoGene backed away. Owen said, "It's not manly to
notice things like women's nails."

"Well, you sure like the way they look wrapped around
your—"

Owen held up his hand. "All right, honey, we get the
point."

Charlotte was looking at Kim's nails, blunt cut without
a speck of polish. It was clear why Kim hadn't commented. "Speaking of getting the point, these are why
Owen gets to sex the gators now. Kim, you know how to
sex a gator?"

"No, and I'm pretty sure I don't want to know."

"You stick your finger right up in their hole." She
demonstrated. "And feel around some. Can't hardly do that
with these, now can I? I'd eviscerate the poor thing," she
said, pronouncing the *c* in *eviscerate*. She patted Owen's
cheek. "He's dang good at it, too."

Kim was too grossed out by the mental picture of that to
point out Charlotte's mispronunciation. She gratefully
took an order from Amy before returning to her bar
patrons. Charlotte was tapping those nails again, but her
gaze was on Kim. "So, how long you going to be staying in
town?"

Kim had expected those words to be the first out of her
mouth, actually. She may as well have asked, *When are
you leaving?* Kim glanced at the crowd of people, the glaring Billy Bob and Clem, and then to JoGene. "You want to
know how long I'm staying?"

"It is the question of the week, after all," Charlotte said.
"Followed closely by, What are you going to do with the
bar?"

"Well, I'm going to answer both questions." She walked
around the bar and over to the jukebox. When she pulled

the plug on Ricky Skaggs, sounds of protest filled the room, including a, "Hey, I paid for that song!"

Well, she had their attention. "There'll be free music for the rest of the night. I have an announcement to make." She cleared her throat. "I'm staying in town and I'm keeping the bar. Now, I know that several of you won't be happy to hear that. Some of you will be downright annoyed. If you want to boycott my place, well, there's nothing I can do about that. If you want to bust out my winders"—she looked at Smitty, and he winked—"well, there's nothing I can do about that, either. The truth is, though you may not like me, you like Southern Comfort."

She gestured at the pictures. "Most likely your family is up on those walls. You've got a history here. You've got your favorite table. I don't intend to change much around here, other than maybe adding some tunes to the jukebox and someday building a screened porch out back. I intend to honor Elva's memory, and I hope you'll do the same. She wanted this place to go on, and she wanted me to have it."

She leaned against the jukebox and caught sight of Zell standing by the front door. For a minute all her words flew out of her head. She coughed to recover and shifted her gaze away so he wouldn't distract her. "So, yeah, you could get the whole town to boycott me out of spite and run me out of business. Then what would you have? No place to go. I still wouldn't sell it to any of y'all, out of spite, too. Some tin-canner might buy it and jack up the prices and take all the country music out of the juke. Or maybe turn it into a bait shop and compete with our locals." She gave Lou a look, since he owned Master Bait and Tackle, the biggest bait and tackle shop in town. He hated tin-canners, what the old-timers called tourists. "I'm willing to bet that you need this place as much as I need customers." She studied the faces around her. Most registered some state of shock; some even showed a smidgen of respect. "Any questions?"

Oscar, obviously sensing something of import was up,

ambled over to her side. She reached down and scratched his head in appreciation of his support.

One man shot to his feet. "You're not gonna take Merle off that jukebox now, are you?"

He looked so worried she nearly laughed. She was on the edge of a bubble of laughter anyway, relief at not being stormed or booed. "I'll leave Merle and Skaggs and even Willie. We just won't have every album they ever made on the juke."

"Well, all right then." He slowly sank to his chair.

Another man bellowed from his place, his arms crossed in front of him. "What about Oscar? Saw you had an ad in the paper giving him away."

"Since I'm staying, so is he."

No one else said a thing. Billy Bob and Clem shoved up from their seats and pushed past Zell to walk out. A couple of others threw their bills on the table and walked out, too, leaving the door open. No one else moved or said a thing. Until Zell started clapping. It started out slow and increased in speed. Her face flushed with heat. A couple of the women clapped with him, and a couple of men even joined in. Amy let out a whoop.

"Thank you," she said, because it seemed appropriate. Hopefully nobody noticed the squeakiness in her voice. As promised, she plugged the jukebox back in and fed a bunch of dollar bills into it. She walked on shaky legs over to Zell. He was wearing an old, white T-shirt and brown camouflage nylon pants, dressed for egg hunting, she supposed.

"You didn't have to do that," she said. "Clap, I mean."

Something in his eyes drew her in and made her heart pound even faster than it already was. "Damn, woman, you sure do make it hard for a man to hold a grudge." He ran his hand back through his hair and shook his head. "You got bigger balls than most of the men in here."

A comment like that might have insulted a woman in Tallahassee, but down in Cypress, it was the biggest compliment a gal could get. "Thanks."

He wandered to the bar with a gait that said he was way too comfortable in his skin. Even Amy was watching him with some appreciation, and she was related to him. Kim met a few people's eyes as she made her way back to the bar. She'd only lost a few customers.

"You seen Dougal?" Zell asked the threesome at the bar. "He was supposed to meet me at the house an hour ago. I was hoping he'd just forgotten and was here having too much happy hour. I hope he hasn't disappeared again."

"I haven't seen him," Kim answered. Last time she'd seen Amy's brother, he was a gangly teenager who looked a lot like Zell. She was sure she'd still recognize him.

Owen said, "I'll go."

Kim could see that prospect didn't warm Zell. "I'll keep that in mind. Maybe we crossed paths and he's back at the house. See you all later."

Was she imagining that he'd left his gaze on her a second longer than on the others? Why did he have to be so damn gorgeous? It just wasn't right. Even in the old T-shirt and camos.

Angus, wearing those crabbing boots as always, waved Zell down. "You nailed it again. Or should I say, *I* nailed it, heh heh. I threw her down on the bed like you said, and she jumped all over me." He shook Zell's hand. "Thanks, man."

"Glad it worked out."

Kim rolled her eyes, remembering Zell's advice. That man could be dangerous.

As Zell walked toward the door, his cell phone went off. He raised his hand to them, indicating it was Dougal. Owen's shoulders slumped.

JoGene was watching him walk out, but it wasn't appreciation on his face; it was fierce anger. "That son of a bitch walks around here like he owns the world. He does whatever he wants, no questions asked." When he realized that Kim was watching him, he erased the anger. "So you're gonna stay," he said. She couldn't tell exactly how she felt about that at first, but then he winked at her. "Maybe we can pick up where we left off."

Owen snorted. "Oh, yeah, your daddy would sure love that."

"Well, first I have to tell the current boyfriend," Kim said to buy time.

That got a snort out of the three of them. Kim knew it sounded cold talking about Simon like that. He wouldn't miss her, just her company. It was going to be weird being the one saying good-bye. She always hung around until the guy said it first. Well, she was sure walking out of her comfort zone now. What she didn't need was to get involved with anyone until she was settled in here. That could take a while.

"Does that mean I get to keep my job?" Amy asked.

"If you'd like it."

"I would. This is so much fun, it almost ain't fair taking money for it. My tootie's been pinched twice already, and by a cute one, too." She gave Bo a lascivious wink. "Need a rum and Coke and two MGDs."

Kim walked around the bar and hoped a tootie was Amy's butt and nothing more personal. She met Charlotte's gaze, but she was hard to read. She was tapping her nails again. Once Kim had processed Amy's order, she leaned against the bar in front of Charlotte. "Go ahead, say whatever it is you're wanting to say."

Charlotte's mouth twitched until one side lifted into a smile that reminded Kim of Zell. "Well, it sure is gonna be interesting around here."

That wasn't nearly as bad as she'd expected. Maybe this wasn't going to be so hard after all. A warm feeling alighted in her stomach. Maybe—

"Oh, my God, Zell!"

Charlotte's voice rocked Kim out of her thoughts. Zell had walked back in covered in blood. Instinctively, Kim rushed toward him as he approached the bar.

Charlotte beat her to it. "What happened? You just left here a minute ago!" She grabbed up a paper towel from one of the tables and started dabbing at the blood.

A few of the men at the bar had gotten to their feet and

walked over. Upon closer inspection, he wasn't exactly covered in blood, but there was a fair amount of it running from a cut above his eye down his cheek. He had a cut on his lower lip, too.

That didn't keep him from giving them a wry smile. "Billy Bob and Clem didn't much care for my applause." He waved Charlotte away. "Stop fussing, woman! I didn't come in here to get coddled, I just didn't want to get blood in my truck."

Three of the big fellers rushed out the door—to look for the offenders, Kim guessed. Smitty came over and pulled up a chair so he could watch the ministrations. Even Oscar wandered over and looked up at Zell, who grumbled, "What are you looking at, piggy?"

Kim said, "We have a first-aid kit in the back. I'll get it."

Charlotte pushed him down into a chair and ordered Owen to get some wet towels. "I'll coddle you all I want. It's a sister's right and duty." She turned to Kim when she returned with the kit and popped it open. "What do we got in there?"

"Not much." Kim shifted to block Charlotte from taking over the kit. She could be a caretaker, too, dammit. And it was her bar. Her fault. When Charlotte took the towels from Owen and wiped away the rest of the blood, Kim pushed a chair in front of Zell and sat down. She ripped open the last medicated wipe and brushed it across each cut. He hissed and swore but didn't move other than that.

"Sorry." She meant it in more than one way.

It was only then that she realized how close they were. That made her pause for a moment, the same way he'd thrown her off when she spotted him during her speech. She focused on opening the antibiotic packet. It had expired a few months earlier, but she figured it was better than nothing.

"Look, it's fine, just a couple of little cuts." He started to get up, but she held his chin in place before even thinking about it.

"They're not that little. Let me do this."

His muscles relaxed, and she wiped the cream over each cut. They weren't bad, probably didn't need stitches. It didn't matter; he'd sustained this because of her. No wonder he wanted her to leave. Her presence was probably causing him lots of trouble. There was as much pushing her to leave as there was pulling her to stay.

"You're not putting a bandage on me," he said, getting to his feet. "This'll be fine." He grabbed his cell phone, which had obviously taken a skid across the gravel. The plastic was scratched with white streaks.

The posse came back in. "They're gone. Hope you got 'em as good as they got you."

Kim said, "They were two against one! How good could he have gotten them, especially since they obviously ambushed him?"

Zell put his hand on her shoulder. "No need to protect me, darlin'," he said in a low voice. To the men he said, "Got Billy Bob in the nuts. He can't move as fast as the little guy. I gotta get out of here. Dougal's going to wonder what happened to me."

Charlotte gave him a quick hug and didn't see him wince. "Once you're out there collecting gator eggs, you'll forget all about those cuts."

Zell gave Kim a pointed look. "Be careful. Keep that stuff you have handy."

As soon as Zell walked out, Charlotte turned to Kim. "See what your presence here is doing. Zell never fights, never. Since you been here, he's been in a near-brawl, got kicked out of your bar, and now been attacked by two dickless weasels."

Kim didn't need this piled onto the guilt she already carried. She turned to JoGene. "They work at the club, don't they?"

"Yeah, but I'm not their keeper."

Kim crossed her arms over her chest. "I bet they're doing this for your dad, maybe even on his orders. Can't you say something to them or Buck?"

JoGene, Owen, and even Charlotte laughed. JoGene's

smile faded fast, though. "I can't tell my dad nothing. He holds a worse grudge than the Macgregors." He eyed Charlotte. "Or at least the way they used to."

"We still do! We're the best grudge-holders in town. But Kim's right. This is the town bar. Why should we deprive ourselves of a drink now and then just because of her?"

JoGene didn't look as though he believed her, but he shifted his gaze back to Kim. "Forget talking to my dad. Or to those knuckleheads. They're all as hardheaded as a cypress tree. And don't you get any ideas about talking to him yourself. He'd just as easily have you for supper as give you the time of day. Maybe you ought to rethink your decision to stay."

All the fight drained out of Kim as she eased into the nearest chair. She should rethink it. But she also knew the decision was made. Now she had to live with it.

# CHAPTER 10

"You was flirtin' with him," Smitty said as they cleaned up at closing time late that night.

"I was not." Kim slipped a surreptitious glance toward Amy, wondering how much she'd pass on to the Macgregors. "I was treating his cuts. It was the least I could do."

Smitty had a smug expression on his face, like he knew everything in the world. "Flirtin'," he said under his breath and carried off a bin of garbage.

Amy supposedly found some dirt beneath a nearby table that Kim was sure had already been swept. "There was something going on between you two," she said with a sly smile.

Kim tapped the palm of her hand against her forehead. "There was not. I was getting into the nurse Nightingale thing, that's all."

Amy leaned against the broom handle and shook her head. "I don't blame you. That man has it going on. If he wasn't my cousin—"

Kim held out her hand. "Stop right there! There are just some things I don't want to know about my employees."

"Don't be silly. I can admire a gorgeous man, no matter who he is. Acting on it is another matter, and if you'll recall, I said *if* he wasn't my cousin."

Kim wiped the fingerprints off the jukebox. Smitty set the chairs on one of the tables. Zell's table. He murmured, "Flirtin'."

"Was not!" She turned around and leaned back against the jukebox. "Even if I hadn't testified against his stepfather and even if he hadn't lied about me on the witness stand— talk about your ifs—we're all wrong for each other. He's so . . . so . . . intense. When he talks about his work, I mean."

"He's got a passion about him when it comes to gators, and his family, and anything he feels strongly about," Amy said. "Which I bet translates nicely into the bedroom."

She didn't want to think about Zell and bedrooms. "I like calm, sensible guys." She thought of Simon. A good point, she thought. Saying good-bye wasn't going to hurt all that much. If he'd said good-bye first, that wouldn't have hurt, either. *That* was sensible.

Amy rolled her eyes. "Sounds boring to me."

"And then there's the alligator thing," Kim said, ignoring Amy. "He loves them, I hate them."

"Well, now, that could be a problem," Amy said.

Smitty set the last chair on the table. "There's the gator test, after all. She'd never pass it."

Kim pushed away from the jukebox. "What's the gator test?"

Amy and Smitty shared a conspiratorial look. "Knew she'd ask," Amy said, looking proud of herself. "'Cause she likes him."

"Oh, just tell me. It doesn't matter anyway."

Smitty said, "Any gal who thinks she wants to get serious with Zell has to pass the gator test. It's a series of questions about gators that only someone who really likes the animal will know. And then she has to hold a gator."

"And enjoy it," Amy added. "He said if he's gonna marry a gal, she's gotta love them gators as much as he does. And he can tell if she's faking, too. Two gals failed on that part alone. Being able to stand going in the gator farm is the last part. One gal passed the first two parts and then passed clean out on that last part."

"Sounds like he just wants to avoid commitment. How many girlfriends has he had?" When Amy gave her that annoying grin again, Kim added, "Not that it matters."

"Oh, a few," Smitty said. "Truth be told, I don't think he gets attached to any of 'em. Not that he leads them on or anything. If they start talking marriage, he throws the test at them."

"He treats those girls good, though," Amy said. "Takes 'em out for nice dinners, picnic lunches out on the marsh in dry season when the skeeters aren't so bad. Buys 'em little gifties, just to show he's thinking about them when he's out of town. He's a good dancer, too." She got that if-he-wasn't-my-cousin look again.

"Okay, I think we're done now," Kim said, meaning both the bar and the conversation.

Smitty chimed in with, "Why, when he took Linda May out for their first date, she come right out and said she loved him! He never did take her out again."

"That is a little fast," Kim had to admit.

Amy issued a little sigh. "He's an Everglades cowboy."

"Don't you have to have horses to be a cowboy? And a ranch?" She pictured him in his alligator boots, but doubted any self-respecting cowboy wore tropical shirts.

"He has a ranch, but they've got gators instead of cows and horses. Zell may not have a horse, but he's got that sexy airboat. That's his horse. He goes out hunting alligators and has to wrangle one at the farm once in a while, too. I saw it once. You've been to the big gator house, right?"

Kim was ashamed to say she hadn't, not once in the two years she'd lived there. She merely shook her head.

Amy had the sense, jobwise, not to call her a scaredy-cat, but she did give her the look. "Well, the main door is cut in halves, see, and you always open the top half and take a look to make sure no gators have gotten out of the holding areas. On one harvest night, Owen just walked right in without checking first. He was so excited to be part of it, I guess. I was pretty excited to be there, too, so I can kinda understand. Anyway, Owen, he walked right past a six-footer."

Smitty added, "Them's the nastiest gators, even more so than the big'uns. They're big enough to do damage and agile enough to whip around you real fast like."

"Owen didn't even see the guy until Zell told him to move back slowly. Owen panicked and jumped, and the gator lunged at him. I swear, I thought my heart was going to shoot right out of my chest! The gator had its mouth open, hissing, and was moving right toward Owen. Zell just swore, pushed back his sleeves, and walked in. He straddled the gator quicker than spit, grabbed hold of the gator's mouth and pulled it up and back toward him. By then, Charlotte had grabbed a rope and she wrapped it around the gator's mouth."

Smitty interjected again. "A gator's got tons of power to close his jaws, but not much to open 'em."

Amy didn't seem to mind the interruptions. "Zell led the gator out the back to the slaughterhouse."

"No wonder he didn't seem crazy about letting Owen go egg hunting in Dougal's place," Kim said. "How do they kill the gators?"

Amy said, "Well, as Charlotte likes to say, 'you just stick the knife in their head right behind their eyes and pop out their brain.' " She demonstrated with nails as long and dazzling as Charlotte's, holding up the pointer finger and giving it a knifelike twist. "She does the killing herself without batting an eye. It's very humane. Severs all function instantly." She snapped those fingers. "Just like that."

Kim said, "As charming as this conversation is, I must pull myself away. I'm beat. Come on, Oscar!"

The pig trotted to the door and waited with his tail wagging like a dog. Kim's mouth tugged into a smile.

" 'Course," Amy added, "the hardest test would be having Charlotte as a sister-in-law!" She hooted and slapped her knee.

Kim couldn't help but smile, though she didn't comment. Sometimes it was better to keep your opinions to yourself. She didn't know where loyalties ran yet.

Smitty hit the lights at the bar, and the three of them walked out into the heavy night air. The moon was blazingly bright above them, lighting up the river and the mangroves. The parking lot had a few lights at the corners; Kim was going to have three more installed to cover every inch. They all took a moment to check the surroundings. She had her tear gas ready at her side. Smitty walked Amy to her car, and then walked Kim to hers.

"Gonna have to get yourself an American car now that you're staying," he said.

"I know. It was cheap, what can I say? I've always wanted a truck. Like an F-10, something like Zell's, shiny and coolish." Before she closed the door, she said, "Do you think I'm crazy to stay?"

"Yeah, but crazy's all right. Worked for me all these years. Comes down to whether you can stand the fallout. G'night, young'un. Call me if you need anything."

She had a crazy urge to hug him but figured that was probably just a little too crazy. "Thanks," she said instead.

She knew what he meant. If she had trouble at home. She didn't want to think about someone coming to her home—*my home, wow, did that sound incredible?*—and hurting her. Or damaging her home.

When she drove up to the house, she took an extra couple of minutes to scan the area. She kept her canister in hand as she let Oscar out. She took another look, and this time noticed the way the moonlight dappled the ground through the leaves. It pooled over the house and made it look like something out of a fairy tale. All around her sang the symphony of frogs happy to be alive on a summer's night. It was so beautiful her heart started beating faster. She slapped at the swamp suckers and continued to take it all in while she turned in circles. Though she'd hated the mugginess down here, it wrapped around her like an old, favorite blanket. The moon was overhead now, still as bright and detailed as before. Brighter than she remembered. The stars looked brighter, too. It wasn't her imagination, wasn't because she'd missed this place so much. The stars didn't have to compete with city lights and pollution.

She could hear Oscar rooting around in the shadows. At least she hoped it was Oscar.

"This sucks, being afraid. That's what they want, for me to run away with my tail between my legs. Well, that's not going to happen." She wanted to yell it out, but there was no point in scaring the wildlife. She felt a surge of that Lyons orneriness. Before it could really take hold, a scream like a newborn's rent the night air. Just as suddenly, it died to silence. Even the frogs ceased for a few moments before resuming again as though nothing had happened. Kim had frozen, staring into the darkness of the trees.

"Oscar?" she managed through a tight throat.

She heard a splash in the near distance. Closer, footsteps pounded on the damp earth. Where was that Lyons bluster now when she couldn't move? The steps grew louder, and then a shadow separated from the background darkness. Oscar rushed past her toward the porch and eased through the dog door with a scraping sound. Only then could she step backward and grab for the door handle.

Once on the relative safety of the porch, she turned back toward the darkness. Her mind did a search on that eerie scream that had died so suddenly and found a match. A raccoon had gone down to the water's edge for a drink and had become a meal for an alligator. Probably the one that had left the tracks.

She shivered. That's how it was here in the wetlands. Life and death, hunter and hunted. She just hoped she didn't become part of that cycle anytime soon.

Tullie had heard her mama come back from the bar and had gone downstairs. She saw Charlotte tap on Grandpa's door and then step inside. Tullie hovered in the hallway to listen to their conversation.

"What the hell are you doing waking me up in the middle of the night?" he'd said, grumbling like a bear.

"I got gossip. First off, Amy's working at the bar now."

"That doesn't surprise me. That girl'll do anything for money. Lying on her back would be a more respectable way to earn it, though."

"There's something even bigger. Kim's staying in Cypress. She made an announcement tonight, right in front of everybody. She said we could boycott the bar and even run it out of business, but she knows Southern Comfort's the only place in town folks like to go. Some folks left, and those two creepy cons of Buck's stalked right out. Then they beat up on Zell."

"What?"

Her mama said, "Well . . . he did applaud when Kim finished her speech. You shoulda been there. It was quite the show."

"She won't last."

Her mama's voice changed from the sharing-gossip tone to low and serious. "What if she does? You know how determined she can be. Do you think she'll cause trouble?"

"I sure hope not. If she does—"

"We'll just have to make sure she doesn't, won't we, Daddy?"

"Won't hurt to keep an eye on her."

Tullie crept back to her bed just in case Mama finished the conversation and stuck her head in her bedroom to check on her. Sometimes she did, but a few minutes later she drove the truck to the farm to get the incubators ready for the eggs. Her daddy was already out there.

Kim was staying, and Uncle Zell got beat up. Mama and Grandpa were worried. About what? Could Kim hurt them in some way? Her bad feeling was coming true. The problem was, she liked Kim, though she'd never tell anyone. She'd expected not to like her at all when she'd offered to take her to Uncle Zell. But she wanted to find out for herself, wanted to see if she could feel her badness like she could with some people. There was a good feeling about Kim instead.

There were other people whose badness she picked up on. It scared her.

She slid out of her canopy bed and crept down the stairs. Grandpa's workout-room door was open and light spilled out of the opening. When she peered through the opening, she saw that it was the moonlight, so bright and silvery, it didn't look real.

Grandpa Winn was struggling to pull up his legs on one of the machines. Tullie would have knocked softly on the door then, but there was something in his face that stopped her. He looked like he was in pain, and there was a darkness in his eyes that gave her that bad feeling. Maybe it was just the light and shadows. Still, she went back to her room.

Her alligator was stirring in his tank. Mama had given it to her a few months ago; the gator wasn't growing fast enough and would have probably died from starvation. She'd told Tullie not to name it, because when the gator was big enough, it would go back to the farm and become a meal and somebody's purse. Tullie had secretly named him Runt. She tapped on the glass in greeting, and Runt lifted his head in interest.

But Tullie had other things on her mind. She climbed onto her window seat and looked out over the front yard. She loved full-moon nights, loved how the world looked magical. But tonight she couldn't enjoy it. The feeling was getting bigger inside her. Since Uncle Zell was going to be out until about four in the morning, she'd have to wait until midday to check up on him. But it was her mama and Kim she was worried about. She felt like she was crossing her mama by liking Kim. Maybe she'd talk to Uncle Zell about this. She could tell him anything. But how could she tell him something she couldn't explain to herself? The dark, scary feeling that someone she knew was going to die. And that it might be her.

. . .

JoGene pulled up to one of the hunting cabins he called his own. If his father had heard Kim's speech, would he give her credit for standing up there and announcing her decision to stay? Nah, probably not. As much as he hated her, he'd have thrown a bottle at her.

JoGene looked at the small front porch—where his dad was waiting for him on the rocking chair. He looked mean and drunk, which was typical for this time of night. JoGene took his time getting out of the truck, but that didn't ease the lump in his throat. Damn, he was a grown man. He shouldn't be afraid of his dad anymore.

"Heard you were at Southern Comfort tonight," Buck said.

JoGene leaned against the column, making sure to keep his back straight and look him in the eye. "Yeah, so what? It's the only real bar in town. 'Sides, Smitty's there."

"Well, Smitty ain't any better than the rest of 'em. But you, you're my son. You got no business hanging around that woman. She's the enemy."

"I have a plan, that's why I was there." He hadn't told Buck about his intention of buying the bar and finally getting out from under his control.

"Well, now, what plan might that be? Getting in her pants? You'd screw anything with a hole in it."

JoGene's jaw clenched so hard, he felt a muscle pop. "I'm trying to scare her a bit so she don't get too comfortable here. I put a dead rat on her porch. I got her good when she was poling around the mangroves."

"Yeah, and that worked real well, now didn't it?"

"Look, I'm working on it. I'm trying to be careful, doing things that can't be traced to me." As soon as Kim was out of the way, he was going to get that bar, and by the time Buck knew about it, he'd own it outright. Wharton had been sworn to secrecy; JoGene had reminded him about lawyer-client confidentiality, just in case.

Buck stood and hitched up his saggy jeans. "Wail, all

right, but don't get too friendly with her. And don't take too long, or I'm going to take care of Kim myself."


For the first time, Kim slept in Elva's bed. Her bed now. She was having an interesting dream about kissing the cut on Zell's lip when a cold, wet something prodding at her dragged her right out of the dream. She opened her eyes to find a dark, ugly face peering at her from the side of the bed. Early morning light peeked in through the crack in the closed curtains.

"Oscar," she whined, rolling to the other side. A minute later, she heard a sound from that side and opened her eyes again. The face was still looking at her.

"You must have to go out." She pushed herself up. "Well, you're sort of like having a dog." She scratched his head and swore the pig was grinning.

She didn't even brush her hair. There was no Simon, after all, to tell her that she looked like a ragamuffin. Since that reminded her of him and that unfortunate task, she left him a message and walked around checking the outside of the house while Oscar attended to his pig pellet duties. Nobody had been up to mischief while she'd slept. No new gator tracks marred the yard, either: another bit of good news.

She walked through the hothouse next and misted the orchids as Zell had shown her. She was sure Elva had an orchid-care book around the house, and Kim intended to find it. When she returned to the house, she called her boss and put in her resignation. He gave her a hard time and said he wouldn't miss her. But she knew he would, just a little. Who else could he harass and get away with it?

Afterward, she set out to make this place a real home. She cleaned the kitchen, scrubbed the floors, and purged the refrigerator of several unidentifiable containers and sale items Elva had overbought.

When the phone rang, her heart skipped a beat. Even though breaking ties with Simon was the right thing to do, it wasn't going to be easy. Doing it over the phone probably wasn't the best way, either, but she wasn't going to be able to get back to Tallahassee for a week or more.

She wiped her hands on her jeans, grabbed up the portable, and went out onto the porch where Oscar was enjoying the day.

"Sorry I missed you," Simon said in a casual way that meant he wasn't really all that sorry.

Kim knew she was trying to justify breaking up with him and pushed the snippy thought aside. "Where were you? I don't think you've been home since I left."

He gave her an uneasy laugh. "I went out with the guys from work again. We had so much fun at the hip-hop clubs we went out again. I was sound asleep when you called. How's it going down in the swamps with the rednecks?"

"I'm a redneck." He'd teased her about her language whenever she lapsed.

"I know, but you've pretty much shed all that, thank goodness."

"I'm still a redneck, and you know what? I'm proud of it. This is my heritage, for better or worse."

"No need to get testy. You know I only mean it in fun."

"Well, you never did have a good sense of what was fun." As it turned out, Simon launched into a coughing attack, probably brought on by the club smoke, and hadn't heard that.

Oscar moseyed over and shoved his butt against her for a side rub that quickly became a belly rub. Just like Smitty had said, the pig rolled right over and made a sound of pleasure.

"Excuse you," Simon said. "Was that a burp?"

"That wasn't me, it was Oscar. The pig," she clarified.

"You haven't gotten rid of that thing yet? Isn't there an animal shelter there? Maybe you could let it loose in the swamp."

She looked at Oscar and realized he was a better roommate than Simon had ever been, lack of sex notwithstanding. "I'm keeping the pig."

"Kim, we talked about this. You can't—"

"I'm staying in Cypress."

That stopped all form of conversation for a few moments. "What?" he said at last. "I must have misunderstood you."

"I'm staying. You know how I've always wanted a place of my own and my own bar. Well, I've got it here. I love this place, and I realized that this is home for me. Tallahassee was never home."

"You met someone, didn't you? An old boyfriend, I'll bet."

She rolled her head back against the rocking chair. "This has absolutely nothing to do with a man." Even if Zell did flash through her mind. "Nothing. This is about me. This is about me being able to hang up my neon lizard sign and all of my other so-called tacky stuff. This is about me being able to leave my keys where I damn well please and not get yelled at like even my own daddy never yelled. It's about making someplace *my* home." She scrubbed her fingers through her hair. "And you know what? I haven't even brushed my hair yet today."

Simon made his disgusted sound. "You even sound like a redneck, and you've only been there a few days. Fine, if that's what you want. What do you want me to do with your things?"

"Most of them are still in boxes in the second bedroom. My clothes are all in that closet, too, so my stuff shouldn't be in your way." It never had been, now that she thought about it. Simon had so many things that he needed his own closet. Same with the bathroom. "If you don't mind, just stick whatever might belong to me in the second bedroom. I'll be up in maybe a week or so, once I get things settled down here."

"Fine. Just let me know when you're coming. I'm going to have the locks changed."

"Fine," she said, mirroring him. He'd taken her plan to move down here as a breakup. Not once had he thought about whether he wanted to live here, too. "I'll talk to you later then."

After she hung up, she felt deflated. She slid down to the floor and continued scratching Oscar's belly with abandon. He continued to make those interesting sounds. After a few minutes, she laid her head on his side. For the second time in her life, she was totally alone.

When Zell returned from collecting eggs, the whole Macgregor clan helped with the process of checking them in. All those eggs were a beautiful sight, lined up in incubators that matched the original temperatures of the nests. Alligator nests had two chambers for two different temperatures, which determined the sex of the hatchling. The eggs were smaller than hen eggs, but a little longer. And in almost every one an alligator waited to be born. The days the eggs hatched were even more exciting.

The sun was just starting to come up, and the pink rays were beginning to light up the small house where the young gators lived. The roof was made of an opaque film that filtered out most of the light. Shar had taken the data and gone in the office to put it into the computer. She and Zell would be keeping an eye on the eggs until they hatched.

Winnerow had already given him hell for getting beat up, as though he could have helped it. "Now folks think you're on her side," he'd said. "First interfering with Billy Bob and Clem and then applauding."

Zell lifted a shoulder. "It was a heck of a speech."

Winn had dropped a few choice words at that and wheeled out of the incubation room. He hadn't asked if he was all right, hadn't given Zell an ounce of sympathy. Well, what had he expected?

When Zell finished in the room, he closed the door and stepped into the hallway between the four large pens where the smaller gators were kept according to size. Dewey, their groundskeeper and handyman, was at the end spraying down the concrete floor. Owen was standing by the wheelbarrow that carried the Purina Gator Chow. The gators learned that the scrape of the shovel meant feeding time. The two-footers were already clamoring on their concrete beach for their daily ration.

As Zell passed, Owen said, "Be careful about that girl."

Zell paused, wondering if he'd heard the underlying threat. He couldn't help tensing his shoulders. "You telling me what to do?"

"I'm just saying to be careful, is all. For your sister and your daddy and the Waddells, too. There's lots of girls in town who'd be happier than a gator in a mud hole to take up with you." He avoided Zell's gaze by scraping the food into the gator holding tank.

Zell couldn't believe it. Owen was advising instead of kissing butt, which was how he got by in life, how he'd gotten into the Macgregor family. Shar was too strong for most men, for men who had backbone, anyway. Owen must have figured it was worthwhile to set aside his manly pride. Zell didn't know if he was just calculating or beaten down by life and poverty. It was odd and a bit disturbing to see him out of character.

Now Zell, he'd learned that sometimes keeping your mouth shut was a better way to handle things than jumping into a fight mouth and fist first. But if he let Owen get away with that, who knew what else he'd get up to? If Zell had had any sleep behind him, he might have tapped Owen on the nose with the stick they used on the gators. Just a quick tap when a gator got a bit full of himself and opened his mouth. He let his words do it this time.

"Owen, I'd advise you to keep your nose in the gator business and out of mine."

Zell headed out into air that was comparatively cooler and closed the door behind him. Out of the corner of his eye, he glimpsed pure animosity on his brother-in-law's face.

# CHAPTER 11

Kim woke up exhausted on her birthday. At first she thought she'd dreamed the whole breakup conversation with Simon before realizing it had happened the day before. Why didn't she feel sadder about it? She had loved him, hadn't she?

*As much as you can love someone,* Becca's voice echoed.

Kim pushed out of bed with a grunt. "I can love someone with all my heart." She glanced over at Oscar, who was waiting beside her bed. "Maybe even you. If you stop rooting through my clothes and shoving your butt at me."

She slipped on her robe and started boiling water for jasmine tea. "And tearing up my newspapers." Shreds of the local paper littered the floor. Some had become spit wads. Soggy spit wads she discovered when she stepped on one. "Ewww!"

She walked out the front door to let Oscar take care of his morning rituals—and take in her present to herself. The used Ford F-10 she'd purchased yesterday in Naples sat where she'd parked it so she could take it in first thing in the morning. It wasn't fancy like Zell's, just a simple truck for a gal who lived in the swamp. The dark blue paint looked nearly black in the morning shadows. She'd had a running board installed that would help Oscar climb in and out.

Yesterday she'd gotten most of the house cleaned. Since the bar was closed on Mondays, too, Kim had all day to accomplish the same with the bar. She poured pig food into one of Oscar's bowls and put fresh greens into another. Her breakfast was a cup of tea and a couple of spoonfuls of peanut butter.

Once she got ready, she and Oscar headed out to Southern Comfort.

"Oscar, don't you even think about it!" He was very interested in the small birthday cake she'd bought for herself at a bakery in Naples that was sitting on the seat between them. "You're not supposed to have sweets, Zell said so." The pig snorted at that, as though he didn't think much of Zell's advice.

When she pulled down the short road to the bar, her stomach dropped down to her feet. The building was covered in graffiti, most of it unsuitable for even her eyes. Three different colors of spray paint had been used, and the letters were sloppy and large. She used one of those words herself before closing her eyes for a moment.

"What did I ever do to these people?"

Oscar grunted in answer, not offering anything useful. Leaving him in the truck, she unlocked the door and checked inside. Nothing else had been touched, though the graffiti went all the way around the building. She called the sheriff's substation and asked someone to come out. When they gave her a fifteen-minute ETA, she decided to go to the hardware store.

She returned with several gallons of brown paint and all of the fun stuff to go with it. The deputy was out front taking pictures with a digital camera. She vaguely remembered him from school; he'd been a few years younger.

"Hi, Dave. Or should I say Deputy DeBarro," she said, taking in his badge.

He nodded. "Hey, Kim. Got yourself a mess here."

"A bit of one." She lifted one of the gallon cans. "And

I'm going to clean it up as soon as you're done. Any ideas who would have done this?"

"They didn't exactly sign their artwork. Or leave any evidence like empty cans." He touched one of the red letters. "They must have done it sometime during the night; it's dry. Honestly, there's not much we can do about it unless we have some evidence or catch 'em in the act. Do you have any ideas?"

She opened her mouth to name the two Bobbsey Twins from the lodge, but closed it before a word came out. No point in sending the law out there to question them. It wasn't as if they would confess, and the visit would just rile them up even more. That was the last thing she needed.

Kim had painted the front and one side of the building by midafternoon. Her arms were so tired they felt rubbery. She glanced down to where Oscar sat in the shade and watched her. "You could help, you know."

He snorted and rolled onto his side.

"Just what I thought you'd say. Come on, let's get out of this heat."

She dragged herself inside where the cool air chilled the sweat on her body. After collapsing in one of the chairs for a few minutes, she pulled herself up and went to the file cabinet in the back office. "Hey, happy friggin' birthday to me. Might as well celebrate the big two-seven. First, we need music. I'm not enjoying my little birthday celebration with George Jones." She had a few of the CDs she'd brought on the trip. It wasn't much of a selection: the soulful angst of Sarah McLachlan, *Erotica* by Madonna, and *Nkalakatha* by Mandoza. She was definitely in the mood for the more upbeat South African artist. She figured out how to replace some of the CDs in the jukebox. "Sorry, George, but we've got like all of the CDs you've ever made in here. They won't miss one or two."

Once the rhythmic beat started, she lit a candle on the cake and carried it to Zell's usual table. Only because it was the coziest. She cut a piece of the cake, set it on one of the paper plates, and called Oscar over. "Heck with it, it's my birthday. Here, have a piece."

She left the candle burning as she cut another piece for herself. "Gawd, this is so pitiful." She sank her fork into the moist yellow cake coated in chocolate. She'd wanted chocolate on chocolate, but this was all they'd had in the when-you've-got-no-one-in-the-world-but-yourself size. "At least there's no one around to witness it."

A slash of sunlight swept in as the door opened. Her heartbeat tripped when Zell walked in, a questioning look on his face. He was wearing a tight, white undershirt and a shirt with fish swimming against a black background unbuttoned over that. His gaze went right to her and he walked over.

Embarrassment made her snap, "What are you doing here? We're closed."

He took in her cake. "Your birthday?"

She nodded, blowing out the candle and wiping off the icing that was probably all over her mouth. Then she saw the brown paint spattered on her arms and her old Cher concert T-shirt and figured it didn't matter anyway. Besides, it was only Zell. She started to get up. "I'll get you a plate."

His hand on her shoulder stilled her. "Don't worry about it." Even worse, he must have picked up the rejection on her face, because he said, "I don't eat that stuff."

"Everybody eats this kind of stuff once in a while."

He turned the other chair around and sat backward on it. "Not me, but go right ahead."

There was something about Zell that made her so completely aware of herself. Which made it hard to eat in front of him. Still, it *was* cake, so she did her best.

He didn't seem to notice her discomfort. "My granddad Zelwig spent his birthday alone once, up on Red Ant Camp. You know why it's called that?" When she shook her head, he rambled on. "Whenever he'd put up on one of the shell mounds for a few days to fish or hunt, he'd set up

his skeeter bar, to keep the skeeters out, and look for somewhere to make a bed. Gator nests make a nice soft bed, so
he laid his bedding over that mound of leaves and dirt and
went right to sleep. Until the red ants got him. Ants also
like old gator nests, you see, because of all the unhatched
eggs. He was covered in 'em before he realized it. He went
screaming into the water and said he looked like he had
measles afterward."

Zell's voice had taken on a smooth, Southern twang
when he'd started the story, and Kim enjoyed listening to it.

"Anyhow, his friend Lizard Jones was supposed to come
get him in four days. Lizard had gone on to another mound to
do some hunting. Well, ole Lizard had a skiff full of gator
skins, so he headed on back to unload them, thinking he'd
come back on time. But he got the opportunity to sell his
skins for a better price to a fellow in Miami, so he drove over
there before heading back out to get Zelwig. By the time he
returned, a week had passed. Granddad Zelwig spent his
birthday on that mound all by himself. He caught some mullet and cooked it up and sang 'Happy Birthday' to himself.
He sure was mad at Lizard, though, and never did let him live
it down."

Grudges. The word hung between them, a reminder that
they shouldn't be there sharing an old story and some
laughter. It made her feel even worse that his bruises
matched some of the colors in the shirt. If she hadn't
returned to town, he wouldn't have been ambushed.

He reached down and scratched Oscar's head. The telltale empty plate was bad enough, but Oscar had frosting all
over his snout. She didn't know why she felt ashamed
about feeding him cake. He was *her* pig!

Instead of chastising her, Zell said, "Whose truck is that
outside? Saw the truck and graffiti and wondered what was
going on."

"The truck is mine, the graffiti was a gift."

"The graffiti's not very nice, but the truck is. You really
are settling in, then."

Her smile faded at the chagrin in his voice in the last

part. "Whether anyone likes it or not. It's going to take more than some smashed winders and paint to chase me out of here."

"Well, I . . ." He stopped then and turned to the jukebox. "What in the hell are you listening to, anyway?"

"Mandoza. Some guy from South Africa brought the CD into the club I worked at and asked the DJ to play it. It was so cool, I ordered it."

He shot out of his chair and started scanning the selections. "You didn't take out Kenny Wayne, did you?"

"No, but some of George Jones went on vacation."

He turned around and leaned against the jukebox, looking completely comfortable and all kinds of interesting. "Folks are going to love that."

She pushed away her plate and walked over. "There ought to be variety. You don't like that old country music, either. Elva put something in there for you. Seems like the owner ought to have something in there for her, too."

He lifted a shoulder. "Can't hardly argue with that. Just don't play this during happy hour. They might toss the juke right out." He reached out and touched her belly button ring. The small diamond caught the light with his movement. "City girl."

Her stomach trembled, and she laughed to cover it. "I guess I am, a little. I do miss calling for pizza delivery, I can tell you that."

When Oscar nudged her leg and gave her the "potty break" look, she let him out. Zell walked outside too and checked out her paint job. Then he wandered around the side that she hadn't gotten to yet. "Nice."

"Didn't know those two could even spell words like that," she said. "I'm not even sure some of them *are* words."

He chuckled. "You think it was Billy Bob and Clem?"

"They're the most vocal of the I-Hate-Kim Club."

He swiped at a mosquito. "Sometimes it's the quiet ones you gotta look out for."

She crossed her arms in front of her and walked to the

river's edge. "I suppose you're a charter member of that club yourself."

He slid her a sideways glance as he walked up beside her. "I orta be," he said, reminding her of another Cypress word she hadn't heard in a long time. "It's in the family doctrine, after all."

But he wasn't? She didn't want to ask, mostly because she figured he wouldn't answer anyway. "But you want me to leave."

"Doesn't matter what I want. You're staying, aren't you?"

"Yep."

"Well, there you go." He walked to his truck, and she caught herself watching his easygoing stride and his easy-on-the-eyes backside. "See you around," he said when he opened his door.

She waved in answer. He didn't look too awfully bummed at that prospect. The sky to the east was darkening into the almost-daily storm. She grabbed up the gallon of paint and tray and headed inside. Hopefully it was dry enough to withstand some rain. She should have thanked him for checking on the bar, but for some reason the words clogged in her throat beneath a lump of disappointment. She hadn't expected him to wish her a happy birthday anyway.

She heard his truck pull away as she headed to the door to call in Oscar. He was waiting on the steps. "Oscar, what on earth have you been into?" Some weeds were tangled in his collar. As she tugged them free, she realized they weren't tangled; someone had tucked them there. And they weren't just weeds, but weeds with small pink flowers on them. Loose gravel indicated where the weeds had been growing; the broken-off stems were lying nearby. She leaned against the doorway and looked at those tiny blossoms. Redneck flowers.

"Dammit, Zell, why can't you just be a hundred percent jerk? You're góod at it, after all." She could hear gratitude thickening her throat now, though she was sure she hadn't sunk so low that tears were pressing against the backs of her eyes. "Keep doing this, and I'll start thinking you're a good person. I know you don't want that."


Billy Bob drove in from the lodge to pick up some supplies at the hardware store. When he handed Evan, the owner's son, the company charge card, Evan said, "Somebody painted up the bar last night. Kim was in this morning buying paint to cover it up. You wouldn't happen to know anything about that, would you?"

Billy Bob chuckled. "Nope, but I'd like to shake the hand of the man who done that and the winders."

Evan's gray eyes narrowed. "She ordered tempered glass. Harder to break."

Billy Bob signed the slip. "They'll figure out some other way to get her out of here. There's always something you can do to a woman to send her packing." He headed out to the beat-up truck and threw the bags in the back. The sky rumbled and started spitting rain. Before long, it would be a downpour. He got in the cab and looked across the street to the corner of the bar he could see.

He bet JoGene had something to do with that. He sure had encouraged him and Clem to give Kim a hard time. Scare her a little, even. And JoGene was their boss, after all. Well, Billy Bob bet they could scare her a lot. Yeah, and they'd have a good time, too. She wasn't bad-looking. She'd be lots of fun on a hot summer night.


Kim settled in for an evening of reading, but guilt nagged at her over those hundreds of orchids that required her care and attention. No one had called on her ads yet. She brewed some spicy chai tea and settled in the second bedroom where Elva kept her office. "No wonder I kept putting this off. What a mess."

Elva wasn't the best housekeeper in the world, but this room far surpassed the rest of the place in clutter. It looked as though she'd been searching for something in a big hurry.

Kim threw papers, a broken conch shell, and lots of paper clips into one box. She started to pull out the top drawer of the filing cabinet, but could barely budge it. When it finally came loose, she could see why: it was in total disarray. Papers were vertical in the folders, making them catch. That was strange, since the drawers at the bar were in perfect order. Elva had always been a savvy businesswoman, and that meant being organized. Or so she'd always told Kim.

All of Elva's personal files were in here, categorized with neat file tabs. Elva kept paperwork for years, like the payoff on the house and repair records for vehicles she hadn't owned in forever. Kim set all the displaced papers on the floor. She was halfway through organizing when she stopped cold at the sight of a small piece of rubber on one of the hanging folders. Why would Elva be going through here wearing gloves?

No, something wasn't right. Individually, the strange occurrences meant little. Together, they were beginning to paint a disturbing picture: the mess of the files, the recent adding of Kim's name to the bar and house, and now that she thought about it, that it had been changed around the same time the payments started on that ledger. A woman at home in a skiff in the swamp tips it over and hits her head, right around the time all this other stuff is going on. Smitty seemed way too uncomfortable talking about her death.

Something at the window above her caught her eye. For a second, she thought a face blended with the darkness outside. Her heart hammered and sent blood pulsing in her temples. Then she realized that the shadows and leaves outside only made it look like a face. She got to her feet and faced the curtainless window, trying to ignore the flutter in her chest. All she could see was her own white face with eyes a little too wide. Shadows and a dash of paranoia.

She released a breath and looked over the mass of papers on the bed. What was someone looking for so hastily in here? Had they found it? She placed the piece of rubber in a baggie and walked out to the living room where the urn sat on the coffee table. "Elva, what were you into?"

Elva's body had conveniently been cremated, but there had to be a report on her death. Kim gave Oscar a pat on the head. "I'll be right back. I need to read that report."

The moon was still bright as she headed to the substation.


The taillights on Kim's truck faded and then disappeared as she turned right and headed toward town. What had she found in that filing cabinet? It had been gone through thoroughly, but, admittedly, left in a mess.

The extra set of keys would come in handy. No matter where Kim had gone off to in a big rush, there was time to check things over and make sure nothing had been missed.

Hopefully Kim wasn't on to anything. It was hard to kill someone you knew. Killing Rhonda and Elva had been necessary. If Kim kept digging, she would have to be taken care of, too.


By the time Kim arrived at the sheriff's substation, her fingers were locked on the steering wheel. She pried them off and walked into the brightly lit building.

"Is Dave working tonight?" she asked when she saw Kinsey behind the desk with his feet perched on the corner.

"I'm the only one here right now. Surely I can help you, Miss Lyons." He flashed her the most insincere smile she'd ever seen.

"I need to see the report on my grandmother's death."

The smile disappeared as he pulled his feet down. "Now why would you want to see that? Might be disturbing."

"Police reports are open to public viewing, are they not?"

"Yes, ma'am, they are. Hold there for a minute."

He made her wait for twenty. She wouldn't give him the satisfaction of knowing how much it irritated her, and holding it in made it all the more irritating. When he finally reappeared, he made no apology for the delay. She took the report and walked to the small waiting area. It pinched her chest to see her grandma's name on that cold, official report titled "Death Certificate." Elva's life was laid out in typed text. Under cause of death: "accidental drowning and submersion; blunt trauma to head." She'd probably been unconscious when she'd drowned.

The certificate had been prepared by Len Watkins, funeral director and city coroner.

A shadow fell over the paper. "Something I can help you with?" Kinsey said.

She pointed to where it indicated accidental death. "Are you comfortable with this finding?"

"Of course. I made the determination based on the facts."

"Did you find the object she'd hit her head on?"

"There were lots of logs and cypress knees in the area. She had floated an undetermined distance, and her body had been in the water for two and a half days before Smitty discovered she was missing and went looking for her."

"Did you even consider that someone may have knocked her unconscious, taken her out in her skiff, and held her underwater?"

He rested his scuffed cowboy boot on the small coffee table. "Who would want to kill your grandma? That is what you're suggesting, isn't it? That someone killed her and made it look like an accident?"

"I think it's a possibility. Did you?"

"We look for suspicious circumstances and order an autopsy whenever a body is found. There had been no threats made against her, no known motive for someone to murder her, and her injuries were consistent with a fall."

"I may have found some suspicious circumstances." Kim told him what she'd found, leaving out the mysterious payments since she didn't know if they were connected. She held up the baggie. "I found this piece of rubber glove on one of the files. Elva wouldn't be looking through her own files with gloves on." She realized it wasn't much. She thought of Tullie's premonition. "I have a feeling there's more to her death than an accident."

"A feeling." He rubbed his hand down his face. "Based on the evidence you've given me, I see no crime. Your grandmother was getting on in years. She shouldn't have been out there by herself. She probably just lost her balance and fell. Nothing sinister about it." His voice lowered. "If I were you, I'd stop making everything into a crime. Remember the girl who cried wolf?"

She didn't respond, only walked out of the station. Had someone murdered her grandma? She didn't want to believe it, but her gut said it was a distinct possibility.

When she got home, Oscar was pacing madly. "What's wrong?" When he didn't want to go out, she wondered what else could be bothering him. She grabbed her tear gas and searched all the rooms. She looked out the windows, just to be sure. "I don't see anything, Oscar. Maybe you just missed me."

Oscar still looked uneasy. "Come on, let's go to bed." She took the urn, grabbed her jar of peanut butter and a spoon, and went into the bedroom, closing the curtains tight. He settled on his pile of blankets, though he kept his gaze on the door. "Oscar, stop that! You're creeping me out." Her insides were already wound so tight, if she sneezed, they'd probably split apart.

She set the urn on the nightstand. Morbid maybe, but it was like having her grandma there in a way. She sat on the bed facing it while she dug the spoon into the peanut butter. "Elva, what kind of mess have you left me in? I can handle a lot of things, but this, too? If I pursue this, I'm going to end up just like I did before." Her voice went lower. "Or worse. And if I let it go . . . then three murders have gone unpunished in this town. Could I live with myself?" She rubbed her temples, but the shooting stress pains continued. "Well, I'm older now. Smarter. Maybe I can put this together without alerting anyone. 'Course, I just alerted the entire town by telling Kinsey what I know. But he didn't believe me. Or pretended not to believe me. Who knows, he could be in on it, too."

She stared at the urn. "You could help me out here. If you wanted to show up as a ghost, I'd be okay with that." She thought of the face she'd imagined in the window. "I need your help. It's the least you can do after dropping me into this. You had something somebody wanted, maybe wanted badly enough to kill you for. But why not just take it when you weren't here? Unless you caught them in the act. But I'll probably never know unless you appear in an ethereal vision and tell me. The evidence is all gone, including your body."

She slid beneath the sheets, her can of tear gas at her side. She knew she'd keep looking. But she was going to need some real evidence to get this to the attention of law enforcement personnel who cared. As Kinsey said, no one was going to listen to her cry wolf again. And whoever killed Elva, how far would they go to keep the truth concealed?

# CHAPTER 12

After tossing and turning all night, Kim woke to the nudge she was getting used to. She cracked an eye to find a smooth, brown object bobbing in front of her. She jerked out of bed with a muffled scream. Before fright could take hold, she realized what it was: her jar of peanut butter firmly attached to Oscar's snout. And he wasn't too happy about it by the way he kept jerking his head up and down.

"Oscar!" She plucked the jar off his snout, and he proceeded to rub the peanut butter off his snout and onto the carpet. She could only shake her head.

After getting ready, she drove straight to the bar, tensing as she made the turn into the parking lot. Nothing looked out of place. She let out a breath of relief and drove to the hardware store.

Evan smiled at her. "Your glass orta be in sometime this morning."

"Great. I also need two sets of locks rekeyed. Who does that around here?"

"Doyle Cannon. Got his number here somewhere."

While he looked, Kim ran the name through her memory bank. No relation to the Waddells. "Is Doyle related to the Macgregors at all?" She wanted to make sure no enemy could get a key.

Evan laughed. "No, there's bad blood 'tween 'em. Doyle and his brother Don sold Winn a shotgun that didn't work, see, and wouldn't take it back. That was, oh, about eight years ago."

"Great, thanks." She took the number he'd jotted down. "Uh, you wrote the number on a check."

"I know. It's bad anyway."

"Okay, then." She folded the check and tucked it in her pocket. "Thanks for your help. Can you deliver those windows when they come in? I'd like to have them by two if I could so I can install them between lunch and dinner."

"During the storm time?"

She'd forgotten about scheduling life around summer storms. "I suppose so."

"You gonna install them yourself?"

"Can't afford to hire anyone." The bar's reserves were beginning to dwindle. "It's easy, right?"

He blew out a breath. "Easier than building a building, maybe. If you got a few minutes, I'll have Ed give you some pointers."

Kim smiled. "Thanks, I'd appreciate that."


Doyle came out mid-morning and re-keyed the bar. She then led the way to her house, where he re-keyed the front door lock. Kim finished the painting just as Smitty arrived. She waved him to the back. "Here's a new key to the bar. I need to talk to you, and promise me you won't stomp off in a huff this time."

He stiffened. "Can't make a man promise something when he don't know what it's about."

She rolled her eyes but reined in her impatience. "Did you ever think that Elva's death was suspicious? Be honest with me."

For a moment he didn't say anything. "Thought it was wrong," he said finally.

"Smitty, you know what I'm talking about. She was into

something, wasn't she? That's what she was making those payments for."

"I don't know what they was for. I didn't get involved in her personal affairs. I just helped her out here and . . . well, and at other times."

He started to walk around the corner, but she snagged his arm. "I need some answers. I think Elva was murdered, and I think you do, too."

He wouldn't meet her eyes. "I don't know what she was up to." He released a long breath when Kim kept her scrutinizing gaze on him. "But I thought she might be into something, yes. She wouldn't tell me, just got secretive. I asked Zell about it—"

"Zell?"

He ran his fingers down his scraggly mustache. "Not about what she was up to, but what to do about it. Him being the Sage and all. He said I should let her do what she needed to do; that women need to go off and do their thing sometimes."

She suppressed her groan about Zell giving advice on love. "But you didn't think Elva was cheating on you, did you?"

"We didn't have that kind of thing going. We just did the Yankee Doodle Dandy once in a while, is all. Zell, he thought I was asking about cheating, and I let him. Figured it applied just the same. Wasn't none of my business anyway."

"But you were worried about her."

"A bit. Never thought I'd be worried about Elva."

Kim started to lean against the building but thought better of it because of the paint. "Did you love her?"

"Love." He chuckled and shook his head. "Zell says the most common kind of love is the friendship kind mixed with a little somethin' extra. That's what Elva and I had. It's all she wanted."

Zell's sage advice again. Oh, brother. Then she realized they were getting sidetracked. "Why were you worried about her?"

"I could tell she had something on her mind. Something serious. She looked around the parking lot when we left for the night and kept a closer eye on Oscar. Like she thought something might happen. She wouldn't tell me what."

Was he telling the truth? How much did he know about Elva's comings and goings? "I'm just trying to figure out what she was up to."

"Seems you got enough going on without getting yourself into trouble around here."

"You'd think," she answered as he walked around to the front when a car pulled up. Trouble seemed to be her middle name.

Smitty didn't talk much to her during lunchtime, other than to say yes, he'd help her set the windows as best he could. Evan from the hardware store delivered the panes of glass right before the last customers left.

Smitty regarded the glass leaning against the front of the building. "You know how to install these things? Ain't never had to install a winder before."

"I got instructions from Ed."

He raised a white eyebrow. "Plumb Crazy Ed? Oh, boy, this is gonna be fun."

Kim assembled the tools Ed said she'd need along with the diagrams he'd drawn. "He didn't seem crazy to me."

"The craziest people never do. You'd best remember that, young'un."

The seriousness in his voice made her look at him, but he was sizing up the windows. She remembered Zell warning her about the least vocal people.

Smitty said, "We orta do one at a time so we don't get stuck with a buncha open winders when the storm blows in."

The eastern sky was just hinting at a storm with the clouds a darker shade of blue. "Good idea," she said even though she'd already decided on that route.

She climbed up on the stepladder and pried off the

plywood. Smitty took hold of one end and she the other as they set it on the ground.

"Oscar, are we doing it right?" The pig was watching her every move.

Smitty turned around. "I think that pig loves you. Hasn't taken his eyes off you."

"Smitty, I'm beginning to think you see love everywhere, you old cynic."

He gave her a wink as he followed her inside. "I know you was flirtin' with Zell."

"All right," she said, pointedly ignoring him and studying the diagram. "First we need to push those two big tables together to use as a worktable and then cover them with newspapers." Once they'd accomplished that, she said, "Now we need to remove the window—er, winder—and lay it on the table."

She was busy chiseling away the old glazing when she heard a vehicle pull into the parking lot. She wasn't ready to deal with anybody. Even though the air was on, the humid heat came in through the opening and drenched her in sweat. She'd wrapped a light blue handkerchief around her forehead and had stripped down to a tank top, jean shorts, and hiking-style boots. She walked to the opening and groaned.

Zell and Tullie were getting out of his truck. He looked as good and fresh as he had the day before in a pair of white pants and a reddish-orange sunset shirt. His yellow music player was strapped to his arm. Tullie skipped along in front of him as they walked to the bar while Zell talked on a cell phone. His eyes were on her, framed in the opening as she was. She wanted to tell him to halt and go back to wherever he came from. She didn't need to feel shabby around him and she sure didn't need any distraction.

Somehow the words didn't come out of her mouth, and before long, the door opened and the two walked in. Tullie ran over to Smitty and gave him a hug and then she gave Oscar a hug, too. Zell was saying to whoever was on the phone, "Looks like you got some gopher tortoises and red

cockaded woodpeckers. I'll have my report ready next week
and we'll get together and come up with a strategy. Let the
state have their say and we'll have ours. I'll be the bad guy.
Hell, to them, I always am. By the time I'm done, we'll
prove that everybody can live peaceably and you'll have the
land you need. Okay, sounds good. Bye."

He disconnected and looked at Kim. She wanted to say,
*Go away!* And yet, as bad as she looked, there was some
warped part of her that was glad to see him.

"We're not open," she said instead, hearing vanity put
an edge to her words.

He took in the window on the table. "I can see that. Southern Comfort's never officially open in the 'tween time. I just
brought Tullie over to play with Smitty." When Kim raised
her eyebrow questioningly, she followed Zell's gaze to where
Tullie was carrying a backgammon game from the office to
the tall table by the side window. "She usually comes over
after school and hangs out for a bit. Shar decided she could
start coming again." He walked over and ran his finger along
the place where Kim had just removed the glazing.

"I can't spare Smitty right now. We're replacing the
glass."

Tullie had walked over and was looking at Kim with
those beautiful, haunting eyes of hers. "Hi, Kim."

Kim braced her hands on her thighs to lower herself to
Tullie's level. "Hi, Tullie."

"I like your hair that way. Don't ever cut it, okay?"

Kim raised her eyebrows. "Well, thank you. I'll keep
that in mind. Uh, Smitty can't—" She stopped when Zell
started working on the remaining glazing as though he
knew what he was doing.

He said to Tullie, "You two go on." The cut above his
eyebrow and on his lower lip were starting to heal. It gave
him a rough, dangerous look and for some strange reason
that appealed to her. She ran her hand across her stomach
and felt the belly ring he'd touched.

Kim was at once grateful and uncomfortable with his
help. And curious. "Why are you doing this?"

"So they can get a game in." If there was more to it, he wasn't saying. He left her in limbo, making her want to like him when she should be remembering all the things he'd lied about on the witness stand. "Start sanding down the wood channel behind me." He worked the pieces of broken glass out of the grooves with a deft hand.

"Shouldn't you wear gloves?"

"Can't work as fast with them. Too bulky. But I will lose this." He shrugged out of his shirt, leaving only a white, sleeveless undershirt that clung to the contours of his body.

She grabbed up a piece of sandpaper and ran it along the grooves, finding herself leaning way too close to him in the process. He smelled good, all soap and clean man. He looked all kinds of good, too, with his muscles flexing as he worked.

"So, why are you a bad guy?" she asked when her thoughts were getting too wrapped up in his physical presence. "The call you were on."

"The state environmental agencies call me a biostute. Biological prostitute. They think I sell out nature for money because I believe man and nature can coexist. They told this landowner that he could only use two out of his fifty acres because of the red cockadeds and tortoises. I'm going to show them how he can use forty acres and still give the creatures a safe habitat in which to live."

"You do all kinds of things, don't you?"

"If I could survey alligators full-time, I'd do it." He was nearly done with his part of the window.

She sped up the sanding and shook her head. "I still don't understand how you can be so into those creatures."

He looked at her. "I don't know how anyone couldn't be impressed by them." He walked over to the panes of glass. "Are these cut to fit?"

"Yes."

"First we have to coat the bare wood with sealer."

Kim popped open the small can and came over with a brush. He took it from her and ran it over the wood. "You've done this before, I take it," she said.

"A time or two. Between helping friends and building my own house, I got handy with this kind of thing."

When Kim glanced over at Tullie and Smitty, the girl was watching them. She quickly averted her gaze to the game. What had she seen in her vision? Kim didn't really believe in that kind of thing anyway, so why think about it? But she *was* thinking about it, and she realized something: Tullie had been right about Kim seeking the truth, before Kim even knew she was seeking it.

"I brought my hair dryer," she said, pulling it out of the bag she'd brought from the house. "Ed at the hardware store said it would help the drying process."

"Plumb Crazy Ed?" He watched her run the dryer over the wet surfaces. "Not a bad idea."

"Would you like something to drink? It's the least I can do."

"I'll get it. You want something?"

"I'm fine, thanks."

He poured a root beer into a glass of ice, checked Tullie and Smitty's game, and scratched Oscar's back on his way back. Zell removed the music player from his arm and set it on a nearby table. George Thorogood belted out "Bad to the Bone." Not her type of music.

He touched the sealer. "It's dry enough." He grabbed the putty knife and glazing compound and started pressing it into the grooves. She was glad he hadn't put on gloves. He had great hands, long fingers. She was starting to have dangerous feelings about him. Zell might be hard to get to know, but she sensed a deep well of passion beneath his easygoing surface. She preferred her men to be easygoing all the way down, so why was she drawn to him?

As though even God Himself were warning her, the sky rumbled in the near distance. Kim decided to explore one of the other reasons why having any kind of feeling for Zell was a bad idea.

"Heard you have an alligator test for potential girl-friends," she said as she wiped away a bit of excess glazing.

When he looked at her, she quickly added, "I'm not vying for a spot, just curious."

The corner of his mouth quirked. Did he think the possibility of her vying for a spot was ludicrous? She, who hated alligators, who was hated by the Macgregors. It *was* ludicrous.

"Yep, there's an oral quiz and a tactile part."

She shivered at the mere thought of cuddling up to one of those things. "Has anyone ever passed the test?"

"Nope." And he seemed pretty pleased about that. "But I feel honored that some of them study up."

"You are so full of yourself."

"I prefer to say that I'm comfortable with myself and where I am in life." He finished. "We're ready for the glass. Give me your gloves a minute and I'll bring one of the pieces over."

"I can do it," she said even as he slid the gloves from her hands.

"Let me do it. Makes me feel like I'm a gentleman once in a while." A minute later, he carried one of the pieces over. "You got glazing points?"

"Right here."

When J. Geil's Band's "Love Stinks" came on the music player, she said, "I think you're afraid of commitment. That's why you have the alligator test."

He chuckled as he pressed the glass into position. "Put those glazing points flat against the glass surface about ten inches apart. You think because I have a song called 'Love Stinks' I'm afraid of commitment?"

"And 'Love Hurts' and 'Love Bites.' "

He followed her as she pushed the points in with the putty knife. "You forgot 'Ain't Love a Bitch.' Rod Stewart," he added at her questioning look. "It's a reprisal of the Maggie May story."

"I don't remember that one being on there."

"I just added it. Track forty-seven."

She finished with the points, walked over to the music player, and chose the track. Rod Stewart started singing about his experiences with love, ending each one with "Ain't Love a Bitch."

"I threw 'Tainted Love' by Soft Cell on there, too, track forty-eight, just to be sure."

"Sure of what?"

The corner of his mouth quirked again. "Just sure."

She gave him a rolled-eye look, but he was busy applying a bead of the glazing compound along the edge of the glass. He ran his finger along the bead to smooth it in. After he wiped his finger on the newspaper, he caught her watching him.

She crossed her arms in front of her. "Why, Zell, between the gator test and the music, I think someone broke your heart along the way."

He smiled and then started singing a song about everybody having the blues someday. Dammit, he could even sing well, which particularly rankled because she couldn't. When he was finished with the chorus, he stepped back. "The glazing has to skin over before you can paint it."

"So who was she?"

"Huh?"

"The girl who broke your heart. Come on, there had to be one." It was becoming a challenge, getting him to answer a personal question.

When he saw that she was waiting, he said in his Southern accent, "Wail now, there was a gal I had a particular likin' for, but she couldn't pass the gator test. It was a sad day in Zellville when I had to let her go." He even patted his heart for effect and looked for all the world like a man with a broken heart.

Yeah, right.

She was on one side of the table and he was on the other. She leaned forward and said in her best challenging voice, "I don't think you've ever been in love with anyone. Except maybe yourself."

He put his hand on his heart again, this time pretending to be wounded by her words. Just as quickly, he dropped it. "All right, you got me. But you know, it is a lot easier to just keep track of myself. I can control how much trouble I get into."

Though he was being a smart-ass, she picked up something else in those words. "Just because you love someone doesn't mean you have to take responsibility for them and their behavior."

All humor had left his face when he said, "Oh yeah, it does."

Thunder cracked across the sky, and he walked to the window and looked out as the afternoon torrent of rain started. The cool breeze ruffled his hair and chilled her damp skin. She was too caught up in his words to take advantage of it, though. Throughout most of his life, Zell had had to take care of his father. After his mother's death, he'd probably had to take care of Charlotte, too. No wonder he didn't want any responsibility. No wonder he didn't want to love any woman who might become another burden. Heck, he didn't love her and she'd become a burden anyway. He'd watched Oscar, taken care of the orchids, gotten beaten up, and was now helping her with her windows. No doubt his family wasn't happy about any of it.

Aerosmith's Steven Tyler crooned about his angel, making her wonder if he didn't have a romantic side after all. She walked up behind him, resisting the urge to slide her arms around him and rest against his back, to offer some bit of comfort in return. Keeping her distance was best for both of them. She'd already caused him enough trouble, and she was bound to cause more when she started nosing around the circumstances of Elva's death.

She felt her body lean into his, just slightly, and caught herself. Smitty and Tullie were probably watching them, and she didn't need to hear any more accusations of flirting. She wasn't flirting; she just needed . . . what did she need from Zell? His forgiveness, his acceptance . . . something more visceral than that?

She was so caught up in her thoughts and the line of his shoulders flecked with freckles and carved with lean muscle, he took her by surprise when he turned around. For an instant, he took in her eyes and then her mouth, and something primal lit in his blue-green eyes.

"Someone just pulled up," he said, only then making her aware of the car that had parked right outside the window they'd been standing at. She'd been so caught up in the moment, it took her more than another few seconds to realize she recognized the car: it was Simon's.

# CHAPTER 13

"Hey, JoGene, you gonna buy those binoculars or become a winder display?"

He gave Evan a sneer and returned to what he'd been doing: watching Southern Comfort. It was across the street, a short distance away. She was fixing the windows. It was the same thing as thumbing her nose at him. Or giving him another rude gesture. She was serious about this staying thing, then. His fingers tightened on the glasses. Damn her. Why couldn't she have just stayed where she was up in north Florida?

The worst part was Zell helping her, that traitorous son of a bitch. What was he up to, anyway? Could be he was just gaining her trust on the outside and seeing what it would take to make her leave on the inside. Owen had said Winn was giving Zell a hard time about helping Kim; looked like he was going to get more of it, but apparently he didn't care.

JoGene had wanted to be the one to help her. That would have enabled him to wiggle right into her good graces, and maybe even her tight jeans. Cold sweat popped out on his face. Could Zell be after the same things? The guy who had everything, could do whatever he wanted, and sure enough, probably wanted the bar, too. He wouldn't even have to borrow the money to buy it, either, he bet.

He was glad Billy Bob and Clem had beat the crap out of Zell. JoGene couldn't help smiling at that thought, but his glee was short-lived. Zell had the upper hand, as usual. Look at them getting all cozy. He frowned and set the glasses on the display counter.

And the graffiti? Had even one of those crude words offended her? Or had she simply marched right over here to buy paint and brushes, letting them all roll off her back? He'd wanted to help her paint, too, but Buck had gotten in the way that time, ordering him to weed around the cabins. Criticizing him for not keeping up the grounds.

His mouth tightened into a hard line. It was time to do something more drastic.


Charlotte double-checked her figures on the eggs as she counted them in their incubating boxes. Inside the boxes was the same material alligators used to make their nests: leaves, twigs, and decaying matter. She liked seeing her dazzling nails against the backdrop of those eggs. She checked the temperature before closing the lid on the box. Nice and toasty, just like this room. She brushed at the fine hairs stuck to the base of her neck.

Thanks to Zell's diligence, ninety-five percent of these eggs would hatch. The best part was watching the babies pop out of the shells. Their grunts were like music to her ears as they called for their mama. *She* was their mama. In fact, she'd do more for these babies than their real mama would have. She'd feed them at least, as well as keep them from danger and ill health. They'd grow fast and strong and eventually get moved to the big gator tanks in the next building. And sometime after that, they'd get slaughtered and become meat and purses and souvenirs. It wasn't like they got attached to her. All gators cared about was eating and having space. They'd eat her without remorse if it came to that. That's how it was in the gator world.

"Hey, Shar," Owen said, peeking his head in the incubating room.

She closed her notebook and opened the door. "I was just finishing up."

She loved watching the young ones in the tanks. Most women she knew fawned over baby chicks or bunnies, but Shar, she loved baby gators. Just watching them scramble around the pen taking in the world with their bright yellow eyes filled her heart with joy.

Owen leaned on the railing next to her. "JoGene just called. Zell's over there helping Kim fix the winders. I told Zell he orta leave that Kim alone, but he didn't listen to me."

She lifted her eyebrow at that. "You *told* Zell?"

His shoulders stiffened. "Yeah, I did."

One of the things she liked about Owen was his easygoing nature. She called the shots, in the business, their marriage, and in the bedroom. Zell had his alligator test with women; she'd had her testosterone test back in high school. If she told a guy to finish his plate of fried chicken and mashed taters and he did, she stuck around to see if he was just being polite. After growing up with a brother telling her what to do, she didn't want any husband taking over the role. No way. Owen passed the test—or should she say failed it? He'd been so in love with her—and her family's money and prestige; she wasn't blind—that he'd swallow crickets if she asked him to. Made life easier, even if it was boring at times.

"You told him not to see a woman?" This was a departure, and she wasn't sure she liked it.

Two young gators got into a tangle by the pile of salt that sat at one end of the beach. As it seeped into the water, it helped the young hides heal from occasional scraps.

"I told him to be careful about that gal. I remember what it was like when she turned on us."

She nodded, touched by his bravado. "It did rip us all apart, didn't it?" She slid him a look. "So what did Zell say?"

"He said to mind my own business. But I'm not going to let him hurt this family by listening to his pecker."

She couldn't help it; she grabbed him right through his jeans. "What are you going to do, Owen, if he keeps seeing her?" Her voice sounded breathy.

He'd jumped when she'd grabbed him, but now he was growing hard beneath her hand. She hadn't given him any in a while. She'd been bored silly for so long she was already in a rut with her vibrator. But this side of Owen was exciting. Maybe he had a hidden aggressive side.

"I'll have me another talk with Zell first. I'll push him down in a chair and make him listen."

She tightened her hold. "And what if he tells you to mind your business again?"

His voice was getting stronger in direct proportion to his pecker getting harder. "I'll tell him that this family *is* my business, dammit!"

Normally she would have chastised him for raising his voice in the alligator house. Since the only sound the gators ever heard was the scrape of the food barrow, noise stirred them up. Right now she didn't care. She unzipped his pants. His breath caught as her fingers slid around him. "Then what?"

He ripped open her blouse, sending buttons skidding across the concrete walkway. He mashed her breasts and ravaged her with his mouth. His voice was muffled now so the gators wouldn't be disturbed. She was the only one getting disturbed.

"I'll tell him that he ought to damn well settle down and start contributing to this family in a gene-pool kind of way. Find himself a nice, compliant gal who'll help out, or maybe one that'll stop him from doing exactly what he pleases. But he don't need any trouble like Kim'll give him—give all of us. I'll poke my finger in his chest and tell him what's on my mind and make him see."

"And if that don't work?"

"I'm already working on it, darlin'."

She whispered in his ear. "What are you doing?"

"Just let me take care of things for once."

Hmm, intriguing. Mysterious. He had been out late at night recently. She'd pushed his pants down and then her own as he was talking. "Owen, you beast. Give me some of that passion and anger and brute force."

He shoved into her as she braced herself against the railing. It was so hot in there that even her eyes were sweating. She closed them and focused on her mild husband slamming into her, crushing her buttocks against the railing. In some dim portion of her mind, she heard the door open at the end of the hallway. She cracked open one eye and saw Dewey with a bucket in his hand. She closed her eye. Owen was sliding into the final zone, and she wasn't about to do a thing to disrupt him. Dewey probably didn't even know what sex was.

She checked on him once more. He was still standing there watching. Oh, yeah, he knew what sex was. Sometimes she suspected he wasn't nearly as dumb as he pretended to be. Shar had much better things to do than be modest. She held Owen tighter and felt him rocket to the moon.

Could it possibly be Simon? Kim watched him run through the rain with an umbrella carefully dodging puddles. Oh, yeah it was Simon all right. He'd gotten more soaked opening the car door and fumbling with the umbrella than if he'd just made the dash. People in Cypress rarely reached for an umbrella. They either waited it out or got wet. Simon shook out the umbrella and set it by the door. He brushed the water from his brown hair and only then did he look at her. She thought it appropriate that Matchbox 20's "Bent" was playing just then.

Nothing in her heart betrayed a longing or regret at her decision; she checked just in case. He was handsome, no doubt, and looked successful and well put together. Comfortable. Safe.

"Simon, this is a surprise."

He glanced around at the bar and the people inside. "This is your bar?"

She detected the slightest distaste in his voice, but not enough to call him on it. "It's not glitzy like City Lights, but it's mine." She glanced at Zell. Well, mostly hers. "I have plans to fix it up."

"Like repairing broken windows?"

"That was an accident."

He gave her his skeptical look. Had he always been this condescending, this annoying?

"This is Zell Macgregor," she said before anything more derogatory could slip out. They shook hands and murmured whatever it was that men who didn't really want to meet each other murmured. Zell seemed to be studying Simon's reaction to his name, maybe to see if Kim had told him about the Macgregors. "Over there is Zell's niece, Tullie, and Smitty, also part of the Macgregor family." Oscar trotted over to check out the new arrival. Simon jumped back, definite distaste on his face when Oscar's twitching snout touched his pants. "This is Oscar, the pig I inherited." She gave him a scratch on the head, and Oscar shoved his butt into her. She regained her balance and looked at Simon. "What are you doing here?"

"I—" He looked over at Zell, who was fiddling with the window, and then steered her toward the open window where the rain continued to pour down. "I stopped by your house first. I remembered where you'd said it was, off the road on the way down, tucked in the swamp."

"What'd you think?"

"Well, it's tucked in a swamp." He shot another look at Zell, who was still within listening range. "Is that an ex-boyfriend of yours?"

She almost laughed at that. "No. Simon, what's this about? Do I owe you money for rent? Just take my part of the last month's rent."

He looked pained for a moment, or maybe she imagined it. "I think . . ." Another glance at Zell. "I think you're making a mistake."

"That's why you came? To tell me what I should do?"

He looked at a loss for words. Finally he grabbed her hands. "When I was packing up your things . . . four boxes, plus the three you had in the second bedroom, I saw how little you had and realized why it's so important to you to have a home. I understand it now. I don't know what happened when you lived down here, but I do know you haven't had a home of your own in a long time. I'm sorry I didn't see that until now. I found a place, Kim. A place we could buy. We could get married." He glanced at Oscar, whom Zell was petting now. "They don't allow pigs in the neighborhood, but we could get a dog."

Her head was swimming. He was offering her what she'd always wanted, what she'd wanted from him. Zell was listening to all this and hearing way too much about her.

Simon saw her looking Zell's way. "Look, I don't want to discuss this in front of your hired help. Can we go somewhere and talk?"

A bubble of hysterical laughter escaped at that notion. "He's not hired help. He's just . . . helping me out so his niece can play with Smitty. Oh, never mind," she said at Simon's confusion. It was probably a good idea to go somewhere else. Zell was distracting her, and his music reminded her of trying to find his soul on that first lonely night back in town. "Let's go out back. The rain's lightening up now."

She felt a tightness in her chest as they walked outside. The air was cool and damp. Rain dripped from the overhang, adding a steady rhythm. As soon as she closed the door, she turned to him. "Did you just ask me to marry you back there?"

"If that's what you want, then yes, I did. I didn't listen to you, Kim. I should have."

*If that's what I want?* "Why now, Simon?"

He forced a sheepish smile. "They always say you don't know what you have until it's gone. I liked what we had, and I got too comfortable with it. That's why I didn't want to change anything. But I see why it means so much to you now."

"Because I'm pitiful?"

"No. That's not what I meant. I just . . . Kim, you're not making this easy on me."

She was staring at his beeper. "What?" he asked at last.

"Isn't it going to go off? Every time I ever brought up marriage or a buying house, it went off. Strange how it's silent now."

He ducked his head and ran his hand through his damp hair. "All right, I didn't make it easy on you, either. But I've seen the light. Isn't that what a woman dreams of, for her guy to see the light and give her what she wants?"

Was it? She let out a long breath and leaned against the back wall. When she remembered the wet paint, she decided to just stay there. "You're offering me a home. Marriage. Dog."

"Yes. I'll even try to work through the after-sex shower thing. I know that really bothers you."

He *was* giving her everything she wanted. She felt his offer tug at her sensibilities. "Did you even think about moving down here?"

"No." He glanced around. "This isn't me. And I couldn't keep my job. Even you wouldn't be happy living here, not after living in a city. There's nothing here for either of us."

She watched Oscar, who'd followed them out, as he snurfled in the gravel parking lot. She looked at the backside of the bar covered in brown paint. She took in the mangroves and river.

"Come on, Kim. Don't keep me in suspense any longer. Are you coming back with me or not?"

"Not."

His face paled. "Not?"

"I wanted a life and a home with you in Tallahassee, but you wouldn't listen when I wanted to talk about it. You didn't want to hear about my dreams then. You wouldn't give me what I wanted, so I changed what I wanted. Going back with you would be easy, sure. Would I be happy? Marginally. But I'm tired of taking the easy way. This"—she gestured to include the bar and the river—"is what talks to my soul. I never belonged in Tallahassee, something you often reminded me of. Well, this is where I really belong. On my own." When she saw his shoulders slump, she said, "I'm sorry, Simon." That apology had come easier than usual. Then again, she'd had lots of practice lately. "Now that I've come back, I have to stay. I know that now. Maybe I always knew it."

He put that impassive look back on his face. "All right, if that's what you want. I brought your things just in case."

If he'd been a passionate man, he would have bought a ring and driven down with no intention of returning without her. But not Simon. He had a contingency plan. She followed him around to the front of the building. Nickelback's "This Is How You Remind Me" floated from the open window where Zell was preparing to rehang the window with Smitty's help.

Simon opened the trunk of his BMW via remote as they approached the car. He took out one of her boxes and scanned the parking lot. "Where is your car?"

She took the box he'd handed her and walked to her truck. "What do you think?"

He shook his head. "You do belong down here."

"Guess I do." She took the next box to her truck. The third box held some of her "tacky" keepsakes like the bar lights. She looked at the four other boarded-up windows and set the box on the steps.

When the last of the boxes and her clothes had been removed from his trunk, she said, "Thanks for bringing my stuff." In the end, it was better that he'd had a backup plan.

"Have you called Becca yet? She left a message for you at the apartment."

"No, but I will." She hadn't yet told her friend about her crazy decision to move down here. Becca would no doubt applaud her dumping Simon. She met his gaze and tried to ignore the fact that Zell was only a few feet away. She gave him a quick hug that he, as usual, didn't give back. "Bye, Simon. Good luck."

He glanced at the bar. "Yeah, you, too." *You'll need it,* he didn't say.

She didn't even watch him pull away. Instead she turned to take the box inside and found Tullie standing on the step. She had that deep look in her eyes again, the one she'd had when she told Kim about searching for the truth.

Kim laughed, though it sounded hollow to her ears—and probably Tullie's, too. "That's true love for you."

"It wasn't true love," she said. "When people are in love, really in love, it feels different."

Kim hefted the box, but paused. "How'd you know I'd be searching for the truth?"

"I just know things. I can't explain how. Like I know that you're not going to like the truth once you find it. But that's not going to stop you from trying to find it." She tilted her head. "Do you believe me?"

"I don't know, but the thing about searching for the truth . . ."

"Creepy, isn't it?"

"No, not creepy. Eerie, maybe." She took a step to go inside, but Tullie's next words stopped her.

"I had a bad feeling about Elva, too. I told her to be careful, but it didn't help her." Her grief over that shadowed her face. That shadow contrasted the baby fat around her cheeks and chin, both wizened adult and child.

Kim set the box down. "What kind of feeling?"

Tullie shrugged. "I just had the feeling about her. I knew something bad was gonna happen, but I didn't know what."

"You said you had a feeling about me and Zell. Was that a bad feeling, too?"

Her mouth tightened and she nodded.

The door opened and Zell stepped out. He'd donned his tropical shirt again. For a moment their gazes locked. She wondered what he'd heard.

He averted his gaze to Tullie. "Ready to go home, angel? I've got to get back to work."

For some reason the word *angel* tickled through her. When Kim also looked at Tullie, the girl was shifting her gaze from her to Zell and back again. A sly grin replaced the shadow. She looked at Zell. "She's your match, Uncle Zell. Not like those other girls."

Zell blinked but recovered and ruffled the girl's hair. "You must mean the boxing kind of match. Let's go. Say bye to Smitty and Oscar."

Tullie ran inside.

"You believe her?" Kim said. "In general, I mean, not about us being a match."

"She's been right about a lot of things. Besides, it's not my place to disbelieve her." When Tullie rushed to the door, he said, "Got the one window in. It's a start anyway."

"Thanks for your help. I . . . well, I didn't know Simon was coming. I didn't mean for you to finish the job by yourself."

His mouth quirked. "The course of true love never did run smooth, isn't that what they say?"

"And you'd know, I suppose."

He full out smiled at that, probably remembering their earlier conversation. "They do call me the Sage."

"So what would you have advised me to do, O great Sage?"

"Just what you did."

Tullie said, "It wasn't true love."

" 'Course it wasn't," Zell said in his know-it-all way. He turned to Tullie. "One of them would have been on their knees, either him begging her to come back or her begging him to stay. Somebody would have said the word *love*. It would have been much messier"—he gave Kim a pointed look—"and much more interesting. Let's go, angel. Your mama said you could come by for a game, not open a seer shop." He nodded his head at Kim and guided Tullie to the truck.

"What's a seer?" she asked him.

"It's someone who sees things and has feelings about them."

Tullie gave her uncle a smile that tweaked Kim's heart. "I like that. Seer. It's better than *freak*, isn't it?"

He helped her into the truck. "That it is, angel. That it is."

Before the happy hour crowd started arriving, Kim drove over to the Watkins Funeral Home and House of God. One Watkins brother had gotten into the business of death, and the other had gotten into the business of saving souls to assure eternal salvation. In an odd way, it made sense. Though she probably ought to be attending services—she could use all the help she could get—today she was there to see Len, the nonreverend brother. He also doubled as the Cypress coroner.

"Ya did get your granny's ashes, didn't ya?" Len asked after they'd exchanged greetings. "Wharton picked the cheapest of the urns, but if you intend to keep Elva around, ya might want to upgrade to one of our finer models." He gestured to a wall of urns.

"I'm not sure what I'm going to do with the ashes, but I'll keep that in mind. Actually, I'm here about her cremation. Who gave you the authority to do that?"

Len stuck his finger in his ear and worked it for a few seconds. His wrinkled face was scrunched up, from thinking, the ear scratching, or maybe both. Finally he said, "Well, now, that was confusing. See, with you being next of kin, you should have been the one to advise us on how to proceed. But Wharton couldn't find you at first, and then we got a call saying to go ahead and cremate her. The wife said it was from Wharton, but he said he never called, so I dunno. I hope it's not a problem. Elva was a practical woman, and she would have preferred cremation, I'm sure."

Kim was running what he'd said through her mind. Someone had wanted Elva cremated before any autopsy could be done. Before Kim could be found. She merely nodded. "You did the autopsy, Len. Was there anything at all that struck you as odd?"

"I wrote it all up on the death certificate."

"I know, but I was just wondering if there was something else you may have remembered after the fact that seemed off. Did it look like she'd fallen out of a skiff and hit her head?"

"Sure. What else could have happened to her?"

No one was willing to look beyond what was convenient, that Elva had died accidentally. "Thanks."

As she walked out, he said, "Think about that urn upgrade, okay? I got some overstock I can give you a discount on. They play 'You Are My Sunshine' every time someone walks near 'em."

She waved her answer and stepped out into air so heavy, she could feel the water in it. The storm had passed and the sun was turning all that moisture into a steam bath. She was covered with a sheen of perspiration by the time she reached her truck. She got in and headed back to Southern Comfort. Who had called to have the body cremated? This was like one of those mystery puzzles where you don't know what the picture is and you have to blindly put the pieces together. Why was every piece pointing to something foul?

"Because it is," she said. Or was she just looking for trouble again? The best thing for her to do was to let it go and try to earn her place in town again. Except that she'd put everything on the line to get justice for Rhonda Jones, a woman she'd known only peripherally. If she'd done that for Rhonda, she had to do it for Elva. It was only fair. Besides, she'd promised not to let Elva down again. But where did she go from here?

Was Kinsey involved or did he just want to take the easy route? He'd been more than happy to chalk up Rhonda's vicious murder to some wanderer. He hadn't wanted to look too closely into her father's death, either. While Kim didn't think Winnerow had shot her father on purpose, he still should have been prosecuted for involuntary manslaughter. Instead, he'd volunteered for a life sentence with Kitty and her angry daughter. Maybe going to jail would have been easier, after all.

Kim spotted Rhonda Jones's younger sister walking out of Tiger's Grocery Store and pulled into the parking lot. Kim and Grace were the same age and had been friends through most of school. Once Kim had moved in with the Macgregors, it had put her in a strange place with many of her previous friends. She wasn't one of "them" anymore. She wasn't a Macgregor, either. When she testified against Winnerow, everyone gave her a wide berth.

Grace had one barefoot child in tow, a girl as far as Kim could tell. When Grace saw Kim, she paused almost warily.

"Grace, it's good to see you. You look great." She looked years older than Kim.

In an automatic gesture, Grace smoothed her bright blond hair. "Good to see you, too. Heard you were in town. Sorry 'bout your grandma."

"Me, too. Why don't you come over to the bar sometime? I'll buy you a drink."

She glanced at the black-haired child who was fussing. "Don't have time with this one. This is Martha Lee, named after my mama." Martha Lee hid behind her mama's faded dress. "I married Tommy Osceola. 'Member him from school? I'm a hairdresser at the Everglades Hair Salon on Tilapia Street. Come on over if you need a trim or something."

"I sure will. How's Ernest? I still think about him from time to time."

That was an understatement. She'd never forget that little boy who looked so lost at the funeral. Rhonda's son had been five at the time of her murder. If Kim had had any thoughts about backing down, he had sealed her decision. She knew that feeling of being lost, of losing someone you loved in a sudden and wrong way.

Grace shook her head. "My mama did her best by him, but he never was the same after Rhonda's death. Acted up in school, got himself arrested for stealing a swamp buggy with some friends, you name it, he was into it. I think he's into something even bigger, but he won't say. The family won't tolerate him being into anything harder than marijuana." She laughed nervously. "We've had enough trouble over the years with the law. We don't know what to do with him."

Kim hated hearing that. "Maybe I'll visit him, see how he's doing."

"Whatever he's into, you ought to know that your granny was into it, too."

Elva and Ernest into something together? "Are you sure?"

"Sure as I can be. All right, little 'un," she said to the fussing Martha Lee. "We'll be going in a minute." To Kim she said, "I think Elva was buying something from him. She came once a month for a few months till she died."

"You saw Elva give him money?" Her grandma into drugs or other illicit dealings? Elva wasn't perfect, but she was a God-fearing woman. It made no sense.

"Yep, though Ernest denied it when I asked. The next time she come by, I hid around the corner of the house and watched them."

"What did he give her back?"

She shrugged and grabbed hold of Martha Lee's hands, which were bunching her skirt tight around her legs. "Never saw what she got for her money. They was right sneaky about it. I better get going. Gotta get dinner started. Daddy's bringing home fish tonight, ain't he, honey?" she asked her daughter.

"Big fish!" the girl said.

Kim forced a smile. "It was good seeing you, Grace, and good to meet you, Martha Lee. I'll head over tomorrow and see Ernest. Tell Tommy I said hey."

Kim sat in her truck for a few minutes before heading back to the bar. What was Elva up to? And how did her visits to Ernest fit into it? She was damn well going to find out.

# CHAPTER 14

"Tuesday nights was buy-one-get-two-free night, I swear it," Dennis Purdy was telling Kim when Zell walked up to the bar.

"And you're full of it," Zell said, leaning against the bar next to Dennis. He'd showered and changed since helping her with the window. He wore another of his sunset shirts, black jeans, and alligator boots. Not that he was dressing up for Kim, of course.

"Dammit, Zell, you spoiled it for everyone. She was that close to believing me."

Zell said, "No she wasn't." He'd been watching the exchange and could see skepticism in her eyes. "You're a two-bit lying cheat and that's the truth."

Dennis's eyes narrowed. "You Macgregors hold a grudge like it was a thorn in your asses. I was gonna help you all paint, I really was." He turned to include Kim and maybe get her on his side. "See, Winn and Zell and Owen helped me paint my place, what was it, eight years ago? A couple of years later, Winn asked me to help them out when it came time to paint their place. And I was gonna help, but I threw my back out." He rubbed the small of his back as though it were still bothering him.

"Then why were you seen tearing up the mud flats on your ATV that same day?"

Dennis's face reddened. "It got better?" he offered weakly.

"Yeah, right."

"Hell, Zell, how long are you gonna hold that against me?" He turned to Kim. "He won't even give me advice, and with Misty, heaven knows I need it." His face brightened. "Hell, Zell. I like that. Hell Zell." When he saw Zell's unamused expression, he paid for his beer and went back to his table.

Kim placed a drink in front of him. "It's on the house for helping me today."

His match. He'd never once heard Tullie say something like that. If anything, Kim was his complete opposite. Hated gators, probably hated his family just as much as they hated her. He had to admit she intrigued him, though. Her sass was something to behold, as was her body. *And I'd like to be holding that body*. The inane phrase floated through his mind. She wore a white tank top and jean overalls that gaped just enough to show a swath of her side. Her blond hair was shiny clean and flipped up at the ends. It looked all kinds of soft, and was just long enough for a man to curl his fingers into as he was driving into her . . .

He blinked and pushed away that particular image. He was already getting hell for helping her out, and it was getting harder and harder to sell his self-serving reasons. What he needed to do was go sit at his table and not talk to her anymore. The only reason he'd even stopped by was seeing Clem and Billy Bob's hunk of junk out in the lot. They giggled at their handiwork, but he gave them a look that cut those giggles to silence. Calling the cops for assault just wasn't done in Cypress. It was tantamount to tattling. He'd show them that he wasn't afraid of them, and that he wouldn't be caught unawares again.

Amy sidled up to the bar. "Hey there, sweet cousin, how's it hanging?"

"It is, and that's always a good thing. How's business?"

She glanced at the half-full bar. "I'm keeping busy. Heck, this is more fun than selling real estate, and I had to get a license for that. Kim, see that guy over there, the one that's waving at you?"

They all looked. Zell didn't recognize him, which meant he was probably a guest at the hunting lodge.

Amy said, "He wants to buy you a drink. He knows it's your bar and all, but he still wants to do it."

"Tell him thanks, but I don't drink."

Amy shrugged and headed back over. "All rightee."

Though he knew he should mosey on, he couldn't resist. "A bartender—a gal who *owns* a bar—who doesn't drink?"

"That's right."

"You allergic to alcohol? Religious zealot? A recovering alcoholic?"

She shook her head at each question.

"Well, what then?"

"I'll tell you when you tell me the second reason you want me to leave town."

He raised his hand in surrender, took his drink, and headed to his table. There were more than a couple of other reasons he wanted her to leave. Liking her was one of them.

The man who'd wanted to buy Kim a drink intercepted him. "Hey, what's up with the chick who owns the place? She a lesbo or something?"

Zell couldn't help but look at Kim reaching up a bottle high up on the shelf. "She likes men well enough, I suspect." Well-dressed boring men, at least. Is that what Kim wanted? That and a home. No wonder she was fighting to make a go of it. Being born here, she was apt to be out of place in Tallahassee. He sure would be.

"Pardon?" Zell asked when he realized the guy had said something.

"I'm going to go tell her I could eat her all night long."

Surely Kim was used to guys coming on to her if she

worked in bars. "You think she'll go for that? Does that line actually work?"

The guy, a middle-aged businessman taking a week off to play redneck, grinned. "Once in a while. I think it'll work on her. She looks just hot and gutsy enough to take it for what it is. A supreme compliment," he added at Zell's questioning look. Before he could tell the guy to think better of it, he'd marched up to the bar. Zell stood back and watched the show.

She gave away nothing in her expression after he'd obviously delivered his romantic line, but she did survey the bar to see if someone had put him up to it. Her eyes alighted on him and narrowed slightly. She'd probably seen them talking. Then she turned back to the man and said something that wilted his shoulders and probably something else, too.

He walked back to Zell. "Probably a lesbo."

Zell bet this bozo ran into a lot of lesbos, as he put it: every woman who turned him down. "What'd she say?"

He seemed to consider not telling him, but gave in. "She said, 'You might could eat me all night, but I got a big appetite myself, and your little cocktail weenie would hardly even whet it.'"

Zell let out a hoot of laughter. "Damn, but she is something else." He headed to his table.

His cousin Dougal was standing at the jukebox with a puzzled look on his face. A lot of folks thought they were brothers if they didn't know better. He turned to Zell. "What the heck is Mandoza? Never heard of 'em."

Zell tried to keep a smile from his face. "Maybe it's a new country group. Give 'em a try."

Dougal put his dollar bill into the machine and made his selections. Then he dropped into the seat opposite Zell's. "Cuz, I got to tell you about my woman troubles. You're the only one who can make sense of the lovely creatures." He was halfway into the story about Sue-Ellen and how she kept changing her mind on whether she loved him or hated him when he stopped. The South African artist had just started singing words that no one could understand. "What the heck kind of music is this?"

Everyone in the bar had stopped talking and was looking at the jukebox like it had morphed into an alien. Zell couldn't answer; he was too busy laughing.

After a night of mostly old country music, Kim was enjoying the silence as she, Smitty, and Amy cleaned up for the night.

Amy was laughing as she wiped down the tabletops. "And the look on Dougal's face, I'll never forget it! What did he say to you, anyway?"

Kim grinned, remembering the Zell look-alike stalking up to the bar. "He said, 'What kind of weird foreign music are you desecrating that jukebox with?' I have a feeling Zell had something to do with his selecting it. I'm also pretty sure he had something to do with that creepoid coming up saying he wanted to eat me all night."

Both Amy and Smitty laughed. Kim had already told them the story.

Smitty said, "Zell wouldn't tell anyone to say something like that to a gal. Likely the guy told Zell what he was going to say and when Zell couldn't talk him out of it, he just enjoyed the show."

"Hmph," Kim said as she ran the numbers for the night. But she couldn't help smiling. She was doing that a lot where Zell was concerned, and that wasn't a good thing at all.

She'd been surprised to see Sam Wharton step through the door earlier that evening, his expression sour as he scanned the bar. Kim wasn't sure if he was looking for someone or just seeing who was going to be crossed off his Christmas list. After laying a cold look on her, he'd left. Kim had resisted thumbing her nose at him.

"It was a busy night," Amy said as she threw her washrag in the bin and grabbed up her purse.

"Not busy enough. We're down by forty percent from a normal Tuesday night. Between a downturn in business and repairs, the reserve is going down fast." At Amy's worried look, she added, "We'll see how we stand next week. Maybe folks will start coming back when they see that I'm serious about staying."

"I hope so. I'm liking working here. Good night, Kim, Smitty." She leaned down and scratched Oscar's head. "Night, sweetie pig."

"I'll walk you out." Smitty walked her to her car and returned a few minutes later. "You ready?"

Kim closed up the ledger books and turned off the calculator. "Just about." She was about to tell him he didn't have to stay around but remembered Zell's words about doing just that and stopped. "Thanks for sticking around."

She grabbed up her bag, readied her tear gas, and turned off the rear lights. Smitty hit the front lights, though they were leaving the outside lights on from now on. The two jerks had come and gone without any trouble. She was hoping that was a good sign.

"Oscar, come over here!" she called when he wandered to the hedge.

"Nice truck you got," Smitty said as they approached it.

"Thanks, I—"

Everything happened so fast it was a blur. She saw someone come up behind Smitty, wrap an arm around his neck, and jerk him backward. At the same time, she felt an arm doing the same to her. She tried to twist around and aim her tear gas at whoever was behind her. Before she could get it into position, the can was wrenched out of her grip and thrown to the ground. She smelled sweat and stale smoke on the man behind her. It was definitely a man. Not only was he strong, but the fact became evident as he repositioned her against the front of him.

When the man who'd grabbed Smitty came back from around the back of her truck, she recognized him as the skinny one of the two jerks. She couldn't remember his name, but she did remember Billy Bob was the big guy— the one who had a grip on her.

"Clem, give me a hand here," Billy Bob said.

Clem rubbed his hands together and walked forward

with his gaze on her breasts. "Sure I'll give you a hand. I'll give you two hands. You can't have all the fun."

She couldn't see Smitty but didn't have time to worry about him at the moment. She jammed her heel into Billy Bob's shin, doubled over, and shoved him with her butt. Clem was already on her, grabbing at her arms. She cupped her palms and clapped his ears, something she'd learned in self-defense class.

"Dammit, I can't hear anything!" he said, giving his head a shake. Unfortunately, he recovered quickly.

Still, it gave her the chance to yell for help before Billy Bob slapped his hand hard over her mouth. It covered most of her face. "Grab her legs 'fore the bi— Dammit!"

She'd jabbed at him again and shoved backward, catching him off balance and sending them both crashing to the ground. Clem jumped on them, pinning her down. From her position down on the ground, she saw Smitty lying on the gravel behind her truck. He was moving, but not much. She tasted blood where her front teeth had been smashed into her lip. Billy Bob climbed out from beneath her and shoved Clem aside. He was pushing her into the gravel with his knee, and his hand was still covering her mouth. "We got a fighter here, don't we? Well, let's see what kind of fight you put up when we're giving you the best ride you ever had."

Clem giggled. "Free dick rides, just like it says on our bumper sticker."

She tried not to betray her raging heartbeat or the fear pulsing through her veins. The anger she had no trouble letting them see. Rocks were digging into the back of her head.

"Clem, get her keys. Find which one opens the bar door. Get the old man inside."

"Free drinks *and* free woman, this is gonna be fun!" He grabbed her keys. "We'll even get the jukebox going to cover the noises she's gonna make." He made sounds of ecstasy as he walked to the door.

As soon as Clem left, she tried to pull her leg up, but Billy Bob's more than two hundred fifty pounds of bulk had her pinned down hard. She tried to get a tooth hold on his hand, but the palm was too smooth. Sensing what she was trying to do, he pressed down even harder, jamming her teeth into her cut lip again. That made the rocks dig even deeper into her scalp.

"Got the door open!" Clem called, excitement in his voice. He started dragging Smitty into the bar, grunting under the effort.

"Maybe this'll get the message across that you aren't welcome here," Billy Bob growled. "Nobody's gonna fault us for the way we're handling this, 'cause they all want you out of here, too. We're gonna have fun, you and me and Clem. If'n you say a word to anybody, we'll come back and kill you. Got that?" Using his hand, he forced her head to nod yes. "You're going to sell the bar and house and leave, aren't you?" Again, he made her nod.

If she'd gone with Simon, some distant part of her mind said, she'd be safe right now. *No, forget that . . . They're not going to chase me out of my home.* When he jerked her to her feet, she thought, *Oh, God, they're going to rape me in my own bar. But not without a fight. I can take Clem. I'll knock his balls clear up to his throat.*

Tough thoughts for someone getting shoved toward one of the worst fates a woman could experience. She could hardly breathe for the fear coursing through her. At least Oscar wasn't around. He was hopefully still snurfling in the bushes. They would make a ham roast out of him probably.

The sound of tires on gravel made Billy Bob turn around, forcing her to turn with him. The sight of Zell's truck nearly made her melt in relief. But he wasn't much of a fighter, and unless he'd brought firepower or backup, these boys weren't going to give up the prize.

Billy Bob let out a curse as Zell stepped from the truck still wearing his tropical shirt and alligator boots. He took in the situation as he approached—a rifle hanging casually from his hand. "What's going on here, boys?"

Billy Bob had her hands gripped behind her. He'd pulled her close to him when Zell had arrived. "Just go on home, Zell. This ain't your concern."

"If you're putting a hurting on that woman, then you're wrong about that. Let her go."

Kim thought she heard faint footsteps, but her heart was racing too loud to figure out if they were real or in her head. As Billy Bob started to answer Zell, she stomped down on his foot and shoved him backward. This time she pushed away so he wouldn't take her with him. In the rush, she thought she saw Clem, who had sneaked up behind Zell, shove him forward.

As she started to scramble away, Billy Bob grabbed her ankle. Clem and Zell were going at it. Clem had jumped on top of Zell, taking advantage of his surprise. Zell was trying to buck him off with his hips, all the while moving closer to the rifle lying on the ground. She was trying to reach it, too, but Billy Bob now had a hold on both her ankles.

She heard the sound of broken glass somewhere, but didn't have time to focus on that. She kicked at Billy Bob, smashing his hand. Footsteps sounded on the gravel nearby, and before she had a chance to see who it was, Smitty was holding a broken bottle against Billy Bob's neck. "Let her go."

Smitty had a bloody bump on his forehead, but he was obviously all right. She jumped to her feet and turned to Zell, who had just knocked Clem off and grabbed the rifle. He swung it in a perfect arc at Clem's head as he got to his feet. The sound of a siren finished the excitement as a sheriff's vehicle skidded into the parking lot.

Deputy Dave DeBarro jumped out of the car with his gun in hand. "What the hell is going on here?"

Smitty dropped the bottle and took a step forward, the only one who had enough breath to talk. "These two creepoids tried to rape us," he managed before collapsing to his knees.


Billy Bob and Clem were loaded into the back of the car in cuffs once everyone had had their say.

"You sure you all don't want to see a doctor?" Dave asked before he got into his vehicle.

They all nodded and watched him drive off. Each of them turned to the others and asked simultaneously, "You all right?" They laughed, and Kim never knew how good it felt to laugh until then. Oscar had finally come out of the bushes, licking his chops after apparently finding something edible in there. She knelt down to scratch his back. "I'd pull out the first-aid kit, but it doesn't have much in it. I haven't had a chance to refill it."

Zell said, "You're both coming back to my place. I have a complete kit at home."

She was too tired and achy to think better of going to Zell's place. Besides, Smitty would be there, too.

As they gathered up their things, Smitty said, "I'm just gonna go on home."

"No you're not," Zell said. "You got quite a knock on the head. You're coming with us. You can ride with me or drive behind me." That he said to both of them.

"I'll drive," they both said, though she really just wanted to sit back and let him drive. But then Zell would have to drive her back here to get her truck.

"I'll be right back," she said, enjoying in a sick kind of way how Zell followed her into the bar to make sure she was all right. Sick because she didn't need a man looking after her, and she shouldn't like Zell being the man who was looking after her. She grabbed an unopened bottle of Captain Morgan and locked the door. "I presume you have root beer at home."

"I also have spiced rum."

"Well, this one's on me." She paused near Billy Bob's truck when one of the bumper stickers on the rear window caught her eye. FREE DICK RIDES, Clem's crude phrase. She shivered and turned away.

A few minutes later, they pulled up in front of Zell's octagon home. She was somewhat heartened to see the stuffed alligator still standing sentry on the small entrance porch. Smitty took several steps back when he saw it. Even

Oscar wasn't too sure; he backed right up into Smitty, sending him staggering farther backward.

"It's stuffed, Smitty," Zell said on a laugh. "Keeps the salesmen away, though."

Smitty took a closer look at it. "That's Elva's gator, isn't it?"

"I gave it to Zell, sort of a peace offering for kicking him out of my bar. Who knew I'd need him to rescue me so many times?"

Zell opened the door and stepped aside. "Yeah, I'm just a regular hero nowadays."

She felt a hitch in her chest at the sight of him, still banged up from the last scuffle and now with a few new scratches. "I'm sorry, Zell." There, that hadn't been so bad. It had come out all on its own and made her feel a little bit better.

"Hey, I'm the one who drove by to make sure they weren't hanging around. It was my choice."

She suspected it went deeper than just being a choice with Zell. He felt compelled to protect her—only because she was a woman, she quickly reminded herself when something close to adulation started filling her chest. She walked inside the house and came to a stop.

"Wow. This place is incredible." She'd never seen anything like it. The shape of the house was one thing, lending interesting angles to the common areas. The living room, dining area, and kitchen were on the left side of the house. In the center was a fountain; water bubbled over a stone alligator into a copper basin. Two stories of windows opened the house to the night. Upstairs was an open loft.

"My bedroom," he said right behind her.

She jumped at both his nearness and his words. "Pardon?"

"That's my bedroom you were looking at. I've got another bedroom over there." He pointed to one of the doors behind the fountain. "Office is in here." She could see it through French doors, lined with built-in shelves and a desk. "Bathroom's over there. I'll get the first-aid kit."

Smitty said, "Let's get this forced doctoring over with. I want to go home."

"You sure you don't want to crash here in case you die in the night or something?" Zell said as he walked into his office.

"Naw, I want to die in my own bed."

"Suit yourself. But ladies first."

"I'm fine," she said, glad for a few minutes alone to let the adrenaline drain. "Do Smitty first."

"All right, old man, come on in and let me flash a light in your eyes."

"Need some help?" she asked. Oscar started rubbing against one of the corners, and she quickly shoved him away. She'd seen the dirt marks from where he did that at home. So he rubbed against her instead.

"I've got it," Zell said at the same time that Smitty said, "Don't need no woman fussing over me."

Kim pressed her hand against the back of her head as she walked around the living room area. Blood dotted her shaking fingers. She focused on the unique décor instead, keeping bad thoughts at bay. There were old pictures, paper rifle shells in a glass case, a bottle of some clear liquid, and even an old jail cell turned into a small wet bar. The place looked more like a museum, the many items showcased against every bit of available wall space. There was a lot of gas station paraphernalia. An old pump sat in one corner, topped by a lighted Texaco sign. Old tin signs, some rusted, touted things like Socony aircraft oils, Dr Pepper ("When Hungry, Thirsty, or Tired"), and Welch-Penn motor oil. One sign read, "Authorized dealer Stewart-Warner South Wind car heater. Heats *HOT* in 90 seconds." A large frame held a sepia-toned hand-drawn map.

"Those are from my granddad Zelwig's service station, before he started the alligator farm," Zell said from behind her, making her jump. "The map is one he drew up before there were any maps down here. When he was a kid, he took surveying crews into the swamp." He walked into the kitchen and filled a glass with water, then grabbed a bottle of aspirin from the cabinet.

Smitty followed, sporting a bandage on his head. "No

concussion," he said to Kim's unspoken question. "Just a little knock on the noggin." He took the glass and pills from Zell and downed them in one long gulp. After setting the glass on the counter, he looked Kim over. "You gonna be all right, young'un?"

She nodded. "I'll be fine." The shakiness in her voice gave her away; she could see it in Zell's expression.

Smitty bid them farewell and headed out. Zell pulled one of the stools from the long counter around to the kitchen. He patted it and set the first-aid kit on the counter. As she settled onto the stool, he fixed two tumblers and handed her one. "Sounds like you need it."

"I'm fine," she repeated, but took a long swig . . . and nearly choked on it. She took another sip. "It's not bad." The spices in the root beer blended perfectly with the spiced rum.

His first-aid kit put hers to shame. He opened a medicated pad and gestured for her to turn around. "I take this whenever I go out," he said, nodding toward the wetlands north of the house. He touched the pad to the back of her head. "Ouch. Does it hurt?"

She hissed. "It does now. You don't have to do this, Zell. I can handle it." It felt strange to have him fuss over her like this. No one had fussed over her since her dad had died.

"How can you tend to something you can't see?" He continued to swab at the assaulted skin.

She gave up and enjoyed it. Well, as much as she could, being in pain and all. "You're pretty good at this. Did you get a degree in nursing, too?"

He chuckled. "No, just read up on it. Had to, working with gators and being so far from civilization at times. And Dad, he was always getting into scrapes of some kind or another." He drifted into silence.

Zell had had to grow up awfully fast. She couldn't blame him for not wanting someone else to look after. She wasn't even his girlfriend, not even his friend, technically, and look at the trouble she'd caused him.

"Is it bad?" she asked.

"Just some small cuts." He moved in front of her, face to face. "You've got some down the back of your arm, too." His finger skimmed down her skin.

"He was sitting on me," she said as it came back. She shuddered. "He was sitting on me telling me what he was going to do to me."

He brushed his thumb against her lips. "Shh, don't think about it. You're all right now. It's over. 'Sides, they probably would have chickened out."

"Zell, why are you doing this? Why did you come by the bar tonight? You don't owe me anything. Just the opposite, in fact."

He let his hand drop away from her mouth. "I'm not thinking about the whys, just what needs to be done." He turned her head back and continued administering first aid.

She saw crayon drawings on the refrigerator, signed lovingly by Tullie. One was obviously Zell wrestling with a gator. She felt all tight inside. His gentle touches weren't helping. She tried focusing on the living room instead. A traffic light with only red and green lights hung from the center of the ceiling, alternating between Stop and Go. Yes and no. She wanted to tell him to stop and she wanted him to never stop touching her. "What's in that bottle up there on the shelf?"

"My granddad's moonshine. The bowl of the fountain is the top of his still. Granddad Zelwig learned shinin' early on from his dad. Between the Depression and the hurricanes it was tough times back in the twenties and thirties. The family put up on shell mounds, trying to make a living by farming and trapping whatever was in fashion at the time."

"Like poor egrets."

"Their feathers were all the rage. They were hunted to near extinction."

Kim had heard about the old-timers camping on the mounds of shells that made up small, barely habitable islands. "It must have been a hard living."

"So hard that after a while, they had to resort to illegal activities, like hunting gators and making shine.

"Even when Prohibition ended, Zelwig continued with the shine. The old-timers said he made the best in the area. He used to set up fake stills all around the swamps to throw off the law. Had to move the real one around a lot. They had a big cowbell on the front porch, and when word got out that the law was coming, someone rang the bell. Everyone in the family got together and moved the still to a clump of mangroves until it was safe."

By the time he'd finished the story, he had put salve on her scalp and had started on her arms. His fingers felt warm against her neck as he brushed away loose bits of gravel. His hands skimmed down the front of her arms as he cleaned the scrapes on the back. When she turned to watch him, he was totally focused on his task. She couldn't quite read what was in his eyes other than a burning intensity. Anger at the two men, maybe? She hoped, because she didn't want to see that intensity aimed at her.

Once he finished her other arm, he took her hand and inspected it. Her palms were all right, but her knuckles were bruised where she'd hit Billy Bob. Very slowly, he raised those bruised knuckles and brushed them against his mouth. She shivered. His gaze met hers, and she could *hear* the silence in the room. She pulled her hand back and whispered, "I should take care of you now." Yes, that's what she needed to do.

She turned to the kit and pulled out another medicated pad while he positioned himself between her legs, leaning against the counter where she sat. He had a wide scrape on his right cheek where he'd hit the gravel. He didn't move as she ran the pad across his skin. Didn't move his gaze from hers, either. Her voice came out low when she said, "This is beginning to be a habit."

"Mmhm," was all he said.

As she smoothed on the antibiotic with her thumb, the tips of her fingers slid into his hair. She dropped her hand

and wiped off the rest of the salve. "Is there . . . are you
hurt anywhere else?" A loaded question, she realized.

"Just a few new bruises."

She took a drink, just a small sip. Not enough to bend
her sensibilities and make her think Zell had been very
close to kissing her.

"You're obviously not against alcohol as a rule. Why don't
you drink?" he asked, leaning against the counter between her
legs again. She felt his breath against her chin, smelled the
spice of the soda and the husky scent of the alcohol.

"I don't like losing control."

He nodded. "Is that why you pick guys like Simon?
Cool, calm, and professional?"

"Yes," she heard herself answer much too honestly. It
was hard to lie when he was so close. She could feel them
moving toward a line, enemy and friend.

"Why, Kim, I think someone must have broke your
heart along the way."

She couldn't help her soft laughter at his using her earlier supposition. "I don't want to talk about it."

His voice was low and coaxing. "I am the Sage, you
know. Maybe I can help."

She closed her eyes and leaned her head back. Oh, man,
could he help. Except that he didn't mean that kind of help.
"The only man I ever gave my heart to broke it." She took
a breath and opened her eyes. "He played reckless and got
himself shot."

"Your dad. I'm sorry about that."

She lifted her gaze to him. "Why would you want to
give me advice? Last I heard, you wanted me out of town."

"For good reasons."

She tilted her head. "I don't think I heard all those
reasons."

He braced his hands on the counter on either side of her.
"I knew you were going to be trouble the minute I heard
you were in town. I just never imagined what kind of trouble. Your being back is putting me in a weird place."

"Like between my legs," she said with a wry smile, glancing down when he clearly thought she'd meant it some other way. "The way you're standing."

"Ah." But he didn't move.

She realized he'd actually answered her quasi-question. He'd stepped on that line. "What's the weird place?" she asked.

"I should hate you because of my family, but I'm having a hard time hating you. I want to make sure you're safe, but I get a hassle every time I get between you and those boys. It's got me turned upside down."

Her heart was thumping low and heavy in her chest. She brushed her finger over the healing cut above his eyebrow and caught his slight intake of breath. "I didn't mean to cause you trouble."

"Yeah, that's the other thing." He gave a long shake of his head. "I want you to be this coldhearted bitch-on-wheels." He pulled her off the counter and set her on her feet. "It's damn impolite of you to be so appealing." He swept her with his gaze, one part annoyance and two parts something much more interesting.

She tried hard not to grin at those words. "Sorry about that. I'll try to step on your feet once in a while. Maybe kick you out of the bar again. Would that help?"

They shared a smile, and her heart tripped over that smile of his. No man should be armed with a weapon like that around a vulnerable woman.

"Don't kick me out. That was too embarrassing. Why don't you just call me names instead?"

She rolled her eyes. "Let's see . . . dork, dog breath, bonehead—"

He kissed her. His mouth covered hers as though he'd been doing it for years. She hadn't realized how much she'd wanted this, but the rush of relief that was mixed in with surprise was proof enough if she'd needed more than the sigh she'd let out. The kiss was tender, sweet, and short enough to make her want more.

"Stay here tonight."

She blinked. "Boy, you move fast."

He laughed, and she swore she saw a tinge of color brighten his cheeks for a second, "I meant in the guest room. Once Buck hears his two boys got arrested, you never know what he's likely to do, especially after drinking all day." He rubbed her chin, but his gaze was on her mouth. "Just for the record, I don't think it'd be a good idea at all for you and me to start anything."

"No, probably not," she said on words as light as a breeze. She cleared her throat. "Definitely not. We have a lot of . . . history. And you have loyalties."

His laugh was humorless. "Loyalties. Yeah, that about sums it up."

"You were willing to lie on the witness stand—to perjure yourself for those loyalties."

"I was. I did. Back then, loyalty was more important than the truth. Or even the law."

She looked into his eyes and wondered if she saw regret. "And now?"

"I don't know anymore. Told you I was turned upside down."

He slowly, perhaps reluctantly, pulled away, walked to a linen closet, and took out a pile of towels. "For Oscar," he explained. "The bed in the guest room is made. I'll be next door if you need anything. I've got some work to finish." He nodded toward the office. "I may be gone by the time you get up; I've got to present my report to the state in the morning. Just make yourself at home."

Those last words twanged at her heart and made her realize just how at home she did feel here. "Thanks," she said in a softer voice than she'd intended.

"Do you need a shirt to sleep in?"

"No, I'll be fine." She wasn't sure what to make of Zell. That she wanted to make something of him scared her more than anything.

# CHAPTER 15

Kim woke the next morning and discovered that it wasn't morning at all—it was two minutes past noon. She pushed out of her bed and discovered that it *wasn't* her bed. Everything rushed back and swirled around in her head with the dizziness that came from moving too fast. The attack, fear, and Zell's tender kiss. When she managed to push back those disturbing images and regain her mental footing, she looked down to find Oscar missing. No wonder she'd slept so late.

The back of her head ached like someone had taken a meat tenderizer to it. She checked the pillowcase; at least she hadn't bled during the night. The only marks were the residue from the antibiotic. She felt out of sorts, achy, and dragged out.

Hanging on the inside doorknob was a shirt—a tropical one with pink hibiscuses scattered over a background of a blue-green that matched Zell's eyes. Without even bothering to put her bra on, she slid into the shirt. It smelled new and felt store-crisp. She slid into her overalls and stepped outside the bedroom.

The house was quiet. She remembered Zell saying he probably wouldn't be there. A sun-gilded peace filled the place and soothed her soul. With the white carpets and beige and brown furniture, it felt warm and sit-right-down-and-make-yourself-at-home comfortable. She wandered over to the hand-drawn map and found Red Ant Camp. Macgregor's Landing was to the east of that. Oscar lifted his head from a pile of towels near the kitchen, and then trotted over to greet her.

She was getting used to the strange feel of his skin and hair, and even that ugly face was beginning to grow on her.

"Good morning, sweetie pig," she said, borrowing Amy's phrase.

Amy! The bar! Oh, crap. She searched for a phone and called Southern Comfort. Smitty answered.

"It's Kim. I overslept. You got it under control?"

Smitty chuckled. "Overslept, eh? Yep, it's fine here. Wednesdays are usually slow, so if'n you want to snuggle on in with Zell—"

"I'm not snuggling with Zell, so just get those dirty thoughts out of your mind. I slept in the guest bedroom. How are you feeling?"

"Ah, got a bit of a headache, but I'm okay. How 'bout you?"

"I'm achy and I want a shower really bad, but otherwise, I'll make it." She took in the room filled with Zell's legacy. "I just hope I didn't cause more trouble for Zell."

"Ah, he can handle it. The important thing is that you're all right. I was serious about you relaxing for a while. I can cover lunch."

"I may take you up on that. I've got someone I need to see. Did you know about Elva buying something from Ernest Jones?"

After a pause, he said, "You aren't digging again, are you?"

"You thought she was up to something. If Elva was murdered, don't you want to find out who did it and why?"

"Not if it sullies her name and gets me killed in the process." The warning in his voice was clear. "Sometimes the truth's not worth knowing. If you mean it about staying here, let it go. You, especially you, have a lot more to lose by pointing fingers."

She walked into the kitchen and found a note from Zell, hydrogen peroxide, and the tube of ointment. "I'm not going to point fingers at anyone. I'm not going to specu-late. I'm just going to see what I can find out. I'll see you tonight then." She hung up before he could talk her out of seeing Ernest and leaned over to read the note.

*Kim, put another dose on those cuts. I heard Oscar mak-ing noises so I let him out. Also hung a shirt you can wear. Shar gave it to me for Christmas a couple years ago. It's too girly for me, so you can have it. Bye.* He signed his name with a flourish. She smiled. Then frowned. Zell was obviously used to taking care of people. Now she had inad-vertently come under his care. Exactly what he didn't want.

It was strange being in his house alone. Like they'd shared some intimacy the night before. Like they'd had wild, crazy, heavy-breathing sex. Not that she knew what that was like. Outside the windows she caught a glimpse of decking, and off to one side was a large barbecue grill and picnic bench. He'd left the deck unscreened so it wouldn't obliterate the view, no doubt. She wondered what it was like to wake up to a sea of golden marsh prairie every day. She glanced up at the bedroom loft and decided that think-ing about regularly waking up here was not a good idea.

"Come on, Oscar, let's go home." She'd take a shower there.

She bundled up the sheets, found the small utility room, and started a load of laundry. She jotted a thank-you on Zell's note and let him know about the load in the washer. As soon as she opened the front door to leave, she came face-to-face with Charlotte Macgregor. Perfect, just perfect.

She'd been touching the stuffed alligator, probably trying to figure out if it was real. At the sight of Kim, she popped straight up and her face went white. "What are you doing here? And wearing Zell's clothes?" She looked around Kim. "Is he here?" She wore a flowered summer short set that accented her trim figure and made her look as fresh as a hothouse flower. At least until she whipped out a cigarette and lit it, as though she needed fortification at the sight of Kim.

"No, he had a job to do. This isn't what it looks like." A trite line, she knew, but accurate. "Smitty and I were assaulted at the bar last night."

Charlotte narrowed her eyes. "I know, that's why I came over, to see if Zell was all right and to find out what the hell happened. Knew you were involved somehow." She looked Kim up and down. "Didn't realize just how involved."

Kim might have told her to mind her own damn business, but she'd caused Zell enough trouble without trying. "Billy Bob and Clem jumped me and Smitty as we left the bar. Zell happened to be driving by and stopped to help. He insisted Smitty and I come here so he could see to our cuts. He let me stay the night in the guest bedroom when he saw how tired I was. That's all there is to it."

Charlotte crossed her arms and tapped her long, now gold-flecked nails against her arms. Trails of smoke followed her movements. "You in love with my brother?"

"No." She was trying really hard not to be, anyway. "He's not my type of guy." Not even close.

"You sure? 'Cause you could get him in a lot of trouble with his family. He doesn't need a woman who causes him problems, know what I mean?"

"Sure do." Kim stepped farther out and closed the door. Oscar had already meandered out to her truck. Despite their past, she was beginning to like Zell too much to cause him trouble. Especially with his family. "See you later." She started to walk past, but Charlotte's words stopped her.

"Are you all right?" She didn't have the gleam of someone who wanted gossip. She looked sincere.

Kim showed her the backs of her arms, the bruised knuckles Zell had brushed against his mouth, and finally the back of her head. "I'll be okay. Smitty took a hit on the head." At Charlotte's widened eyes, she added, "He's okay, too. Billy Bob and Clem are in jail." She found that talking about it made her edgy. "I have to get going."

She felt sloppy around Charlotte, and it didn't help that she watched Kim give Oscar the heave-ho to get him into the truck. When she walked around to the driver's side, Charlotte said, "You ought to come around when the baby gators start hatching. It's the most precious thing you'll ever see, even if you don't like gators."

Kim was so startled by the invitation she didn't immediately say *Forget that.* "I'll take your word on the precious part. But I'll keep it in mind."

Charlotte watched her back around and head down the road, a contemplative expression on her face. Even as a teenager, Charlotte hadn't been easy to read. As pretty as she was, she could cut someone down with a tongue that could be rapier-sharp one minute and then honey-sweet the next. So why did Kim feel touched that Charlotte had asked how she was? After moving to Heron's Glen, she had wanted to earn her stepsister's friendship. Strange how she kind of felt that way again.

"Just what we need," she said to Oscar. "To become friends with the Macgregors."

A part of her did need that, though, as much as she wanted to deny it. That sense of home and belonging pulled at her like a drink pulled at an alcoholic. It was bound to cause problems, though. Winnerow would never forgive her . . . and she wasn't sure she could ever forgive him, either.

Kim had showered, changed, and started unpacking some of her boxes. She replaced some of Elva's paintings with her framed prints of the Everglades. Her bottle of tequila earned a special place on the mantel. She added her pictures to Elva's. She opened some of the *Good Housekeeping* and *Better Homes and Gardens* magazines to the pages where she'd bent down the corners and eyed several places in the house that needed decorating improvement. She jotted down a list of things to get at the hardware store in the near future.

"Oh, Simon." He'd just thrown her philodendron and fern in one of the boxes. They'd tipped sideways and their roots were exposed. She stuffed them back into their pots, gave them a good watering, and set them out on the porch.

At noon, she was ready to head out to Ernest's place when JoGene's truck pulled into her drive. The sight brought back old memories when seeing him pull in made her heart do a little dance. Now she wondered how much he knew about the previous night's events and if Charlotte would be out telling people that Kim had spent the night with Zell. Or for that matter, Smitty could be enjoying telling that tale, since the old coot liked to blab.

Like a watchdog, Oscar walked right over to JoGene when he stepped out of his truck and checked him out. "Hey, Oscar," JoGene said, giving the pig a scratch on the head. He was dressed up, wearing new jeans and one of those western-style shirts with the opalescent buttons. "Hey, Kim."

Luckily she wasn't wearing Zell's shirt, which would have been a giveaway since he was the only one in town who wore those bright shirts. "Hey, JoGene."

"You look good," he said, nodding toward her white pants and gray shirt.

"Ah, thanks." She'd purposely dressed in her least attractive outfit after last night.

"Stopped by the bar, but Smitty said you'd taken some time off. You doing okay?"

Thank goodness he hadn't said anything about her being at Zell's. It didn't surprise her that JoGene knew about the assault. Probably everybody in town did by now. "I'm fine as long as they keep those two creepoids in jail. Bet your dad's mad at me for getting them put away."

He waved away his dad and jammed the tips of his fingers in his front pockets. "He's mad about everything. I told him to lay off you."

Kim wasn't exactly comforted. "You're standing your ground with him. Good for you."

Determination gleamed in his eyes. "Yeah, I am. Glad

those two didn't do more than put a few scrapes on you. They'll probably think better of it sitting in jail."

"I hope so. I was just heading out." She hoped he'd get to the point.

"Want some company?"

No way did she want JoGene knowing what she was up to. "I'm taking care of some personal business, but thanks anyway." She waved Oscar to the passenger side of the truck. "What brings you out here?"

He swallowed hard and grabbed hold of her arm. "I'm scared for you, Kim. Billy Bob and Clem, they're just the beginning. And they're not the ones that vandalized your bar; they were out with my dad that night."

She tried to pull free of his grip without making a big deal of it but couldn't. "If you know something—"

"I couldn't rat on someone, Kim." He tightened his hold on her. "But I can tell you that there are people in this town who don't want you here. People who'd do anything to run you out now that you're snooping around Elva's death. They think you're just here to cause trouble again. They're mad at Zell for interfering last night. I don't want you hurt, or worse. You need to leave, the sooner the better. Cut your losses, sell out, and go. No matter what happened ten years ago, I still care about you." He finally loosened his grip and awkwardly put his hand on her shoulder.

She resisted the urge to step back. "Who, JoGene? Who wants me out?"

"Plenty of folks. I can tell my dad not to mess with you, but I don't know how long I can hold him off. Wharton wants you gone. Owen says Winn's real edgy about you being back. Even Owen, out of loyalty. Speaking of, Zell might seem like your friend, but don't forget he's a Macgregor. He may do what he damn well pleases, but you ain't got a future with him."

That last stung because she knew it was true. "There's nothing between us."

"For all you know, he might be spying, seeing what you're up to."

"I'll keep that in mind."

He gave her shoulder a squeeze and let go. "I hope you do. I'm just thinking of your best interests, and staying alive is a good idea, don't you think?"

She waited for him to leave before getting into her truck. What did he have to gain by her leaving? Maybe Buck was giving him a hard time, the same way Zell's family was giving him trouble over her. She hated not being able to trust anyone.

She drove past Southern Comfort just to make sure all was well. There wasn't any sign of the scuffle the night before other than the skid marks from both Zell's truck and the deputy's vehicle. Billy Bob's truck was gone, too. Since it was past two, the bar was closed and Smitty had obviously gone home.

She headed south. The main road split off at the southernmost portion of town. To the right were the docks and her old neighborhood. To the left it crossed the Snake River. The RV park where Smitty lived was on the left, and the Gun and Rod Club was straight ahead. She veered right where the road turned to gravel and into the section known as Otter's Tail. If it weren't for the thick layer of mangroves buffering Otter's Tail from the bay, the ramshackle homes here would have a great view. This was po's po country, the poorest of the residents. This was where the Joneses carried on their illegal activities far from the eye of the law or anyone else who cared.

The homes were spread out among the thick forest of cypress. The road here wasn't even gravel, just hard-packed dirt with water-filled ruts. Despite the road and ramshackle homes, the area was beautiful in its own way. Majestic old cypress trees were covered in air plants and draped in moss, their knobby knees protruding from the waterlogged areas. Like the vastness of Zell's marsh prairie and solitude of her hammock, this place made her feel far, far from civilization.

A rusty old washing machine sitting on the corner of the first street brought her back. Several yards from the road sat the ghost of an old truck grown over with weeds and vines. The houses were set way off the main road.

Kim remembered coming here after Rhonda's death to visit Ernest. He and his mother had lived in his grandmother's house. Ernest wouldn't be that quiet little boy anymore. He'd be almost a man now, left with a bitter legacy. His grandmother had passed on a few years earlier. Ernest was now living in his childhood home as an emancipated minor.

His house was on the end of what could barely be called a street considering the three inches of water that covered most of its surface. She had no idea how she'd be received, but surely he'd remember her and what she'd done for his mother.

A light green truck roughly in the same shape as the one she'd spotted in the weeds sat in front of the small house. The hood was up, and she saw someone working on it. The young man peered around the hood as her truck splashed down his driveway. He was a nice-looking guy, with blond hair and startling blue eyes that narrowed suspiciously as he approached her. No one knew who his father was; Rhonda had kept her mouth shut on that.

"You stay in here, Oscar," she said, waving to the young man. She stepped out and tried to place that boy's face against the one she saw now. "Ernest?"

"Yeah? Who're you?"

"Kim Lyons."

She waited until the recognition dawned on his blunt features. "Kim, yeah, I remember you. You left town on account of . . . well, everything that happened." He wiped his hands on his faded jeans. "You come to see me?"

"Yeah." She took in the place. Not too bad, considering. At least there wasn't a toilet in the front yard like the first house on the street. "How are you doing?"

"Gettin' by. Heard you was back in town. Sorry about your grandma."

She gave him the opportunity to say more, but he didn't. "Thanks. I'm going to miss her."

He ran his hand across his perspiring forehead, leaving a smudge behind. "Me, too."

"I understand you were friends."

"Ah, I don't know that you'd call us friends. We didn't hang out or anything like that. But she was good to me."

She leaned casually against the fender of his truck. "Ernest—"

"They call me Ernie now."

"Okay, Ernie, I need your help on something. I need you to tell me the truth."

He hesitated, but said, "Suppose I owe you that, after all you did for my mama. Even if they didn't get a conviction."

She'd failed. She remembered his face when Winn had been proclaimed not guilty. He'd been sitting with his grandmother during most of the trial. "Sometimes murderers get away. It's not fair, but it happens. Maybe a little too often. Ernest—Ernie, I need to ask you something. Elva was coming to see you before she died. Every month, Grace said." When he nodded, she continued. "She was buying something from you."

He ran his arm across his forehead again. "I wasn't supposed to tell anyone about it. Elva made me promise."

"I'm sure she did, but she's dead now. I'm her granddaughter, and I'm looking for some answers. There are payments on the books at the bar, and I'm trying to figure out what they're for. Did she borrow money from you?"

He made a sound between a laugh and a snort. "Me loan someone money? I don't think so. Ain't got nothing to sell, neither. She was just giving it to me, I swear."

He looked uncomfortable, shifting and fidgeting. She outwaited him, and finally he said, "She come here a few months back, out of the blue, and gave me two hundred fifty dollars. Just like that, no explanation or nothing. She came the next month and did it again. Someone don't just give you that kind of money for nothing, right? I wouldn't let her leave until she told me, and she made me promise not to tell anyone." He agonized over it for a few more seconds. "She said the money was coming from the person that killed my mama. She said they owed it to me."

Kim couldn't talk for a moment. "Elva gave you money from the person who killed Rhonda," she clarified. "You said *they.*"

"She wouldn't say who it was, or if it was one person or more. At first I thought it was nice of 'em to give me money like that. I figured they musta felt guilty."

The payments of five hundred dollars—they weren't outgoing, they were incoming. Elva was collecting the money and giving half to Ernie and half to Zell in payment for the loan. "Oh, God, she was blackmailing Rhonda's murderer."

He raised his hands. "I don't know nothing about blackmail. She just gave me the money and said it was owed to me and I'd be seeing it for two years. Told me not to tell anybody about it. Not even Gracie knows. She seen Elva out here once, but I wouldn't tell her why. When Elva died, I got kinda worried that it had something to do with that money, but I couldn't tell nobody. And then I kinda pushed it out of my mind 'cause it was uncomfortable thinking about it."

Kim drooped against the truck. This was not what she'd expected. Elva knew who had murdered Rhonda. But how had she found out? Kim would likely never know. She remembered the messy files. The murderer had been looking for something, probably whatever evidence Elva was holding over his head. Then he'd killed her and made it look like an accident. Kim rubbed her hand over her face as she tried to comprehend it all. Once again, Tullie was right; the truth was looking worse and worse. She glanced up at Ernie. "No one knows about this?"

"Nope. No one but you, me, and Elva, her being in the past tense nowadays."

She pushed away from the truck with shaky arms. "Keep it that way. Don't even tell anyone I came here."

As she walked away, he asked, "It was just an accident, what happened to Elva, wasn't it? I'd hate to think it was because of her getting that money for me."

"Yeah, it was an accident." She was surer than ever that it wasn't.

When she pulled back onto the road, she spotted another vehicle way up ahead, though she couldn't see what it was. From a distance, it looked like the cypress trees flanking the road eventually closed it up completely. Once she reached the gravel portion of the road, she saw no other vehicle.

She turned her thoughts back to Elva. She couldn't go to the sheriff's office with this information. They probably wouldn't believe Ernest anyway, thinking Kim was cooking up another conspiracy plot.

"Oh, Elva, why didn't you call and tell me you knew who had murdered Rhonda? Or at least leave me a letter?" Maybe there had been a letter in the file cabinet telling her who the killer was.

The killer. Her first thought was Winnerow, but he was wheelchair-bound now. He'd have a hard time sneaking into Elva's home and hitting her on the head, much less taking her out in the skiff. Unless he wasn't as helpless as he wanted people to think. Or probably he had someone else do it. Loyalties ran deep around there. It could be anyone: Zell, Owen, Buck, even JoGene or those two creepoids. Which one? How many?

Or she could let it go. Her fingers tightened on the steering wheel. Someone had killed her grandma, maybe the same person who had killed Rhonda and gotten away with it. Maybe even the same person who had killed her father and gotten away with it. No, she couldn't let this go, couldn't let Winnerow keep getting away with murder. Not now.

Like the clever and persistent raccoon, Kim had scented on the truth and was now digging for it. Her truck passed the hiding spot in the thick forest of cypress and continued on. She had talked with Ernest. What did he know?

Oh, she could have visited with him to see how he was

doing. But folks rarely came out to Otter's Tail to just visit. You either knew the resident well enough to feel at home here, or you met them in town. No, Kim was foraging, just like she'd done looking through the file cabinet. Kim suspected that Elva had been murdered; she knew just enough to be dangerous.

Sometimes raccoons were eaten as they foraged. Like the coon near the shore at Kim's house. The gator had snapped it up, a drama of life and death played out in the darkness. *Wonder if that raccoon knew what had eaten it. Well, Kim would know if she kept digging. She would damn well know who was going to kill her. Just as Elva had known. Now, how to find out what Ernie told her. There were ways to find out just about anything here in Cypress.*

Kim's biggest fear was alligators. Everyone knew that. That was the big joke years ago, how she'd hated gators and ended up living with Macgregors who had a farm full of them. Maybe one of those beasts would see her as a morsel and tear her to bits.

"Keep digging, Kim. You'll dig yourself right into a grave."

# CHAPTER 16

Zell knew he'd be the reason Winnerow had summoned the family to dinner that evening. He didn't know which was worse, looking after Winn like he was a child or being subjected to his new role as family patriarch. They ate a pleasant dinner and discussed the farm and Zell's next egg-collecting foray. He noticed all of them taking in the newest scrape across his cheek, but no one except Tullie asked if he was all right.

As soon as Gisella had cleared the dinner dishes and brought in a slab of strawberry shortcake for dessert, Winn leaned forward and let him have it. "What the hell were you thinking, boy, taking up for her like that—*again*?"

Shar was giving him a cat-that-ate-the-canary look, whatever that was about.

He hated having to defend his actions, something he hadn't had to do since his mother's death. "I'm supposed to see those two guys attacking her and Smitty and just drive on by? Smitty's family, or did you forget?"

Owen asked, "What were you doing there, anyway? The bar was closed."

He narrowed his eyes at Owen, who was becoming a real mouth lately. When he glanced at Shar for her reaction, her mouth had gone slack and her eyes were heavy.

She was looking at Owen like she wanted to eat him up.

"Where I drive and why is my own damn business. We had a talk about that very subject, I believe."

Owen's cheeks reddened and he looked to Winn to back him up.

"Are you interested in her or not? That's what I want to know," Winn said.

Zell took a forkful of shortcake and ate it slowly. She interested him, that was the truth. "I'm not going to stand by and watch someone beat up on her or any woman."

"You didn't answer my question," Winn said, narrowing his eyes. "Or maybe you did."

Shar had aimed that grin at him again. Tullie was silently taking it all in like she always did. She was no doubt thinking of her proclamation that he and Kim were a match.

Zell started to pick up his plate. "If all you want to do is interrogate me, I'll just take my dessert and leave."

"Sit down," Winn said. "You might think you ran this family before, but you don't anymore, not until I'm dead. If you got some point to prove to me, prove it with someone else I don't like."

Shar said, "There are plenty of 'em, too. I can name six right off the top of my head who'd be more than glad to take up with you."

"I've been out with half of them, and there's a reason I'm not dating them. Besides, I have no intention of settling down, so stop worrying about my love life." He hoped no one got wind of the fact that Kim had spent the night. No one would believe he'd set her up in the guest room.

Owen looked way too pleased by this turn of events. "She's up to something. JoGene saw her going out to Otter's Tail today. Only one person she could be seeing out that way."

"Ernest Jones," Shar said, a trace of dread in her voice. "She wouldn't be stupid enough to dig up that mess again, would she? If she's still got Daddy in her sights, he can't be retried."

Zell said, "Maybe she just went out there to see how he

was doing." He finished the last of the whipped cream on his plate and stood. "Well, it's been nothing but lovely, but I've got a report to write up, so I'll bid you all good night."

"Zell, did you sleep with that woman?" Shar asked, stopping his escape. "I saw her at your place this afternoon, wearing that shirt I gave you for Christmas that I've never seen you wear." She made sure he knew how that made her feel.

"I knew it!" Winn stood, actually *stood,* threw his fork across the table, and spewed words unfit for Tullie's delicate ears. "Have you forgotten what it means to be a Macgregor? Are you trying to disgrace this family, Zell?"

He had to hold his tongue on that one as well as his temper. He shot his sister a cool look as he stood. "The shirt's too girly for me. I told you that when I opened it." He headed to the kitchen and set the plate on the counter.

"You didn't answer my question!" she called after him.

"No, I didn't." He walked past the dining room on his way to the front door.

"Well, what did he mean by that?" she asked the other members of the family. "That he didn't sleep with her or didn't answer us?"

Winn's voice sounded as hard and edgy as the gravel Zell had gotten so intimate with the night before. "I'm not going to let that girl destroy our lives again."

Owen said, "Neither am I," in the same tone.

Zell stepped outside into the muggy air. As usual, everything was wet from the afternoon storm. The mosquitoes were out full force, scenting his flesh immediately and swarming on him. He walked to his truck and got in. Before he could start it, Shar dashed out the door and ran to his truck. She was breathless when she jumped into the passenger seat.

"I'm sorry, Zell, I didn't mean to cause you trouble. It just came out 'cause I wanted to know so bad. I've been holding it in all day." She sounded like a little girl pleading for forgiveness and explaining herself. She knew exactly what she'd been doing: causing trouble.

"You could have asked me when we were alone. You know that kind of thing riles Dad."

Shar's contriteness had passed. She scooted closer like she was sharing gossip about someone else. "I couldn't believe it when I pulled up and there she was coming out like an easy girl on a Sunday morning. If it makes it better, she did say you hadn't slept together. Said she slept in the living room on the couch."

"In the guest bedroom," he said, knowing she was trying to trip him up. "The only company she had was the pig. Now scoot. I've had enough of my family."

She gave him a little pout, kissed his cheek, and got out. "Be good, brother of mine. You'll give Daddy another stroke if you take up with that girl."

"I'll keep that in mind." He started the truck, but his escape was thwarted again when Winn waved him down from the entrance. As much as Zell wanted to ignore the man, he couldn't. For a moment, Zell even felt sorry for him as he made his way down the walkway with his cane. Sometimes he thought Winn was milking his ill health, but recently he seemed stronger. He walked shakily to Zell's window.

"Whatever has passed between us, find some other way to punish me. I'm asking you, not as my son but as a Macgregor, encourage that girl to leave town. Please, Zell."

Those last words, laced with desperation, got his attention, "What are you afraid of her finding?"

Shame colored Winn's face. "I just want her out of here so she doesn't cause trouble again. Promise me you'll stop fighting her fights and helping her fix up her place."

"Not until you tell me why you want her out of town so bad."

Winn seemed to consider telling him, but let out a sigh instead. "Just do it, Zell. Just do it for me. For all of us."

Zell backed away. Taking up with Kim wouldn't amount to all of his old man's sins. Or the sins he'd made his children commit, the secrets they'd had to keep. What secret was Winn keeping from them now?

Winn's desperate plea bothered him more than if he had gone off on him. What bothered him most was the realization that he didn't know his father at all.

Kim took a few of the magazine pages she'd earmarked to the hardware store the next morning. When she returned an hour later, she discovered a blue Ford truck at the house. Owen was kneeling at the steps leading to the porch. She hadn't really gotten a bead on him yet, other than that Charlotte seemed to run the show as far as their marriage went and he wasn't real happy about it.

He came to his feet when she approached him, hammer at his side.

"What are you doing?" she asked, very aware of that blunt instrument in his hand.

"Replacing the steps. I told Elva I'd take care of it for her a couple of months ago." He nodded toward the new steps. "Had these built before she passed on, but haven't had a chance to bring them over."

Kim walked closer and tried not to sound skeptical. "You did this out of the kindness of your heart?"

He lifted a shoulder in answer. Sweat dripped down the sides of his face and neck and dampened the neck of his T-shirt. "Well, she paid me for it. I helped her out from time to time. I'll be done in a minute."

Helped her out, or had Elva coerced him into doing household things in addition to the payoff Winnerow had to make? All right, she was getting paranoid. Owen was a big guy, but he didn't look like he had the guts to tell someone off, much less off someone. Still, his loyalties would run deep. But why had he come to finish the job? Most likely he'd been snooping around.

He put the final nails into the wood and took a step back to look at it. "I think that'll do. You'll have to put a coat of paint on them, of course."

"Was Elva close to the Macgregors?"

"We liked her well enough." He ran his sleeve across his

sweaty forehead. She noticed he kept his gaze on the steps and didn't look her way much. "Zell was probably closer to her than anyone."

She felt a pinch of guilt that her enemies had been closer to her grandmother than she had been. But had one of them murdered her? "Did you help her out a lot?"

He slapped the head of the hammer against his palm. Those moonflower-blue eyes narrowed. "What are you doing, Kim? Questioning me?"

"Just making conversation."

He sneered at her. "Just making trouble. I know what you're doing and I'm not going to let you hurt my family again."

She eyed that hammer. "What am I doing?"

"Digging up the past. The Macgregors are good people. The thing with Winn and your dad, well, that was a shame. But it was an accident." He grabbed up his tool belt and started walking toward his truck. "Let it go, or you're going to find yourself in a world of trouble."

"Why—" Kim held back her words. Owen had closed the door and started the engine. Was the wimpy Owen threatening her? Or had someone else sent him? This was probably why he'd really come over, so he could warn her off. She turned back to the house and whispered a prayer. "Please don't let the Macgregors be involved in Elva's death." She did not want to make war with them again.

Smitty had been avoiding Kim; she was sure of it. As soon as the lunch group had dispersed, he'd headed right out. She'd asked him to come in a little early that evening. When he arrived, Kim met him outside and asked him to come around back to look at something.

Reluctance etched his face as deeply as his wrinkles. "But what about the customers?"

Two vehicles were parked in the lot. "Amy can handle them. I need to talk to you." When they reached the area behind the building, she said, "She was blackmailing

Rhonda Jones's murderer and giving Ernie half of the monthly payment."

"Amy was blackmailing someone?"

"Not Amy, Elva!"

Disbelief colored his expression. "Blackmail? Why would she blackmail someone?"

"She must have had some evidence tying someone in town to the murder. In her own warped way, she was doing good—helping out Ernie. And taking her cut, too; probably figured it was only right considering she was risking her life to do this. Whoever killed her probably took the evidence. That's why the filing cabinet was so messy." She slapped her hand to her chest. "What was she thinking? Why didn't she just turn it over to the police? Unless she knew Kinsey was either in on it or might cover it up. Did you know?"

Smitty looked pained. "I knew she was up to no good. But you know how she was; she'd get her mind wrapped around an idea and wouldn't let it go and wouldn't tell me nothing, either. Not that I pressed her. I knew I couldn't talk her out of whatever it was she was up to, so I figured it was better not to know. She wouldn't have wanted to drag me into her trouble, and she'd feel the same way about you. If she was fool enough to blackmail someone, and I'm not saying I believe she was, and you got no evidence, why keep going after it?"

"I can't walk away from this, Smitty. Somebody killed her. How am I supposed to walk away from that?"

He was shaking his head, giving her a look that said, *It was nice knowing you.* "The bottom line is, someone was willing to kill her to keep their secret. What makes you think they won't kill you if you get too close?"

She got a chill from his words. It seemed everyone was warning her to back off. But who had the most to lose if she didn't? "Smitty, has Owen ever done repair work for Elva?"

"Not that I know of, but as I said, I didn't know all of Elva's business. Why?"

"He was out at the house earlier, said he helped her once in a while. He was fixing the front steps."

He narrowed his eyes. "Oh, boy, you're really opening a big can of worms again, aren't you? A big, Macgregor can of worms."

"I've got to look at everyone."

"I suppose you do." Smitty started to walk to the rear door, but paused. "Tullie wanted me to give you a message. I wasn't sure about giving it to you, but now . . ."

"What was it?"

"She said to be careful who you trust. And she looked real worried."

# CHAPTER 17

The crowd wasn't bad for a Thursday night. Laughter filled in the lulls between the songs on the jukebox. Charlotte, Owen, and JoGene came in together and sat at the bar. Charlotte had purple polish today with a starburst design airbrushed on the surface.

"Groovy nails," Kim said, remembering how Charlotte had complained that no one commented on them.

Charlotte spread her fingers to show them off better. "Why, thank you for noticing." She shot the two men a *See* look. "I heard you did fancy drinks. I want something different, something from the city."

"How about a rumrunner?"

"Sounds good. I'll try it."

Kim made the multiliquored drink with a flourish, enjoying the attention of most of the patrons. Charlotte looked impressed as she watched Kim pass the bottle of banana liqueur from one hand to the other behind her, flip it, and catch it at a perfect angle to pour a splash into the glass. She even clapped when Kim set the frozen drink in front of her.

Kim got the guys their beers and took an order from Amy before returning. "Owen, I never got a chance to thank you for fixing the front steps." She watched the others' reactions.

That got Charlotte's attention. "What steps?"

Owen waved it off. "Elva paid me to fix her front steps awhile back. I went out today and finished it."

Charlotte clearly didn't like not knowing what her husband was up to. She forced a smile. "That was nice of you, honey."

Had he been lying about helping Elva out from time to time? Had he used the steps as an excuse to threaten her, as she suspected?

It was Charlotte's turn to surprise Kim next. "So, how's Ernest Jones these days? Heard you went out that way, figured it must have been him you were seeing."

Kim said, "How'd you know I was out there?"

"JoGene told me, isn't that right?"

He looked uncomfortable at being pointed out. "Someone at the camp saw you driving by and mentioned it to my dad. Not many people go out that way who don't live there. It caught their attention."

Great, everyone knew she'd been out to see Ernest. "How are things at the hunting camp?" she asked JoGene, trying to divert the conversation away from her visit.

"We've added another six cabins since you were out there last. We got a big corporate party coming in this weekend looking to hunt wild boars."

Charlotte lit up a cigarette, and Owen instinctively shifted away from her. Kim soon saw why when Charlotte's hand flew out as she spoke. "What's Ernie doing these days? For a living, I mean."

"I'm not sure."

Her eyes narrowed. "Funny, you paying a social call and not finding that out."

"Yeah, it is funny," Kim agreed. Crap. She'd given herself away. "Mostly we just talked about his mama, reminisced a bit." Kim doubted anyone would believe that, but it was her best shot. She decided to change the subject. "So, where's Zell tonight?"

Charlotte lifted her shoulder in a coy shrug. "I'm not his keeper. Maybe he's out on a date." She studied Kim for a moment and then leaned closer. "You were telling the truth the other morning, weren't you?" She indicated the morning she had caught her leaving Zell's house, and obviously her claim that she wasn't in love with him. Thankfully JoGene didn't seem to know about that. "You're looking a little pale."

"I swear it on the Bible," Kim said, and busied herself wiping down the bar.

Owen was watching her, too. Knowing the Macgregors, her exit from Zell's place had probably been the topic of dinner. No, dessert. Winnerow liked to save his haranguing for dessert for some reason.

Charlotte had a lazy smile on her face by the time JoGene and Owen wandered over to talk with Angus. She leaned against the bar and said, "You should come out to Heron's Glen for lunch sometime. Just you and me, you know, girl talk. When Daddy's out of the house, of course. We could have some real cormodity."

"You mean camaraderie."

She narrowed her eyes, but waved off the correction. "Yeah, that. We should be friends."

"Why? I mean, why are you so nice all of a sudden?" Kim asked.

Charlotte ran her finger down the side of her dewy glass. "Well . . . it could be because you own the bar and maybe I'd like a free drink now and again. Or it could be that I'm bored with all the jealous, spiteful women in town and maybe I think you'd be interesting to hang out with. Or maybe I want to keep tabs on you, see what you're up to." She waited to see what Kim's reaction would be.

Kim eased her suspicious expression into a smile. "Or maybe it's all three."

Charlotte gave her a look of reluctant respect. "Maybe that's what it is."

Kim poured the remainder of the rumrunner from the blender into the glass. "You're not getting free drinks, but lunch sounds good sometime."

"Good. I'll have Gisella whip us up something provencally."

"Do you mean Provençal?"

"You keep correcting me, and I'll rescind my invitation. I'm trying to improve my vocabulary." She crossed her legs. "Everybody's around during the weekend. Can you do lunch during the week?"

"Mondays I can. And sometimes other days if it's slow."

Charlotte mentally checked her calendar. "Tomorrow Owen and I take Daddy into Naples for a doctor's appointment. He's been working himself to death lately. Let's keep Monday on the burner, shall we?"

"Sure thing." How wise was it to become her friend? And what was her motivation? One thing Kim remembered about Charlotte in years past was that she couldn't be trusted.

Charlotte finished her drink with a loud slurp as the two men returned to their stools. "It's a pretty good drink. I'm feeling a little buzzy." She slid off the stool and leaned just a bit. "Owen, honey, take me home and sass me around some." She winked at Kim. "He's got a tiger inside him."

Owen steered his wife toward the door before she could say anything else. Kim looked at JoGene. "A tiger?"

"Yeah, right. That woman has him ball-and-chained for sure. Not that he don't enjoy it. Owen was heading for trouble when he met Charlotte. Who knows where he would have ended up if she hadn't cut his line short."

It was an odd marriage, but Kim wasn't about to say that to Owen's best friend. "If it works," was all she'd commit to. She had to wonder if the good little submissive-husband act was just that: an act. How far would he go to protect what he had?

JoGene was still leaning against the bar when Amy and Smitty started ushering out the clientele at closing time.

"Thought I'd watch over you," he said when she looked his way. "Zell can't get all the credit around here for saving damsels in distress."

Kim rolled her eyes at the phrase. "Thanks, but it's not necessary."

He stayed anyway. He even helped clean up and then he

stayed after Amy and Smitty took off, assuring Smitty he'd take care of Kim. As she was running the totals for the night, he slipped a dollar into the jukebox and chose the sultry Garth Brooks song "Shameless." Her pulse tripped, not out of anticipation but trepidation. She wasn't up to anything romantic with JoGene.

"What's the matter? Don't like this song?" he asked.

"I'm not much into country music these days."

He grinned. "I also picked something from that Madonna CD."

Oh, jeez, not something from *Erotica.*

"How's the bar doing?" he asked, nodding toward the receipts.

"It's getting better. Business is still slower than normal, but people are beginning to come around. I think I'll make it." She stuffed the cash and credit card receipts in the bank bag and put it in the office safe.

When she came out, he was leaning against the end of the bar. "Is there something between you and Zell?"

Heat flushed her face. "Zell? No. He's not my type."

JoGene wrapped his arms around her shoulders, but kept a casual distance between them. "What is your type these days?"

She thought of Simon and the guys like him that she'd dated before. *Comfortable, safe . . . boring.* "No one right now."

He kissed her without much warning. There was something comforting and familiar about that kiss, the way he still held her head at an angle and covered her mouth completely. Did anyone ever tell him to cut down those interminably long kisses, so long her mind began to wander? She realized her mind *was* wandering. Her body didn't feel like melted chocolate the way it had when Zell had kissed her. While her heart was beating a little faster, it wasn't crashing around in her rib cage.

Apparently no one had told JoGene about those long kisses. He tasted like beer. She rode the kiss, maybe to see if any leftover teenage lust remained. Apparently it did from his side; she could feel him hardening against her. He finally did bring it to a close. He didn't notice her lack of enthusiasm, obviously.

"Just like old times," he said with a smile.

"Exactly."

Madonna started singing about erotica and romance in her sultry voice, which was way too bizarre, mixing JoGene with Madonna. He was a country boy from way back.

He cupped her face. When he was going to kiss her again, she turned away.

"I'm flattered, I really am, but I'm not looking for that right now. I need to find my place here in town, and that's been hard enough as it is. I just broke up a long-term relationship." She tilted her head. "And I'm not sure it would be the best thing, considering the past. And your father."

He shoved her away and ran his hand through his hair in a jerky motion. "Forget my father! Forget him! I'd like to. I had a talk with him, set him straight on who's in charge of my life. If I wanted to marry you and run this place with you . . . if I wanted that, I'd do it." He regained his temper. "Sorry. It's just that I'm sick of people thinking I cower under my dad's rule."

He did, but she decided not to point that out. "I didn't mean to upset you."

"You didn't." He forced a laugh. "I wasn't kidding about the marriage thing, Kim."

She walked over to the jukebox and turned it off so he wouldn't see the grimace on her face. "Like I said, JoGene, I'm not ready for any of that. I may not be for a long time. Come on, Oscar. Let's go home."

JoGene took the hint and followed them out. She breathed a sigh of relief when she locked the door—until she saw Buck's truck parked next to JoGene's.

Buck was leaning against the front grille with his arms loosely crossed in front of him. "Figured you'd be here," he said to JoGene. "With *her*."

JoGene's jaw tightened. "Go on home. You're drunk."

That surprised Kim. She'd rarely seen JoGene stand up to his father, especially when he was drunk. But he'd had a few beers himself.

She ushered Oscar to her truck and helped him in. As she maneuvered, she got out her tear gas. Not that it had done her a lot of good thus far. Footsteps sounded across the gravel, and she heard JoGene softly saying to Buck, "I told you, I'm handling this."

Buck only grunted in reply as he approached. She kept her back to her truck and faced them, canister at her side. Her heart was beating thickly, as though her blood had jelled. "What are you going to do, threaten to beat me up and rape me like your two goons?"

"I had nothin' to do with that. If I was gonna cause you bodily harm, I'd do it myself and make sure it got done right." He glanced at JoGene. "I wouldn't be no sissy and have someone else do it."

She looked beyond the men, hoping to see the deputy's cruiser coming by. Except for a vehicle on the main road, the town was tucked away in their beds. It was up to her. She had to remember that this man might have killed Rhonda—and may have tried to run her off the road.

Before she could think of what to say, Buck said, "What's it gonna take to get you to get the hell out of here?"

"I'm here to stay, Mr. Waddell. This is my home, and I'm not leaving it again. Maybe I made mistakes—maybe I didn't. I'll probably never know. Threatening, glowering, or hurting me isn't going to make me go away. And if you have any intention of the latter, know that I have a weapon." Her fingers tightened on the canister that she held pressed against her thigh.

JoGene said, "Dad, she's probably got Elva's rifle in that truck. Let's just go home."

Elva's rifle? She hadn't seen a gun. "And I'm not afraid to use it, either," she bluffed.

Buck glowered at JoGene. "She don't have no rifle."

JoGene nodded toward her. "She's got a can of that pepper-spray stuff."

She figured JoGene was trying to scare off his dad, for which she was grateful. "It's police-issue tear gas, and it'll lay you out bad." She opened the driver's door. "The rifle's in the truck."

"You're a brave girl for someone who's standing all alone." Buck turned to leave.

JoGene gave her an apologetic look, but slunk to his truck like a scolded puppy. What had he meant by his assertion that he was handling this? As their trucks pulled away, Tullie's words rang through her mind: *Be careful who you trust.* With a deep regret, she realized that Oscar was the only one in town she could really trust.

She got into her truck, slammed the door shut, and looked at him. "Where is Elva's rifle?"

He didn't offer any suggestions. As soon as they got home, she checked the house and Elva's truck. When nothing turned up, she called Smitty. "Elva had a rifle."

"That's what you called in the middle of the night to tell me? Heck, I knew that. I gave it to her. She said she was hearing noises and was thinking about getting a gun so I gave her one of my old hunting rifles."

"When was this?"

"About five months ago."

Five months. When the payments started and when she'd added Kim to the bar and house. She'd known it was dangerous to blackmail someone. Maybe she thought the gun would protect her.

"When was the last time you saw it?" she asked.

"I dunno, probably just before she died. It was in her truck, which is where it probably still is."

"It's not. I've checked everywhere, and there's no rifle. What does it look like?"

"Do I want to know why you're asking?"

"Probably not."

Smitty let out a groan. "It's trouble, I just know it."

"What kind of rifle is it and does it have any character-
istics that stand out?"

"It's a Remington Fireball. It has my initials carved into
the butt stock."

"One more question, and then I'll let you go. How
would JoGene know about that rifle?"

"I reckon a few people saw it in the rack of her truck."

"All right. If I'm late for lunch tomorrow, go on without
me. Bye."

She didn't give him a chance to question her further.
The less he knew, the better. That's what he'd said, but she
had to wonder just how much he did know.

The rifle was gone, which meant someone had taken it.
Had they thrown it into the swamp and taken the chance
that someone might find it if Elva's death had been deemed
suspicious?

Kim decided to look near where Elva's body had been
found tomorrow.

If they'd thrown it farther into the swamp, she might
never find it. What if they'd hidden it figuring no one
would come looking or make the connection? If they'd
hidden it and if Kim found it, she would probably find
Elva's murderer. But where to start looking?

Charlotte, Winnerow, and Owen were heading to
Naples tomorrow. They'd be gone for a good part of the
day. Charlotte had mentioned a Gisella making lunch for
them. If she worked like their previous housekeeper did,
she'd prepare meals in the mornings, do some cleaning,
and be out of the house by noon. Tullie would go with the
family.

Winnerow and Buck were still near the top of her suspect list as Rhonda's murderers. Owen and JoGene were
also contenders, in their own right or as helpmates. She
didn't think Zell was a killer, but she hoped she wasn't
being blind where he was concerned.

Someone had taken two lives and gotten away with it.
Someone who lived in Cypress. Probably someone she'd

spoken with during the last week. She didn't doubt that he—or they—were keeping a close eye on her.

Shar walked up next to Zell in the incubation room and lifted one of the lids on the wooden boxes. She ran a finger over the eggs. "If you're interested in Kim, you've got competition."

He was measuring the eggs. "What are you babbling about?"

"JoGene couldn't take his eyes off her all night. He's sure asking for trouble with his daddy, going after that one." She gave him a nudge. "Sounds like someone else I know."

He knew Shar was only telling him this to get a reaction. He wasn't going to give her one. She'd always liked playing games and pitting people against people. Generally he tried to ignore that side of her. "She's free to do what she wants," he said as he jotted down the last measurement.

He'd driven by the bar near closing time to check on her and seen only her and JoGene's trucks parked outside. He was surprised by the sharp jab of jealousy he'd felt.

"I think she's going to do him tonight. 'Oh, JoGene, give it to me, baby, oh, yeah, that's how I like it, oh, oh . . . ' "

She was holding an imaginary man by the hips and thrusting, her head thrown back, making theatrical sounds of orgasm. Though the thought of Kim having sex with JoGene wasn't palatable, Shar's ridiculous show actually distracted him from picturing it. When she cracked her eye open to see his response, her enthusiasm drained.

"I can leave you alone if you'd like." He closed the lid and walked out of the room.

At least she looked a little embarrassed as she followed him. "Well, you get the idea."

He did get the idea and he didn't like it. But he wasn't going to let her see that. He stopped abruptly and turned to face her, letting out his irritation in another way. "And what were you thinking, fooling around in here? You'll confuse the heck out of these guys." He nodded toward the baby gators.

"How'd you know—that danged Dewey and his big mouth. And what a perv he was, standing there watching us. Sometimes he just creeps me out. Oh, stop looking at me like *I'm* the perv. Owen's been growing his balls lately and it's getting me excited."

They walked down the central walkway, only the dimmest light to guide their way. "He's been overstepping his bounds, Shar. It's bad enough that Dad thinks he can all of a sudden be a father and tell me what to do. I won't take it from your husband."

She waved him off. "Owen's harmless. Just ignore him."

Zell wasn't sure how harmless he was. Oh, he played the wimp well enough. He'd known that was what appealed to Shar, so he'd become what she wanted. But Zell had seen enough resentment and fire to know that Owen wasn't necessarily harmless.

The next morning Sam Wharton and Buck Waddell were sitting out on the front porch of the shopping plaza Wharton's office was located in. They watched Kim go into the Everglades Hair Salon.

"Well now, ain't that something?" Sam said before taking another puff on his cigarette.

"Yeah, now. First she went out to see Ernest, and now she's seeing Grace. I heard she's been asking questions at the bar, too, about who was friendly with Elva before she died. She's up to something." Buck felt the rage building inside him. She'd tried to point him out as a murderer all those years ago. The truth of what happened to that girl needed to remain buried.

Sam said, "You got that look in your eyes, Buck, that

same one you got when you ran your truck into Bobby's house. Whatcha thinking about?"

Buck flicked his cigarette butt on the concrete and ground it with his boot. "She ain't gonna get away with it, not this time. If she tries pointing a finger at me or my own, I'll break that finger and stick it right up her—"

"Don't let people hear you talk like that. If something happens to her, you'll be the first one they question. You don't want to go through that again. You got lucky last time."

Buck waved that off. "I sure wish it were the days of my grandpappy when, if someone was doing you wrong, you just took care of it. Nobody looked into it too hard. People disappeared in the swamp all the time." He waved his hand at Sam. "Aw, stop looking at me like that. I'm just reminiscing, that's all. 'Sides, JoGene's got something in the works to get rid of her. I'll give him a little more time. I'm worried that he's going to go soft on her, like Zell Macgregor did. And unlike Winn, I won't put up with that. The sooner she's gone out of here, the better, as far as I'm concerned." He stared at the front window of the beauty shop. "The sooner the better and by whatever means necessary."

# CHAPTER 18

Hair in the morning, trespassing in the afternoon. Kim flipped through a copy of *Good Housekeeping* while Grace finished with her current customer. "Decorate Your Home Like a Pro and Stay Within Your Budget," one article proclaimed. "Discipline Your Kids with Love," another header read. It reminded her too sharply of what she wanted and didn't have. She picked up *Cosmopolitan* and opened it right to an article about keeping your husband happy in the bedroom. A few months ago she would have been picturing Simon as that husband, maybe even have thrown a couple of kids into the picture. Now the happy image of home, husband, and children seemed a far cry from possible. She needed articles on "How to Find a Killer" and "Questioning People Without Giving Yourself Away."

That's what she was doing at the Everglades Hair Salon, hoping to mine some nugget from Grace's memory. Her search for the rifle had turned up nothing.

"It's your turn," Grace said, breaking into her thoughts. "And none too soon. You'd have destroyed that magazine 'fore long."

Kim looked down to see she'd mangled the header "Using Your Mouth for More Than Words." She tossed the magazine on the table and let Grace wash her hair and lead her to one of the chairs. Outside and across the street she could see two of her least favorite people. They looked as though they were staring right at her.

Buck was mean enough to kill Rhonda and Elva and arrogant enough to think he could get away with it. So far, the killer had. She remembered JoGene saying they had a corporate group coming in that weekend. That would be a good time to take a peek. Checking the main lodge or Buck's house for the rifle would be tricky. Though Buck was often out hunting or checking his animal stock, his cowed wife usually stayed at home.

She wasn't sure what she'd do if JoGene caught her snooping around his cabin. Maybe apologize for blowing him off and tell him she wanted to be friends. Buck, on the other hand, would be a much harder sell. He'd probably just shoot her.

"Whatcha thinking?" Grace said, picking at strands of Kim's hair. "Can't go much shorter, really, without looking butchy."

"I'm just looking for a trim." A trim that she didn't need since she'd recently had her hair cut.

Grace started combing Kim's hair. "How's Oscar doing? I heard you're keeping him."

"Yeah, he kind of grew on me."

"We bought one of Elva's pigs when she was breeding them. Miss Piggy's almost as much our child as Martha Lee is."

"Does Miss Piggy like to tear paper?"

Grace laughed. "Oh, yeah. We buy her packing paper so she can have at it once in a while."

"So it's a pig thing, then, huh? I woke to the sound of tearing paper this morning. Stepping on a gooey, wet wad in the hallway totally woke me up. Oscar was in the living room tearing out pages from my magazines. He'd shake the page free, take it into the back room, and prance around with it for a few seconds before chewing it up and depositing it on the floor with the other spit wads."

Grace nodded her head. "Oh, yeah. Ain't it cute?"

"*Cute* wasn't quite the word I used, though it has the same amount of letters."

Kim had run into the living room to retrieve what was left of her decorating ideas. Then she went around the house picking up spit wads, all before having her morning tea.

"Ernie said you stopped by. Did you find out what Elva was buying from him?"

"Ah, no. But I don't think it was drugs. I hate thinking about him getting into trouble. It's a shame, him losing his mother so young. Maybe he would have turned out better if Rhonda had lived."

Grace snorted as she snipped Kim's hair. "Not likely. Rhonda wasn't exactly a pillar of the community, you know. Oh, she did try her best by Ernie, I'll give her a little credit. But her way was getting someone to take care of her. She wanted the easy ride. Can't say as I blame her. Guess we each have our ways of bettering ourselves."

Kim led her a bit. "I wish they'd found out who killed her."

"Well, you tried to pin it on Winnerow and Buck. That sure was ugly."

"You don't think they did it?"

Grace measured out the ends of Kim's hair with her fingers as she talked. "Well, I dunno. Buck, he can be ornery and all, but I can't say nothing bad about him. My hubby works for him at the club. Winnerow did give her a ride a few times, but so did a lot of guys around here. Heck, even JoGene gave her a ride every now and again, and I ain't only talking about the driving kind."

"JoGene was seeing Rhonda? When?"

Grace flushed red, and her movements became more hurried. "I forgot about you and him dating. It was nothing serious, mind you. He came by a few times, maybe in the year before she died. He was always complaining because his girlfriend wasn't giving him any." She gave her a sheepish look in the mirror. "I guess that was you." She shrugged. "It's no big deal. If a guy's got a need . . ."

JoGene had slept with Rhonda. The thought twisted inside her. Not only because JoGene had cheated on her, but because he'd had a sexual relationship with a woman who was later murdered. During the trial, the prosecution made the point that Rhonda had known and trusted her killer. She'd known JoGene.

"What do you think?"

Kim had hardly been paying attention to Grace's performance as they'd talked. Now she looked at the reflection, and her heart did a somersault. Crap. She looked like a boy.


Kim had called Heron's Glen just to be sure. No one had answered. She had no idea what Zell was up to, but since he lived so far from the main house, she should be safe. She pulled down the road and paused at the intersection. The farm was straight ahead. She saw a truck parked near the buildings, but saw no one outside. Zell could be at his house to the right. That made a strange, itchy feeling run across her skin. She took it as a warning and quickly turned left.

Her heart started hammering as soon as she pulled up to the house. Was she crazy? Did she really want to do this? The real question was, did she have a choice?

There was no place to hide her truck, so she parked out front and looked at the house. "If I were a rifle that someone had stolen from a murdered person, where would I be?"

She rang the door chimes and waited an interminably long time to make sure no one was around. People in Cypress weren't especially worried about robbery, but she figured the front door would be locked. It was. She walked around to the back.

Her mother's voice echoed with all the excitement of a girl's: *Wow, Kim, look at this pool! We're going to have a good time here. All the hard times are behind us now, I swear. Please, Kim, let's just be happy.* Though in the end, Kitty discovered the money and name hadn't made her happy after all.

The pool cage was as tall as the house and kept the

immense pool and upstairs balconies within its mosquito-free confines. She walked inside the cage, wishing she could find the peace her mother had found at the sound of the waterfall that splashed into the pool. Rocks, palms, and bromeliads added to the tropical look. She walked to the bank of French doors surrounding the leisure room and tried a handle. Bingo.

First, she checked the garage, but found nothing. In the gallery she found an elaborate rifle case and tugged on the door, but it was locked. Good, she supposed, since there was a young girl in the house. Bad for Kim, though. She looked at the rifles mounted inside, but saw nothing like an old hunting rifle.

Why would the murderer have taken the gun? Elva hadn't been shot. But she had been bludgeoned with something. Maybe the murderer had used the rifle and then taken it so no evidence would be found. Of course, if it had been treated like a potential crime scene, investigators would have found particles of whatever had been used embedded in Elva's skin.

The study had been turned into an extensive workout room. If Winnerow were working out here, then maybe he was capable of murdering Elva after all. She remembered Charlotte saying he'd been working himself to death lately. Had she meant working out?

She caught her reflection in the wall of mirrors and started again at the sight of her haircut. Not only did she just plain hate it, something else bothered her about it. She pushed it from her mind and left the room.

Winnerow's suite was past the study. Kim had hated the thought of her mother sleeping with him. Kim slipped into the room and went right to the massive walk-in closet. She could hear her mother's voice the first time she'd shown Kim the room. *Look at this closet! It's as big as our old living room.* She dropped down to her knees and crawled beneath the hanging clothes. She searched the upper shelves and then beneath the bed, but found no rifle.

She tiptoed up the curving staircase, looking out the

terraced windows as she went. She remembered Zell sliding down this banister. He'd taunted her into doing it once, and she'd gotten in trouble when Winn caught her. There were three bedrooms upstairs. The one at the top of the stairs used to be Zell's. As she walked in, she guessed it was now Charlotte and Owen's room. They had a tall waterbed with a headboard filled with alligator skulls, statues, and knick-knacks. A large sitting area held a blue couch and an exercise bike. Like Winnerow's room, this one overlooked the bay. Would Owen hide a gun nearby that he couldn't explain? Doubtful. She searched the closet . . . and found nothing.

She walked across a bridge that looked down to the living room and foyer. Charlotte's old room, which now belonged to Tullie, was rich with little-girl graces and pink ruffles. She wondered if Tullie liked this style or if Charlotte was forcing it on her. Tullie seemed too old and too serious for this kind of room. Kim's eyes lit on the aquarium containing a baby alligator, about the size of the one Charlotte and Zell had put in her bed. That seemed more suitable for the girl than the ruffles.

Kim's old room was now a storage room, a perfect place to hide a rifle. Only she didn't get to look. The sound of a garage door opening shot adrenaline into her veins. She was blinded by the glint of sun against glass as a door opened. Two vehicles had just pulled up, one inside the garage and one parked out front. She didn't take time to investigate. At the top of the stairs, she gripped the banister . . . and perched her behind on the smooth wood. She pushed off and slid down the banister, jumping to the tile at the bottom. Voices filtered in from the utility room, where the garage door entered.

"She won't be in the house, Daddy," Charlotte said.

"She'd better not be."

They would walk into the gallery any second and spot her at the base of the stairs. Her throat was so tight she could hardly swallow. She darted across the gallery to the study. Her feet slid on the tile just as their footsteps sounded on the floor. She had to weave through the maze of workout equipment toward the French doors leading out to the lanai. Their voices grew louder, though Kim's heart was pounding so loud, she couldn't hear what they were saying. Something grabbed at her, pulling her back. She twisted around to see that the pocket of her pants had caught on one of the handles. She extricated herself and lunged at the brass lever.

It was locked. She fumbled at the lock and jerked down on the lever again. The door opened, and a rush of humid air enveloped her. She pushed it closed and started toward the screen door to the right just in time to see Zell coming around the corner of the house.

Buck and Sam wandered into the hair salon. Buck removed his cap and smiled at Grace.

"Hey there, Mr. Waddell, Mr. Wharton. You in for a cut or a shave?"

"I just might be in for a shave." Buck rubbed his grizzly chin and sat in the chair. Grace went right to work, rubbing warm lather on his face. He said, "Saw Kim Lyons was in earlier."

She gave him a nervous laugh. "Yep, sure was. Don't think she was too happy with my cut, though. I think I snipped it a little too short for her."

Wharton had taken a seat in the waiting area. "Was she asking you questions?"

Her gaze darted around a bit. "I . . . well, I suppose she was. Made me a little uncomfortable, to be honest. I know you didn't hurt my sister, Mr. Waddell. I never thought that, not even back then."

Back before her husband didn't depend on him for a job, she didn't say. "I appreciate that, Grace, I do. Are you saying that Kim was accusing me?"

"No, sir! No, not at all. She was just asking who I thought had done it."

Buck traded a look with Sam. Yep, just like he thought.

She was digging into Rhonda's murder again. "What'd you tell her?"

Grace ran the blade over his skin, but she was tripping over her words. "Just how I didn't think you'd done it, and how Mr. Macgregor wasn't the only one that gave Rhonda rides." Her face flushed red. "I told her what I figured she already knew."

"What was that?"

She dropped her hand. "That JoGene had been seeing Rhonda. I thought everybody knew. I guess she didn't."

Buck needed to see Winn, and he needed to talk to JoGene. That boy had to be careful what he said around Kim. The fact was, he needed to just stay away from her. Buck was going to move ahead with his plan. If things had been done his way ten years ago, none of this would be happening now.


Kim knew she had all the telltale signs of someone caught doing something she shouldn't be as she walked around the pool toward Zell: flushed face, her words rushing out like a waterfall, and shaky hands. Had he seen her coming out of the house?

"Hi, Zell! Fancy meeting you here. I was looking for Charlotte."

His expression was eerily blank. "Kim," was all he said. Not an accusation exactly, but close enough.

Charlotte walked out of the house, followed by Winnerow, who was . . . walking. His left leg dragged a little, but he still made good time. They'd known she was there, of course, as soon as they'd pulled up to the house. But what were they doing back so soon?

"What the hell is going on?" Winnerow demanded when he saw her. "What is she doing here?"

Tullie and Owen followed the war party. Kim had to fight the urge to look toward the door for escape. Instead, she pasted on her best, most innocent smile and focused on Charlotte.

"You mentioned us having lunch and it turned out I had time. Anyway, I came on over and when no one answered, I walked around to see if you were out here." It wasn't the best excuse, but it was all she had. "I see you refinished the pool in black. It looks pretty cool. How do you know if there's a dead scorpion or a snake in the pool, though? I don't think you could see it down at the bottom."

Winnerow turned to Charlotte. "Did you invite this woman here for lunch?"

"Yeah, but not today." She gave Kim a stern look. "Remember, I told you I was taking Daddy to the doctor in Naples."

"Oh, I thought you said Owen was taking him." She casually walked closer to the door—and away from the encroaching circle of Macgregors. "Sorry for the misunderstanding."

Winnerow wasn't buying it by the red infusing his face. He walked forward and blocked her way. "When will you Lyonses learn that breaking into other people's homes can get you killed?"

Charlotte squeezed Winnerow's shoulder. "Daddy—"

But that wasn't going to stop his tirade, not now. "You're just like your daddy, nothing more than a two-bit thief! I trusted him, and he broke in here and tried to steal from me. But I'll never trust you!" His finger shook as he pointed at her. His mouth was open, as though he were going to say more. But it gaped silently as the rage in his eyes turned to cold realization at what he'd just said.

Kim looked at Zell and then Charlotte. "My father wasn't a thief."

"The hell he wasn't," Owen said, and would have said more if Zell hadn't given him a look that silenced him.

"You'd better go," Charlotte said to Kim. "Now."

Her gaze skipped from one person to another. There was something going on here. A conspiracy that colored Winnerow's and Zell's faces with the tint of shame and pity. "Not until you tell me what's going on. My father wasn't a thief."

Desperation threaded through Charlotte's voice when she said, "We don't have to tell her anything. She'll make trouble for us just like she did before."

Zell said, "No she won't, not when she knows the truth." He went ahead without consulting them further. "The night your father was shot—it wasn't a hunting accident."

She'd known that, deep in her heart, she'd known. "Then . . . what?"

Zell said, "There had been a string of robberies in town. Someone had broken into our hunting camp and stolen a radio and some ammo. Other people in town discovered guns, equipment, and cash missing. And there was a robbery at the convenience store heading toward Naples. Everyone was thinking transients or folks from Miami, but it didn't make any sense them coming to Cypress. There wasn't much for them to take in this town. Everyone was on alert.

"One night we heard someone downstairs and came down to investigate. Dad was the first to hear it. He saw someone standing by the rifle case, just a silhouette of a man taking two of the rifles out. When Dad told him to stop right where he was, the man jerked around with the rifles in his hands. Dad thought he was going to fire, so he shot him out of instinct. When I turned on the light . . . it was Donnie."

"No," she said, backing away from them. "You're all lying." Her blind devotion to her father warred with the truth she saw in their somber expressions and the sympathy in Zell's.

Winnerow spoke now. "Of course we called Kinsey over. He looked at the evidence, but it was clear what had happened. Donnie's face was smudged with black charcoal, he was wearing black clothing, and he was in my house in the middle of the night. He'd come in through a side door."

Charlotte said, "There were some guns in his truck that he'd just stolen from Angus."

Zell moved a little closer, as though he thought she

might bolt. Or maybe it was a way of offering comfort without touching her. "There had been rumors going around that your dad was into something pretty bad. We think he was running drugs for someone in Miami. Not regularly, but on a once-in-a-while basis. The trouble seemed to have started right after a tropical storm blew through here. Do you remember that, about a week before he died?"

Kim nodded, feeling numb. Her father had taken out the boat earlier that day and was going to head up the west coast of Florida for another one of his fishing excursions. Excursions that netted him a wad of cash. An unexpected storm blew through and capsized his boat. Kim remembered being surprised at how upset he was over losing that old junk heap of a boat. He left the house to make phone calls and became a chain-smoker. Then he started going on overnight hunting trips.

"We're thinking that he lost a shipment and was trying to come up with the money to make up for it. We stayed up half the night trying to figure out what to do. We could tell the truth, and my dad would probably be acquitted. Donnie did have the rifles in his hand. Meanwhile, your family's name would be dragged through the mud along with ours, and if he had any life insurance, they probably wouldn't pay out. Kinsey looked at everything and decided the truth would hurt more people and wouldn't help anyone. Your mother was the one who gave us the hunting story."

"My mother . . ." Kim's eyes widened. "She knew about this?" She didn't think her chest could hurt any more, but that sentence proved her wrong.

"Of course," Winnerow said. "We brought her to the house and told her everything. She agreed to our plan. She didn't want you to suffer for what your father had done. She had nothing to gain by having the truth out."

Kitty, who had been so unhappy as Donnie's wife. Kim remembered hearing an argument over Donnie's fishing excursions. Had Kitty known about the drug running?

"Did Elva know?"

Zell nodded.

Kim felt her legs weaken and locked her knees. "If I'd known the truth . . ." She looked at Tullie, who had warned her she wouldn't like the truth.

Charlotte stepped forward. "You wouldn't have believed it. Even if you had believed, you still would have hated Daddy. Either way, it was a lose-lose situation."

Kim turned to Winnerow. "Whose idea was it to marry my mother?"

"Mine. I felt I owed it to her. And to you. There wasn't any insurance money, as it turned out. The bottom line was, I killed your father, even if it wasn't intentional." He stepped closer to Kim. "I liked Donnie. He was a friend, but he betrayed me. Not that he deserved to die for that, of course. You and your mother didn't deserve to starve because of it, either. So I did what I felt was right."

Kim's head was spinning. Her father a thief? Winnerow a good guy? No, the world didn't change like that. "I have to go."

Winnerow called after her. "Talk to Kinsey about it. I'll tell him to tell you the truth."

She couldn't respond, could only tighten her arms around her and keep walking to her truck. Was it a lie, a vicious lie they'd made up to cover their butts?

She didn't think so, not deep inside. Because even in Winnerow's eyes, she'd seen pity.


Zell watched Kim leave and felt a tug to follow her. Not only to comfort the shock in her eyes, but to get some answers. He had to let her go . . . for now.

Shar whistled. "Well, that was something interesting. I suppose it's best for her to find out. Sometimes it's better for the truth to come out."

Winn rubbed his hand over his mouth, as though he could take back his blunder. "And sometimes it's not."

Zell opened the French door. It had been a lie to protect family honor—Kim's family. Still, he wondered if it was right. But it was too late for wondering things like that. The lies had been told, and the secrets had been kept. He wondered if Winn was thinking about other lies and secrets as he filled a glass with ice at the wet bar.

"So, Shar, did you really invite Kim to lunch?" Zell asked as he opened the refrigerator and poured two iced teas. He intercepted his father pouring bourbon into the glass by handing him one of the teas. Winn grudgingly took the tea but eyed the bottle of bourbon. He'd be back for that. Zell was sure that Winn had never figured out he'd been watering down his drinks for years.

Shar helped herself to the tea, too. "I did, but not for today. I told her we should have lunch together."

Winn scowled. "Why would you do that?"

She gave them a coy smile. "So I can keep tabs on her, see what she's up to." She crushed a mint leaf into her glass. "Besides, she's interesting. And she's got balls, something I admire in a woman."

Winn was still scowling, whether it was the forced iced tea or Shar's choice in friends, Zell didn't know. Winn walked over and pressed the blinking light on the answering machine. Buck's voice boomed out an urgency to talk to Winn and he walked into the living room.

Owen said to Shar, "I don't think it's a good idea bringing that woman into our home and our lives."

She chucked him on the chin. "And when did I ever give a hoot'n holler what you thought? I'll be friends with whomever I like, irregardless of what anyone thinks." She shot Zell a look. "That principle doesn't apply to you, big brother."

He leaned back against the counter. "Excuse me?"

"You can't be friends with her. It's a double standard, 'cause she's a woman. You become friends with her, she'll fall in love with you, and you'll be sleeping together. That'll make things all kinds of complicated around here." She swigged the rest of her tea and wiped her mouth with the back of her hand, "There's no chance of me sleeping with her."

Tullie was taking all of this in as she usually did. The girl was so quiet it was easy to forget she was even there sometimes. She met Zell's gaze, trouble darkening her expression.

Winn came into the room after calling Buck. "It's just like I thought: Kim coming back to town is nothing but trouble. She's investigating that girl's murder again. First her trip out to Ernest Jones, and now she's questioning Grace, asking her who she thought killed Rhonda. Who she was seeing at the time of her death." He looked at Owen. "It's time to run her right back out of town."

Zell didn't like the sound of that. "What are you going to do?"

"You just never mind. Doesn't concern you." This time he filled his glass with bourbon and dared Zell to do something about it. That was a fight Zell wasn't in the mood to take up. Bigger wars loomed on the horizon.

Winn said, "I'll bet you a bottle of Kentucky's best she was looking for something here. I want to know what it was."

So did Zell. "I've got to go." He was going to find out.


Kinsey made Kim tell him what she knew of the story. He'd made her walk outside the station before he parted with anything so no one else could hear them.

"Yep, that's about how it happened," he confirmed when she'd told him what she'd heard.

She leaned against the outside of the building and swatted at mosquitoes. "Do you think he was running drugs?"

"I'm pretty sure he was. I know he was your daddy and all, but he got in over his head sometimes. People aren't always what you think they are." Kinsey lit a thin cigar. "See what happens when you dig too much? You find out things you don't want to know. That's the least of your worries."

"What else should I be worried about?"

"Now that you're scratching around Elva's grave, a lot.

With the way you point fingers, it's making people nervous. All you're doing is looking for trouble . . . and all you're gonna do is find it."

"Someone murdered my grandmother, and I intend to find out who it was. Her rifle is missing."

"Didn't know she had a rifle."

"It was Smitty's; he lent it to her. She was afraid. Now the rifle is missing."

"Then Smitty ought to come in and file a report on it."

Kim let out a long breath. It was useless telling him anything. She left him standing there with a smug look on his face and a cigar dangling out of his mouth. She got into her truck and headed home, still having a hard time believing that awful story. Her father was a good man with bad judgment perhaps, but he wasn't a drug runner and thief. It had to be a big misunderstanding.

The ache in her chest that had started with Winnerow's words was growing. She remembered a police car coming to the house once, one of the deputies questioning her father. Afterward, he'd ruffled her hair and told her not to worry about it. They had the wrong guy. He said he'd always be there for her. She'd loved him with all of her heart, a heart she'd never given to anyone else. As fragile as she felt, safe men like Simon were sounding pretty good. At least she'd never get her heart broken again.

When she pulled up to her house, anxiety washed over her. Zell was leaning against his shiny black truck waiting for her. He looked casual, his arms loosely crossed in front of him, but there was nothing casual about his eyes. He reminded her of an alligator, sitting in the water looking like a harmless log but waiting to pull flesh apart at the first opportunity.

She wanted to stay in her air-conditioned cab for a long time and listen to her Pink CD. That Pink was singing about getting the party started struck her as sadistically ironic.

She pushed out of the truck and walked forward like a woman who wasn't feeling all kinds of trepidation. "I've got to let Oscar out," she said and stepped onto the porch. Oscar lurched out and down the steps, and headed off to attend to his pig business.

Zell had strolled to the hothouse. The easy sway in his walk reminded her of Amy's comment: Everglades cowboy. With his alligator boots and faded jeans, it fit.

She realized she had just stood there watching him walk away. Of course, he expected her to follow him. On principle, she should stay put, but she wanted to get this over with.

While it was muggy outside, it was downright steamy in the hothouse. The smell of earth and bark overpowered the orchids. He was poking at the bark of a mounted orchid. "You're letting them dry out."

He was going to drag this out. "I haven't been a good mother to the orchids, I admit. I've had a lot on my mind."

"Elva had planned to install automatic misters in here when she started making some money." He took his time inspecting the plants. She tried not to look bothered by his making her wait or the wilting orchids. Finally he walked back to her and leaned against the nearby wood post. "You okay?" He studied her, and for a moment, she let herself think that was why he was there, to make sure she could handle the news she'd just been given.

"I talked to Kinsey."

He nodded, knowing Kinsey had confirmed the news and probably seeing by the defeat in her eyes that she was beginning to accept it. "Sorry you had to hear it that way. Or at all. Sometimes it's better to leave the truth where it is."

"That seems to be the sentiment around here. I don't buy it."

He lost that shade of sympathy and took the look he probably used when lobbying in Tallahassee. "What were you doing out at Heron's Glen?"

"I told you, I was looking for Charlotte."

"And you're a liar."

"So are you."

He pushed away from the post, and she hated the way

she flinched at his advance. He stood inches in front of her. "You tell me the truth, and I'll tell you the truth."

"About what?"

"Anything you want to know."

She wanted to kick him in the shin and she wanted to pull him close and kiss him. More sadistic irony.

"I saw you coming out of the house. Now, if I'd told Winn about that, he'd have really gone off on you. I figured I'd find out and then decide if *I'm* going to go off on you. What were you doing there, Kim?"

That hard, lean body wasn't going to move until he got what he wanted. And dammit all, she was at a loss to come up with a viable lie. A trickle of sweat sliding between her breasts made her more aware of the drop sliding down Zell's neck. With a sigh of defeat, she gave it to him. "I was looking for Elva's rifle. It's missing."

"You were searching our house for her rifle?" His face transformed as he processed that. "I thought this was about Rhonda."

"It is. It's about her and Elva." She didn't want to tell him everything. He was the enemy, or at the least, an unknown factor. But she was already in too deep to back out now. "Elva was blackmailing Rhonda's murderer." She nodded toward the hothouse. "She was using the money to pay off your loan." She left Ernest out of it. "And I think her blackmail target killed her."

"Elva wasn't murdered; she fell out of her skiff and hit her head."

"That's what they want us to believe. Think about it: Elva poled through these waters all the time. She was an expert. She was in good health. The death certificate said blunt trauma to the head. Elva was only five foot three. How much blunt trauma could happen from falling out of a skiff?" She had his attention. "I found a piece of a rubber glove in the filing cabinet. Someone had been looking for whatever Elva was holding over the murderer's head. He made a mess of the filing cabinet."

Zell idly reached out and touched one of the pink

orchids. "How do you know Elva was blackmailing Rhonda's murderer?"

"Trust me on that part."

"Trust you? You sound like a one-woman posse hell-bent to wreak havoc. I just caught you sneaking out of my family home. How am I supposed to trust you?"

Maybe she did sound like a one-woman posse. Maybe she was hell-bent to wreak havoc. She needed Zell to believe her. It was important somehow, so she gave him the rest. "I found five entries on her ledger for five hundred dollars each. At first I thought they were payments to you, but the amount wasn't right. Then I discovered Elva was giving Ernie two hundred and fifty dollars every month for five months. She'd told him it was from the person who killed his mother. She was trying to make up for it in some small way. In Elva's way."

He rubbed his hand over his mouth as he considered it. His gaze shifted back to her. "You still think my dad killed Rhonda? And now you think he killed Elva?"

"I'm not sure it was Winnerow who killed Elva. It could be Owen."

He laughed. "Owen? You might as well accuse Dewey. And Shar. And me while you're at it." His eyes darkened. "Or maybe you already have. Did you plan to check out my place, too?"

The truth was, she couldn't trust anyone. She hoped she could trust Zell. "No, I wasn't planning on checking out your place."

"If I catch you in my house, you'd better be naked and lying on my bed."

He'd said it to shock her; at least she was pretty sure he had. He had that arrogant gleam in his eyes, the one that had always tickled straight to her stomach and farther on down. Even when they lived at Heron's Glen, she realized. Even then. She tried not to look shocked by his statement; she'd heard a lot worse in her years of working at bars. Apparently something had slipped through; his mouth quirked up in a satisfied smile.

"Did you get a look to your satisfaction?" he asked.

Her gaze darted down his yellow shirt with palm trees and his faded jeans, and then she realized he'd meant at Heron's Glen. "Mostly. I didn't get a chance to check out the upstairs storage room since everyone had the nerve to show up. I thought they were going to be gone all day."

"It's darn irritating when people show up at their own house, isn't it?"

She allowed him a quirk of her mouth. "A bit, yes."

"There was an accident on US41 that had traffic backed up for miles. They rescheduled and turned back. Dewey called me when he saw your truck head to the house. We all got there at the same time."

"Did they believe my story about being there to see Charlotte?"

"Maybe, maybe not. But Winn knows you're digging again. Buck called him right after you left."

Buck knew. How? Had he asked Grace what Kim had talked about?

"Why can't you let this go?" he asked, running his long fingers up and down the length of an erotically shaped white orchid petal. "Why do you have to keep pushing at this?"

She had to pull her gaze off his fingers. "I don't know." It was Kitty's words that came back to her, her exclamation about the closet, actually. Kitty had been determined to better herself. She'd been determined about a lot of things. Stubborn and hardheaded, some said. People had said the same thing about her. "It's a family trait, like the way Macgregors hold grudges."

"Uh-huh. You'd been better off with early graying hair or bad skin."

"Someone murdered Rhonda and Elva. Maybe the same person or persons. I can't walk away from that. I can't walk away from a miscarriage of justice."

Sweat tickled down her back and made her shimmy a little. Zell looked as cool as a bottle of Bud just plucked from the ice bin. He was draped against a post, watching her while absently stroking that petal.

"All right," she said, bringing her mind back to the conversation at hand. "I've answered your questions. Now you have to answer mine."

"Wait a minute. I've got one more." He advanced on her with a raised hand. "What the hell did you do to your hair?" His hand slid over her cap of hair.

"Grace. I used a haircut as an excuse to question her. I distracted her and wasn't paying attention to what she was doing." His fingers lingered against the back of her neck, twining in the short ends of her hair. She brushed her own hand through her hair, brushing his away in the process. She didn't need his touch messing with her mind. "Does it look butchy?"

He took her in. "Nothing butchy about you, angel. I liked it longer, though."

Angel. That's what he'd called Tullie. Maybe what he called all the girls. So why did it snake right through her like a sensual wave of smoke curling up from a candle?

Maybe it was the steamy air that was affecting her mind, or the earthy, flowery scents. Were orchids aphrodisiacs? She pulled her thoughts together, but they came sluggishly. Maybe it was because he was still standing in front of her, adding aftershave and his own scent to the mix.

"My turn now," she said. "You said you'd answer any question I asked." She'd see about that; he was good at skirting questions. "Do you have any idea who killed Rhonda? Or Elva?"

"None." Tiny beads of sweat now dotted his upper lip. "Kim, let it go. It was a shame what happened to Rhonda, but she would go home with anybody. She just picked the wrong guy one time."

"And that guy is still walking around free."

"But he's not still killing women, or at least not around here. He was probably a transient."

"Did she go home with you?" She hated herself for waiting on the edge during those milliseconds before he answered. Hated his smile for seeing right through her.

"No, she didn't. I guess I was the odd one, because I didn't want a girl who would open her legs for anybody. I liked the one who wouldn't."

Those words dropped on her insides like lead weights, punctuated by the call of a nearby heron. She wasn't sure why she said, "I never slept with JoGene."

"I know." He knew. He'd meant her. Maybe. "He complained about it for hours, and I commiserated with him while silently cheering you on. Maybe I wouldn't have cheered if it'd been me with the blue balls."

She choked on those words, easy since she'd been holding her breath. Forget about the insinuation and especially the blue balls! "Who did she open her legs for?" Diversion was easier. Fighting her feelings for Zell was becoming a bigger battle than she'd bargained for. It was pressing down on her chest and making her legs feel wobbly.

"Probably half the guys in town. Yeah, JoGene did her, too." He didn't look very troubled about telling her, either. "Every now and then."

"Grace told me." She was amazed that it still hurt all these years later. Maybe it hurt because Zell had known. "For days, weeks sometimes, he'd bug me. And then I wouldn't see him for a while and he'd be, 'Oh, let's wait,' again, sweet and calm as could be. I figured he'd jacked off."

She supposed she wanted to shock him with her bluntness, but he only chuckled. "Yeah, well, we all did that now and again. When it became necessary."

"You weren't an innocent, either. I remember Terri, Marie . . ." She remembered too well, listening outside his bedroom door late at night after everyone had gone to bed. She remembered how she'd felt, as though he'd betrayed her. It made no sense, since he owed her not an ounce of chastity.

It didn't help that he chuckled again. "I didn't have to be an innocent. I was a teenage boy with his choice of pickings."

She kicked him in the shin, not hard, but enough to make him jump. She wasn't acting rationally. So what if he'd screwed a hundred women? It really shouldn't matter a whit. But it did, obviously, and that annoyed her.

He rubbed his shin. "I thought we were having a conversation here. If you don't want to talk about my former sex life, why'd you bring it up?"

She wanted to kick him again but held herself back. She figured he'd taken enough bruises for her lately. "I'm asking the questions now, remember?" She steered her mind back to the matter at hand. "Who else was doing Rhonda? Owen?"

"And risk Shar's wrath?"

"Maybe he liked being the dominant one for a change. What about Winnerow? Or Buck?"

He shifted his gaze away. "Kim, I wasn't her pimp. Why do you think I'd know exactly who was doing her?"

She didn't like the shadow of guilt on his face, but she decided not to push him at the risk of losing his cooperation. "Have you ever seen an old rifle around Heron's Glen that didn't belong there? One that had the initials S.G. on the butt end?"

He met her gaze directly. "Nope."

"Were you aware that Owen was helping Elva with things around her house?"

"He might have been. Folks help each other around here. Nothing strange about that."

"Why'd you kiss me that night at your house?" The question just slipped out. She could blame it on the orchids or the muggy heat, but she let it stand between them.

Without any warning, his hand slid behind her head, and he pulled her against him. His mouth covered hers, no, possessed hers. He dipped his tongue into her mouth and wandered lazily around to explore.

His kiss felt different than JoGene's had. Made her feel different. She tried to objectively compare them, like a scientific observer. That lasted for about three seconds and then she was lost in the kiss for the rest of the minute that his tongue lathed hers. The temperature jumped up another twenty degrees with their bodies pressed together. With her crazed thoughts, she didn't realize she'd returned his kiss, matching his lazy rhythm with her own. Her mind could object all it wanted, but the rest of her didn't care about the concept of friends, enemies . . . or lovers.

Her father was a thief, her grandmother was a black-mailer . . . and now she was a traitor to everything she believed in.

She could tell by the way he kissed, demanding her whole mouth, holding her close with the merest touch of his fingers against the back of her neck, that he would demand everything from her—her heart and soul. He would demand passion she didn't possess.

She was ashamed to admit that she wasn't the one who finished the kiss. Zell released her, but he didn't step back. The fire in his eyes scared her in some deep way. This was not a man who was easy to know. But once she did know him, he would consume her.

He ran his thumb over her mouth, regarding her with that sage look on his face. "Because despite the fact that kissing you would be a bit of bad business, like consorting with the enemy . . . despite that, getting involved with you would get me into all kinds of hot water, not only with my family but also with the Waddells, who are almost like kin. Much as that displeases me," he added in a low voice. "Despite that kissing you goes against every principle I have, I wanted to."

He wanted to. Well, that was simple. Even as simple as it was, the words tingled through her. "So, you wanted to kiss me, but you didn't want to kiss me."

"Exactly."

"And you're not happy about it."

The fire and hunger in his eyes turned into something harder. "Not a bit." His finger continued to trail over her chin and down her damp throat. "You're walking across the backs of gators. This killer you're looking for . . . maybe he is one of us, maybe he's not. It doesn't matter, 'cause some of these folks will see your digging as accusation. Loyalties run deep around here. Be real careful who you point a finger at. And if you think you've found a killer, be damned sure you have proof this time. I don't want to see you get hurt, angel." The expression on his face changed, and he dropped his hand. "Your hair is short."

"Well, yeah. You already asked—"

"Like Tullie saw. When she 'saw' you in her bad dream, she said your hair was real short. And now it is."

While she shivered at that, he turned and left. Tullie's visions, the ones that came true sometimes. She remembered the girl's plea for her not to cut her hair.

She remained in the hothouse long after, her heart still pounding. Her thoughts shifted from Tullie to the conversation. She'd seen concern in his eyes. But she wasn't sure if the rest of that was warning—or threat.

# CHAPTER 19

Zell hadn't liked that conversation at all. First of all, he was going to have to do penance for kissing her. Since he was Baptist, there would be no Hail Marys for him. No, for Zell Macgregor, penance consisted of singing "Love Stinks" forty times. Just to remind him that kissing the woman who had caused his family so much trouble—and was bound to do so again—was a really bad idea.

He hated to admit it, but the fact that she'd cut her hair scared him. Tullie wasn't always right, but the coincidence that Tullie had seen Kim with short hair, and now she had short hair, was too much to ignore. That was probably why the girl had looked so disturbed after Kim's visit.

He drove home to work on a report he had a feeling wasn't going to get done. Not with all this other stuff crowding into his mind. Elva blackmailing a murderer and then being killed? No, couldn't be. Kim was on another blind pursuit for justice. She believed it, just as she'd believed his father had murdered Rhonda Jones all those years ago—and probably still did.

Zell had been able to bury his secrets and his doubts. Now Kim was digging around that shallow grave. What worried him more was that everyone knew she was digging. Rhonda's murderer—if he was still around—knew she was digging, too. It was likely he wouldn't hesitate to kill Kim if she got too close to the truth.

What really bothered him, more than his doubts and the protection of his family, was how much it scared him to think about Kim in danger. Against his better judgment, she was beginning to mean something to him. He wouldn't have been happy about it in the best of circumstances. Now she was putting herself in a bad position. There wasn't much he could do to protect her if she kept sneaking around people's private property.

As he pulled up to his house, he started singing his first song.

Kim called the Gun and Rod Club to ascertain that the hunting party had, indeed, gone out that early morning and that JoGene had gone with them. She'd already asked Amy to help Smitty with the lunch shift at Southern Comfort. She dropped Oscar off at the bar early that morning, only opening the front door and letting him in. Then she headed to the club.

Fifteen minutes later, she drove into the cypress and pine forest. To the right a gravel road led to the lodge, where guests could stay, eat, and buy hunting and fishing supplies. To the left was the road leading to the cabins, and just beyond that was the boat launch.

They had added more cabins and refurbished the existing ones. They were set in a circle with picnic tables and a large bonfire in the center. To the north was the large tract of land the Waddells let their guests hunt on.

The parking area was filled with sedans and luxury SUVs, but the place was quiet. She'd decided on the forthright approach as she pulled up to the hunting cabins. She walked purposefully through the scattering of numbered cabins to the one set back near the Snake River. The small wooden sign out front read LODGING MANAGER.

Zell's warning echoed in her head. She preferred to think of it as a warning and not a threat. A man who could kiss her like that couldn't hurt her, right? She wouldn't dwell on the fact that he'd probably do a lot to protect the Macgregor family honor, especially after spending so much of his youth doing just that.

She knocked on the door and prepared her spiel should JoGene be there. No answer. She scanned the area again, but heard only the chatter of birds. The front door was unlocked, so she stepped inside the dark cabin. She didn't take time to analyze the mess of hunting magazines, plate holding two crusts of pizza, or any of the rest of the place. She went right for the closets, where one was likely to stash a rifle.

With one ear tuned to outside noise, she looked in the utility room, kitchen, and then the bedroom. Zell's provocative words about catching her in his house came to mind as she glanced at the rumpled bed.

She found a rifle in the second bedroom. In fact, she found a lot of rifles. A long table held bits and pieces of several guns in varying states of being cleaned or reworked. She searched through them, looking for an old butt stock with initials carved into it. Nothing. His gun cabinet wasn't nearly as elaborate as the Macgregors', but it was jammed full of rifles. Better yet, it wasn't locked. She sorted through those, but came up empty-handed again.

The storage shed might be a place to stick a gun you didn't want anyone to find. Of course, she knew there were plenty of places to get rid of a gun: rivers, swamps, and even the area where someone had spooked her among the mangroves. She walked the several yards from JoGene's cabin to the large shed. She'd spent a few afternoons there, watching JoGene tune up a tractor or his ATV. There was something masculine and slightly primitive about a man fixing machinery that she used to find irresistible. Thinking back to Zell working on his airboat, she realized she still did.

The shed was locked. She jiggled the padlock just in case, but it held firm. The sound of an ATV in the distance sent her back to JoGene's cabin as she scanned the woods.

Even though she hadn't been caught at anything suspicious, her heart was still beating faster than normal. She debated on getting in her truck and leaving, but she could see an ATV coming down the road.

JoGene was looking right at her as he rode toward his cabin. He pulled off his Gun and Rod Club cap and wiped the sweat off his brow, cut the engine, and pulled his lanky legs off the bike.

"Is everything all right?" he asked, looking puzzled but not suspicious.

"I came by to apologize for the other night at the bar. I'd like to keep the door open . . . for us, I mean. And I'd like to remain friends for now." She held out her hand.

He took her hand, a half-smile on his face. "Buck would have fits if he saw you here." His smile grew wider.

She pulled her hand away. "I'm sure he would. He's out with a hunting party, isn't he?"

"No, we came back early." He glanced at the upscale vehicles in the parking area. "Guess the wussies thought the place would be air-conditioned. All they did was whine about the mud and bugs. They're all taking a break at the lodge, plumb tuckered out."

"Well, I'd better go." She walked to her truck before he could get any ideas about kissing her again or keeping her around until Buck did find her there. When she started the engine, she saw JoGene trying his front door and then looking at her. Did he wonder if she'd been snooping inside? And more importantly, had she made another enemy?

She saw the lodge through the trees as she drove down the main road. Beyond that was the Waddells' house where JoGene had lived when they'd dated. That was the place she really wanted to check out. She'd have to give some thought as to how she might achieve that. Sneaking into Buck's house would be like crawling into an alligator cave.

When she pulled up to Southern Comfort near noon, the sight of a squad car parked out front made her chest tighten with dread. Not again. And then a more terrifying thought: Oscar! Smitty's and Amy's cars were out front along with two others. A quick scan revealed no visible damage other than the boarded-up windows she hadn't replaced yet. She skidded to a stop and ran inside.

"Oh, my God."

The place had been trashed. Stools and chairs were broken, tables tipped over, and the bottles of liquor behind the bar smashed. The fumes were overwhelming. If somebody lit up, the place would go up in flames. Her gaze darted to the pictures along the walls. They had been knocked down, but weren't damaged. The jukebox's glass cover had been cracked. Elva's dead animals had been smashed. At least the one fixed window hadn't been re-broken. The vandals hadn't touched the plywood covering the other windows.

Amy rushed over and took Kim's hands in hers. "It's awful, just awful. We found it like this when we came in. We've been worried sick about you. Been trying your house for an hour."

Angus was walking around taking it all in. Kinsey was snapping pictures. Smitty walked over and awkwardly patted her shoulder.

"Where's Oscar?" she managed through a throat tightened by grief and anger.

"He's out back. He's fine, just fine. I didn't want him cutting himself on the glass."

She took in the destruction again, hoping tears wouldn't blur her eyes. "I didn't even look inside when I dropped him off."

Angus walked over. "I don't guess you'll be serving lunch today."

She could only shake her head. He also patted her shoulder and walked out. She blinked to clear her eyes. Anger overtook the shock and sorrow, and she stalked over broken glass to Kinsey. "Find out who did this."

"Well, we know it wasn't Billy Bob or Clem. They're still in jail. Know anyone who might have a grudge against you?"

She wanted to laugh but was sure it would come out hysterically. Since he was toying with her to begin with, he'd get too much satisfaction from that.

"Could be half the town, don't you think?" he said.

"Take fingerprints. They had to have left fingerprints."

"Them and everybody in town who's ever been in here. I did find this. Figure they used it to smash the bottles." He indicated a new bat with the pointy end of his boot. "Dusted it, but there weren't any prints on it. We'll see if we can trace where it was bought." He pointed toward the half-open door. The door frame was cracked where someone had jimmied the lock. "They gained entrance through the back door." He finished the report and handed her a copy. "For insurance."

She hoped Elva had good insurance that paid promptly. There weren't enough cash reserves to fix this. "What about finding the person or persons who did this?"

"Let me handle this." He nodded toward the bar. "You've already made enough enemies. In all the years that Elva owned this place, she only had one break-in— and that was for money. This is a message to you. You can't seem to keep out of trouble. Just like your dad. You best remember what happened to him." She got a chill, but kept her expression bland. "Rest assured, Miss Lyons, we'll be focusing all of our attention on this crime. You are, after all, our best customer these days."

He said good-bye to Smitty and Amy and walked out. Kim surveyed the mess again and tried not to let tears bubble to the surface. Every bottle of liquor had been smashed. If this was a message, what did it say? Get out of town? Stop snooping? It made her even more determined to disobey both commands.

Kim picked up a broom. "Let's get this place cleaned up."

Smitty said, "You seen the kitchen yet?"

She hadn't thought past the main area and all the lost liquor. She followed him into the kitchen where the mess continued. Thawed chicken wings littered the floor, adding a dead flesh aroma to the air. Bread was scattered every-where, lettuce and tomatoes strewn all over. Her box of beer signs was still in the corner where, thankfully, she hadn't unpacked it yet. They, or he, hadn't messed with the desk other than to clear the surface. The drawers and files within were intact. The safe was in the floor beneath the desk, hidden by the carpeting. The vandals hadn't been interested in money, only in making as much of a mess as possible.

"Let's get this place cleaned up. I don't want to see it anymore."

She fed dollars into the jukebox and crossed her fingers when she pressed the selections. She smiled in relief when Mandoza played.

"I chose some Skaggs for you," she told Smitty. "And 'Mustang Sally' for you, Amy."

She put a large CLOSED FOR REMODELING sign out front and hated the fact that whoever had done this would take satisfaction from that. But they'd never see her break down.

By three, they'd piled all the broken chairs and stools out by the Dumpster. Luckily, the tables were so sturdy they'd only sustained a few bumps and scrapes. She'd already gone over to the hardware store and ordered replacement chairs, using up the last of the reserves with the deposit alone. They wouldn't be in until mid-week, which meant she'd be closed until then. Couldn't ask your customers to sit on the floor, after all. She tried not to think about the lost income just when she needed it most. She was going to make the best out of this. In fact, she'd rented a sander for the following day and planned to take down the top layer of grime and old varnish on the wood floor.

"Hello!" a man called from the front door. Kim didn't recognize him, and judging by the dress shirt and tie, he surely didn't live in town.

Amy walked over to him, a few steps ahead of Kim. "We're closed."

"I'm William Berlin, from South Florida Liquor Distribution." He nodded at Smitty, who was scraping up the last bits of broken glass behind the bar.

"I'm Kim Lyons, Elva's granddaughter. I own this place now. Boy, am I glad to see you. As you can see, we had some trouble last night. I'm going to need some basic stock to get me going again."

He squinted as though his hemorrhoids were acting up. "Actually, I'm here to collect payment for your last order. I'm supposed to collect on delivery, but Elva was a long-time customer and I gave her a few days to get the money."

Kim glanced at Smitty for confirmation. He said, "She took money from the bar to build the hothouse, and it put her behind a little. The distributor had just come last week and stocked us up. Didn't I mention he'd be coming for payment?"

"No, Smitty, you neglected to mention that small detail." She knew how the system worked. Unfortunately, she'd used most of her savings as a down payment on the truck. She pushed past the dread in her chest and put on her sweetest smile. "Mr. Berlin, I'm going to need a few more days—and some basic stock."

Berlin had been tracing his finger across the crack in the jukebox, which had gone silent a short time ago. "All your stock is gone?"

"Every last bit. I won't be able to afford a full bar right away, but I'll need the basics." If he'd only extend her a little more credit, she could raise the money.

Berlin got the hemorrhoid look again. "Well, see, we have a problem. You're already behind by one invoice. I can't sell you any more until I'm paid for that, and for whatever you want to order now."

She held back all the nasty words that wanted to gush out of her mouth and took a deep breath to be absolutely sure they wouldn't sneak out. "You extended credit to Elva."

He held up his hand, maybe to ward off the words he sensed were just below the surface. "And I'm not supposed to do even that. By law, I'm to collect payment upon delivery. Elva was a good customer for a number of years, so I gave her extra time once in a while. But she is not our customer any longer—you are. You're an unknown quantity. The bottom line is, I can't give you any stock until you've paid in full."

"All I'm asking is that you reconsider. I've worked in bars for years, I've got a BA in business, and I know how to run one. This is the only real bar in town, and it's a favorite of the locals."

He was backing toward the door, not a good sign. "I'm sorry, but I have to follow the law." He bumped into the door. "Until you pay in cash for the last shipment and the next, I can't give you one bottle. And I need payment on the last shipment right away." He ducked out the door and walked briskly to his panel van. He didn't even look back at her, just hopped in and quickly backed out of the lot.

Rage and frustration coalesced to helpless defeat by the time the dust had settled in the parking lot. She felt a hand on her shoulder and turned to find Smitty standing beside her. "Wish I could help you, young'un."

"Me, too," Amy said. "I've only got two dimes to rub together these days, but you can have 'em."

Kim was touched by their support. "Thanks. I'll figure out a way, I swear I will. But until then, we're going to have to close." She hated that most of all, that someone out there would be enjoying watching her bar sit closed day after day. "If I could sell those damn orchids, I'd have the money." Well, after she paid off Zell, which probably wouldn't leave much.

They finished the bulk of the cleaning by the end of the day, and Kim paid them. It was dark by the time they walked out to their vehicles.

"You gonna be all right?" Smitty asked after Amy had left.

She felt her lower lip quiver and bit down on it. "I'll be fine. I'm not going to let them win, Smitty. I can't."

"You're a lot like Elva, you know. When she got something in her head, she'd go after it no matter what. She'd never give up. And if someone stepped on her, why, she'd brush off the dirt and keep on going." He gave her shoulder a squeeze and headed out to his small truck.

Being compared to Elva was a compliment. She'd been a strong woman who had survived being an outsider, a divorced woman when being divorced wasn't common, and the female owner of a bar when that wasn't common, either. But Kim wasn't completely sure he'd meant it as a compliment. After all, Elva had ended up dead.

# CHAPTER 20

All it would take was a tug on the trigger and Kim would be dead. The end of the rifle was pointed right at her as she lay in bed, no doubt exhausted by all the cleaning she'd had to do that day. Even the pig was asleep.

This would the easy way of handling Kim. Pull the trigger, *bang,* and it'd be all over. Oscar started to stir. Okay, check out the rest of the house while he resettled into sleep. Take one last look to see if anything had been overlooked. Like that tiny piece of rubber glove. Just a stupid little thing, maybe not even incriminating, but still . . . it didn't pay to take any chances, especially now that Kim was snooping around. A plastic bag held the piece of the glove. It would disappear.

The pig was standing in the doorway. Good thing it wasn't a dog. Though Oscar didn't bark, he let out a loud snort as his snout twitched. Pigs didn't have good eyesight, but they had great noses—and he smelled an intruder.

"Oscar?" Kim's voice trailed from the bedroom.

Damn. After a quick survey of the room, the closet seemed the best place to hide. The door had just closed when Kim's voice sounded from the hallway.

"What are you doing, sweetie pig? You startled me."

Sweetie pig, eh? Through the slats, Oscar could be seen

walking into the room. Kim walked in, too, and looked around. She was carrying a small canister, probably tear gas. She opened the closet door. The coats must have covered everything, because she closed the door and padded into the hallway. More noises followed as she checked the living room and kitchen.

"Come on, Oscar. Let's go back to bed."

It was silent again after a few minutes, but Kim was no doubt listening intently from her bed. Soon, though, she'd relax and drop back to sleep, and it would be safe to leave the closet. And to leave one small gift for Kim.


Kim was jarred out of sleep by the sound of a gun going off. She lurched out of bed, her heart slamming against her ribs. She grabbed her canister of tear gas that she kept beneath her pillow and went to search the house. Oscar went tearing past her out of the second bedroom, squealing wildly.

What was happening?

Early morning light crept into the house and spilled onto the floors. She could see droplets of blood in Oscar's trail. "Oh, my God, Oscar! Oscar!"

She looked into the bedroom he'd come from, expecting to see someone standing there holding a gun. Something struck her as odd, but she couldn't place what it was. She checked the bathroom before she ran into the living room where Oscar had gone. He was burrowed into his pile of blankets, still squealing in pain. Blood smeared the blankets.

She knelt down beside him. "Oscar, what happened? Let me see."

When he lifted his head, she saw that a small portion of his ear had been torn. Someone had shot him. The thought prickled through her, both terrifying and infuriating. "Hold on, big guy. I'll be right back."

Nobody shot her pig and got away with it. Well, unless they shot her, too. She ducked down as she crept to the bedroom and looked out through the blinds. No one was out there. She made her way to the front and peered out. No vehicles, no sign of anyone. What was it, a phantom sniper? No, wait. She'd heard a shot, but not breaking glass. Which meant someone was in the house.

Her finger twitched on the canister. The closet. That was what bothered her about the second bedroom. When she looked last night, she'd closed the closet door. Now it was open. She walked on shaky legs into the room, canister raised and ready. She shoved the bifold door open the rest of the way and aimed—at a rifle.

"What the hell?"

The rifle was lying on the floor. She pressed the back of her hand against the barrel; it was warm. How had this gotten back in the house?

"Oscar." She grabbed tissues, peroxide, and antibiotic and ran back to the kitchen. She held on to him as best she could while pouring peroxide on his ear. "I know, sweetie pig, I know. It'll only hurt for a minute." It was a small tear. Luckily the bullet had only nipped the edge of his ear. He could have been killed. Strange how the thought squeezed her heart over a pig she hadn't wanted in the first place. She hugged his big, warm body. "Oscar, what did you see last night? Was someone here . . . in the house?" She shivered violently at the thought.

Whoever it was had probably been hiding in the closet with the rifle. As much as she didn't want to believe that, she knew she hadn't missed seeing the rifle in the closet.

"Did you go investigate this morning?" she asked as she dabbed at his ear with tissue. "Maybe you bumped the trigger or pushed it into something else. Maybe it was set to go off."

Should she call the substation? And tell the deputy on duty what, that the rifle no one had even reported missing had just shown up in her closet? Kinsey would love that story. She finished treating Oscar's ear and went back to the closet. If she could get someone to do a close scrutiny of it, maybe they would find a hair or other fiber that might help. No way would that happen, so she'd do it herself.

She carefully picked up the gun with two towels and carried it into the kitchen. Smitty's initials were carved into the stock, just as he'd said. There was also a sanded-down patch on the wood. Blood or any other indicator that this had been used to strike Elva was gone. Still, she put on Elva's reading glasses, sat under the brightest lights in the house, and went over every inch of the gun. She saw nothing, though she could have missed a tiny fiber. After searching the house, she found some bubble wrap that was swaddling a Chia Pet Elva had stashed in a closet, and wrapped the gun in it. When she got more proof, she'd hand it over to the authorities.

Except she'd now lost her way of finding the killer. A killer who had figured out she'd been looking for the gun or some piece of evidence. She'd told Zell everything. Had he mentioned it to his family? Could one of them have panicked and brought the gun back? She'd also mentioned it to Kinsey.

Kim settled in next to Oscar and rubbed his belly. "We're going to find out who did this to you. I promise."


Charlotte let out a long whistle as she walked inside the bar. "Wow. They weren't kidding."

She looked as fresh as a wild orchid and just as pretty. Her white dress hugged her small waist and accentuated her cleavage. Tullie was dressed in a flowery pink dress that was at odds with her somber expression.

Kim felt gritty compared to them, but she was too tired to care. She turned off the sander when the two walked in. Flecks of varnish and wood coated her skin.

"They?" she said.

"The folks at church." Charlotte was still taking it in. Tables were pushed against the walls, and the pictures were stacked on the end of the bar. She ran her finger down the crack in the jukebox.

"Anybody at church brag about doing this?" Kim asked, brushing off some of the dust.

"I didn't hear anything. Kinsey said there wasn't any evidence to point to the purporters." Before Kim could correct her, she added, "Perpetrators, I mean. This is a shame, a damn shame. Where are folks supposed to go drinking now? Can't listen to Waylon Jennings at the Everglades Inn's lounge."

Tullie was running her fingers over the broken backgammon board.

"It's still playable," Kim said. "The pieces are in the office."

Charlotte asked, "When do you think you'll be open again?"

Kim wasn't going to tell her about the supplier problem. "Oh, might be a week or so. I've got to get chairs and a new supply of liquor. Figured I'd tackle the flooring while we're closed." She tried to keep her voice as upbeat as possible, but she could hear the phony echo.

Charlotte said, "Hey, frog, got any vibes on who did this?" She wiggled her fingers. "Maybe one of your *feelings*?"

Tullie shifted her gaze away from her mother.

Kim said, "I could use all the help I can get. Really," she added when Tullie looked at her skeptically. "Not that it'll get a conviction, but it'd be nice to know who my enemies are."

Charlotte leaned against the jukebox and leveled her blue-green eyes at Kim. "It's always good to know a person's intentions." Her long nails tapped rhythmically against the thick glass.

When Kim suspected Charlotte was about to ask why she'd really been sneaking around Heron's Glen, she quickly said, "Where's the rest of the family?"

"Owen don't go to church. Said if there was a God, he'd have been born rich and good-looking. Daddy was too hungover to go this morning. And Zell—he's the one you're really wondering about, isn't he?" She gave Kim a sly smile. "He had an emergency call from a client. Some environmental group shut down a construction project in Naples."

She seemed overly interested in Kim's level of interest in Zell, so Kim kept her face bland. She wanted to clarify that she didn't care what Zell was doing but got sidetracked by Tullie who screamed, "What happened to Oscar's ear? A piece of it's missing!"

"He accidentally caused a rifle to go off." There was no point in telling the rest of the story. "He's all right now, but he was sure scared when it happened." That last part could be said of her, too.

Charlotte said, "You've got to be careful about keeping guns around. Pigs are like children, you know. Curious as all get out. We keep ours locked in a cabinet. Our guns, I mean, not our children." She started the tapping again, looking at Kim. "Was it true what you told us Friday, about coming out to see me? To have lunch?"

"Yes," Kim lied, wondering why Zell hadn't told them she'd been trespassing. Maybe because he could be trusted. "I'd like to be friends." That much was true, anyway. "I like you and Tullie."

"And Zell," she said in a teasing voice. "Well, if that's what you want—to be friends—you need to set things straight with my daddy. And if you have any designs on my brother at all, even ones you haven't admitted to yourself, that would sure help your cause. It'd make things easier on Zell, too."

Kim felt herself tense. "Set things straight?"

"Yeah. Apologize. After all, you did accuse the man of murder." She lifted an arched brow in challenge. "If that's what you were really out there for, then making things right shouldn't be so hard. You apologized to Zell for kicking him out of your bar when he was defending you, after all."

"But I knew I was wrong then. I honestly don't know whether your father killed Rhonda or not."

"He didn't." She waved her gold-tipped nails in the air. "He might have been reckless in the old days, but brutally kill a girl? No way. 'Sides, if he was into killing women, more of them would have died between then and now. If you want to live here, you got to let the past go. You're like a bulldog, grabbing onto something and not letting go. You moved into our house full of anger and a need for justice." She pushed off from the jukebox and walked to where Tullie was crooning over Oscar, who was on his back loving every minute of it. "Let's see what happened to you, big boy."

Apologize to Winnerow? Charlotte was right, though. Kim had moved to Heron's Glen full of anger. Had she only seen what she'd wanted to see? Anybody could have taken the family truck, another fact that had helped create the jury's doubt as to Winnerow's guilt. She'd been so sure. Could she have been wrong? It was something she couldn't bear to contemplate.

"Oscar, my goodness, you poor thing," Charlotte said as she examined his ear.

Tullie had wandered over to where Kim still stood near the jukebox. "Do you believe my feelings?" she asked softly.

Kim leaned closer to the girl. She tried to phrase an answer about not necessarily believing in psychic feelings but admitting Tullie had been right about the quest for truth. The words *I do* came out instead. When Tullie was clearly eyeing her shorn hair, Kim felt compelled to say, "It was an accident."

Charlotte strolled toward the front door. "Tullie, we better get on home. We've got two large orders of gator meat to get ready to ship tomorrow."

With those haunting blue eyes, Tullie held Kim's gaze for a moment. She wrapped cool fingers around Kim's arm and whispered, "Be careful," before meeting her mother at the door.

Charlotte said, "Oh, one thing I gotta ask you, and there's just no polite way to do it. What in the name of bad haircuts did you do to your hair?"

Kim automatically ran her hand over her head. "I thought I'd try something new." If she implicated Grace, it would be all over town by that evening.

"Well, remember this: new ain't necessarily better." She

started to walk out, but swung back through the doorway. "Daddy'll be around all day if you decide to come over for any reason. We'll see you later."

Charlotte seemed so sure Kim would come out. Maybe an apology was in order. Smoothing things for Zell would be worth humbling herself after all he'd done for her. And Charlotte wouldn't have suggested it if she thought Winnerow would throw her apology back in her face.

Or would she?

She remembered how Charlotte had enjoyed creating strife. Nothing lethal, just a dose to liven things up. She liked to play both sides, pretending loyalty while enjoying the show. Tullie's words came back: *Be careful who you trust.* And then just the warning to be careful. The girl was worried, no doubt about that. Kim had every intention of being very careful about who she trusted. She had a feeling her life might depend on it.

A couple of hours later, Kim called it quits for the day. She drove home, running her apology through her head like a speech. It occurred to her that Charlotte had pressed her into this apology using her own lie against her. Was she orchestrating another display of humiliation or was she really trying to make peace for her family, and Zell in particular?

All right, she'd prepare for humiliation and hope for the best. That Zell wouldn't be around would make things easier. He had stepped into the role of reluctant ally. She didn't want to put him in that uncomfortable place if Winnerow refused her apology.

As soon as she pulled up to her house, she knew something was wrong. She couldn't pinpoint what it was at first. She sat in the truck and scanned the house. Her gaze homed in on the open hothouse door.

She grabbed her tear gas, left Oscar in the truck, and walked to the hothouse. Pieces of bark and leaves littered the ground. When she walked into the hothouse, she saw that those bits were all that was left. She'd had to fight tears that morning at the bar. She couldn't handle one more assault.

But there it was. Not vandalism this time. Her legs went weak, and she held on to the nearest post. Every orchid had been stolen except for the few that had been nailed to the posts. How much was she supposed to take? This wasn't just thievery. Like the vandalism at the bar its aim was simple: drain her and run her out of town.

What pissed her off was that it hurt. It was rejection at its worst. She dropped to her knees and gave in to the tears for a few minutes. She needed this release of grief and frustration. She sure as hell deserved it. How was she ever going to repay Zell?

She pulled herself up, not out of a desire to pull herself together and buck up, but to check out the house to see if further damage had been done. A quick tour showed no sign of thievery or vandalism. She let Oscar out and took in the empty hothouse again. It looked as though someone had dragged a length of board over the ground to cover up footsteps and tire tracks. Not that she expected any resolution, but she still called the sheriff's substation and reported the crime.

A deputy she didn't know came out and wrote up the crime. While she'd waited for him, she'd taken a shower and actually considered drinking one of the beers Elva had left in the fridge. She nixed the idea. What she didn't need was a loose tongue when she went to see Winnerow.

After the deputy left, she put Oscar in the house and drove to Heron's Glen. She hated leaving the pig behind, but it was too hot to leave him in or near the truck. She whispered a prayer for his safety. Besides, they'd done their deed. Now they'd sit back and wait to see what she did.

Funny, she thought as she drove between those two fancy columns with herons on them; when she'd first come back, she'd sworn to steer clear of the Macgregors. And now here she was driving onto their property for the third time in less than two weeks. As a perfect backdrop to the visit, storm clouds roiled the dark sky above her. She was hoping the storm would hold off just long enough to be used as a reason to make a quick getaway.


JoGene stomped into his father's house. "What the hell were you thinking, trashing her bar like that?" It was the first time he'd had a chance to confront Buck about it.

Buck was sitting in the living room with his usual can of discount beer. "Someone had to take matters in hand."

"I said I'd handle it! And I am!"

"She's still here, ain't she? I wouldn't call that handling it. I'm just helping things along, that's all."

He hated that Buck didn't trust him—not that he deserved it. And in fact, he could use this to his advantage. Yeah, that's exactly what he'd do.

# CHAPTER 21

Zell's black truck was parked in front of Heron's Glen. Kim tried to sell the jump in her belly as nervousness about her apology and nearly succeeded. As she walked up to the house, she ran her speech through her mind once more. Short and sweet and to the point. She took a deep breath and pulled on the fancy brass knocker.

A few minutes later, Tullie answered the door. She had her little gator slung over her shoulder. Both were dotted with water, and Tullie had a towel wrapped around her bathing suit. She smiled when she saw Kim, who involuntarily stepped back at the sight of the gator.

"Been swimming?"

Tullie nodded. "Runt needs his exercise. You come to apologize to Grandpa?"

"I'm going to give it my best shot. Is he here?"

"They're all down at the farm checking on the eggs. Wait a minute, and I'll take you there."

A few minutes later Tullie reappeared, thankfully without Runt. She'd thrown on shorts, a tank top, and flip-flops. "Okay, ready," she said breathlessly.

When they got into the truck, Kim said, "It's nice of you to take me there."

"I like you. You don't treat me like I'm weird."

Kim felt a jab in her chest as she remembered the snide way Charlotte had referred to Tullie's "feelings." "You're not weird. There are lots of people out there like you."

Tullie's eyes widened with such hope, it was painful. "There are?" Tullie hadn't been out in the world to know.

"There sure are. Some people believe in them and some don't. But it's not considered all that strange."

"Uncle Zell says I'm different, not strange. He says being different is good."

Damn, why did he have to be so nice? She'd much prefer to think of him as arrogant and self-absorbed. "He's right."

Tullie directed her to the two white buildings with plastic roofs. To the left was the large water tank. Kim knew that every day they flushed out the water in the gator holding tanks. Beyond the gator houses was the slaughterhouse and cool storage for the meat. Part of the slaughterhouse building was the office.

She pulled into the parking lot and cut the engine. This was as close as she'd ever come. The smell alone was enough to keep one away, let alone the gators inside. Even with constant fresh water, gator excrement in great quantity was strong enough to peel off skin.

"Is Zell here?" Kim asked.

Tullie shrugged. "I think he's on a call."

She hopped out and headed to the building on the right. Kim envied her ease. Like Charlotte, she'd grown up around gators.

Kim slowly followed, hoping against hope that it wasn't a drop of rain she felt on her arm. The sky rumbled in answer, and a shimmer of light in the east preceded another rumble of thunder a few seconds later. If Tullie hadn't been with her, she would have gone on home and waited for another day. The storm was going to end up stranding her there.

Tullie stood by the half-doors waiting for her. No backing out now. She was one of the few people who seemed to like her. She didn't want to lose the girl's respect by chickening out.

When she got to the doors, Tullie said, "Open the top door and look inside. Even though there are smaller gators in here, it's still good to make sure none got loose."

"Very good," Kim agreed.

She remembered the story of how Owen had forgotten to do that once. She flipped the bolt and pulled it open. The smell wasn't as bad as in the big gator house, but the air was still hot and steamy. It was dim inside; the only light came through the opaque roof. With the storm overhead, that was minimal. The walkway was painted white, probably to highlight any gators that might have escaped.

"They're in the incubator room. Come on, I'll show you the eggs." Tullie grabbed her hand and started pulling her toward the doorway at the end of the long walkway.

Kim tugged the girl back despite the enthusiasm in her voice. "Why don't you tell them I'm here? I'll wait. Don't want to disturb them."

The rain started coming down, sending a gust of wet, cool air through the top opening of the doorway. She could feel the mist against her bare neck, and it sent a shiver down her spine. Tullie tugged harder. "Come on, see the eggs."

She allowed the girl to pull her along, but her gaze was drawn to the large holding tanks on either side. This was her worst nightmare, only in miniature. Even small, gators could deliver a nasty bite with their needle-sharp teeth. Each tank held a different-sized gator. The one at the end held the smallest specimens.

"Aren't they cute?" Tullie said, sounding like a normal little girl . . . except for the fact that she was talking about gators.

"Uh . . . no. Not evenly remotely cute."

As soon as those words were uttered, she came face-to-face with Zell. He had opened the door and was about to walk right into her. Which wouldn't have been a good idea considering his sweaty, naked chest. Not much better, she instinctively put her hands out and made contact with that chest, which was how she personally became aware of just how naked and sweaty it was.

"I thought you were out on an emergency call," she blurted out because nothing sensible came to mind. She pulled her hands back and wiped them on her jeans.

He had his shirt wadded up in his hand and used it to wipe the sweat off his face. "I managed to mediate until we can get a court date. What are *you* doing here?"

She pulled her gaze away from his face and looked beyond him. Charlotte was in a large room lined with shelves and wooden boxes. She said, "Tullie, where have you been? I've been trying to call the house. Some babies are hatching!"

Tullie darted inside the room and peered in the box that was sitting on a table in the center. Now that Kim had a chance to collect her senses, she could hear the high-pitched grunt of hatching gators. The grunt was a call to their mother, who would help them out of their shells and carry them to the water.

"Come here, Kim!" Tullie called, her face in total rapture.

"I came to talk to Winnerow," she stammered, but Zell steered her by the shoulders to the box.

Charlotte had stripped down to a silky peach bra in deference to the heat in the room. Neither Owen nor Winnerow were within sight. Charlotte leaned down and stroked one of the eggs with her manicured finger. It shook and jiggled. "Come on, baby. Come on out or mama will help you." She made the same type of grunting sounds the babies were making. "I heard them on the monitor." She sucked in a breath when the egg cracked. "Too bad Owen isn't around. He hates missing a hatching. He and JoGene are out fishing."

Two tiny gators were curled up inside their eggs trying to break out. Charlotte used her nails to help them. Her face looked rapturous too, even though this was something she had to have seen a hundred times.

When Kim looked at Zell, he was watching her. His gaze shifted to the box, though he wasn't bothered that she'd caught him. She watched a bead of sweat making its slow journey along his jawline as he leaned over the box. Sweat already trickled between her breasts and down her back, and she understood why the two had taken off their shirts. Not that she was going to do it.

She decided it was a safer bet to watch the gators than to get caught staring at Zell. She moved into the space between him and Tullie, feeling his damp arm brush against hers. The two gators had broken free of their confines and were rubbing against the nesting material to shed the bits of shell. The first baby was sitting on Charlotte's hand as she continued to grunt.

Zell picked up one of them and held it in front of Kim, who made a point not to back away. The gator's grunts quickened. "Cute little fella, huh?"

"Cuter than the full-grown ones," she allowed.

Two more eggs cracked open, and she watched the babies emerge. Zell picked up the one on Charlotte's hand and took both gators to one of the holding tanks. He returned and waited for two more to get their bearings before taking them off. Kim followed him and found his fantastic derrière perched up as he bent over to put the babies in the tank.

She came up beside him in the open doorway and watched the babies instantly take to the water. They alternately swished through the clear water and assumed the gator pose: floating in the water with only their eyes and nostrils above the water and their legs akimbo. Rain pounded on the plastic above, catching their attention.

Zell turned around to face her and whispered, "Now if I had a big ego, I'd think you'd braved gators to get another lip lock."

"You do have a big ego," she whispered back and nudged him. "I came to see Winnerow."

He affected a shot-in-the-heart stance. "Thrown over for my own father."

That earned him another nudge. "Don't be ridiculous."

"And I do not have a big ego. I just happen to be wildly good-looking and fun to be around."

She caught a spark of humor in his eyes and a twitch at the corner of his mouth. When she realized she'd been looking at that mouth for a second too long, she shifted to his eyes. She disliked him and liked him; sometimes he seemed threatening, and other times she was afraid of him for reasons beyond bodily danger. He wasn't her type, yet she was drawn to him like sweet ants to sugar. She'd never been kissed like that before, and the way it had made her feel scared her more than anything.

Her heartbeat was speeding up, and he was only looking at her. Lightning flashed above them, lighting up the dim building. It felt as though an arc of electricity jumped from him to her. His hand went to his chest in the shot-through-the-heart way again. "Whoa, what was that?"

At first her mouth was too dry, her throat too tight, to respond. "Lightning?" she finally said.

He shook his head. "That wasn't lightning."

She took a deep breath, her mouth hanging slack. No, it wasn't lightning, at least not the kind that shattered the sky outside.

The door at the end of the hallway opened, and a very wet Winnerow walked inside. He managed quite well with his cane, she noticed. His displeasure at seeing her was evident on his face, but apparently silence among the gators was more important. Was that why Tullie had insisted she come inside, knowing he couldn't yell at her? He walked up to her, killing both her and Zell with his eyes before going into the incubation room.

When she met Zell's gaze again, she thought she read *Don't worry, I'm here* in the blue-green depths. Just what she didn't want. She followed Winnerow, and Zell walked in behind her. Charlotte held up one of the babies. "You're a grandpa!" she crowed in a whisper.

Winnerow closed the door. "Why is it that every time I turn around, this woman is on my property?" He glared at Zell. "Or on my son's property."

Kim cleared her throat and faced Winnerow, who hadn't looked at her through his whole whispered tirade. "I'm sorry to intrude, but I wanted to apologize." Of course, her perfectly planned speech fled her mind. "For everything. If I'd known the truth about my father . . . who knows how I would have felt? I came here with a lot of anger toward you. When I saw your truck going down that road, well, maybe I saw you because I wanted to see you. It seemed very clear back then, but I could have been wrong. I caused a lot of turmoil in the family, I know." She took all of them in. "I just wanted to say that I'm sorry."

Winnerow Macgregor was speechless, something rare for him. The heat felt heavy, making it hard to breathe. The only sounds in the room were the grunts of the gators, the rustle of nesting material as they moved, and the gentle patter of the lightening rain. Since she didn't expect him to absolve her, she started to leave.

"Wait," he said. "You mean that?"

"Yes." She was pretty sure she did.

He regarded her for a few long minutes. She glanced toward Charlotte and Zell, finding surprise on his expression, satisfaction on hers. Tullie was taking it all in as she usually did. Kim turned back to Winnerow, who said, "Why are you doing this? Are you in love with my son?"

Kim shifted her gaze to Zell and quickly back again, trying not to think of that lightning moment. "That's not it at all." Though she had to admit she was doing this for Zell, and she clearly had feelings for him to put herself through this ordeal. "I just want to make peace."

"Are you saying you now don't believe I killed Rhonda Jones?"

"I believe that I convicted you without enough evidence."

He considered that. "At least you're honest. If I accept your apology, I'd better not catch you snooping around my property again."

"Fair enough." She glanced at everyone standing around the nesting box. "I'll leave you to your work."

She was glad to open the doors and step out into the relatively cool air outside. The rain still fell, but she gratefully stepped into the light shower. She lifted her face and let the drops of water wash down over her. That hadn't been so bad. In fact, a weight had lifted off her shoulders.

And a different one had taken its place as she remembered Zell's words: *Whoa, what was that?* He wasn't about to let either of them believe it was mere electricity.

A touch on her shoulder sent her spinning around. Zell stood there, still naked from his waist up. "That was pretty big of you, apologizing like that."

"It was about time, really."

He brushed her hair off her forehead. "You're something else, you know that?"

"I was thinking the same thing about you just recently."

"Is that when you realized how big my ego was?"

She laughed. "Sometime around then."

"You could have made things a lot easier on me by just being a pain in the ass. You're good at it."

"Are you trying to lay the charm on me?"

He tilted his head, looking devilishly cute. "Just telling you like it is. That's how I am."

"Ah, if I can get an answer out of you in the first place, you mean. Which brings to mind the fact that you can be a real pain in the ass, too."

He moved close enough to trip her heartbeat and brushed her hair back again. "It helps, you looking like a boy."

She brushed his hand away. "Helps what?"

"Helps to remind me that you are not, in any way, shape, or form, the type of woman I'm usually attracted to. I like a woman with long hair who's sweet and quiet, appreciates gators, of course, and doesn't cause trouble." He drew his fingers up her throat to beneath her chin and rubbed his thumb across her lower lip. "Not one who's full of sass and makes me want to kiss the sass right out of that mouth of hers. Not a woman I'm supposed to dislike on principle. Not a woman who's got half the town wanting her to leave."

"I can see why you've got a reputation with the ladies, Zell. I'm about to swoon right now." The truth was, she could hardly breathe.

His laugh vibrated through her body. "What I'm saying is, stop doing things that make me respect you and, even worse, like you."

"Or?"

"Or I just might have to kiss you again." And he did, after tipping her chin up for a better angle. For a few seconds, she forgot about the rain and the alligators and even the smell in the air. She forgot that she wasn't supposed to like him, either. She forgot everything except his mouth moving over hers and the way that was making her feel all alive and tingly everywhere. He finished the kiss and said, "Now scoot before I really lose my head."

She didn't know whether to take him seriously or not. Especially when she could hear him singing the words to "Ain't Love a Bitch" as he walked back to the building. He had her all confused and tangled up. She was used to men cloaking their intentions and burying their feelings. Zell was another creature altogether. He would demand full disclosure from her if this went any farther, and she didn't know how to disclose her feelings.

Her body gave some indication as she walked to her truck with a bounce in her step—until she saw the broken orchid petal lying on the muddy ground. She picked it up, remembering how Zell had stroked a petal just like it in the hothouse. A few more leaves and pieces of bark littered the road going past the buildings. Maybe it was a coincidence that this petal was here.

Fat chance.

She was startled to see Winnerow watching her from the open doorway. He quickly closed the door.

Why did something happen every time she thought things might be looking up?

She got into her truck but sat there for a few minutes rolling the bruised petal in her fingers. She could call the deputy who had taken her report and ask him to check out Heron's Glen. She could tell Zell about it and see if he knew anything. Either action would seem like an accusation, and old wounds had barely begun to heal.

She tossed the petal on the floor of the truck and started the engine. She felt just like that broken petal.

Winnerow had seen everything: the kiss and Kim finding the orchid petal. Zell hadn't looked surprised when he'd turned toward the doors and seen him there. He'd kept his expression bland, and Winn realized Zell had probably gotten that from him. The kid could slip a mask of nothing on his face to cover whatever he was feeling. Where Winn was concerned, it had often been embarrassment and derision. Winnerow deserved nothing less, of course. Zell had also gotten his passionate nature from his father, though Winn's passion had died long ago. The stroke and then Kitty's death had crushed it into the ground. He couldn't get past that he'd been responsible for her husband's death and then hers. They'd been drinking and fighting when Kitty found out he'd been cheating on her. She'd rushed out in anger, driven into the ditch, and drowned. His fault.

Somehow he'd been blessed that his children had managed to forgive him, if not respect him. Charlotte particularly had stayed by his side. Zell was much harder to win back.

Winn could live with that. He had no choice. But he'd hardly had time to assimilate Kim's apology when he discovered his son kissing her. Was he doing it to test Winn's patience, to dare him to intercede? Zell had met Winn's eyes with nary a hint of sheepishness. He'd just continued on to the incubation room.

Even that wasn't the worst of it. He knew what she'd found in the mud. Strange, but he'd felt a jab in his chest at the pain on her expression. She'd looked right at him, not accusingly even, and then gotten in the truck. Would she call the police?

He watched the rest of the babies hatch out, waiting for a knock on the door. When Owen walked in, Winn said, "Outside."

Tullie called out, "Daddy, you missed the baby gators hatching!"

He glanced at his daughter, but recognized the seriousness in Winn's face. "I'll check 'em out in a minute,
honey."

The two men walked down the ramp and across the
paved walkway to his truck. "Kim was here."

"What?"

"She came to apologize for accusing me of Rhonda's
murder. Yeah, I know, surprised the hell out of me, too.
Where'd you put the orchids?"

"Out behind the gator houses for now. I never figured
she'd come out here again, especially to the gator houses.
Did she find 'em?"

"She found a petal on the ground. I think she put it
together. So far, no visit from the sheriff's substation. Let's
not take any chances. Get rid of them."

Owen nodded. "What do you think she'll do?"

"Hard to say with that one." He'd almost rather she
accuse him of stealing. He didn't like feeling guilty about
it. "Just get rid of them now and don't let anyone here see
you."

What was done was done. He'd just discovered what
JoGene and Owen had been up to. Buck had asked him to
find out through Owen. That this might be the final nail in
Kim's financial coffin, which would send her back to Tallahassee, had been a bonus to him.

Winn might feel bad for the girl, but that didn't make
him want her to leave any less. She was still trouble eight
ways from Sunday. Adding Zell to the mix made it a real
problem. No, she had to go. He pulled out his cell phone
and punched in a speed-dial number.


Tullie woke in a panic in the middle of the night. The room
was silent, though the frogs sang their exuberant chorus
outside her window. Her eyes adjusted to the dim light cast
by her alligator nightlight. Nothing had changed.

She scrambled out of bed and went to Runt's cage. He
was trying to catch the crickets she'd put in his aquarium

before going to bed. She tried to rub the goose pimples from her arms.

The dream. It still clung to her as real as the memories of watching the baby gators hatch earlier that day. But this wasn't a dream about baby gators. This had been a nightmare about the big gators fighting over flesh and blood. She shivered again. She'd never witnessed anything like that before. Sure, they sometimes fought over the food, but all they got was Purina Gator Chow. They'd never eaten anything that was alive, though Uncle Zell had warned her that instinct was strong enough to never trust them. They weren't tame and never would be. Not even Runt.

In the dream, they were tearing flesh. She didn't know whose flesh, but the terror had been so stark, she knew it was a person, someone she knew. She remembered the foreboding she'd had about someone dying, and maybe that someone being her.

She couldn't look at Runt anymore, so she clambered back into bed and pulled the covers over her head. She'd never had a scary dream about gators before. She was so shaken she couldn't be sure that it was a dream. All she knew was, she had the sudden urge to cry.

# CHAPTER 22

Kim finally broke down and called her friend Becca that evening. Becca had worked in accounting for City Lights when Kim had started there but now worked for an engineering company.

"Well, it's about damn time," Becca said when Kim identified herself. "You've been down there almost two weeks now and not one call. So I call you, and guess what I find out? Just guess."

"I broke up with Simon and am now living down here."

"Imagine that."

Kim pulled up her knees and hugged them. "I know, I'm a terrible friend."

"I'd chalk it up to your dislike for saying good-bye if you hadn't chucked your boyfriend in the process. Goodness, girl, what are you thinking?"

"That I'm crazy. You were right about Simon and my need to pick men who didn't challenge me. And about my being too chicken to step out of my comfort zone. So, I took your advice. Now I have a house, a bar"—she scratched Oscar's head—"a potbellied pig, and some direction. I think."

"Any interesting men? Any ex-boyfriends who still spark your flame?"

Kim's laugh sounded dull to her own ears. "No," she said firmly. "I'm sorry I didn't call you earlier."

"You're sorry? You, Miss I-hate-to-apologize, sorry?"

"I've been learning how to say those words on a regular basis lately. It's just been crazy from the beginning, and I was waiting until my life had settled down to call you." She wasn't sure that was ever going to happen. Becca didn't know about her past life here, and Kim had no intention of telling her.

So when Becca told her to spill on what had been happening in her life, Kim forced a smile in her voice and told her about the beauty of the area. She left out the dangerous part.

The next morning, Kim's first stop was at the bank to see about getting a small loan. Mr. Smythe had processed her loan application, but he'd been frank with her. "I doubt you'll be able to use the bar as collateral. It is closed, after all, and in danger of going out of business."

She hated those words but only nodded in understanding. "What about my house? It's paid off."

"That's a possibility, though the house is pretty old and not in a great location. Let's see if this goes through. If it doesn't, we'll try for an equity loan."

His smile did not ring with much hope. She hated that he was looking at worst-case scenarios: *if* she defaulted, and *if* they had to take possession of the house and find a buyer for it. Didn't he realize that she'd fight to the end before she'd let the bank take her house? She gave him the best smile she could manage. "Thanks for whatever you can do. I appreciate it."

His smile sagged, but he revived it and thanked her for coming in. Unfortunately, one of the larger banks in Naples would be even less likely to take a chance on her. She pushed the defeated look from her face and walked out of the bank as though she'd just procured a loan for half a million . . . just in case anyone was looking.

JoGene was waiting for her, leaning against his truck that he'd parked behind hers. Great. She hoped he wasn't ready to move their supposed friendship to a supposed romantic relationship already. He always had been impatient.

"You seeing about getting a loan?" he asked, nodding toward the bank.

"Yeah. They're processing the paperwork now."

"I've got a proposition for you," he said, causing her muscles to stiffen.

She leaned against her truck's tailgate. "Go on."

"We draw up a partnership. Find out how much the bar is worth, I give you half, and we're partners. You're solvent and you've got help financially from here on out. We're in it together, running it and everything." When she continued to look wary, he held up his hands. "If you decide you want to extend the partnership to more personal areas, that's fine with me, too. But this is a business-only proposition."

When she had dreamed of owning a bar, she'd pictured owning it by herself. Never once had she envisioned, say, Simon running it with her. She wanted to make it on her own. On the other hand, she did want to make it. JoGene had no idea how desperate she was now that the orchids were gone, too. "I'll think about it."

"Don't mention it to anyone while you're thinking about it, okay? I don't want it getting around until it's official."

She nodded in parting and got into her truck. JoGene as a partner? She didn't like the idea a whole lot, and what made the knot in her stomach even tighter was the fact that she might have to accept his offer if she hoped to keep her life here.

When she drove to Southern Comfort, Zell's truck was in the parking lot. He hopped out, wearing a white under-shirt and old jeans. Oscar moseyed over to greet him, and Zell knelt down to scratch his head. "Oscar, what happened to your ear, buddy?"

"It was an accident." She left it at that. "What are you doing here?"

"Thought I'd help you with another of these winders before I head up to Clewiston to look over a client's property."

She leaned against the side of his truck. "I appreciate that, Zell, I really do. But I'm going to hire someone to finish them. I'm reworking finances right now, and I'm not sure I'll be able to make your payment this month until I do. I will make good on the loan, I promise."

"I'm not worried about the loan. Haven't you been able to sell those orchids?"

She had to look away at that. "Not many." He didn't know, she had to believe that. He had nothing to do with the theft of her orchids. But his family did, some of them. After all he'd done for her, she refused to put him in the middle of a bad situation, especially one with his family at the other end.

He was analyzing her. "You all right? I didn't shake you up by kissing you yesterday, did I? I didn't think a little ole kiss would shake up the indomitable Kim Lyons."

She couldn't help but laugh—or respond to the challenge he'd slipped into his words. "You didn't shake me up. I just don't think you and I getting together is a good idea. Like you said, you have a family obligation to dislike me. And I need to get my head together before I can think about getting involved with anyone." Especially someone like Zell.

He stood right in front of her and demanded that she meet his gaze. "What's going on, Kim?"

"Nothing. Something." She shook her head. "I don't want to drag you into it. Forget what I told you about Elva. Forget everything."

She called Oscar and unlocked the front door, trying hard not to look at Zell. Distancing herself would be better for both of them. What she really didn't need to do was fall in love with Zell Macgregor. She was getting dangerously close to doing just that, and that was trouble she didn't need.

. . .

Zell couldn't stop thinking about Kim all day, even as the property owner drove him around on his swamp buggy and Zell tracked the alligators and nests. Something was going on with her. Oscar's injured ear, her inability to make a payment, and more than anything, the defeat on her face had him worried.

His and Kim's getting together wasn't a good idea; she had that right. He wasn't any happier about the attraction than she was. He'd also never felt anything like this before. He wasn't about to let the bad idea of getting involved keep him from exploring it.

He'd never forced his friendship on anybody, though. She'd made it clear that she didn't want that or his help. When he'd driven into town later in the day, she'd been working on one of those windows by herself.

Fine by him. He picked up a steak and a six-pack of beer at the store and headed home.

Tullie was sitting on his front stoop when he pulled up. At first he thought she'd brought her little alligator with her. Then he realized she was talking to the stuffed gator.

Her eyes looked as haunted as Kim's had. "What's the matter, angel?" He realized he'd accidentally called Kim angel a couple of times.

"Uncle Zell, you ever seen a gator eat a person?"

He sat down beside her. "Never. Seen one eat a deer once. Gators rarely eat people."

"What about our gators? Would they eat a person if someone fell into the holding area?"

He ruffled her blond hair, wishing she could be a little more normal and smile more often. "Why are you asking all these questions?"

"I've had dreams about gators the last two nights. They were eating a person. I've never been afraid of gators before, but I'm even getting a little scared of Runt."

"Runt?"

She blanched. "My gator."

He gave her an affectionate tap on her nose. "You weren't supposed to name him."

"I know."

He leaned back against the side of the porch. "Are these dreams like your feelings?"

"I don't know. That's the strange thing about them. All I know is they make me so scared."

She was scared, and he didn't like that. "Could you see who was being eaten?"

She shook her head. "But it was someone I knew." Tullie seemed on the verge of tears, something he hardly ever saw. "Kim got her hair cut real short."

"Yeah, I know." That bothered him, too. Tullie had "seen" Kim with short hair and now she had short hair. Cold fear trickled down his veins. "You don't think it's Kim you're seeing, is it? You know she'd never go near a gator."

Tullie only shrugged, but she didn't look comforted.

He glanced longingly at the six-pack. "Let me put my groceries away and we'll go to the farm. Seeing those big guys might help you put things in perspective."

He hoped seeing them in their usual placid state might help. The most she was ever likely to see at the farm were the gators fighting each other. They were fed regularly to prevent cannibalism. The only time things got dicey was during breeding season when the males bellowed in a symphony that was accompanied by a water show. The vibrations were so strong they sent the water above the gator's back shooting up into the air.

He put her bike in the back of his truck and drove to the farm. Both JoGene's and the family's trucks were parked out front. They were probably checking on the babies. He took Tullie into the large gator house.

After checking to make sure there were no loose gators about, he led the way inside. The last of the day's light was the only illumination in the place. He watched Tullie's face as they stepped up to the first pen. Each pen was a mass of as many as three hundred gators. True to form, they were lying around looking as harmless as gators could look.

"See, no attacking gators here," he whispered.

Tullie was holding her nose. "They're just laying there," she whispered back.

She took them in with her big, blue eyes for a couple of minutes. The worry had eased a bit. "Okay, we can go now."

They both took gulps of fresh air when they stepped outside. "Feel any better?" he asked.

"A little. I hope it's just a regular dream."

"I'm sure it is. Nobody's ever been killed by a gator around here."

She looked at her dad's truck. "I can go back with my daddy."

"All right. Let's go see what they're up to." He put Tullie's bike in the bed of the other truck and headed into the small gator house.

"I'm going to wait out here," she said, climbing into the truck's cab to get away from the mosquitoes. "I've seen enough gators for a while."

He didn't like that she was getting afraid of gators. Being part of the Macgregor family meant being close to the creatures. That was partly why he had the gator test for any woman who had a mind to become part of the family. He remembered how Kim had accused him of using the test to keep women away. How she'd suspected he'd had a broken heart once. She was right. He did use the test to keep away marriage-minded women. He'd never had a broken heart, because he'd never given it to anyone. Until recently, he'd doubted that he would ever give it away.

He walked into the small gator house and headed toward the incubation room. Just as he reached for the doorknob, he heard JoGene's voice.

"I offered Kim a partnership."

Winn said, "A what?"

"I thought you wanted her out of here like the rest of us," Owen said. "What the hell have we been doing all this time, then?"

Zell froze.

JoGene said, "I'm still going to get the bar. The way I figure, I get what I want and eventually she'll fall for my charms. Then I can keep her in line."

Owen said, "What if she don't take your offer?"

"She's running out of options. We made her use all her money fixing up the bar, stole them orchids, and now she can't get booze. I'd say she's done."

Winn's laugh was bitter. "She'll find a way. She always does."

Owen said, "She was out there fixing the winders today. No, JoGene, we gotta get rid of her. I'm with Winn on this. No partnerships. We gotta do something drastic."

Zell's anger was building with each word. He wanted to bust in on them, but that wasn't his style. His style was to mull things over, think about the ramifications.

JoGene said, "Let me handle this. Probably she'll just give up and sell out to me, after I was such a nice guy and all. And if I get a roll in the hay in the meantime—"

Zell opened the door and shoved JoGene against the empty shelves.

JoGene's eyes were enormous. "What the hell?"

"It's not going to go down that way. No partnership, no roll in the hay—nothing." He knew the defeat he'd seen on Kim's face was fueling him; it made him shove JoGene harder.

JoGene said, "Zell, you don't like fighting, remember?"

Winn barked, "Zell, let him down!"

Owen just stood there with his mouth hanging open.

Zell gave him one last shove before releasing him. "Did you have anything to do with those two goons jumping her?"

JoGene stumbled and had the audacity to look mad. "They acted on their own. I just broke out the winders and painted up the bar."

"And stole the orchids."

"Well, yeah, that, too. Look, I'm not trying to hurt her. She's still going to end up with money and she can open a bar somewhere else. I'm just trying to put her in a bad financial situation. I planned to sell the orchids and add in the money to what I offer her."

"You just have it all figured out, smart boy, don't you?" Zell said. He wasn't sure how much was a load of crap. He shifted a hard gaze at Owen. "How do you fit into all this?"

"I was just helping JoGene out, is all. Since you won't let me work with you, I figured I'd help him at the bar some."

Zell knew where they were coming from; two power-less men kept down by a wife and family. It still didn't excuse them. "What about trashing the bar this last time?"

JoGene said, "That was Dad. I told him I was handling things, but he had to jump in like always. I didn't think I'd have to go this far. I figured she'd give up and leave long ago."

"Or you'd get into her pants first?" That pissed Zell off almost as much as the vandalism.

"That would have been a bonus. I figured if we were friendly, she might be more susceptible to selling me the bar. Or maybe I'd marry into it and get both bar and pu—"

Zell shoved him before he could finish the crude word. He turned to Winn. "How much of this are you involved in?"

Winn's expression was as hard as it had been when he'd seen Zell kiss Kim. "I suspected these two were up to something. I want to make sure it's handled the right way."

Zell ran his hand back through his hair. "For the first time, I'm ashamed of being a Macgregor."

Winn's face reddened, and he clenched his fist. "Don't you ever say that! I'm going to do whatever I have to do to protect this family."

"Just what are you trying to protect us from?"

Winn's face paled for a moment, but he recovered quickly. "False allegations. You are a Macgregor in any case, and you won't say a word about any of this."

"I won't incriminate our family . . . if you give me him." He pointed to JoGene. "He and I have a little busi-ness to discuss."

JoGene looked at Owen and Winn for help. Neither said a word. No one had ever seen this side of Zell before. He liked their reaction and hoped they remembered it. Especially Owen.

"I'll see you outside," he said to JoGene and walked out. Yeah, he had some business to give him.


Two in the morning and everyone was sound asleep in their beds. Moonlight slanted in through the bedroom windows, illuminating Oscar on his big pillow. It was too bad the pig would die. To save him would mean waking Kim, who lay in the shadows sound asleep. Hopefully both would succumb to the smoke before the flames reached them.

When Elva and Pete had built this place, they hadn't put in a back door. Obviously code enforcement officials weren't as strict back then. There was a door out the kitchen, but that wouldn't help Kim.

A series of wood strips wedged into the bedroom door would jam it closed. The strips would burn with the house and leave no evidence. Of course, the authorities would know it was arson. Gasoline left a trace. But no one would know who had set the fire.

With the door closed, the smell of gasoline shouldn't reach the bedroom before the house was consumed with flames. By then it would be too late.

Gasoline splashed along the wood floors and soaked the old furniture. The smell burned the nostrils and stung the eyes, but soon it would be over. Hopefully for good this time.

At the front door, the match lit up the night; then lit up the house. Flames took hold instantly.

Ah, so this was why pyromaniacs set fires. The roar and the intense heat were exciting . . . almost sexual. The flames shimmered, and smoke curled along the roofline. Maybe it was because fire was so all-powerful, taking lives and buildings at once.

There wasn't time to gloat or get off on the scene. Time

to leave before anyone saw the smoke. The plants beneath the bedroom windows came to life in flames, blocking the only other way out of the bedroom.

Now the truth would be safe.


Zell still couldn't drop off to sleep. He sat up in bed and looked out over the prairie. He could only see the palmetto heads sticking up out of the vast grayness of grass.

As angry as he was with his father, he was more disgusted by Winn's expectation of silence. Maybe it was Zell's attraction to Kim that had made Winn want her out of town more urgently. Was that the source of his desperation? Or was it something bigger, darker? After his talk with JoGene, he'd questioned Winn alone. Winn had said that Buck had wanted to know what his son was up to and figured Owen would be involved. He'd asked Winn to check it out. Supposedly as simple as that.

What bothered Zell most was the turn of events. Kim had found herself in that same uncomfortable place he'd been in: between him and his family. That's why she'd backed away from their growing relationship. Winn had told Zell that she'd seen the petal and likely knew someone in the family had stolen the orchids. She hadn't accused anyone, hadn't reported them to the police. She hadn't even mentioned it to Zell.

So was she really trying to break off things between them or just protect him? All he knew was he'd hated seeing defeat in her eyes instead of that sass. He pushed out of bed and threw on a pair of jeans and a shirt. The clock on his nightstand read two o'clock.

He walked out onto the back deck. The night air was warm and muggy, the same as it was during the day. For those few moments when he'd shoved JoGene against the shelving, he'd felt primitive. That was the passion that had driven his father during his younger years. Giving in to his impulses before thinking the consequences through was Winn's nature. Maybe it was Zell's nature, too, and he'd fought it after watching his father self-destruct.

He picked up the scent of smoke and searched the night sky for its source. It was too wet for a wildfire. He saw no glow toward the north, so he walked around to the front of the house. There, to the southeast, was a subtle orange glow. Smoke, somewhat lighter than the black sky, billowed into the air.

Even in the warm night air, a chill washed through him. That was where Kim's house was.

# CHAPTER 23

Kim dreamed of fire. She was standing in a field of flames. Oscar was nudging her and making odd grunting noises. She was sure it wasn't time to get up, but she wanted out of this dream so she forced her eyes open. The air was hot, just like the dream. And the smoke was real, too. She shot up and gathered her murky senses.

Oscar's front hooves were up on the bed in his efforts to wake her. She pushed him to the floor and scrambled off the bed. Flames licked outside her windows. She ran to the door and tried to open it. The doorknob was warm. It turned, but the door wouldn't budge.

"Stay calm, stay calm," she chanted, assessing the situation.

Smoke poured in from beneath the door. She yanked the sheets off the bed and jammed them in the crack. The scent of gasoline was strong. She could feel heat coming through the wood door, which wouldn't hold off the flames for long.

She coughed, feeling her chest constrict. "Oh, God . . . oh, God, help me."

Flames blanketed the window on one side of the house. Was the whole yard up in flames? If so, there wasn't any hope. She looked out the other window. Only a small fire had been lit below. The yard wasn't on fire—yet. She started to open the window, but pulled back from the hot metal frame. She grabbed a towel out of the linen closet and used it to push open the window. Smoke spilled in through the opening. She ran to the bathroom and turned on the faucet, then searched for something to put the water in. All she could find was a drinking glass that Elva had once used. She filled it up and dashed to the window.

The flames hissed when the water hit them but didn't go out. She raced back to the bathroom and filled the cup again. She saw a large bottle of hand lotion and grabbed that, too. A quick read of the ingredients revealed no alcohol. She poured the water and dumped out the lotion onto the flames. As she filled up another glass, she searched for more lotion. Elva was a fanatic about her skin. She was also a bargain fanatic and had stocked up on a few large bottles with *Sale* stickers on them. Kim dumped more lotion and water onto the remaining patch of flames.

Now, she thought as she turned to Oscar; she had to figure out how to get him out of there. Getting a hundred-and-twenty-five-pound pig through a window was not going to be easy. Oscar was pacing and making high-pitched grunting noises. He kept looking at the door and then nudging her leg. Only a few wisps of smoke drifted from around the edges of the sheets, but the wood was making cracking sounds.

Kim grabbed up one of the nightstands and swung it at the window. She'd meant to keep a hold on it, but it broke through and landed in the yard. She took one of the lamps and used it to break away the shards of glass left in the frame. Smoke started coming from a black patch on the door. The fire was coming through.

She grabbed hold of the chest of drawers and pulled it toward the window. It tipped over and fell facedown in front of the window. "Come on, Oscar!"

He was too preoccupied with the growing dark stain on the door and the thickening smoke coming from it. "Oscar!" she screamed, and he turned toward her.

"Come on! Now!"

She helped him climb onto the back of the dresser. With the expertise she'd gained helping him in and out of vehicles, she maneuvered him to the window's ledge, lifted him rear first, and shoved him through. He landed with a heavy thud and limped away from the house. She turned back to the room. Her purse was lying on the far nightstand. She grabbed that and threw it out the window. She climbed through the window, falling just as ungracefully as Oscar had, and scrambled away.

The house was engulfed in flames. They rose up through the roof and licked away at the sides of the house. The only exterior fires had been the two set outside her windows. Someone had wanted her to die. This wasn't about trying to ruin her financially or sending her a message. This had been about murder.

*Forget about that right now.* She checked Oscar over and found just a few scratches. He was still limping, but he was able to walk.

Her truck! She called Oscar and headed around the house. She couldn't even see the front porch with all of the smoke. Headlights swept down her driveway. Was this her would-be killer, checking to see if he'd done a good job?

When she recognized Zell's truck, her knees went to jelly. He parked off to the side and ran toward her. She fell into him the moment his arms went around her. His hands searched her face. "Are you all right?"

She could only nod and cough.

"Oscar?" After he saw Oscar running to the edge of the hammock, he turned back to her. "Where are the keys to your truck? I'll move it."

She handed him her purse. He found her keys, corralled Oscar into her truck, and parked it behind his. Sirens obliterated even the sound of the flames and cracking wood, and a few moments later a fire truck came around the corner. Zell had left her truck lights on so they'd see the vehicles.

He pulled her out of the way as the men rushed forward

shouting instructions. One man came over to them. "You own this place?"

"I do," Kim managed to say before coughing.

"Anyone else in there?"

"No."

"You all right?" he asked them.

Kim nodded, but felt herself sink against Zell again. He wrapped his arms around her and pulled her close. She didn't want to need his strength or comfort, but she was too scared and shocked to fight it. He stroked her hair and whispered softly, though she couldn't hear what he was saying. It didn't matter; his voice soothed her anyway.

When she thought she could handle it, she turned back to the house. It hit her then, that this wasn't a nightmare. It wasn't fixable. The house was gone. Two of the men shouted and backed away as one of the exterior walls caved in. Her home was going to be gone, along with her shell frame and pictures. She had nothing and no one . . . no one but Zell, temporarily, holding her.

Another fire truck pulled in and the men started assisting the first group. It was hopeless. They were only trying to get the fire out to save the hammock.

Hopelessness, the fear of nearly dying, and the relief of escape . . . everything crashed in on her. She felt the sting of tears and tried to hide them from Zell, hoping that turning away from him would do the trick.

No such luck. He turned her to face him, tilting her chin up. His eyes were filled with grief for her. His fingers trailed down her wet, sooty cheeks. "I'm sorry."

She nodded, because she couldn't say anything. She was afraid to open her mouth and let out the sobs she was swallowing with all of her might. But with every touch, every gentle gesture, he drew her closer to the edge. Behind her, she could hear the shouts of the firemen, the water gushing out of the hoses, and the sound of the flames gobbling up what was left of her home. She didn't want to watch. She wanted only to stare at Zell and try to draw from his strength.

It backfired. His strength somehow gave her permission to let go and crumble. She did. The tears came, as powerful and consuming as the flames that ate her home. She collapsed against him and cried out everything she'd been holding in for so long. He held her, rocking her back and forth and pressing his mouth against the top of her head.

Kinsey and DeBarro pulled into the driveway and watched the proceedings for a few minutes before walking over to where Kim and Zell stood. Zell wished they'd stay away a few more minutes. He knew Kim would hate them seeing her like this. He wanted to give her comfort for a while longer . . . for as long as she wanted it. But he was also eager to find out how this had happened.

"She all right?" Kinsey asked.

Kim roused herself at the sound of Kinsey's voice and turned around. Her short hair stuck up in places, and tears tracked red streaks down her cheeks. First she looked at the house. The firemen were getting the fire under control. A deep, wracking cough seized her for a few moments. Her dark green eyes were dilated and bloodshot, her face slack. She was in shock. That realization made him slide his arm around her and pull her close again. Her vulnerability ripped his heart out, but he couldn't even recite any antilove songs in his head to rebuild the wall.

"What happened?" Kinsey asked Kim, and then turned to Zell. "Were you here when this started?"

"No, I saw the fire from my house, called the firefighters, and came over."

Kim's voice was hollow and weak. "Someone set it. They came into the house and poured gasoline all over. My bedroom door was jammed shut. They set fires outside the windows so we couldn't get out."

"We?" Kinsey asked, looking at Zell again.

"Me and Oscar." She turned to Zell with concern in her features. "Is he all right? He was limping after he fell to the ground."

"He's fine. He wasn't limping when I put him in the truck."

"Are you saying someone tried to kill you?" Kinsey clarified.

Kim nodded. Gasoline? Jammed her door shut? Set fires outside the windows? The rage poured through Zell again, making him squeeze her even closer against him. "Yes, that's what she's saying," he said through clenched teeth. Impatience riddled his voice.

Kinsey said, "You accuse Winn and Buck of killing that girl, then you claim someone killed Elva—I guess it's no surprise that now you claim someone tried to kill you. How did you get out of the house?"

"I broke the window and put the fire out below it. I poured water and lotion on it." She let out a watery laugh. "Elva loved her body lotion."

Other people had started to arrive, people who had either heard the sirens or seen the fire from a distance. Zell shifted so they couldn't see her teary face.

"Any ideas who would have done this?" DeBarro asked, his notepad at the ready. "Do you think it's the same people who vandalized the bar and stole your orchids?"

"I'm not sure," Kim said, her gaze still on the flames.

Zell's insides felt as heavy as clay.

Kinsey said, "I'm sure the state fire marshal will be down tomorrow first thing to talk with you further. We'll keep someone posted here so no one messes with the crime scene. And we'll need a statement from you."

"Oh, my God, what happened? Are you all right? Zell, what are you doing here?"

Zell turned at the sound of his sister's voice. She and Tullie ran up to them wearing clothes they'd obviously thrown on in a hurry. Tullie wore a faded Kermit the Frog nightgown tucked into her jean shorts. Owen walked slowly up behind them, meeting Zell's angry gaze. Zell answered Shar's questions as well as he could without imparting the murder plot. Tullie was already looking haunted as she watched the flames.

Shar was also watching the flames, though she seemed mesmerized. "It's beautiful," she said to herself.

"What?" Zell asked in a harsh voice.

"Flames are beautiful. The colors, the intensity. Wicked beauty." She looked over at Kim, and then took over, putting her arm around Kim's shoulders. "Are you all right? I can't imagine waking up and finding my home on fire. Is Oscar all right?"

Kim only nodded.

"Thank goodness. We've got to get you out of here, get you cleaned up." She gave Kim a once-over. "I won't have a lot of clothes you can borrow, but maybe a few things will fit."

As Shar tried to steer Kim away, Kim protested. "No, I can't leave yet."

Zell shook his head, giving Shar the message to let it be. Kim needed to watch the final death throes.

An ambulance pulled into the driveway and paramedics jumped out. Zell steered Kim over to them.

"I'm fine," she said, but let him guide her.

As they checked her over, Zell took Owen aside. Owen obviously expected the questions. As soon as Zell got close, he said, "JoGene and I had nothing to do with this. I know he wouldn't have done this. He wanted to be her partner," he added derisively. "That's what he said, anyway."

And Owen had said they had to do something drastic. "If I find out—"

Owen held up his hand. "You won't, Zell. I swear, you won't."

"We all need to talk tonight. As soon as I get Kim settled at my place, we're having a family meeting." He glanced at the house again. He wanted to hurt someone for this. Now he knew the taste for justice Kim had experienced. He walked back to the ambulance and watched while they finished their examination.

"You're lucky," one of the paramedics said as they released her.

Shar came over as Zell and Kim walked back toward the house. "Is she all right?"

"She'll be fine." *After the shock wears off,* he didn't say. Tullie tugged on his shirt.

"I had the dream again, Uncle Zell. Seeing the gators didn't help. I was having it when the sirens woke me up."

"See, it didn't mean anything. This has nothing to do with gators." But did it have to do with Macgregors? He hated thinking it. It reminded him of the doubts that had plagued him years ago. How badly did his father want Kim out of town? And why *did* he want her out so badly? Revenge? Spite? Fear?

A car he didn't recognize pulled through the obstacle course of vehicles. A man got out and obviously instructed bystanders to clear the road. Kinsey and DeBarro met him on his way toward the house. Zell watched them discuss the situation, pointing toward Kim on occasion. After several minutes, they walked over.

Kinsey gestured toward Kim. "This is Kim Lyons, the owner of the house and intended victim. This is Detective Tony Minotti."

Minotti shook her hand. "You all right?"

"As fine as she can be," Zell said. "I'm Zell Macgregor."

The two men shook hands. Minotti said, "I'd like to have a word with you, Ms. Lyons. If we can just step away." He nodded toward a place away from the fray. "We'll only be a few minutes, Mr. Macgregor."

Zell got the hint. He wasn't to be included. He watched as Kim did most of the talking, gesturing occasionally toward the house or the swamp beyond. When she wasn't gesturing, she kept her arms tightly around her. She was probably telling him everything, including her suspicions about Elva's death. Whatever the detective was saying tightened her features. He wasn't sure if the detective was finished, but Kim stalked away from him anyway.

"He thinks I set the fire myself," she said when she approached. She gestured wildly toward the house, which was still partially in flames. "For insurance!"

"Why does he think that?"

"No doubt Kinsey told him I was a nutcase who was

having financial difficulties and might be looking for a way to get some money. He suggested that I was clever enough not to burn down the bar since that would be too obvious."

He smoothed back her short hair. "He's just testing you. Stay cool about it."

She pressed her forehead against his shoulder. "How much can I take, Zell? How long can I keep fighting them?"

He slid his arm around her. "Don't give up, angel. Not yet."

Zell arranged for Shar to drive Kim's truck to his place while he took her, Tullie, and Oscar. Kim was quiet—too quiet. She sat in the truck slowly running her hand down Oscar's back, staring at nothing. Tullie looked as though she bore all the responsibility for the fire. The smell of smoke permeated the air inside the cab.

Shar and Owen went to Heron's Glen, where Shar would try to find some clothes Kim could wear.

He helped Kim and Oscar out of the truck when they reached his place.

"Uncle Zell, Oscar's cut!" Tullie said.

"He'll be all right. We're going to fix him up." He ruffled her hair before turning to Kim. She looked lost, even swaying a little. He took hold of her and turned back to Tullie. "Do me a favor and give Oscar a good rinsing with the hose. Then we can see where he's cut."

Tullie led Oscar toward the hose, and Zell guided Kim inside.

"Is he all right?" she asked in a thready voice.

"He'll be fine, angel. We'll take care of him. The question is, are you all right?"

She nodded. "I need to take a shower. I can't stand the smell of this smoke and I feel all gritty."

That was a good sign. "You going to be all right standing in the shower?"

He was relieved to see a glint of sass in her eyes. "Are you offering to take a shower with me?"

He cleared his throat. "Only if you insist."

She gave him a little shove, making him feel even better. "I'll get you a robe," he said, steering her toward the guest bathroom.

After hooking the robe on the outside doorknob, he took a couple of towels out to Tullie and helped her dry off Oscar. "See, he's feeling fine," Zell said when Oscar shook off the water. He chucked her chin and corralled Oscar into the house. He knocked on the bathroom door to check on Kim before taking the first-aid kit into the kitchen. "Bring the patient in here, nurse," he said, getting a ghost of a smile out of the girl.

The sound of the fountain soothed him as he dressed the cuts on Oscar's dark skin. "Go check on Kim, will you?" he asked Tullie halfway through.

She ran off and, in a few minutes, came back. "She said to stop bugging her."

"Means she's feeling better."

Tullie was studying him. "You like her, don't you?"

"Yeah," he said, sure he'd heard a trace of regret in that answer. "I do."

She smiled. "Your match."

"We'll see about that." When he was finished, he gave Oscar a pat on his flabby bottom and instructed Tullie not to let him rub off the salve. "And check on Kim again. I'm going to take a shower, too." He was also sick of the smoke smell.

Kim had emerged from the bathroom by the time Shar returned with a bag of clothes. "I threw in some dresses and a nightgown and a couple of Owen's shirts. Something ought to fit." She gave Kim's arm a squeeze. "We're just glad you're okay." She looked at Zell. "She staying here tonight?"

"Yep." Whether she wanted to or not. But she didn't look like she'd put up too much of a fight in any case. He didn't think it was possible, but she looked small in his oversized white robe. Her face was red from scrubbing and her blond hair was sticking up in places from towel-drying it.

"All right, give me a call if you need anything. Come

on, Tullie!" Shar headed outside, but Tullie walked over to Kim first.

"I'm sorry I didn't see the fire. I only saw the gators."

Kim knelt down to her level. "It's all right. You can't see everything. It doesn't work that way."

Something softened in his heart just as the torment in Tullie's eyes softened. The girl only nodded and ran after her mother.

"Gators?" Kim asked when the front door closed.

"She's been having nightmares about gators. Never mind that. Let's get you to bed. You look flattened."

She let him lead her into the guest bedroom. He grabbed up the bag Shar had brought and set it by the closet door. Oscar stretched out on some towels Zell had laid on the floor.

Kim dropped onto the bed, staring at nothing again. He should leave her alone, give her some quiet time to absorb recent events. And he would have if she hadn't looked so damned lost sitting there on that huge bed by herself. He sat beside her, not knowing if he should touch her or say anything at all.

She was shivering. Her chin trembled, and her eyes filled. "My home," she said in a raw voice. "Someone burned down my home."

Her home. He remembered how much she'd wanted that very thing, how her ex-boyfriend had offered it to her. He couldn't give her back her home, but he could pull her into his arms and hold her for a while. She curled against him. Holding her close, he could feel waves of tremors. The shock was wearing off and reality was setting in.

He stroked her back and kissed the top of her head. "It'll be all right," he whispered. "The most important thing is you and Oscar got out."

She held on tighter, maybe thinking that someone hadn't wanted them to get out. That thought made him squeeze her, too. He pushed away the rage, the same rage that had washed over him when he'd overheard JoGene in the incubation room. Time for that later. Now she needed him to be calm and soothing.

She needed him. That thought alone pushed out the rage and questions in his mind. He didn't want to be needed. He didn't want someone to take care of. But here he was, relishing the role of caretaker. It felt right holding her when she cried in his arms as they watched the house burn. Just as right as it felt now.

She lifted her face to his. Her green eyes were still glazed. He brushed away her tears with his thumb. It took everything within him not to lean down and kiss her. He cradled her head, feeling strands of her wet hair slide between his fingers. He couldn't kiss her, not when she was so vulnerable.

She surprised him by kissing the bottom of his chin. Then she kissed along the line of his jaw. Then the corner of his mouth. He held his breath. She slid her hands around his neck and her mouth, warm and soft, covered his. Her eyes were closed. No man could be expected to resist her, not in this moment. Not when his heart was racing and his head was spinning. Her tongue slid against his, and her hands slid down his bare back. He'd forgotten to put a shirt on, eager to get back downstairs and see how she was doing. As her hands moved over his skin, he was glad he'd forgotten. The honorable part of him that warned not to go too far was receding in his hazy brain as he lost himself in her.

She pushed her robe back over her shoulders and moved closer. Because she continued to kiss him, he couldn't see her, but he could feel her. His hands slid over her shoulders and down her arms. They flattened against her stomach and moved over the curves of her breasts. She inhaled softly as his thumbs brushed her nipples. He wanted to hear that sound again and again. He pushed her back on the bed as his body strained to be free of the cotton drawstring pants he'd thrown on.

He felt dampness when his cheek brushed hers. It snapped the honorable part of his brain back to attention. Her eyes were still closed, and tears mingled in her eyelashes.

"You're crying," he whispered.

She shook her head and kissed him even harder. She didn't want him to see this side of her. Would she go all the way just to keep him from seeing her vulnerability? Kim probably would. And he couldn't let her. It edged way too close to taking advantage of her. As he continued to kiss her, lighter and lighter each time, he maneuvered her beneath the sheets. She probably thought he was going to slide in with her, but he covered her with the sheet that now separated them.

He must be crazy; one part of his body thought so. She opened those hazy eyes and realized there was too much distance between them. The sheets barely covered those deliciously soft breasts he'd allowed himself to touch when he was out of his mind. Her hair was mussed, her cheeks flushed.

Before she could say a word, he lay down beside her. He slung one leg over her, one arm over her shoulders, and pulled her against him.

"Zell . . ." she said in her hoarse voice, plaintive, questioning, maybe even a little pleading.

"Shhh." He stroked her cheek, letting his fingers continue their stroking motion through her hair.

He hoped she wouldn't take his actions as rejection. His desire was plain enough, pressing against her thigh. More so, he hoped she wouldn't test him further. He wouldn't turn her down again. His body was disappointed when she closed her eyes. Then again, his body knew nothing of honor and responsibility. At least his mind did, and that had kept him out of trouble over the years.

Before long she had fallen asleep. He continued touching her, because he couldn't stop. She felt right lying there beside him. Of all the women he'd been involved with over the years, why this one? She had somehow gotten past his walls, but she had walls of her own.

"Love stinks, love hurts, ain't love a bitch, and love sucks," he whispered as he traced the shell of her ear.

He glanced at the clock on the nightstand. Even though he had to attend the meeting that he'd ordered, he couldn't stop watching her—or thinking that someone had tried to kill her. Whoever it was would try again unless Kim gave up and left town. He had a bad feeling she wouldn't give up, not now. He had a really bad feeling that whoever had tried to kill her was someone he knew. And even worse, that it was someone in his own family.

That thought finally pushed him out of bed. "Keep an eye on her, Oscar." He threw on some clothes and headed to the main house. It was going to be a long night.

# CHAPTER 24

Zell found Shar, Owen, Winn, and JoGene in the family room, each halfway through whatever they were drinking. Zell wanted a drink, too, but having a clear head was a better idea. Tullie had been put to bed, but he suspected the girl was lurking somewhere. He leaned against the fireplace mantel and waited for them to come to order.

Winn was the first to speak. "JoGene says you're making him fess up to Kim about what he did to the bar. That isn't going to happen, especially in light of what happened tonight. Not only does it implicate him in the fire, it implicates the rest of us. Buck, too," Winn added, because it was so damned important to protect the son of a bitch.

Zell narrowed his eyes at his father. "You should have thought about that before you got involved in all this." He looked at JoGene, who was running his fingers through the oil slick on his brow. "Did you set the fire?"

"Are you crazy? That's *murder,* Zell."

Winn's mouth was a firm, tight line. "No one here tried to kill that girl. I don't want to hear any more questions like that out of your mouth. We've got to figure out our plan of action. She's been digging into Rhonda's murder again, we know that. Asking questions, talking to Ernest. Kinsey said she thinks Elva was murdered."

Owen said, "Elva wasn't murdered. She fell out of her skiff. She was old, for Pete's sake."

Winn said, "Doesn't matter, you know how Kim is when she gets an idea in her head. She's going to cause all of us some serious problems unless we get a handle on our stories."

More cover-ups. Zell was sick to death of covering up the truth. The alternative, though, was to confess his knowledge of the scheme to run Kim out of business, thus implicating them in the fire—and attempted murder. If he told the truth, he'd be turning on his family. He hated this. "I insist on JoGene making amends for what he's done."

Shar said, "Fine, let him make amends. But if he admits to the vandalism and the stolen orchids, he'll be tied to the fire and so will Owen."

Owen finished his whiskey in one gulp.

JoGene said, "I'll make it right, okay?"

Zell narrowed his eyes at the weasel. "I'm glad to hear that, JoGene. First of all, you're going to be responsible for the loan Elva took to buy those orchids. Since I let her make payments, I'll extend you the same courtesy. Two hundred fifty dollars due at the beginning of the month. I'll tell Kim it's being taken care of by an anonymous benefactor. Then you're going to arrange to pay her liquor bill. Not only the outstanding bill but the one she'll rack up replacing the stock. And do it so she thinks the company is extending her the courtesy."

"Zell, dang it, I don't have that kind of money."

"You were planning to buy her bar, weren't you? You've got to have some money stashed somewhere."

He lowered his head. "Yeah, I have a few bucks saved up."

"Good. Then you'll have enough to pay for the replacement chairs, too."

Owen said, "Zell, whose side are you on, anyway?"

"I'm on the side of what's right. You don't trash someone's place because you want to buy it."

JoGene shot to his feet. "Elva was gonna sell it to me!"

"But she didn't put it in writing, and now it belongs to Kim. Give it up. The bar's not yours, it's not going to be yours, and if I catch wind of anything screwy going on with that place again, I'm busting your ass. And if you try kissing up to her for it, I'll bust another part of your anatomy."

JoGene dropped back into the chair. "You're just mad because you want her."

Owen said, "You're sleeping with the enemy."

Zell leaned down into Owen's face. "I am not sleeping with her, but if I choose to, that's my own damn business. I happen to like her and I don't cotton to anyone trying to hurt her, financially or otherwise."

Winn's voice was low when he said, "We'll talk about that later." He turned to the rest of the group. "No one will know about our involvement in what happened to the bar or the orchids." He looked at Zell again, making that order clear. "JoGene will make amends. That should make you happy, since you've decided to take the girl's side." He turned to the rest of the group. "I don't believe either Owen or JoGene had anything to do with the fire. But there will be an investigation, bet on it. Having an alibi will only do you good."

Owen blurted out, "I was in bed with my wife, sound asleep. We both were, weren't we, hon?"

Shar nodded. "The whole night."

Zell knew Shar would lie to cover for Owen, and he did look just a little guilty.

Owen was clearly sucking up to Winn, trying to be the good son Zell wasn't anymore. "Winn, no way could you get in and set a fire and get away so quick. We can all testify that you don't get around so fast these days. JoGene?"

"I was sleeping by myself. Didn't even know what happened until Owen called me."

"What about your father?" Owen asked.

"Hell, I don't keep tabs on him. My mom will give him an alibi if he needs it. But I don't think Buck would do anything like this."

Zell crossed his arms. "No, he has real morals."

JoGene winced. "Sure, he don't like Kim. He wanted her out of town, but he wouldn't kill her."

Winn took in the group of conspirators. Zell was ashamed to be considered part of that group. Winn said, "So we're in agreement, then? We know nothing about what's been going on with Kim."

Winn made a point to look at Zell, who made a point not to nod. Of course, it was expected that he'd cooperate.

As everyone filtered out of the room, Shar touched his arm and whispered, "I know you like her, and I'm sorry for what happened tonight. But be careful about putting yourself between her and the family. We've survived a lot, big brother. I'd hate to see this tear us apart now."

Winn stayed behind, honoring an unspoken agreement that he and Zell would talk after everyone left. Winn walked to the bar and fixed another whiskey on the rocks. "What does Kim think?"

"That Elva was blackmailing whoever killed Rhonda. And that that person killed Elva. I thought it was crazy talk, to be honest with you. But now, I'm not so sure." Zell gave in and took a beer out of the small refrigerator beneath the bar. He leaned against the back of one of the chairs and waited for Winn to settle into the chair opposite. "Did you kill Rhonda Jones?"

Winn's eyes narrowed to slits, but his anger at Zell's insinuation passed quickly. He looked away. "It's not that simple."

Dread tightened Zell's chest. "Yeah, it is. You either killed her or you didn't."

"Kim doesn't know I'd been seeing her, does she? Ernest was too young to know that."

Ernest. The knot tightened. He didn't quite have the Macgregor eyes. Not quite, but damn close. "She doesn't know."

Winn rubbed the bridge of his nose. Zell wasn't sure if his hand was shaking from the whiskey or nerves. "I loved her."

"That doesn't mean anything."

Winn only nodded, looking more despondent than ever—and guilty.

Zell said, "You know who killed her, don't you?"

Before Zell's eyes, guilt turned to resolve. "I don't know anything. I don't know anything at all."

Zell felt uneasy about that answer. He wanted to believe that, for his family and his own peace of mind. He needed to believe in Winn's innocence, just as he had when he'd testified against Kim ten years ago.

Winn cleared his throat. "Why Kim?"

"Pardon?"

"Of all the beautiful, talented women you've dated over the years, why fall for this one?"

Zell hooked his thumbs on the pockets of his jeans. His first inclination was to deny that he'd fallen for her. He did feel things for her that he hadn't felt for anyone else. Whether that was something close to love he hadn't had time to analyze. "Not to piss you off, if that's what you think."

Winn winced, but Zell went on. "Do you really want to hear the reasons? Do you want to hear how I got to like her better each time someone tried to stomp on her and she didn't crumble, cry, lash out, or give up? She staked her claim here in the face of a lot of animosity. If you'd heard her speech at the bar . . ." That was when she'd started sneaking around the sides of his walls. "I'm tired of holding grudges against people just because I'm a Macgregor. It's too much work."

"She didn't report us," Winn said, his ire softening.

"What?"

"When she came here to apologize and saw one of the orchid petals on the ground. She knew. I could tell by the look on her face, she knew someone here had stolen the orchids. And she never reported us."

Zell could well imagine the look on her face. That was the defeat he'd seen and heard in her voice. She didn't tell him because she didn't want to put him between her and his family.

Winn said, "I see she never told you, either. I suppose

I've just added more fodder for your fire." He closed his eyes and leaned his head back. "That's another Macgregor trait, you know. Fire, passion. When we want something, we go after it no matter the consequences. We have always loved with everything inside us. I loved your mother that way, and I was devastated when she died. And there was Rhonda, so young—too young—and yet so womanly. So wanting, and so giving." His fingers tightened on the arms of the chair. "I knew it was wrong, but I fell for her anyway." Zell thought he saw traces of moisture between his eyelashes. "We love and live without bounds. But remember that it never seems to end well." He fell silent.

Zell left him there and returned home to Kim. Dim moonlight spilled in through the window and silvered her. As tired as he was, he watched her sleep for a while. He didn't like her short hair, but somehow it looked good on her. *She* looked good, lying there in his bed. He started to back away and head upstairs to his room. Then he reconsidered. Maybe she'd wake in the night and need someone. And maybe he needed to be there when she did.

The second bedroom light remained on throughout the night. Zell was in there with Kim. Though the curtain blocked most of the view, there was enough of a gap to see that they were lying on the bed together. So sweet, so touching. Zell had picked the wrong woman to get involved with. One way or the other, she was going to have to go. The fire had failed, but there were other ways to deal with her. Hopefully Zell wouldn't get in the way.

When Kim woke the next morning, the first thing she thought of was the fire. The scent of smoke still clung to her, making it hard to pretend that it had only been a nightmare. It was hard not to remember that all she had in the world was in her purse and at the bar. The bar that would probably have to be sold—or half-sold to JoGene.

Once all the bad stuff had washed over and through her, she became aware of where she was—and the weight of a body next to her. She could hear his deep, even breathing and smell soap and male. Oh, yeah, the rest of it came back, too, her desperate attempt to get him to make love with her, his gentle refusal on the grounds, no doubt, that she was slightly out of her mind.

Hopefully that had been the reason. Even in the midst of personal disaster, a woman had her pride. She turned her head slowly so she wouldn't wake him. He was lying face-up on top of the sheets wearing wrinkled cotton pants. She, on the other hand, was naked beneath the sheets. His hands were tucked behind his head, bulging out his arm muscles. His hair stuck out at odd angles, but he still looked all kinds of gorgeous. In the curious ways of males, though he was fast asleep, a part of his anatomy was fully awake.

It stirred something inside her. Even if she had been out of her mind last night, feeling him around her—inside her—would have taken her away from all that awaited her.

He turned to look at her. "Hey."

"Hey, yourself," she said.

"How are you?"

Hungry, she thought, watching him stretch and scrub his fingers through his hair. He rolled onto his side to face her.

"As well as I can be, considering." She supposed she ought to stop looking at his magnificent chest and think about facing her burned-out house. And the questions. And the state fire marshal. She glanced down to make sure she was covered. "You didn't take advantage of me last night."

"Wasn't because I didn't want to."

"But you're supposed to be this womanizer, this care-free Casanova."

One corner of his mouth lifted in a smile. "Don't believe all the press."

She rolled onto her stomach, pulling the sheets with her. Apparently not all of the sheets by the way his gaze slid down her backside. "Do me a favor. Take advantage of me."

It only took him a second to realize what she was saying. He didn't weigh it, didn't, thankfully, ask if she was sure. Before she could even think about laying herself out there and having him turn her down again, he kissed her the same hungry way she'd kissed him the night before. He ran his hands over her sleep-heated skin, leaving a trail of fire that pooled deep in her belly.

She touched him, too, relishing the contours of his muscles. While they explored each other, their mouths melded and their tongues tangled in mindless fervor. They were breathless when he started kissing from the corner of her mouth down to her chin. When his mouth moved across the skin of her neck, she shivered. He nibbled on her earlobe and then tickled the shell of her ear with the tip of his tongue. She shivered and pulled away from him.

He didn't mind, obviously, because he was already making his way to her stomach, via the valley between her breasts, which he lathed with his tongue. He nibbled on the soft skin of her stomach and gently tugged on her belly button ring with his teeth. When he started going lower, she sat up and started kissing him again.

"Is this the scary part?" he asked between kisses.

"What do you mean?"

"Your eyes are squeezed shut."

She kissed him hard. *Keep it physical. Keep it simple.*

"Open your eyes," he said.

"Why?"

"Because I want to see you seeing me."

That's when she realized she liked the darkness, liked hiding behind it while making love. She'd blamed Simon for wanting the lights off, but she wanted it that way, too. She opened her eyes.

He slid onto his side. He ran his hand across her breasts, down her stomach, and toyed with her belly button ring. The look on his face was part assessing and part mischievous. "What are you afraid of?"

She bit her lower lip as his touch sensitized her nerve endings. "Nothing."

His finger trailed lower, tangling with her pubic hair. His voice was low and smooth when he said, "You sure about that?"

She could only nod when he trailed even lower. "I . . . can't we just . . . do it?"

She tried to take the situation in hand, but he took hold of her hand instead. "What's your hurry? Don't you like foreplay?"

No, she didn't. It was too personal. Sex was physical, two people giving and taking pleasure simultaneously. In an odd way, foreplay was more intimate. There was too much time for eye contact, for connecting on a deeper level, and too much focus on one person at a time. She tried not to remember his discourse about a woman's important parts.

"I thought guys liked to get right down to it."

He smiled. "Sometimes. I thought women liked lots of foreplay."

She shifted her gaze down. "Not me."

He tipped up her chin, forcing her to look at him. "I don't think that's true." To prove his point, he did a little movement with his finger that curled her toes. "Ah, just what I thought."

"Zell . . ."

"That's what I want to hear, you saying my name in that breathy, pleading kind of way." He slung his leg over her legs so she couldn't move.

Even as warm, liquid pleasure rolled through her body, she said, "Why are you doing this to me?"

"Because I want to. And I think you want me to."

She shook her head, but the hitch in her breathing gave her away. He was watching her, demanding that she meet his gaze instead of hiding from him.

"Tell me how much you want this, Kim. How much you want me."

Normally she would have kissed him in answer, but

he'd pinned her down. Zell was demanding more, demanding everything, just as she'd suspected he would. She arched as pleasure built to a peak inside her.

His voice was honey-warm and just as sweet. "Tell me how much you want me. I want to hear you say it."

"Bastard," she said. "You're so full of yourself."

"If I was, I wouldn't need to hear you say it. I want you, angel. I just want to hear you say that you want me."

She squeezed her eyes shut. "All right, all right, I want you, Zell. I—"

"Look at me when you say it." He'd stopped the movements that were sending her so close to the edge.

"You are a bastard," she said, opening her eyes again. "I can't give that much to someone. I've never given that much."

"Then it's time you started."

She took a ragged breath. "Okay."

"Okay, what?"

"I want you to keep . . . doing what you were doing. I want you to take me all the way."

He kissed her, stirring her with just that. Then he started moving his fingers again, sliding in and out of her folds and even inside her. She started to close her eyes but stopped herself. Damn him, she didn't want to go off with him watching.

In the end, she had no choice. Pleasure rushed over her like a tidal wave. She couldn't even contain the heavy sigh that rolled from deep within her and out of her mouth. And oh, yes, he was watching her with those misty-green eyes of his. Even as she swam through the waves of her orgasm, he was still touching her. At first she couldn't handle the sensation, and then she was sure she couldn't come again, and then she was coming again.

Zell was grinning, genuinely enjoying her pleasure it seemed. He leaned over and kissed her while he opened the drawer and grabbed a condom. She took pleasure in giving, too, sliding her fingers over his rigid flesh, relishing each intake of his breath. When she'd teased him to the edge, she smoothed the sheath over him, pulled him back down on the bed, and guided him inside her. As they moved together, she felt the oddest sensation. Not only the building of tension in her belly, but something bigger. Like riding a roller coaster, *click, click, click,* stomach tightening, fear, anticipation, getting near the top, ready to plunge.

All the while, she kept her eyes on his, knowing he would demand nothing less. Did she want him? Oh, my, yes. She didn't want to want anyone like this, didn't want to lose her heart. *Click, click, click.*

She'd reached the peak of that imaginary roller coaster. It was downhill from there at blinding speeds. She held on to his shoulders. "I want you, Zell. I . . . do . . . want you." And then she plunged down.

She shuddered and tightened her grip on him. He kept moving, intensifying the sensation until he exploded inside her. Even then, he thrust in and out, sustaining the feelings coursing through her. He held her tight as they rode the dips and drops and mind-bending curves.

She loved the feel of his weight on top of her, though she suspected he was levering himself up a little. Once they caught their breath, he rolled onto his side. She sneaked a glance at him. He was still breathing heavily, but he gently stroked his finger down her arm.

She felt more naked than she'd ever felt before and resisted the urge to pull a sheet up over her breasts . . . breasts he was now tracing with his finger. *You don't feel naked, Kim; you feel vulnerable.* She shivered at that realization. If he said the wrong thing, she'd probably shatter. Where had the tough redneck chick who always protected her heart gone?

The phone rang out in the living room. She was glad when he didn't move to answer it. The machine picked up, and they heard Kinsey's voice. "I'm looking for Kim. The fire marshal's here and wants to meet her over at the house. I'll try her at the bar."

At the thought of the house, she felt her face go slack. "For a little while, I'd forgotten about all that."

She figured he'd like the fact that he'd swept her away, but his expression was even more shadowed than hers. The shadow of guilt?

"What's wrong?" she asked.

He closed *his* eyes now and rubbed the bridge of his nose. "Nothing. We should probably get over there. I want to hear what he has to say."

He started to get up, but she grabbed his arm. "Zell, what do you know about the fire?"

"Nothing," he repeated, pulling away.

She hated thinking that he knew something. She knew her presence in his house and in his life was already causing him trouble with his family. If one of them had set the fire, he'd be in a worse position than during the trial. Except this time she wouldn't only end up on the losing end; she might end up dead.

Zell insisted that they eat a quick breakfast before heading over. "You'll need the strength," he said, shoving a peanut-butter-smeared piece of toast at her.

She took it and the glass of milk he handed her. "Thanks."

"I want you to stay here," he said, taking a bite of his toast. "At least until this is resolved."

He wasn't giving her a choice, she noticed. "I'll stay at the bar. I can buy a sleeping bag and sleep in the back room until the house is rebuilt."

"The insurance won't kick in until the arson investigation is complete. And if, as you said, they think you had something to do with it, they'll stall. Maybe even refuse to pay out. And that's if Elva had insurance." At her alarmed look, he said, "Some people around here don't have it, despite the threat of storms and hurricanes. In fact, because of it. They can't afford the premiums."

"All of her paperwork is probably gone. I'll have to check at the bar."

He finished his toast, brushed his hands on his jeans,

and leaned down to scratch Oscar's head. "So it's settled."

"What's settled?" she asked.

"Your staying here."

"If you think I'm going to shack up with you—"

He refilled the bowl with Cheerios for Oscar and went looking for his keys. "I have nothing but the most honorable intentions."

"You're a man!" she called after him. "Men have no honor."

Sharing a bed, and her body, with Zell wasn't unappealing. The problem was she had a feeling that being with him would be addicting. Wanting any kind of relationship with Zell was going to be harder than anything she'd ever encountered in her life. He would want it all, every time. She was too scared to ride that roller coaster again . . . and yet, she wanted to feel the thrill again, too. Backing out now would be the smartest thing to do to keep her heart safe and her mind sane.

He returned to the kitchen with his keys. Though she'd meant the comment as a light joke, he looked nothing but serious. He edged up in front of her and tipped her chin back. "I'm not touching you again until you're ready to give me everything. Let's go."

Damn, he *was* honorable. She slid off the stool and located the high heels Charlotte had brought over. They were two sizes too small. She slid into a pair of Zell's sneakers and found them a better fit. "What's wrong with just having great sex?" Talk about role reversal! She followed him to the door.

"I don't want just sex with you."

Those words made her heart jump. "What do you mean?"

He didn't look too happy about it, either. "I don't want just sex with you."

And he was leaving it at that, apparently. Zell wasn't like Simon or any of the men she'd dated before. How did she learn to give everything when she had never done it before?

They walked to his truck, and he opened the door for her. It was nearly eleven. The weight in her chest kept growing heavier as they turned into her drive. A deputy who was guarding the scene waved them through. People were standing around, hoping for a glimpse of the house. What used to be her home, she thought drearily. The images from last night still haunted her, flames licking at the walls and the smoke creeping beneath the door.

When the black wreckage came into view, she still lost her breath. She realized she'd been holding out some impossible hope that part of the house would be salvageable. One wall was standing, but it wouldn't be for long.

Detective Minotti was there with another man she presumed was the fire marshal. She slid out of the truck before Zell could walk around to open her door and, ignoring everyone, stumbled toward the house. The ground was still muddy, and ruts from the vehicles made walking difficult. But she couldn't take her gaze off the house.

"Ms. Lyons, please watch your step. Don't get too close."

She thought it was Minotti's voice, but didn't turn to see. Wisps of smoke curled into the muggy air, giving the structure the sense of being alive. The smell of burnt plastic and other materials stung her nostrils. She barely recognized the couch in the living room. The interior walls had collapsed, as had the roof, covering most of the furniture. The kitchen had been obliterated. She could have been in there. The thought pounded into her head, bringing back the panic when Oscar had woken her and she realized the smoke in her dream was real.

Minotti's voice said, "You're Zell Macgregor, right? You made the call to the fire department."

"Yes."

Kim turned toward the men, who were a few yards behind her. Minotti was consulting his notes. "What were you doing up at two in the morning?"

"Couldn't sleep. I walked out on my deck and smelled

the smoke. Then I saw it and realized it could be Kim's place."

She walked back to the men at the same time as the other man walked from the side of the house to join them. Minotti was taking notes.

"I'm Maynard Burton, state fire marshal," the man said, shaking Kim's hand. He looked like a refined version of Smitty. "I'm sorry for your loss, ma'am. I'm going to do my best to find out what happened here. I need some information from you, though. Tell me what you saw when you first realized the house was on fire and how you left the house."

She described the terrifying events of the night before, even down to the color of the smoke creeping beneath the door. They all followed him around the back of the house. "Was this the master bedroom?"

Kim nodded, barely recognizing what was once the bed she'd slept in. Everything that was left was covered in black soot made muddy by the water. She pointed to the bedroom across the way. "That was the second bedroom." Beneath part of a wall she could see the charred filing cabinet. "I'd like to see if anything in the file cabinet is salvageable. Most of Elva's personal papers were in there."

Burton was sketching the layout of the house. "We'll get you the contents as soon as we're finished."

"There was a rifle in the closet . . ."

"We found the steel barrel, but the stock was burned away."

So much for her evidence, flimsy though it was.

"Detective Minotti's report said you smelled gasoline. You were right; it was used as an accelerant. From what I can tell so far, someone doused the back room, hallway, living room, and kitchen with it."

Minotti said, "But not her bedroom."

"No, the bedroom was the only room that wasn't treated."

Minotti scratched his chin. "That's strange. Seems if I

wanted to burn someone, I'd toss accelerant on them while they slept and throw the match. Seen a few cases like that. That would guarantee that the intended victim would die."

Kim shivered, first from the possibility and secondly from his insinuation that she had set this fire. "Maybe he didn't want to take the chance of waking me. He tried his best to make sure I couldn't escape from the bedroom. Did you find whatever he used to block the door?"

Burton shook his head. "The door and the frame are gone. If something was used, I'll find it somewhere in there."

"What about the fires set outside the windows? That was to keep me from climbing out." She walked to where the windows had once been. The ground and plants were scorched.

Burton said, "I found accelerant there as well. Those were the only windows that were treated."

Minotti turned to Kim. "Who's to say that you didn't start the fires yourself knowing you could put one of them out?" He looked at Burton. "Didn't you also say that there wasn't much gasoline poured under the window in the back, the one she escaped from?"

"There doesn't appear to be as much, no."

Zell said, "Maybe he ran out of gas. Did you find the can?" When both men shook their heads, he said, "How could she have started the fire without a container to hold the gasoline in?"

Burton said, "We've had cases where the arsonist used milk jugs to store the gasoline and then threw the jugs into the fire. We're still analyzing the scene, searching the surrounding area. I'm still trying to determine the point of origin. We have a lot more to cover."

Kim said, "I didn't burn down my house. You don't understand. That was *my* house. My home."

Minotti said, "You haven't been accused yet." Yet. "We're looking at all the angles, questioning people in town to see if anyone saw a vehicle leaving your driveway.

But I can't ignore what else I'm hearing: that you're known for making unfounded accusations and that your bar is in financial trouble. Is in fact closed right now."

"That's because someone has been sabotaging me. Why would I burn down my home? It makes no sense. I have no place to live."

Minotti glanced up at Zell. "I hear that maybe you do." He slipped his notepad in his shirt pocket. "I'll be in touch, Ms. Lyons."

Burton tipped the cap he was wearing and walked back to the house to continue his work. Kim turned to Zell. "Take me back to my truck. I've got a lot of work to do."

"Like what?"

"I'm going to finish fixing up the bar. It's all I have."

# CHAPTER 25

Kim bought some food and toiletries at Tiger's Grocery Store, Pig Chow at the local feed and seed, and headed to Southern Comfort. Her heart filled at the sight of it. It was all she had left, and even that was tenuous. She felt as though she were fighting an undertow. Every time she got a breath, the undertow sucked her down again—and made her more determined to survive.

She hauled in her supplies, including the sleeping bag Zell had loaned her. She was determined not to become his problem as much as she loved knowing she could depend on him. Though he would have canceled his afternoon business appointment with a potential client, she insisted that he keep it. She needed some time to herself.

She started working on the remaining boarded-up windows again. When she'd just begun to maneuver the broken window frame from the opening, an old truck pulled up. She recognized it as the one Ernest had been working on in his front yard. He pulled out a couple of grocery bags.

"Hold on, I'll help you," he said, seeing her struggling with the window. He helped set the window on the table.

"Thanks," she said, eyeing the bags he'd set by the door. "What are those?"

"Grace went through her closet to find you some clothes and other stuff she thought you might need."

That small act of kindness stole away her words for a moment. She finally said, "That was awfully nice of her."

"The fire out at your place . . . someone trashing this place." He looked troubled as he rubbed his forehead. "Is this because you've been looking into my mama's murder?"

She sat down at the next table. "How'd you know I was looking into her murder?"

"People talk. And you were out talking to me. Made sense."

"I guess I am looking. Years ago I wanted her killer punished because I needed to see that sometimes justice prevailed. And I wanted it for you. Seeing you, well, it broke my heart. I wanted justice for the right and the wrong reasons. Now I just want the truth."

"You could have been killed in that fire."

She didn't want to think about that. "Ole Oscar here saved my life." She snapped her fingers, and he ambled over for a petting. "The thing is, if I don't find out who killed your mother, I don't know who to trust."

"They say my mama was a slut."

Kim winced at his bluntness. "She . . . well, I guess she liked men."

"I remember guys coming over, them going into the bedroom for a while. She'd make noises in there, like someone was killing her. I ran in to help her once, and she yelled at me." He gave her a sheepish smile. "Now I know what those noises were about."

Like Rhonda, Ernest had physically matured early. Even though he was only about fifteen, he looked like a man. The faded green tank top he wore showed off muscles and thick underarm hair.

"Maybe she was looking for love," Kim offered. "She just didn't know how to find it."

"I don't fault her, not really. She did her best by me. We always had food, and she hired people to fix up the house. I used to feel bad that my love wasn't enough for her, but now I understand." He grabbed one of the paper towels from the holder on a nearby table and blotted his face. "Are you still looking? Into her death, I mean? Or are you going to leave town? Not that I'd blame you. I wouldn't stick around if someone trashed my bar and then tried to burn me and my house down."

"I'm staying," she said with certainty. Though the sane thing would be to get the hell out of Dodge.

"She was pregnant." He let those words sit for a moment. "I found one of those pregnancy tests. There were two lines in the windows. I didn't know what it was at the time. She grabbed it from me and told me not to say anything about it. She said it was a secret."

Kim tamped down her surprise. "Did you tell the police this?"

He shook his head. "She'd said to keep it a secret. Even after her death—maybe especially because she was dead— I kept her secret. I remember she was real mad about something, too. She walked around the house cussing and ranting in those weeks before she died." He pushed himself to his feet. "I figured you orta know about that, in case it helps."

She stood, too. "But I don't remember the police saying that she was pregnant." Surely they wouldn't have covered up something like that. Kinsey wouldn't tamper with evidence, would he?

He shrugged. "Maybe they didn't test for it."

"I'll check into it and—" Movement at the open window caught her attention. She walked over to find JoGene standing near the door. "What are you doing lurking out there?" She didn't like the thought that he'd been listening to their conversation.

JoGene came inside. "I'm here to help you with the winders."

"You are?"

He removed his red Winchester cap and pushed his damp hair away from his face before settling the cap again. "We're friends, right?"

She had to stop herself from saying, *We are?* Instead, she glanced at Ernest. "I'll be right back, JoGene."

She nodded for Ernest to follow her outside. "Be careful, okay? If people think you're talking to me—and everyone knows everything around here—whoever set my house on fire might hurt you, too."

He nodded. "You be careful, too."

She watched him get into his truck before going back inside. JoGene was looking at the window on the table. "What do we do?"

"I'll show you," she said, remembering Zell helping her with the first window. She wasn't sure why *he* had helped her, either. JoGene's motives were much more suspect. "Where's your truck?" It hadn't been parked outside, thus allowing him to walk up to the open window without her hearing him pull into the lot.

"I parked at the marina and walked over. It's shady over there." In other words, he didn't want his father seeing him here.

She showed him how to break out the bits of glass.

"I'm sorry about your house, Kim. Do they have any ideas how it got started?"

"Gasoline, with intent to murder." She watched his expression, but he was concentrating on the glass.

"Murder? I heard they think you set it for the money. Hell, I told you I'd help you out."

She dropped her hammer on the table before she was tempted to do something else with it. "I didn't set it! Someone tried to kill me."

"Like you think someone killed Elva."

"Someone did kill Elva."

He raised his hands. "All right, all right. I'm not here to argue with you."

"Why *are* you here?"

"To help you." He grabbed a brush. "So who do you think set the fire?"

Sure, he'd love for her to spill her suspicions. "I wish I knew." She had a feeling he wasn't there out of the goodness of his heart. Reluctance strained his features. "Maybe you should go. I don't want you to get into trouble."

He dropped the brush. "My dad doesn't own me!" Rage colored his face, but he visibly contained it. "I need to help you, okay? Let's just leave it at that."

He jammed the brush into the paint. She'd take his help, but she wasn't telling him anything. Maybe she'd use the opportunity to find out something.

While the paint dried, they removed the plywood and took out the last window. Heavy, hot air drifted in through the openings. She had the air-conditioning on, but all of the cool air rushed right out. She felt ridiculous in the dress, but it was cooler than even shorts would have been. Especially considering the bottom hem came to several inches above her knees. Charlotte had said these were her clothes from after Tullie's birth before she lost weight. Even at that, they were way too small. Grace's clothes would probably be a better fit.

"JoGene?" She waited for him to stop breaking out the glass and look at her. "You were seeing Rhonda, weren't you? While we were dating."

His answer was to look away and lift one of his bony shoulders. "Maybe I was. Did Ernest tell you that?"

"No, I heard it from someone else. How much did you hear of our conversation, anyway?"

"Nothing." He used the chisel to scrape out the old glazing.

"Don't you have anything to say for yourself about dating Rhonda?"

"What should I say? You weren't giving me any so I went somewhere else. It wasn't like I was cheating. I didn't love her."

"It's not cheating if you don't love her?"

"Exactly. You're not going to fuss at me now about that, are you? 'Cause you don't have the right to do that, not unless you're thinking of taking up with me again." He gave his head a shake. "And I can't do that now."

"You can't take up with me now? Because of your father?"

"Yeah, that's it," he said, diverting his attention to the old glazing again. What was going on here?

"Rhonda's death must have shaken you up a little, though. I mean, you had been physically intimate with her."

"Of course I felt bad for her. But if you're trying to find out how recently I'd been with her, I hadn't seen her in months. Too long for her to be knocked up by me."

"You did hear us!" Uneasiness seized her.

"Look, do you want me to help you or do you want to jabber about the past?"

She took the chisel from him. "I've got it."

"I guess I don't blame you for not trusting anyone. But the thing is, you might be trusting the wrong person. Zell," he added at her expectant look. "I know you got a thing for him and all, but I've been thinking about Rhonda and your investigation. I think he was seeing her, too. The night she died, Winn called my dad, and he skedaddled right out of the house. He came back much later, looked pretty ragged, too. He burned his clothes in the big barbecue pit out back."

"You never told the police any of this."

"Of course not."

"Because it makes it sound like Buck murdered her."

"He didn't. He was home at the time they figured she was killed." It was JoGene and Buck's wife who gave Buck an alibi. Kim had never been sure. JoGene said, "Dad would never tell me what he'd done that night. But he got mad at Winnerow once and said how he owed Dad big time." He raised his eyebrows, waiting for her to make a connection. "Don't you get it? Owed him. I think Winn's been trying to protect his son all along. I think Zell killed that girl. Winnerow didn't know what to do, so he called my dad."

"I haven't heard anything about Zell seeing Rhonda."

"Not everything gets around this town. Just remember

this: maybe Zell's acting sweet on you because he wants to keep tabs on you." She shivered at that prospect even as her heart objected. He said, "Just be careful, that's all I'm saying. Be careful who you're friends with."

*Be careful who you trust*, Tullie had warned. What she had to wonder was, what did JoGene get out of trying to sway her loyalties?

He snatched up the keys he'd left on a nearby table. "Seems to me that if I thought someone was trying to kill me, I'd stop causing trouble. That's what I'd do."

She went back to the office and phoned Ernest. A tinny answering machine announced that he wasn't there but to leave a message. "Ernest, it's Kim. I'm pretty sure JoGene heard our conversation. Please be very careful. Whoever's behind this has no qualms about murder."

She wished she could tell whether JoGene had meant those parting words as a threat or a warning. Zell had imparted similar words once, but she couldn't believe he was behind any of this. "I've got to trust someone." And somewhere in the back of her mind the movie narrative echoed: *Famous last words.*


Kim finished the last window just before the afternoon storm rolled in. Smitty had come by as well as Amy to check on her well-being. Even Charlotte had called. Kim appreciated their thoughts so much she'd nearly been moved to tears. The stress was getting to her, she knew, but she wouldn't give in to it.

She wondered how long she'd be able to hold on to this place. She didn't have the money to pay off the chairs and stools when they arrived. What good were chairs without liquor? She had no house to get an equity loan on. Elva had had minimal insurance on the bar, saving money on premiums by opting for large deductibles. The few bucks she could get for the vandalism weren't worth the raised premiums. She'd discovered a policy for the house, but the arson investigation would hold that up.

The house. She squeezed her eyes shut for a moment and rocked her head against the glass.

Over at the hardware store, she could see Minotti dashing out into the rain. If he knew how much home meant to her, he'd never doubt her.

The drops of rain running down the glass reminded her of the tears aching to be let out. "How morose, Kim. Get a grip on yourself."

The rain was easing up enough for her to see a large truck backing into her parking lot. She didn't recognize the name on the side of the truck. Two young, buff guys jumped out and walked in. The older one glanced at his clipboard and said, "You Kim Lyons?"

"That's me."

"We've got a shipment of chairs and bar stools for you. You just need to sign here."

"Hold on. I've got to talk to Evan over at the hardware store." She'd scraped together enough money for half of the payment. Maybe she could beg for credit for the other half.

She sprinted across the expanse of parking lot and the empty lot bordering the main road. Even though the rain was light, she was still drenched by the time she reached the store. Evan had just finished ringing up a customer, and she caught her breath while he bagged the merchandise.

"Hold on a minute while I get your invoice," he said before she could explain about the money.

When he handed her a wad of cash, she could only stare at it. "What's this?" she finally asked as he jotted down *paid* on the invoice.

"That's the deposit you gave me."

As much as she needed a break, taking advantage of a mistake wasn't her style. "Evan, I still owe you money for the chairs. And here's the thing—"

"No you don't." He handed her the yellow copy. "You're all set. Just give this to the delivery guys."

"Evan, you don't understand. I haven't paid for them yet. And I can't pay for them."

He held up the invoice and pointed to the *Paid* notation. "You don't have to. Someone took care of the bill. That's why you got your deposit back."

"Who?"

"I can't say." He started to help the customer who'd just walked up to the register, but she grabbed his arm.

"Was it Zell Macgregor?"

"I can't say, but no, it wasn't him. Don't ask me, 'cause I'm not gonna tell you." He went back to the customer.

She glanced at the delivery truck waiting for her, then at the invoice. Paid. Who else would pay it but Zell? She gave up trying to find out and dashed back to the bar to take delivery of her chairs.

Two hours later, the sales rep for the beverage supplier pulled up in his white utility van with the company logo on it. She already knew begging wouldn't sway Berlin.

She walked outside. "I'm trying as hard as I can to pay you, but I still don't have—"

He raised his hand in the same annoying way Simon had when he wanted to halt her words. "Your account has been rectified." He walked around to the side and opened the sliding door. Consulting a list, he started stacking cases of liquor onto a dolly.

No way. This couldn't be happening. "How?"

She wasn't surprised when he said, "I don't know. Accounting called me and said to release your order. You're all paid up." He efficiently stacked the boxes to higher than his own height and wheeled them to the side ramp.

She roused herself and ran inside to unlock the back door. After three more trips, she signed the slip and saw him off. She locked the front door and turned to the stacks of boxes. She was back in business, just like that. And she intended to find out who had done this for her. Just as soon as she iced the beers and hung up the neon signs.

Before she did anything, she called and left a message for Zell. "Come on down to Southern Comfort. I'll buy you a drink."

.  .  .

The lit neon signs drew some of the townsfolk like the
color black did the swamp suckers. Zell, of course, had a
personal invitation. He'd called Shar and suggested it
might be nice to show up and give Kim a little support.
Though he doubted Owen and Winn would ever come
around, Shar seemed at least willing to give Kim a chance.

As soon as he stepped inside, some of the regulars gave
him a hard time about his new shirt. He didn't even model
it this time, just waved them off. The place looked as good
as new. Better than that, he thought, as his gaze settled on
Kim behind the bar as she drew a pitcher of beer. The windows were finished, the bar was stocked, and every table
had chairs. It looked clean and the floors gleamed. Like
with Kim, it gave him a peculiar feeling of vulnerability.
She'd had a house, too, and now it was gone. She'd almost
been killed. Oscar ambled up to him, his ropy tail swinging
happily. Zell knelt down and scratched his back, careful of
the healing cuts. Oscar had almost died, too.

Someone calling his name pulled him from his dark
thoughts. Angus and his wife were sharing a pitcher of
beer. He raised his glass and saluted him. Everything was
going well in Angusville.

"Zell! I got problems, boy, do I got problems."

Zell held up his hand, "Not now, Willie. I got problems
of my own."

"But it's my girl. She's complaining 'cause I'm not last-
ing long enough. You know . . . in the bedroom. What do I
do?"

"When you're just about to come, picture her mama's
face," he said, moving along. When Willie contemplated
that advice, he shuddered. Zell knew what Penny's mother
looked like.

Amy slid up to him, expertly balancing a tray of tequila
shots as she kissed him on the cheek. "Thanks for helping
Kim out. Helping us all out."

"I didn't do anything."

She winked. "Sure you didn't."

"I didn't." He didn't want credit for anything. He didn't want any part of it.

Smitty was shooting the bull with some of his cronies, but when he saw Zell, he pushed out of his chair and came over. "The gossip mill's been going overtime since the bar reopened. Everyone's been saying how you saved the place. Well, boy, you don't have to scowl about it. It's no secret you're sweet on the girl."

"I didn't save the bar." He didn't comment on the sweet part. "I didn't put out a dime."

Smitty picked up on Zell's seriousness. "All right, so you didn't. What's going on?"

Zell met Kim's gaze across the room, but he focused on Smitty. "I'm more concerned about who burned her house down. What are people saying about that?"

Smitty nodded toward the table in the corner—Zell's usual table. Minotti and Burton were sitting there observing the happenings. "Those two have been asking lots of questions 'bout Kim and all that's been happening around here. Local speculation's got it that Buck had something to do with it, maybe that he even got JoGene to do the deed for him."

Now Zell knew how Kim felt about finding the truth. He wanted to know who was responsible. He needed to know. Buck and JoGene were at the top of his list, too, with Owen thrown in for good measure.

Zell said, "Kim thinks Elva was blackmailing someone. You were close to her. Was she?"

Smitty's expression darkened. "All I know is, whatever she was up to, it probably got her killed. It almost got Kim and Oscar killed. And if *you* start asking questions . . ."

Smitty didn't need to finish the sentence. That he looked worried wasn't exactly comforting.

Zell walked up to the bar where Kim handed him a Captain Morgan and root beer.

"I'm paying you back," she said, looking both annoyed and grateful, if that were possible.

He settled onto a stool. "Why? I didn't pay for any of this."

"Sure you didn't."

He let out a low curse. "It wasn't me, Kim."

"Are you getting flack for helping me?"

"I don't care if I do. But I didn't pay for any of this."

She raised her hands. "All right, you didn't. Then who did? Who around here would put out that kind of money to help me? All most of the folks around here want to do is give me a hard time."

That bothered her; he could see it in her eyes and the way the corners of her mouth dipped down for a second. "I need to know who did this, Zell. It's important, just as important as knowing who burned down my house."

Telling her the truth would cause more problems than it would solve. "No, the house is much more important. Focus on that; just accept this for what it is. Hell, the town owed you." He took a long swig of his drink while Kim processed an order for Amy.

When she returned, she said, "Rhonda was pregnant when she died."

"What?"

"Ernest told me that he'd found a positive pregnancy test right before she died. But I checked with Kinsey; the autopsy reports didn't show her being pregnant. I can't figure it out. Did someone at the sheriff's office doctor the autopsy report? I doubt even Kinsey could manage that. And while Ernest was telling me this, JoGene was just outside the open window. He said he came by to help me with the windows, which I highly doubt. I think he was there to eavesdrop." Kim's eyes narrowed. "You knew. You knew she was pregnant, didn't you?"

He wasn't sure what he'd let show on his face, but he hated that she'd picked up on it. "She wasn't pregnant. They tested for it."

She shook her head, her eyes wide and pained. "Maybe

she terminated the pregnancy before she died. But you knew, didn't you? It wasn't common knowledge. Only Ernie knew . . . and maybe the father of her child."

"Kim . . ."

She backed away from him, knocking over a bottle of ketchup in her haste. A few people looked over at the noise but resumed their conversations. Minotti and Burton, however, were watching them with interest.

Zell wanted to walk behind the bar and put an end to that distrustful expression on her face. Only he couldn't, not without lying. He'd been lying so long, why did he find it so hard to do it now?

She wouldn't even look at him, though clearly her suspicions caused her pain. They caused him pain, too, he realized. He'd hurt her once with his lies on the witness stand. This time he'd use them to ease her pain. He stalked behind the bar, took her hand, and hauled her out back.

"Zell, what are you doing?"

He trapped her against the wall, his arms on either side of her. "You think I had something to do with that girl's death? Can you look me in the eye and tell me you think I'm capable of murder?"

She couldn't look him in the eye; she kept shifting her gaze away. "I don't want to think that, but I could see it in your face, that you knew, and JoGene said you were seeing her, and—"

"JoGene said . . ." He pulled back and rubbed his hand over his mouth. "JoGene's lying, all right? He's throwing that out to get back at me. I never touched that girl, not once. I don't know anything about her murder." He tipped up her chin and made her look at him. "Do you believe in your heart and soul that I could kill someone? That I could try to kill you?"

This time she looked into his eyes, searching for the truth. "How did you know about Rhonda's supposed pregnancy?"

"I heard it indirectly from JoGene, who told Owen, who told Shar, who told me. That's how I know."

Could she see the lie in his eyes? Was he going to lose her because of it? He ran his thumb over the softness of her lower lip. Then he kissed her, a gentle kiss that begged her to believe him. He couldn't stand the look of distrust in her eyes, not now.

She slid her arms around him and kissed him back. The back door opened, and Smitty popped his head out. "Kim, we need you."

For a moment she didn't let go of him. Then, with a sigh, she walked inside, glancing back to see if he was following. She'd kissed him, but the indecision on her face killed him.

Shar and Owen were sitting at the bar when they returned. Kim caught up on her orders and then made Shar a rumrunner using her fancy bottle-spinning techniques. He didn't like feeling so much for a woman, especially one like Kim. Just as Winn had asked: why couldn't he have fallen for one of the nice gals he'd taken out in the past? This one was trouble, wrapped in a sinful package, a contradiction if he ever saw one. Strong and yet afraid to give away her heart. From that first encounter with her in Elva's hothouse, he'd been drawn to her, even if it had been kicking and screaming. He wasn't kicking or screaming now.

Owen took his beer and wandered over to a table of his friends. He didn't want to be here to support Kim, that was obvious. Shar had probably dragged him along. Though he laughed at someone's joke, his hardened eyes kept watching Kim.

Shar took a sip of the drink Kim placed in front of her. "Yum-my. I could get used to these things."

When Smitty set several baskets of wings on the counter, Kim grabbed a tray and went to deliver them. Shar swiveled her stool around to face the small group of patrons and tapped her frosty glass with her nails. "I wasn't sure my big brother would ever fall for a woman. Never thought it'd be one who hated gators, especially. What happened to your gator-loving requirement?"

Words denying that he was falling for her didn't jump to

the surface. Just watching her setting the baskets of wings on a table had something inside him going round and round. The gator thing was the least of his problems. "She saw Toopie's arm get pulled off by that bull gator. She was just a kid then. It scarred her."

Shar winced. "I suppose that could scar you, seeing something like that."

"I don't even care if she loves them. Or likes them. As long as she respects them, I'd be okay with that. And I've got an idea about how to work that out."

If Shar was going to comment on his change of attitude, she swallowed the words along with a healthy gulp of her drink.

Getting Kim to like gators was the easy part. Getting her to stop being scared to let her heart go was a major obstacle. This falling-in-love thing was new to him, too. He'd figured they could both take their time getting used to the idea, but secrets and lies were getting in the way. And he couldn't forget that someone wanted her dead. He couldn't afford to forget that at all.

# CHAPTER 26

Kim spent the next morning scrubbing the nooks and crannies of the bar. Unfortunately, the busywork didn't keep her mind from straying to Zell. He'd spent the previous night out in his truck in the parking lot. Protecting her. She tossed a sponge into the bucket in disgust. All right, maybe she'd jumped to conclusions, nothing new for her. Maybe she was looking for guilt everywhere. That it had flashed in Zell's eyes had been more than disturbing. It had rocked her to her core.

When the door opened soon after the lunch shift ended, she hoped it was him. She wanted to apologize. Needed to apologize. She was surprised to see Grace and her little girl walk hesitantly in. By the look on her face, she wasn't stopping in for a sandwich. She pulled the girl behind her and made a beeline toward Kim.

"Ernie's gone. He's been gone since late last night. I saw him get home around midnight. Then I heard a rifle go off, though it could have been a truck backfiring, I couldn't be sure. Then I heard his truck leave sometime after that. He hasn't been home since."

Kim dried her hands as dread seized her. "Maybe he's just up to no good."

Grace's blue eyes flashed defensively. "I know he was here yesterday talking to you."

Kim tried not to react to Grace's unspoken accusation. "He told me that Rhonda was pregnant when she died. Did you know about that?"

"I didn't keep up with my sister's activities." She narrowed her eyes. "You are looking into her murder, aren't you? Is that why your house got burned down? And for what? Justice for a woman who couldn't keep her legs closed? And now Ernie's gone. If something's happened to him, I'm holding you responsible."

With those words, she turned and dragged her daughter back out into the sunny afternoon. The last two men eating lunch quickly resumed eating. They weren't regulars, so at least they wouldn't be spreading gossip about that conversation.

Charlotte had passed Grace on the way in, looking at the woman who was obviously distressed. "What was her problem?"

"Ernie's missing." Kim couldn't stop staring at the door, wondering what had happened to him. She hoped he was just making mischief.

Charlotte didn't ask for further clarification and Kim didn't offer it. After greeting Oscar, she smoothed her green skirt and climbed up on a stool. When Kim asked if she wanted something, Charlotte waved that off. "I came to talk to you, woman to woman. About my brother."

The two men stood, and one said, "We're ready for our bill."

After the men headed out, the place was quiet. Kim locked the front door to keep it that way. She wanted to hear what Charlotte had to say. She took the bar stool beside her. "Go on." Was she going to warn her away? As nice as Charlotte was sometimes, Kim doubted she was truly happy that her brother was seeing her.

"My brother's in love with you. He as much as admitted it right here last night."

Kim blinked at that, unable to really respond. In love?

Even after she'd practically accused him of murder? "Zell doesn't believe in love. He listens to all of those antilove songs."

She waved that away, her glittery nails catching the light. "That's just his way to keep all those money-hungry, boring females at a distance. The thing is, Zell's never been in love before. Infatuated, yes, but not in love. Actually, I'm kind of glad it's you. You're the first gal who measures up to him in terms of spirit."

"I'm in love with him, too." The words had come out under their own power. They were just as surprising as Charlotte's words about Zell being in love with her.

Charlotte smiled. "Well, duh. Like anyone couldn't tell."

Kim decided not to mention that *she* couldn't tell. She really was in love with him, she realized, that roller-coaster feeling sinking in. *Click, click, click.*

Charlotte continued. "*I* even like you, though I'm not in love with you." She laughed at her joke. "Thing is, despite everything, you really are a good match for Zell. Daddy will come to see that. Zell's already had a talk with him about you. Basically he told Daddy that he liked you and that was that. Following one's passions hasn't always been the wisest thing the men in my family have done, but this is the first time Zell's had a passion for a woman to follow. I think Daddy'll come around, especially now that you've apologized to him. He thinks a lot of you after that."

Kim wasn't sure how to feel about that. It depended on how much he'd been involved with the theft of her orchids—and anything else. She remembered how guilty he'd looked when she found the orchid petal at his farm. "I'd like to make peace with the Macgregors. And I like you, too, though I'm not in love with you, either."

Charlotte hooted in laughter and slapped the bar. "I knew I liked you. You've got sass. You'll make a fine addition to the family." She crossed her legs. "And Zell, he'd make a great daddy. He's tender and compassionate and so good with Tullie. Why, you know what he did when I was pregnant? He used to paint my toenails because I couldn't reach them. How sweet is that?"

"You don't have to sell me on him," Kim said, picturing him painting Charlotte's nails. And then picturing him painting hers.

"Now here's the thing. I know Zell has used the gator-loving requirement to keep women at a distance for years. He administers an oral test, as you've probably heard, and then has the lady hold a gator. But it's not only to keep women at a distance. Gators are his life, his passion. Most of what he does for a living revolves around them, and of course, there's the farm. I do understand why you hate them, I really do." She patted Kim's hand. "But you've got to get over that if you're going to be part of our family. So I got to thinking, why don't we surprise Zell?"

Kim wasn't sure where this conversation was going, but she was too pleased by Charlotte's acceptance to worry much. "Surprise him?"

"Come out to the farm. I'll work with you, you know, give you a primer on gators. We'll start with the little guys. You can hold one and get used to how they feel. And I'll tell you everything there is to know about them. I know some of the questions he's asked before. You'll have insider information. You'll get comfortable being at the farm, too. Why don't you come on out now?"

Kim nearly choked. "Now?" She had to think about this.

"Today's a good day, actually. Owen and Daddy are up in North Florida visiting another gator farm. Zell's helping Smitty build some rabbit cages. Everyone will be gone all day." She slid off the stool. "Well, you think about it. Think about showing Zell how much you know about gators and surprising him beyond his wildest dreams. Think how much it'll mean to him. I'll be at the farm for another hour or so."

"I will think about it."

Kim followed Charlotte outside into the moist air. Dark bluish clouds were gathering in the eastern sky as usual. Even dressed up and wearing heels, Charlotte looked at home climbing into the large truck. She waved and backed up.

Kim looked into the bar. She could finish cleaning out the bins and sinks or she could do something for Zell. After all he'd done for her, and especially after last night, it seemed like the right thing to do. This could be the first step in learning to give everything she had inside her.

She gave Oscar a quick belly rub. "I'm leaving you here, bud. You don't want to hang around gators, that's for sure."

She closed up the bar and headed to the farm. Along the way, she searched for Ernest's truck, but didn't see it. She did, however, pass JoGene's truck. In her rearview mirror, she saw him make a U-turn, but when she crossed over the bridge, she lost sight of him.

JoGene had planted that doubtful seed about Zell. Why? As she turned into Heron's Glen, she decided that she would trust him least of all. She parked next to Charlotte's truck outside the farm and stepped out. The smell hit her right away, muggy heat and alligator feces. "I must be in love," she muttered and trudged toward the small gator house that Charlotte was exiting.

The sky to the east looked dark and ugly, contrasting with the trees in the foreground that were still sunlit. Light clouds skittered across the sky below the demon-black landscape. Thunder rumbled ominously. She glanced back to see if JoGene had followed. No sign of his truck.

"You came," Charlotte said, looking inordinately pleased. "Zell is just going to be so captivated, you wait and see." She waved her inside the building.

Captivated. She wasn't sure that was the right word but wasn't about to suggest a better one.

Charlotte put her finger to her mouth, her glittery nails contrasting against pink lips. "You gotta be real quiet in here, especially in the large gator house. Any noise incites them."

Kim envied those beautiful nails, but not the money that probably went into maintaining them. She nodded her understanding, definitely not wanting to incite alligators.

"Where's Tullie?" Kim whispered.

"She's with her uncle Zell. Tullie loves rabbits."

Picturing the girl with the small gator on her shoulder, Kim had to stifle a smile. Both Charlotte and Tullie were contradictions. If that small girl could be comfortable around gators, so could Kim.

Charlotte plucked a two-foot gator from one of the holding tanks. "We'll start with one of these."

"Couldn't we try a smaller one?"

Charlotte laughed. "This is a small one. See, he's still got his stripes." She pointed them out by drawing her finger along the yellow stripes on its side. "Now, here's the trick of holding them. First, you gotta support their bodies. Hold him like this, down by his lower body with one hand and around his neck with the other hand. That way he can't swing around on you. Here."

She thrust it at Kim, who fought the urge to back away and took it. The belly skin was smooth and cool. The gator didn't move, as though it were resigned to being handled like this. "What do I do with him?"

"Just hold him until you feel comfortable." She touched Kim's arms. "Relax. There you go. Now smile. See, it ain't so bad."

After a few minutes, she did feel more comfortable, though she wouldn't do it for fun. She raised the gator up to her face level and looked at him.

Charlotte said, "Give him a kiss, right on the end of his snout. He can't see straight ahead, so he won't know you're even doing it."

Kim raised an eyebrow. "Let's save that for later, shall we?"

"All right, that's a good start." She took the gator and set it back in the holding tank.

A shadow passed over the gator house, and Kim looked up to see darkness above the opaque plastic roof. The thunder was growing louder.

Charlotte said, "Let's head over to the big house."

Kim dutifully followed. The wind had picked up, fling-
ing leaves and dirt into their faces like a naughty kid.
Lightning shimmered in the near distance. At least the
wind also blew away some of the smell and cooled the
interior of the large gator house. The heat that escaped
through the door was stifling.

As Charlotte closed the half-door, it slammed shut,
probably pushed by the wind. Kim heard some of the
gators stir. It was so dim inside she could hardly see the
end of the hallway. Like at the small house, a series of
holding areas flanked the walkway. A half-wall allowed
one to look out over the gators, and a half-door provided
access. Each large area was thick with the creatures, most
in a shallow pool of water. They looked sinister in the dim
light, like something out of a James Bond movie she'd
seen. They were piled up so thick, she could imagine running on top of them as Bond had done.

"How many alligators are in each area?" Kim whispered.

"About three hundred."

"Can we turn on the lights?" Kim asked as Charlotte
came up beside her.

"We never turn them on unless we're getting them ready
for slaughter. This place is set up so they'll grow fast.
That's why it's so warm in here. The plastic on the roof
helps to heat the water. We feed them once a day so they
don't get ornery and eat one another. I was supposed to
feed them this morning, but I waited so you could see them
in action. I know about you seeing Toopie's arm get bit off,
and I thought it might help if you saw them eating what we
feed them: Purina Gator Chow."

Kim raised an eyebrow at that. "I had no idea Purina
made a chow for gators."

Charlotte went into the back room and came out with a
wheelbarrow full of brown nuggets. When she scraped the
shovel against the wheelbarrow, the gators came to life.
Kim heard the eerie sounds of their bodies moving through
the water, hissing and splashing as they fought for position.

The wind howled around the building and snapped the plastic roofing. Or was that the sound of a truck door closing? Had JoGene followed her after all? There were no windows, so she couldn't see. Since Charlotte didn't seem to notice, Kim focused on what she was saying.

"Hopefully this will give you a different image of a gator eating." She opened one of the half-doors and stepped onto a short platform. "Come here."

Hanging over the center of the area was a wooden platform suspended by ropes. Kim stayed just behind the open door and watched while Charlotte reeled the platform closer and dumped chow on it. The gators writhed and tumbled over each other, their mouths open as they warned off those who would encroach on their territory. Kim shivered.

After dumping more food onto the platform, Charlotte reeled it back to where it hovered just inches above the water. The gators rushed it, climbing over one another in their exuberance.

"You say you feed them every day?" Kim asked.

"Yes, but as I said, I waited a bit, so they're pretty hungry. Watch how they eat."

When the rain started in a rush of sound, the gators paused for a moment. Then they went for the food again. They climbed up onto the platform, turned their head sideways, and scooped up the chow.

"They chew," Charlotte said. "Gators in the wild don't chew. They roll their victim over, push it down in the water and drown it. Then they tear off pieces of flesh, which they swallow whole."

The wind shook the doors again, and Kim checked to see if someone had come in.

Charlotte didn't seem to notice. She seemed entranced by the gators. After a few moments, she pointed. "See those ridges on the gator's back? They're called scutes. They're actually solid bone, a nearly invincible armor. That'll probably be on the test, too."

"Scutes," Kim repeated, remembering Zell talking about them.

"Do you know the scientific name for a gator? *Alligator mississippiensis.*"

Kim repeated that, too.

"They've got up to eighty teeth in that mouth, and if they lose a tooth, it regenerates. They can go through a couple thousand teeth in their life." She wheeled the barrow to the next holding area. "Look at that gator there, the one that's submerged. See how you can only see the tip of its nose and its eyes? Can you tell how big it is?"

It was big enough, Kim thought, but only shrugged.

Charlotte opened the door and waved Kim closer. "Count how many inches are between the eyes and the nose." She demonstrated. "Each inch equals a foot of total length. So how big is that one?"

Kim measured with her eyes. "Seven foot."

"Exactly. These are our biggest gators."

Kim remembered the story of Owen's encounter with the loose gator. Smitty had said the six-footers were the most dangerous. A few dozen gators waited below the short platform that reached a foot out from the door. They were eyeing both women with hunger in their beady eyes.

"These guys have never eaten meat?" Kim asked.

"Nope. I suppose they'd know what to do if the opportunity arose. Shall we test them?" Charlotte gave Kim a little shove.

Kim let out a yelp as she grabbed for the edge of the door. "That's not funny!" she shouted in a shaky voice, making the gators stir.

Charlotte closed the door, shutting Kim on the gator side of the half-wall. "I know it isn't." She pulled out a small, pearl-handled gun as Kim reached for the door handle. "But neither is your digging around in the past."

# CHAPTER 27

Zell drilled in the last screw on the third cage. Smitty was working on the bases, and Tullie was playing with the rabbits. Usually the girl chattered incessantly at the rabbits, but since they'd arrived, she'd been quiet. She was lying on her side in the thick grass stroking their ears.

'Course, he'd been quiet, too. He felt a persistent heaviness in his chest he knew had everything to do with Kim. He'd had all night to think about the situation, being uncomfortable as he was sleeping in the truck. He'd decided to tell her the truth; he couldn't risk losing her.

A low rumble drew his attention to the sky. They weren't going to be working for much longer. Black clouds oozed menace. He walked over and dropped down beside Tullie. "You want one of these guys? We could build you a cage."

She shrugged, her blue eyes never leaving the white rabbit she was petting.

"What's the matter, angel? You still blaming yourself for not knowing about the fire?"

Another shrug.

"You still having those gator dreams?"

She looked at him at last. "You said they were only dreams, right? Just regular nightmares." She was waiting for confirmation.

"Only makes sense. You still having them?"

"Yeah. I wish they'd go away. Now I'm really afraid of Runt. I can't even pick him up anymore."

That was serious. She loved that little gator. "Tullie, tell me about the dreams again."

"It's just bits and pieces, least that I can remember. I see you and Kim; last night I saw Mama, too. I see the big gators tearing up something, and I hear screaming. And I keep hearing the screaming." Her face went white at the memory.

He reached over and smoothed her cheek, hoping to bring back some color. "Are they our gators you're seeing? Can you tell?"

She shook her head. "I can't see where they are, just that there's a bunch of them."

If anyone fell into one of the holding areas, it'd likely be Owen. Owen and Winn were at a friend's farm for the day. Shar was supposed to feed their gators this morning. No way would she ever accidentally fall in. He didn't like how upset Tullie was over these dreams. It gave him an uneasy feeling.

"I'll call your mom." He grabbed his phone from the truck and dialed Shar's cell number. There was no answer, but that didn't necessarily worry him. She sometimes forgot to charge it. He called Southern Comfort, too, to tell Kim he'd be coming by in a while. No answer there, either.

When his phone rang, he figured it might be Shar returning his missed call. It was one of the deputies at the Naples sheriff's office. "You wanted me to let you know when those two boys bailed out. Well, they left about an hour ago."

Enough time for them to reach town. "Thanks." Even though they hadn't set the fire, he didn't trust them.

Tullie asked, "Uncle Zell, what's wrong?" when he hung up. "Was it Mama?"

"No, it wasn't. I gotta go," he told both her and Smitty.

"I want to go with you," she said, climbing into his truck before he could say otherwise.

"What's the matter?" Smitty asked as Zell handed him the three rabbits Tullie had been watching.

"Clem and Billy Bob are out of jail. I'm going to check on Kim, make sure she's all right. Tullie, out of the truck."

She crossed her arms in front of her. He didn't have time to wrestle with the girl. He hopped in and headed out. Maybe Kim had just gone to the hardware store.

Her truck wasn't at the bar or at the store, but JoGene's was. Zell stopped and caught him just as he was heading out with a six-pack. Zell wasn't sure what his expression was, but he must have looked a little wild.

JoGene raised his hand as though to ward Zell off. "I don't like that look on your face. I took care of everything just like you said to. She can have the bar. I don't want it anymore. I'm talking to Reverend Macey about taking over his beer and worm business."

He wasn't going to get into JoGene's accusations just then. Later, yes, but not then. "Have you seen Kim today?"

He blinked, readjusting his train of thought. "Yeah, heading north. I pulled into the marina, so I didn't see where she went after she crossed the bridge. I assumed it was to your place or maybe to her place."

Tullie had been listening to the conversation from her open window. As Zell walked back to his truck, she asked, "Is Kim all right? I got that feeling again, Uncle Zell. It hurts right here." She placed her clenched fist to her chest.

"I'm sure she is. Maybe she just wanted to take in her house again, you know, get right inside with what happened."

He headed toward her house. Then he'd check his place. He glanced over at Tullie, who was lost in dark thoughts. And in concert with those dark thoughts, the sky opened up with a loud crack of thunder and dumped rain on them.


"Charlotte, what are you doing?" Kim's strained voice squeezed out of a throat almost too tight for air. This had to be a joke or maybe a test of some kind.

She raised the gun as Kim reached for the door. "I'm protecting my own. Maybe with the last of your family gone, the past can finally rest. Ernie may be a problem, but we'll just have to see about him."

Kim's throat went dry at those words. "You did something to Ernie?"

"No, but I tried. He ran off, scared like a rabbit."

Kim hardly had the wherewithal to feel relieved, not with a gun in her face and three hundred hungry gators behind her. She could hear them thrashing around, fighting for who got to sink its teeth into her first.

"You're doing this to protect Winn, aren't you? He killed Rhonda. And Elva. Charlotte, you don't have to do this."

"Yes, I am doing this to protect my father. Just like I killed Rhonda to protect him."

Kim's mouth dropped open. She gained her senses, wanting to keep Charlotte talking. "But why?"

"Because she was causing trouble, just like Elva did and like you're now doing. Rhonda played up to my daddy, taking advantage of the fact that he was brokenhearted after my mama's death. She might have been a teenager, but she was a vamp. She thought she could get her nails into him, and she nearly did. She got pregnant and demanded that he marry her. What she didn't count on was that he'd be jailed for statutory rape if anyone found out he'd fathered her child. He couldn't marry her."

Her child. "Ernie is your half-brother."

She sneered, "Quaint, ain't it? I overheard Daddy and Zell talking about it. They wanted to protect my feminine sensibilities, you see, keep me out of it. They hashed over their options, and Zell proposed a deal to her: Daddy would pay child support if she'd keep her mouth shut about who fathered that bastard child of hers. She did, apparently, because no one ever found out. Luckily Ernest took after Rhonda and not Daddy. I would have gouged his eyes out if they'd looked like ours." Her talons clenched on the gun as anger flared in her eyes. "When she was about to turn eighteen, she started putting the pressure on him again. I think Daddy intended to marry her, too. No way could I have that girl as a stepmom. No way would I let her win. She'd have ruined the family for sure."

"So you killed her," Kim finished.

"No, I threatened her at first, tried to scare her away. It was her lie that pushed me over the edge."

"She told Winn she was pregnant."

"Exactly. And you even found out about that. Yes, she showed him a positive pregnancy test. See, Daddy had been seeing her on and off for those intervening years. He was lonely, and she filled a need, I suppose. Zell tried his damnedest to keep him away from that girl, but she had him good. Except that right after she turned eighteen, Daddy shot your father. Then he married Kitty because he felt responsible. And that pissed Rhonda off big time.

"Daddy kept promising to divorce Kitty after a bit and marry her, but he kept putting her off. I think he came to like Kitty, even if he was sleeping with Rhonda. So Rhonda got desperate and produced the test. Zell didn't believe her, but Daddy did. But there was something that I knew: if a negative pregnancy test sits for longer than fifteen minutes, it can show a second line. Either way, I wasn't going to stand for it. Either she was lying or we were going to have another bastard child around. While Zell and Daddy discussed how to deal with her—she was threatening to turn him in for the first statutory rape if he didn't marry her—I started planning."

Charlotte's voice, along with the sky-shattering thunder, was irritating the gators even more, particularly since they were still waiting for their meal. Kim kept feeling around for a handle on the inside of the door as Charlotte talked.

"See, Zell's always been the one to clean up after Daddy. They thought I couldn't handle the truth. But I'm stronger than they thought. This time I would clean up the mess and shield my brother from it all. I wanted to be the one to make things right. So I went to Rhonda's place pretending I had money. She got into the truck with me, and I bashed her on the head with a hammer, again and again. Then I drove to the house and told Daddy what I'd done. I thought he'd be proud of me."

Her laugh was bitter, and her eyes filled with moisture. "He yelled at me, told me I was crazy. I was only trying to protect him! That's what I told him. And he held me and said now *he* would protect *me*. That he was long overdue. He called Buck to help him get rid of the girl's body. They jammed a stick up her so it'd look like a sexual crime just in case she was ever found."

Kim touched something that felt like an emergency latch. She felt around for a release lever. "So it *was* them I saw driving out to the swamp."

"Yeah. Buck had suggested feeding her to the gators, but Daddy was afraid something would be left in the tank. I'm going to make sure no one ever finds you." She scanned Kim. "You don't wear a lot of jewelry. I'll be checking after the next flushing of the tanks to be sure that belly button ring of yours isn't left behind or pooped out. Folks around here will think you gave up and left. Someone will see your truck heading toward Miami, I'm sure. I should be back before anyone even knows I was gone."

Kim thought about screaming for help, but she'd never be heard over the torrents of pounding rain. The only person who might hear it would be Dewey, who would probably do whatever Charlotte told him to. Her frantic mind tried to sort through her options as Charlotte said, "Don't think I like doing this. I actually do like you. And Zell, he does love you. That presented another problem. Having you as part of the family would be even trickier. Since you didn't die in the fire, I was hoping you'd at least get scared and leave."

"Mama?"

Kim saw the puzzlement on Charlotte's face before they both turned to find a soaking-wet Zell and Tullie standing near the door.

"Shar, what are you doing?" Zell kept his voice calm despite his utter disbelief.

"Get out of here!" Charlotte shouted, turning the gun back on Kim when she started to move. "Let me handle this."

Tullie started to rush forward, her face wet with tears and rain. "Mama, the dream about the gators! Please, stop! The gators are going to eat me."

Zell grabbed her by her shirt.

"Get her out of here!" Charlotte and Kim both said.

"You have to get back in the truck." When Tullie shook her head, Zell pushed her out the door and locked it.

While Charlotte was preoccupied with Tullie's desperate cries, Kim turned the small knob and pushed the door open. The gun skittered across the floor as Charlotte was shoved backward. She lunged toward Kim, who was moving through the doorway. Kim dropped and grabbed at her legs, sending her to the floor in the open doorway. Charlotte kicked free, screaming unintelligibly. She got to her feet and held on to the half-wall.

Zell pulled Kim against him and grabbed the gun. The gators were churning and hissing now; the sound even overpowered the rain.

Charlotte's eyes were wide in her pale face. "Zell, we've got to get rid of her. She knows too much."

Pain mixed with the shock on his face. "Shar, what are you talking about?"

"We've got to get rid of Kim. I know you like her, but there will be other girls. It's to protect the family. She'll turn me in, even if she promises not to. I know she will. If we get rid of her, we can keep this our secret."

Zell said, "Come here, Shar." He held his hand out to her. "We can work this out."

Charlotte's gaze darted between Zell and Kim. It remained on Zell for a moment, wet with tears of desperation. "Zell, tell me you'll help. You've protected Daddy all these years. Protect me now. I had to kill them to protect our family honor."

"Them?" he asked.

"Rhonda and Elva. I only did it for the family. I didn't

want that girl to mess things up. And Elva, she was black-mailing me. Nobody knew Rhonda kept a diary. She hid it in her sister's shed in the bottom of a box of gardening stuff. Elva bought the box at a church sale, of all the damn luck. Rhonda had written about me threatening her. Elva contacted me anonymously through letters. She said she ought to turn it over to the police. It would reopen the investigation and point it right at me. But she said that wouldn't really do anyone any good now. She was greedy; she wanted twelve thousand dollars. So I paid her, a little every month out of the house account. I was supposed to throw the money into the swamp from the highway coming into town.

"But I knew that the blackmailer would either keep asking for money or eventually turn me in. So I decided to find out who it was. I had Dewey throw the money while I waited in a skiff someone kept at the dock north of Elva's place. And I saw her retrieve the package. See, Dewey can keep some secrets. He never told anyone about that or about helping me dump her body into the swamp. Please don't look at me like that. I had to do it, I had to." Her voice dropped to a whisper. "Please, Zell, push Kim in. We can keep it our secret. Daddy doesn't ever have to know. Or Owen. We can tell Tullie this was a misunderstanding. That I was going to shoot a gator or something, and Kim accidentally fell in."

"No one else is going to die, Shar."

"Then it's all over. I'll go to jail, everyone will know about Rhonda and Daddy's bastard child . . . they'll know it all. They'll say the Macgregors are crazy people. There will be news shows about us, dissecting our lives—me. I'll have done all this for nothing." She glanced at the gators behind her and then quickly turned back to Zell and Kim. He had inched closer but stopped again. Charlotte said, "Promise me you won't tell anyone the truth. If not for me, then for Tullie."

Kim said, "I promise." Anything to get her to walk forward.

She turned to Zell. "Promise me, big brother."

"Just come here," he said, his voice strangled with emotion. "We'll make it all right."

"No. I'll make it all right."

As Zell lunged for her, Charlotte stepped over the edge and into the gators. Kim let out a scream as he reached for his sister. The gators instantly covered her, pushing her beneath the water in a frenzy. Kim grabbed at Zell as he began to climb down into the holding area.

"No, they'll kill you, too!"

He leaned down, searching for Charlotte with the gun aimed at the gators. He was trying to shoot at them without hitting her. Finally he shot up in the air, probably hoping to distract them. But it was already too late. Way too late. The truth of that was in the blood-colored water. Kim pulled him away from the platform and toward the door where the drumming rain washed away the sounds of the gators. He collapsed, and she let him take her with him. Her stomach churned, and she was covered in sweat.

"I'm sorry," she managed to say, looking into his shell-shocked face.

Tullie was no longer pounding on the door. Kim hoped she'd gone back to the truck. Neither of them was ready to face her yet.

"She was trying to kill you," he said in a robotic tone.

She pressed her face against his soaked shirt. "She thought she was doing the right thing, protecting her family. She thought she was protecting you."

"She was crazy. She wanted me to help her cover it up." He seemed to come out of the haze of shock. He shoved away the small gun. "She wanted me to help kill you. Are you all right?"

Kim nodded. "Are you?"

He didn't look all right. He looked pale as he stared past her. "No more cover-ups. I don't expect you to lie about what happened here. We're telling the police everything. I don't want to lose you over this."

After pursuing the truth for so long, Kim thought that the

possibility for justice looked as bleak as the sky overhead. Charlotte was right: there would be reporters, a lengthy investigation, and speculation. The family would be put through hell. She imagined Tullie's solemn face and imposed Ernest's lost face over it. She remembered her own pain and shock over losing her father, and then, just recently, discovering the truth.

"We're not going to the police." She got to her knees and faced him. "Charlotte has been punished." She glanced back toward the holding area. The gators had quieted down again, and the rain had lightened. Thunder rumbled from a distance. "There's no need to punish the rest of the family, especially Tullie." She touched his face as he began to understand what she was saying. "There's nothing to be gained by telling the truth. There's only much to be lost."

"Are you sure?"

"I'm sure."

He pushed himself to his feet and helped her up. He glanced toward the holding tank, closed his eyes, and lowered his head. "What about what Tullie saw?"

"We'll tell her there was an alligator loose on the walkway, and that's why Charlotte had the gun out. That's why we were tense. It's happened before."

He pulled her hard against him. After a few minutes, he said, "Why were you out here? This was the last place I expected to see your truck. I only came here because of Tullie's gator dreams."

She started to tell him about Charlotte's offer to help Kim pass his test but halted. No need for him to know his own test had been used to nearly kill her. "We were just talking, that's all. Let's go tell Tullie the news."

"She probably already knows. Maybe she knew all along."

# EPILOGUE

Zell walked up to the door and knocked. Kim opened it and took him in for a second. It was the first time he'd worn a tropical shirt since what they called the accident. Only Winnerow and Owen had been told the truth. Everyone else in town had mourned only for a terrible accident, even giving Kim condolences for witnessing it. Tullie's feelings told her there was more to the story, but so far she hadn't pressed. Kim knew Zell was having a hard time coming to terms with what Charlotte had done. She hadn't realized how much she'd missed seeing those shirts . . . or the brightness in his eyes.

"You really don't have to knock," she said. "It's your house." Kim had moved into Zell's house while he was living at Heron's Glen to be close to Tullie. They had put their relationship on hold over the last four months while they focused on helping the girl through her grief.

He lifted a shoulder. "It's your place for now. Ready to go?"

"To some mysterious destination? I don't know. I guess I'm game." She glanced behind him. "Where's Tullie?"

Between Kim, Zell, and Winnerow, the girl was never left alone. Helping Tullie heal had been a way for all of them to heal. Old grudges and bad feelings had been set aside . . . hopefully for good. Winnerow had even given Kim a hug good night after dinner last week.

"Owen's back. I guess four months of traveling around Florida helped him work through his grief. He was pretty messed up. I wasn't sure if he was ever going to come back. He seems all right. He's even ready to get back to work at the farm."

She shuddered at the thought of that place. "I have to keep telling myself it was Charlotte who put herself there, not the gators." She let him guide her to his truck. Instead of opening her door, he just looked at her for a few seconds. She self-consciously pulled at her strands of hair. "What?"

"You look good." He leaned forward and gave her a quick kiss. "Real good."

"I've missed you, too." She gave him another kiss, this one not so quick.

Almost dying had taught her that life was too uncertain to waste on safe men. Not that she had a choice on whether to fall in love with Zell Macgregor or not.

When she hoped he'd lead her back into the house so they could *discuss* their future, he helped her into the truck instead. They drove farther out than even Otter's Tail, through the thick cypress in the far reaches of the swamp. The road nearly disappeared, only in evidence by the matted grasses. He parked next to a decrepit truck and helped her out. A rickety hanging bridge led to a house that looked as old as the town itself. The scent of smoke and fish hung in the air, and she saw dark smoke filtering up from behind the house.

"Why are you taking me here?" she asked as Zell took her hand and led her across the bridge. There was something familiar about the place from deep in the recesses of her past.

"You'll see."

An old woman stepped out of the house and stood in the shadows of the front porch. She waved as they approached, showing gaps between her teeth as she smiled. "Heya, Zell. This the gal you was telling me about?"

Kim glanced at Zell again, but turned her attention to the woman. She looked familiar, too, and then Kim knew why. "Toopie," she uttered, making the woman smile again.

"She 'members me." The woman wore a faded black tank top that revealed the nub of her right arm. "Your daddy saved my life, he did. He was a good man."

Kim felt a burst of pressure in her chest at hearing her father described that way. "Thank you."

Zell handed her the cold package he'd brought with him. "Got some gator meat for you."

Toopie took the package with her good hand. "Thanks, Zell." She jerked her head toward the large smoker around the side of the house. "Smoking some mullet. Come on back and have a bite."

Kim glanced at Zell, but he held out his arm to indicate that she precede him. Toopie wobbled a little from side to side as she walked, but she made good time. She grabbed two chairs from the porch and set them out on the lawn. Kim couldn't help looking at the river where the gator had grabbed Toopie's arm.

The woman took her in with cloudy blue eyes. "Heard you was afraid of gators 'cause of what happened to me."

She nodded, trying not to think of other reasons she was afraid of the creatures.

"They shot 'im," she said, coming up beside her. "Didn't want them to, but the government men came out and kilt 'im. He'd been living here longer than I had; it's us who's intruded on their land, not the other way around. Wasn't right."

"You didn't want the gator killed?"

"'Course not. You wouldn't shoot a gator for eating a coon, would you? Or even a dog. It thought my hand flapping in the water was a fish in distress. It was just acting on its instincts." She walked over to the smoker and pulled out a big fillet. Kim was amazed to see her use one hand to skin it, cut it, and set a piece on each of three plastic plates. She handed a plate to Kim and one to Zell. "Best mullet you'll ever taste."

Kim dutifully tasted it and nodded in agreement, but she

couldn't get past Toopie's words. "You aren't mad at the gator?"

She waved her good hand. "Why should I be? I was just in the wrong place at the wrong time is all." She nodded toward the river. "There's another gator in there now. He's a big'un, too. But I don't have to wash my clothes in the river no more. The Macgregors got me a washer and dryer long time ago." She gave Zell a smile drenched in warmth.

They finished their mullet and then their visit. When they left, Zell waited before starting the truck. "What did you think of her?"

"She's pretty neat. I wish I would have met her a long time ago." She reached for his hand and twined her fingers with his. "I see what you're trying to do. Make me understand that Toopie's having her arm bit off was more traumatic for me than it was for her. And I do understand. But I'll never love gators, Zell, and that's a fact."

"That's all right."

"It is?"

"Yep. It's all right if you don't love gators. As long as you love me." He ran his thumb over her lower lip. "You do love me, don't you?"

She kissed the pad of his thumb. "Oh, yes."

"Good. 'Cause if you didn't, that'd make it real tough, me loving you and all. Now then, I have a picnic basket, a boat, and a sunset waiting for us. You and me, we're going to talk about this a little more. I've got a big lonely bed and a lonely body tired of spending every night thinking about you and not doing anything about it."

He looked so serious she tried hard not to crack a smile. She failed. "I've heard about this guy in town who dispenses advice on love. They call him the Sage. Maybe he'd have a few suggestions for a girl who wants to learn how to give her heart away."

He couldn't contain his smile, either. "Why, angel, I have a feeling he'll have some interesting suggestions." He gave her a long, languid kiss. "Some interesting suggestions, indeed."